MEAT

Joseph D'Lacey

OAK TREE PRESS

First published in 2008 by
Beautiful Books Ltd

This edition published in 2013 by
Oak Tree Press
www.oaktreepress.co.uk

Oak Tree Press is an imprint of
Andrews UK Limited
The Hat Factory
Bute Street
Luton, LU1 2EY

Contents

This book is for Foxy, my mainstay and the love of my life.

Acknowledgements

Briefly, to my original publisher and editor, Simon Petherick, thank you for giving me the toehold that allowed me to climb. I'll always be grateful. And thanks to everyone else at Beautiful Books for your wonderful enthusiasm. It was a special time and I miss you all.

Love to my family and in-laws for keeping faith and to my friends for being true.

To Paul Andrews and the whole Oak Tree Press team, who picked up the ball and ran with it, a massive thank you for all the hard graft and dedication that went into this wonderful new edition. A special mention for proof-reader Michelle Finlay, who knows how to make a book shine.

These acknowledgments wouldn't be complete without a nod to Colin Smythe, Lisanne Radice, Stephen Calcutt, Kate Pool, John Jarrold, Kenilworth Writers and Doomey, Deplancher & Theo at www.tqrstories. com and all the reviewers and bloggers who were so vociferously in favour of the first edition.

To Brie Burkeman, for re-imagining my career with such vision and drive, and for your staunch dependability, a huge hug!

And to you, for opening this book, my sincere gratitude.

MEAT - Five Years On

I started writing 'seriously' in 2000. In my case, seriously meant I wanted to make my living as a storyteller. I was in for a very long and painful shock.

MEAT was my sixth novel, completed in 2007. Although I'd placed several short stories by then, getting a novel published remained as impossible for me as nailing the Roadrunner was for Wile E. Coyote.

One day, in my ongoing search for short fiction markets, I found something: at the bottom of a page outlining submission guidelines for Beautiful Books's 'Read by Dawn' anthologies, there was a tiny link. It led to a microsite, just a single page, really. It turned out Beautiful Books were seeking full length horror novels. I had plenty of those, turned down by agents and publishers across the board, so I submitted one.

Predictably, they rejected it. However, they asked if I had anything else. I did and I sent it. They liked it. They liked it a lot, in fact. But they wanted me to rewrite 60% of it from scratch. I loved the novel too much to alter it that drastically. All I had left to show them was a partial document which I'd given up on because the subject matter was so disturbing. I pitched the incomplete idea to owner/editor Simon Petherick over the phone and he told me to send me novel the moment I'd finished.

I hammered out the rest of it in a frenzy and here I am, looking back five years later on everything that happened afterwards.

MEAT was launched early in 2008, though I think it's more accurate to say that the book launched me. It has delighted and disturbed readers in English, Turkish, French, Russian, Hungarian and German. It has turned carnivores vegan and turned the stomachs of many a hardcore horror fan. It garnered high praise from Stephen King - one of my writing heroes - and won me the British Fantasy Award for Best Newcomer in 2009.

In the afterword, written in late 2007, I stated I wasn't a vegetarian. However by the time MEAT was in bookshops, I'd sworn off all flesh and haven't eaten it since. The decision was a direct result of the research I did whilst writing the book.

If there's one recurring criticism of the novel, it has been that I'm preaching vegetarianism or damning those who eat meat. Neither is the case. Being a novelist means being an entertainer. Story comes first. Story is everything. Telling the most thrilling, engaging yet horrifying tale I could was my only aim in MEAT - that's my job. I aim to entertain no matter what I'm writing.

Certainly, factory farming, animal transportation and slaughter are emotive subjects. Exploring them in fiction has been both grim and rewarding. If MEAT, in addition to being a jolting read, causes people to think about some of its themes in new or different ways, well…that's a bonus.

In addition to all the wonderful attention and opportunities MEAT brought me, the novel led to some heartaches too. I should have known something was amiss when, some months after our daughter was born, Beautiful Books rejected what I'd assumed would be my third book with them. Not long afterwards, they went into administration and never came out. Both MEAT and Garbage Man were withdrawn from sale, ending three wonderful years with the innovative, creative publishing house who gave me my start. I was devastated but, I'm quite sure, nothing like as devastated as the owners and employees of Beautiful Books.

Out of nowhere, things looked bleak. My first two novels were no longer available. No publishers were interested in my other books - and I'd written more by then. Even my short fiction was a hard sell. For various reasons, I didn't write anything for over a year. When I did finally return, to write my most ambitious work to date - The Black Dawn series - I couldn't sell that either. I was close to giving up.

Then, one day in 2012, I found a new agent. Not just any agent but the right agent. And, thanks to her, everything changed. New deals and opportunities flooded in. Among those blessings was the novel you now hold: MEAT - reborn, enhanced and updated but just as grim as ever.

I hope MEAT entertains you. I hope it transports you to another world and that it unsettles you as much as it unsettled me. If it does, rest assured I'll be delighted to know I've done my job properly.

In the meantime, all that remains to be said is:

Bon appétit!

Joseph D'Lacey
October, 2013

MEAT

Behold I have given you every herb bearing seed which is upon the face of all the earth, and every tree, in which is the fruit of a tree yielding seed; to you it shall be for meat.

Genesis 1:29

One

Under skies of tarnished silver, towards the granite clouds, Richard Shanti runs home.

Step after crushing step, his breath falling in and out of strange rhythms with the pounding of his feet. Mucus building at the back of his throat – the only moisture left in his body. His legs alternately telling him that they're burning beyond endurance, that they're too weak to go on. He wants to listen.

Instead, he spits out his precious phlegm.

He's out of sweat. The last of it has dried at his temples and his bearded face is aflame. His eyes sting with salt but there are no tears left to clear them. He's desiccating on the run.

He smiles.

His thighs and calves are blowtorched. Blazing, blazing, blazing with every step. His muscles are lava and jelly. There's no strength left in them; not an ounce of goodness or grace.

Not yet.

His shins bend with each burdened contact. He can feel them giving under the load. He imagines hairline cracks appearing in the immaculate bones and a snap – the sound of a wooden ruler breaking under water. It extends his pain. The sound of that damp splintering lingers in his aura; echoes eternal in his ears.

How much will it take to clear the backlog? I'll do anything. I want my purity back.

He runs.

There's a limitless tempo to it. Pain is the punctuation. The percussion of his soles on the stony road is a beat of torment.

Thack-thack-thack-thack-thack-thack-thack. He runs.

It is his only salvation. He runs. He pays.

This life is not long enough to clear him of the ill he has begotten. By his own hand he is condemned. Every part of him must atone. The agony in the soles of his feet lances up into the marrow of his ankles. He visualises stress fractures creeping through his tarsals.

He runs; willing the pain into his body. The pack hammers his back as though it is alive. Every step forces it up and then slams it down against his spine. There is no harmonious pace. The straps chafe his shoulders and the weight threatens to pull him over backwards. Every movement pounds him, grinds him down.

His lungs are dry with the frenetic passing of air. Smoke from the meat trucks clings in his throat until it is distilled to a tainted scum that sickens him.

He runs. He pays. He prays.

The pain is with him all the time now. The damage in his joints and bones scrapes along his nerves each moment of the day. His existence is a whiteness of suffering.

Perhaps I am getting clear.

***

'Hey, Ice Pick!' Bob Torrance shouted from the elevated observation box at the top of the steel stairs, 'What's the chain speed today?'

Shanti checked the stun-counter beside the access panel against the main clock.

'Running at a hundred and thirty an hour, sir.'

Torrance smiled in admiration and delight. High chain speeds meant bonuses for everyone. They made him look good with the men and with Rory Magnus.

'You wipe out cattle like a disease, Rick. Keep it up.' Shanti was the calmest employee in Magnus Meat

Processing and Bob Torrance, the chain manager, loved him. He'd never seen another man like him. They called him the Ice Pick or Ice Pick Rick because of the total cool with which he manned the stun gun. Psychologically, it was one of the toughest jobs on the chain; the most damaging to the mind. For this reason the position was rotated between four trained stunners on the work force, each taking a week of stunning followed by three weeks on other areas of the chain or elsewhere in the factory. No one could kill hour after hour, day after day, month after month without something coming permanently adrift in their head. A break was mandatory for the sake of sanity and, more crucially, to maintain high productivity.

But if anyone could lay a captive bolt gun to the brow of a living creature from this day to retirement without a single day off, it was the Ice Pick, Richard Shanti. If anyone could look into the eyes of the soon-to-be-bled-gutted-quartered-and-packed for the rest of his life without a hint of damage to the psyche, it was he.

2

And look into their eyes he did. Everyone had seen him do it.

For most stunners, it was the eyes that were the problem. Torrance understood why – he'd been a stunner himself in his youth. He knew it was the toughest job in the slaughterhouse. How could you watch the light go out of thousands of pairs of eyes and not be affected by it? How could you not wonder where that light went? How could you not wonder if there was something wrong in what you were doing?

These questions layered up in a person's head. Each passing pair of eyes had their own character and texture. Each pair of eyes was unique.

So what, if Shanti didn't mix with the other workers? So what, if he ran himself to the edge of collapse every night and morning? As long as he turned up on time and did the kind of quality work he always had, Torrance had no complaints.

Every stunner needed a way of counteracting the job. If running helped Shanti cope, that suited Bob Torrance. He smiled to himself as he imagined Shanti sweating his way home of an evening.

It couldn't have suited him better.

Management had learned over the decades that stunners needed time out from the job they were trained for otherwise they didn't last. Torrance had seen it a few times in his long career at MMP. He remembered one young employee in particular:

Stunner Wheelie Patterson had been a jovial, fresh-faced boy when he started out. Pulled the front wheel of his pushbike high in the air on his way out of the yards every evening, thinking it was impressive and making everyone laugh. He was keen, sincere and committed to his work. He told the chain manager at the time – a fool with no instincts called Eddie Valentine – that he could handle two weeks at a time on the stun. It was a mistake for Valentine to let him do it, but back then there had only been religious guidelines for workers to follow – nothing secular or practical.

The kid had worked at the head of the chain like he was one of the machines. The conveyor would roll, the aluminium panel would open bringing a restrained head into view. Wheelie would voice the blessing, 'God is supreme. The flesh is sacred,' then whack the head with a sharp hiss and metallic clunk from the captive bolt gun. The panel would slide closed. He'd hit the proceed button and the conveyor would roll again.

The panel would open. Head.

Eyes.

'God is supreme. The flesh is sacred.'

Hiss-Clunk.

The panel would close.

The stun counter spun higher.

Wheelie worked that way – two weeks on, two weeks off – for six months. Each night he rode home on the bike everyone had come to know as the unicycle owing to his customary flourish in the forecourt. The other two weeks saw him 'on the bleed' or herding the cattle into the crowd pens and single file chute with an electric prod.

After a while, workers began to notice that Wheelie Patterson's smile had changed. He wore it like a mask that was too small and hurt his face. They noticed he wasn't as professional and committed as he had been when he first arrived. He deliberately aimed his prod or 'hotshot' at the genitals of the cattle in the holding pens, sought to shock the sagging udders of the spent dairy cows. Torrance saw him corner a bull from time to time and torment it with repeated electrocutions. Bulls were the ones that fought back hardest.

Wheelie lost his position as stun man the day they found him using the captive bolt gun on every part of a bull he could reach through the access panel except the designated stun point. Torrance had been the one to pull the pneumatic weapon from his hands and end the bull's life with a single, correctly positioned shot. By that time the bull's slaughter had already begun. The bolt gun had split its jaw and broken both cheekbones. Blood drained from the fat round holes the bolt gun created. Wheelie had also managed to shoot through the bull's windpipe and down into the lungs through the tops of both shoulders. The bull could barely sigh its pleas for release by the time Torrance got to it.

But stockmen and slaughtermen were a valuable commodity and Wheelie's behaviour, from the management's point of view, had done nothing worse than retard the factory's chain speed and cost them money. His mismanagement of cattle during the time they spent in the crowd pens and runs had caused some of the meat produced to be affected by PSE. This described a condition in meat cuts that were 'pale, soft and exudative'. The sort of meat people didn't want to buy because it tasted bad and the texture was all wrong. PSE was known beyond any doubt to be caused by increased stress in cattle during the hours and minutes prior to slaughter. Wheelie's games with the hotshot hadn't done anything for the quality of Magnus Meat products.

He'd been fined, sent for guidance and put back on a distant chain position where it was too late to torment the animals or spoil the meat – removing limb ends with bone shears.

4

Even after the 'one week on, three weeks off' statute had been brought into effect by Rory Magnus, the job still got to a few of them. Torrance remembered one stunner opening the access panel, locking eyes with the cow in the restraining box and then shooting himself in the head with the bolt gun. Other stunners over the years had been affected in different ways. Some hurt themselves off duty and bore the scars to work. Others merely went a little nutty and that was fine – plenty of the men in Magnus's employ were a rib shy of a rack.

But these were exceptions to the generally smooth running of the MMP chain. Torrance didn't dwell on the exceptions because he liked things smooth. Smooth and cool like Richard Shanti.

Like an ice pick.

***

Maya Shanti had the evening meal prepared by the time he arrived home.

She worked in the well-windowed kitchen and glanced up often from her cooking in case he came early. He never did. When they were first married, he had often taken the MMP bus home, only running to work with his work clothes and lunch in a small pack a few times a week. Over the years, his running had become an obsession. She was certain it would kill him.

She brought three pans of water to the boil ready to cook the green beans, broccoli and spinach as soon as she saw his gaunt, hunched silhouette plodding up the lane. The rice was already done and warm in the oven. She made a lot of rice and forced both Harsha and Hema to eat at least three full bowls before leaving the table.

Still, the twins looked thin to her.

He would wash with cold water from the steel tub outside using soap as old and hard as a stone, then he would put on a brown body-length tunic of rough material, something he had demanded she make for him, and sit without speaking for five minutes in the bedroom while his breathing returned to normal. He came quietly to the table, not joking or laughing like he used to, and he would make them all sit in silence before eating. When he reached for his cutlery the girls would begin to chatter and giggle and only then did things in the Shanti household appear normal.

MMP workers were privileged and protected. They could have picked a larger house nearer the town or the whole floor of a tower block if he'd wanted. There was plenty of space and choice. But they had both agreed they wanted to see a little greenery each day and Richard had always wanted to grow his own fruit and vegetables – another pastime that had become a fixation. It would have been dangerous to live in such isolation but MMP employees were safe almost anywhere they went and Richard Shanti's family, because of the important job he did, were untouchables, protected forever in the shadow of Rory Magnus, the Meat Baron.

Maya wanted to smile at their good fortune and shower her husband with love. She wanted to enjoy their status in the town and be carefree like the other MMP wives. But when she served the meal each evening and looked at the tiny streams of sweat that still slipped from Richard's temples, she felt a weight across her shoulders like the one he carried on his back twice a day.

Dessert was fresh fruit from the trees, canes or vines at the rear of the house. Richard would eat his fruit, chewing each bite so long that the twins would laugh as they counted each movement of his jaw. He would reach a bony hand out to each of them and touch their faces and their hair. Then he would retire to the bedroom and prepare to sleep. Recently, he had been having problems keeping his eyes open for the whole meal and Maya knew that he was using himself up, burning himself to a useless stump of a man with all his cruel self-punishment.

Something had to be done.

***

Richard Shanti ran every day.

On the Sunday run, his corporal mortification was so severe and sustained he could almost believe he might one day be free of his deeds. On Sundays, he ran only once but he ran further and harder. The route was different to his workday route. It started out the same but once he was on the main road out of the town, he veered onto a path that was kept open only by the passage of his own heavy footsteps once a week.

The path he took led through overgrown hedges, no longer cared for or trimmed. The entrance was marked by a few broken bricks that had once been the wall on one side of a bridge. The only vehicles that came out this way or this far from the town were the MMP buses taking employees to and from work, and trucks transporting meat. No one ever came this way on foot except for him. It was too far from the town to be safe. The bridge was still there, but the walls separating it from the drop on either side were

6

long gone. It spanned a cut that stretched towards town. In the opposite direction, it ran towards the wasteland.

It was five miles to the bricks. That was the first landmark he ran to every Sunday. When he reached them, he turned off the main road and the path took him through brambles, nettles and spiky hawthorn down below the road level. He welcomed the scratches on the skin of his legs. So overgrown was the sunken path that it was like running through a jungle at the bottom of a giant gutter. The growth of plant life was dense on all sides. He had to duck and dodge low strands of needle-lined creepers and the outreaching branches of small trees that had been growing ever since the mysterious byway was abandoned.

He turned left from the bridge taking him away from civilisation. Had he turned right, the disused tracks would have taken him to the very centre of Abyrne, a place he had no desire to visit. Twigs whipped at his face and arms. Fallen branches and roots threatened to trip him. The constant minor damage and the threat of worse if he fell made the Sunday run the hardest and most rewarding of all.

His only rule: once he was running he would not stop for any reason other than being physically unable to continue. That had never happened.

The Sunday run was the only time he was ever tempted to stop and it had nothing to do with avoiding the agonies he caused himself. A few miles along the hidden path, the slopes on each side fell away gradually and the trail became an embankment rather than a cut. The growth of dense brush still surrounded him but now and again he would catch glimpses of the wasteland beyond the town. The wasteland formed a natural, roughly circular border that no one crossed into. His own house was nearer to the perimeter than most people cared to be but there was a broad swathe of fields and woods between. Here, though, as the embankment approached the stagnant waters of the old canal, he could see out into the barren, eroded landscape where nothing grew.

There was no soil with an ounce of nourishment in it.

Instead, a heavy black dust was swept across the dark, carved expanse. It was like looking at a black sea of sculpted waves that never moved, or a black desert of tiny dunes. Occasionally, a glint of white would sparkle from below the dust when funnels of windblown dirt exposed the glassy rock below. There was nothing in the wasteland. Nothing but thirst, hunger and solitude until death. He was tempted by its void. The wasteland was a place where he could run to his conclusion. Death would be slow but certain. It seemed the perfect end to the life of an executioner.

For just a few moments, the dense shrub, usually twice his head height, would thin out and he would be running along an exposed ridge.

Where the ridge met the old waterway, there was a route back towards his house along the outskirts of the town if he turned left again. If he continued straight on, the path, and the embankment it ran upon, ended; swallowed by the wasteland. The canal, at right angles to it, also stretched a little further before narrowing, blunting and ending in the sterile wilderness that held the town in its black fist.

***

Richard lay on his back, eyes closed, already asleep. Maya had banished the girls to their bedroom upstairs. She shut the door behind her as she entered and stood watching the long, shallow breaths coming and going from her husband's diaphragm. He was so thin it hurt to look at him. He seemed not to have smiled at her in a decade. *He could be on his deathbed,* she thought, looking at his pale skin and the lines stitched deep into his face.

She undressed quietly, not wanting him to wake yet. When she was naked, she looked in the mirror, turning one way and then the other in order to catch the curves of her buttocks, stomach and breasts. *Dear Father, I'll be as thin as the rest of them soon.* She put her palm to her mouth to stop the sob that wanted to come out. Recovering herself, she cupped her hands under her breasts and felt the weight of them. They should have been fuller and heavier like they used to be, but now they were slim and less shapely. *Narrow.* She hated to see it.

Richard had only been in bed for ten minutes. She slipped in beside him and slid down below the covers. He wore a nightshirt but he was naked from the waist down. She kissed his soft, lifeless penis and took it between her lips. As gently as she could, so as not to wake him too quickly, she worked it around inside her mouth with her tongue until it began to swell. Soon it was throbbing the way it had every night in their early years of marriage. For the first time in as long as she could remember, she too felt the warm rush of erotic interest and tension fill her belly and seep from inside her.

He stirred. A moan came from him that sounded like pain or torment. She didn't stop. He gasped and she knew that he was awake now. Awake and not stopping her. She made her attentions lighter to prolong it. In the old days he had never wanted it to end and she would tease him until he almost cried for release.

He spoke:

'I don't have the energy to reciprocate.' She paused:

'This is just for you.'

For the next fifteen minutes she worked on him until the skin of it was so tight it seemed it might burst. She knew the final pulses were not far away.

She stopped again.

'Please, Maya. Don't stop now.'

'I want you to do something for us. For me.'

'No, Maya. Don't. You know I can't do it. I won't do it.' She took him back into her mouth, brought him back to the edge and took her mouth away.

'Can't you see how thin they are? They depend on you. We all do. I'm begging you, Richard, just this once. Don't let us starve like this.'

Her head moved over him again. The muscles in his stomach and thighs tightened.

'No,' he said.

She sucked him harder, stopped again.

'Please, Richard, we need it. Just a few kilos. You can bring it in your backpack. Fill it up.'

'Do it to me, Maya. Let me come.'

'Meat. Say you'll bring us meat.'

He was crying, shaking his head but agreeing. Shaking his head and saying, 'I will. I promise.'

He put his hand on her head and urged her downwards. She took him in deep.

Two

BLUE-792 pads a rhythm onto the aluminium wall of the bullpen with the tips of his incomplete fingers. The rhythm is interspersed with 'hhaa' and 'ssuh' sounds that issue like panting from his half open mouth. The padding is too stuttered to be the tapping of a rhythm, too lumpy to be the notes of a tune. Yet the stumps of his fingers are dextrous. The whispered shapes of his exhalations are not practised, repeated lyrics. They are manic sighs of focussed intensity.

BLUE-792 stops padding and sighing and leans his fat, muscular bulk against the cold metal panelling. It bends outward a little but it is strong; reinforced by criss-crossed bars. The metal sends gooseflesh outward across his body in a wave of pleasurable discomfort. He lays his right ear to the steel. His hairless head reflects rows of dim yellow lights above. He is never quite warm enough.

He hears a padding, a sighing within the metal and a smile breaks his face open. BLUE-792 is a bull; a heavy set, club-boned reproductive giant – a fighter honed by generations before him to physical and sexual superiority.

BLUE-792 is round-headed. He is grim-mouthed. He is bulldog-faced. Three hundred pounds of meat and between his legs swings a rare set of testicles. He is twenty-two years old and can procreate all day without tiring. It is this that keeps BLUE-792 alive and he knows it. None of this is enough to make him smile, not even the dutiful rutting.

But sometimes, like now, he does allow an upcurling of the lips and an opening of the mouth into a grin. The smile reveals his slickened, toothless gums and behind them his yellow-coated tongue. Soft drumming comes to him. Rasps and sucks and breaths. His eyes close and the smile broadens. His face is that of a huge child – a deaf child hearing private inner music far to the back of its mind. Saliva spills from the corner of his mouth in a watery string and drips to the straw-covered floor.

A monumental erection rises at his groin as he listens to the noises from the wall. It's a frightening cock with a bulbous helmet, a shaft too thick for fingers to meet around and too long to be anything but painful when in use. He hears footsteps and pads three beats, three times on the panel before moving to the front of the bullpen.

The erection is still beating a silent, swollen tattoo when a face appears at the upper hole in the door. The face is topped by a curly black mop with occasional corkscrews of grey. The beard is even thicker and much darker, no hint of steel or silver in it yet. The eyes in the face are dark brown. Soft, deep eyes. The face doesn't speak. It does not smile. A hatch opens at the bottom of the door and a broad aluminium pan the size of a washing-up basin is pushed through. The hatch closes. The face moves away.

BLUE-792 sits down in the straw, lifts the bowl in his palms and drops his head towards it at the same time. The same smell, the same taste, the same amount as always. Much like a dog with its snout bred flat, he attacks the warm thick mush that is his breakfast with his toothless mouth. The process of eating is more like inhalation. He cannot chew much nor does he stop to bother. In five minutes of chopsy slurping and sucking, the base of the bowl shines dully through. He wipes it out with the stumps of his fingers and licks them. He licks the inner surfaces of the bowl. He smears the mush left on his face with his palms and tongues them clean. The bowl drops from his stubby hands.

He lies back in the straw and belches deeply twice. The erection is gone. Brown flecks of mush still stain his cheeks, chin and neck. Soon, BLUE-792 is snoring so hard that the panel nearest him vibrates in harmony with his breathing.

***

The chain is long but the Chosen pass through it quickly.

It begins in the crowd pens where herds are brought in directly from the fields and feed lots, just a few hundred metres away on the same mega-plot of MMP land. Even for this short journey, the cattle are loaded into gas-driven transport trucks to control them more easily. A ramp slams down from the back of the transporter at the entrance to the crowd pens and the stockmen use electric prods to encourage the cattle down from the truck.

The 'hotshots' as the stockmen refer to the prods, create high voltage static that is harmless to the cattle but impossible for them to ignore. The trucks empty quickly, the speed at which they do so directly affecting efficiency and productivity. Hold-ups whilst unloading mean hold-ups for everyone else on the chain.

Once the cattle are in the crowd pens, stockmen use their hotshots to move them, still as a herd, towards the single file chute. A series of high, barred gates are then closed behind the moving animals to maintain the herd's density as they are funnelled towards the chute.

At the mouth of the single file chute, there is a gradual narrowing until there is space for only one animal. The herd becomes a queue. The weight of cattle behind is usually enough to keep individual animals moving into the chute but sometimes extra encouragement from the hotshots is necessary. A stockman known as a 'filer' remains in position to keep things moving and to prevent spooked animals from reversing out of the chute.

The first in line at the chute will find a 'wall' of steel against which they will be pressed by those behind. When the wall slides open, they will be impelled through either by weight of numbers or by a final prod from the filer. On the other side of the wall, each animal finds itself in a tall, narrow steel box. The box is moving away from the queue in the chute and the animal has no choice now but to be swept along inside it.

This is the stunning box or restrainer. As it moves, a small cage descends from above, trapping the animal's head and preventing it from moving. At this point, the animal's instinct is to bend its knees and sink downwards, away from the cage. However, the moving cubicle will now have encountered a rail at knee height that prevents leg movement. The stunning box is also too narrow to allow lateral movement so the animal is rendered immobile – more by the dimensions of its surroundings, than by actual bindings or shackles.

The box will be moving in a start-stop motion that depends on the skill and accuracy of the stunner. Each time the stunner uses the captive bolt gun successfully, he presses a button that advances the next stunning box in the sequence to a position in front of him. For the animal that has just entered the system, five stops and starts will bring it to a hatch directly level with its face. Within a second or two, this hatch will slide upwards and the animal will be looking briefly out onto the factory floor. The last thing it sees will be the stunner bringing the captive bolt gun towards its forehead.

The captive bolt gun is a humane means of rendering an animal unconscious prior to exsanguination. It is a pneumatic handheld firearm that employs a sudden compression of trapped air to fire its captive bolt. The 'bolt' is a four-inch spike with a groove along the upper part of its shaft. The rear part of the bolt is mushroom shaped. This serves two purposes: first it acts as the piston that is forced forward by the compressed air and second it prevents the bolt from leaving the gun when it is fired. Hence, captive bolt.

Firing the captive bolt gun into the head of an animal has two major effects. The first, obviously, is to pierce the skull and enter deeply into the brain. The second is to cause a massive and sudden rise in intracranial pressure; in other words, to create a very small but significant explosion of force inside the brain, bringing about immediate and painless unconsciousness.

Occasionally, the bolt gun may need to be employed a second or third time. This is rarely to do with the design of the equipment. More commonly, poor maintenance or human error is to blame for the necessity of a second or third firing of the bolt gun. Bolt gun maintenance should be performed daily, between shifts, to ensure proper functioning and all stunners should be fully trained and certificated before being allowed to operate at this point in the chain.

Once the stun procedure is deemed successful by the stunner – a process that should take no more than two or three seconds – the panel will close and the unconscious animal will proceed to the next station in the chain for exsanguination. Viewed from above, this machinery is like a waterwheel lying on its side, with each cubicle acting as a bucket.

Next, the stunning box will open and the animal will fall and roll down an angled steel slope to the 'bleeder'. A bleeder's job is simple and must be performed quickly. They must loop a chain around one or both of the animal's ankles and haul it vertical. In this position exsanguination will occur more swiftly than if the animal is left horizontal. Using a long thin blade, the bleeder must then cut both carotid arteries and the trachea in the neck of the unconscious animal. A bleeder's skill lies solely in speed and efficiency. He should aim to complete the exsanguination process before the animal regains consciousness. Animals that have regained consciousness at this point should quickly lose consciousness again as blood loss continues.

The animal will now move to the next position in the line where it will be dipped into a vat of boiling water for four seconds. This is long enough for the hide to come loose without cooking or damaging the valuable tissue below. It is extremely rare for an animal either to regain consciousness or still be conscious at this point in the chain. The scalded animal now proceeds for beheading – another automated process – then is flayed and disembowelled by skinners and gutters. Skins and organs are all placed on a conveyor for sorting into uniform batches of products and by-products. The lower intestines are reserved and sent for processing at the gas facility. The skin is retained for tanning.

The body of the animal now moves onward for quartering, hanging and boning.

The stockmen watched WHITE-047 on and off over two twelve-hour shifts without getting involved. She was a fourteen-year-old that had mated thirty-seven weeks earlier along with hundreds of others. Her calf would be BLUE-792 stock and it was for that reason that they let the labour continue unaided for so long. Assisted births rarely went well for cow or calf. Stock from BLUE-792 was among the best, and damaging or killing it would be an expensive waste of the bloodline.

The first shift watched her face twist in tightened agony when her contractions came irregularly and infrequently. After the first few hours, WHITE-047 was bent over, hobbling from one corner of the calving pen to another. She kicked up piles of straw, exposing the dirt floor of the barn. She rocked her body, shook her head from side to side, thrust her hands flat against the panels and panted.

From time to time Richard Shanti passed by the calving pens. Though he tried not to, he couldn't help but be fascinated by the arrival of new generations of Chosen, especially the stock from BLUE-792. It was the only time he disengaged that part of himself that was a calm dealer of an endless pack of death cards. It was a fantasy he engaged in, he couldn't help himself. Perhaps, he thought, it's a natural response to all the slaughter. In the fantasy, the calves weren't taken from their mothers to be 'worked'. Their fingers weren't clipped down to the second knuckle, their thumbs weren't removed, their tongues were whole and their vocal cords intact. The males weren't castrated and none of them were hobbled by the removal of their big toes. They were not dipped. They became children not cattle, and they did not die by Richard Shanti's deft, compassionate hand.

It was a dangerous fantasy. The kind of mental process that could cost him his job and more. While the bored stockmen leaned against the walls talking and smoking, Shanti's eyes were drawn to the moment of birth again and again. Maya hadn't made it to the hospital when she'd given birth. If she had, he wouldn't have been allowed in during the labour. Welfare didn't like men, especially MMP employees, to see their wives' birth processes for themselves. They knew how similar it looked to calving. But Maya had gone into labour with the twins on a Sunday when he was at home and though the Welfare had arranged to collect her, by the time they arrived, Shanti had already delivered the twins himself, cut the umbilicals, wrapped the girls in towels and handed them to their mother for their first feed. The midwife, arriving half an hour later, had looked at him with awed contempt. How had a *man* done this? There was nothing for her to do except weigh the girls, ask the exact time of birth and perform the ritual prayers. Somewhere, he guessed, a note was made that the father had been present for the entire labour. His behaviour would be monitored.

But Richard Shanti's name was already an MMP legend. He was the Ice Pick, the most efficient and cool-headed stunner there had ever been. Nothing could cast doubt on his abilities, not even a Welfare midwife's report. Knowing this, the midwife's disgust didn't worry him.

As he walked along the calving pens, spending a moment at each one, he knew he was also the only man in the barn who understood what it was about human labour and bovine labour that was so similar. Would the stockmen have been even a little bit disturbed by it? He doubted it. Every MMP worker in the town was far too inured to systematic cruelty to give it a moment's attention. Look at them now, he thought, not even moved by the sight of new life coming into the world; unaware of the potential and unresponsive to the pain of the cattle as they gave birth to their calves. The stockmen were unmoved by what the future held, not only for the newborns but for the calving cows themselves. After their time of service in the dairy, when their milk yield began to decline below acceptable levels, they would be slaughtered. Their meat, being of a lower standard, would go into pies and sausages and pasties. That would be the end of their story.

He came to WHITE-047's pen and recognised her immediately. This was a cow that had mated with BLUE-792. He remembered their encounter very well.

***

It had been chilly in the mating pens that day. Another unseasonably cold morning at the beginning of Abyrne's short-lived summer. What little heating there was had already been turned off and many of the Chosen were shivering in their stalls. BLUE-792 had been mating with the newest herd of mature cows for three days by then; taken from one stall to the next by an entourage of stockmen and closely scrutinised to make sure he inseminated every cow.

It was another process that Shanti watched from time to time when his week on the stun had passed and he was freer to move around the various buildings of the plant. BLUE-792 was his favourite bull of all time; a powerful, noble creature that went about its business with uncommon energy. Shanti kept an eye on the bull whenever he had a chance. During the annual mating season, BLUE-792 was pushed to the limits of his stamina.

Without exception, BLUE-792 would enter each new mating crate and sniff the air. At the far end of the narrow cubicle would be a young cow of between 12 and 16 years of age, ready for its first mating. Shanti always thought the cows paired with BLUE-792 were the lucky ones. The bull knew exactly what it was doing and always spent time relaxing and coaxing the skittish cows into their duties. He was the most efficient bull in MMP history; larger, stronger, more fertile and able than any other.

Some bulls didn't show enough mastery with their nervous heifers and mated successfully only a small percentage of the time. Others, in ignorance, hurt their cows with their clumsy approaches. A few bulls, despite robust health, off-the-scale sperm counts and great size, were so inept in the mating pens that they were dispatched for immediate slaughter. It was too expensive to keep such animals alive – their meat would fetch good money and offset the loss invested in their upkeep.

BLUE-792 was a bull of a different calibre. Literally. Its huge pizzle was the joke of the stockmen. They'd even made up a song about it that began 'Oh, what a *man* could do, with a cock like BLUE-792'. But it wasn't merely his size. He seemed to lull his cows into a willing trance before he mounted them, stroking and manipulating them to his will. The sighs from the cows were so harsh that Shanti knew they'd be deafening as screams. But somehow they were happy screams, screams of mingled pain and pleasure, silent screams lifting every moment of the mating to a level of experience Shanti could only imagine. As if they were drawing from the mating something that would last them their short lifetimes. Dairy cows usually mated only once and they were the ones that 'screamed' the hardest. Even the meat cows that would produce a calf every year for as long as they were able, sighed as though the pleasure and the pain of mating was the last they would ever have.

When BLUE-792 was involved, the sighs were harshest of all.

Shanti suspected the other bulls were well aware of BLUE-792's abilities. Bulls were always kept separate and in this case it was a particularly good thing. He didn't like to imagine the fight that would have ensued if BLUE-792 ever had contact with any of the other males. There were places in the town where smuggled bulls were baited to fight each other to the death but he'd never been tempted to attend. Even watching the magnificent BLUE-792 sleep was enough entertainment for him.

Shanti had been watching the matings the day that BLUE-792 entered WHITE-047's mating pen. It was subtle; he didn't know if any of the stockmen even noticed – they were too busy shouting encouragement and laughing at BLUE-792's huge pizzle. Something was different about the process that day. The bull sniffed at the air in the crate as he always did but Shanti saw him freeze without taking a single step further. At first, he thought his favourite bull was afraid. Instead of hiding timidly in the corner, nervous and tense like most of the other young cows, WHITE-047 was standing upright and facing BLUE-792. She was staring at him and the bull was staring back.

'Watch this now,' said Freeman, the burly head stockman. 'Gonna be messy, this one. Gonna be a fight.'

The other stockmen pressed closer.

Shanti stayed where he was, near the crate but to one side of the small group of onlookers. Freeman was wrong. From where Shanti was standing, he could see the side of BLUE-792's face. He could see the expression there. He'd watched the bull through the cracks in his pen and in a dozen situations – so many times he understood its behaviour. This wasn't a moment of aggression. WHITE-047 was standing unusually straight for a cow, her shoulders back and her young, unused udders thrust forwards. Her legs were apart so there was nothing she was hiding from her potential mate. But it was her eyes that gave it away, at least for Shanti.

Her eyes flashed excitement. They signalled astonishment. A kind of hunger and recognition. And a softness that no one had noticed but Shanti and BLUE-792. It was as though the pair had known each other for years and were reuniting after too long apart. Then the young cow noticed how Shanti was observing her and her expression became guarded. BLUE-792 tensed in response to her lead and his face hardened into simple determination – down to business.

The bull advanced. The heifer, playing a role now, retreated to the far wall and lost her confident posture.

'Guess the fight's off, sir,' said one of the younger stockmen.

'I should have put money on it.'

Freeman grunted, unhappy to be wrong in front of his crew.

'Not over yet, boy.'

But Shanti could see the man knew there wouldn't be any fight. He glanced over at the younger stockman, a new man he didn't recognise, and wondered if he was the kind that watched the illegal bullfights in the town.

He was a small man but he wore his mean streak like a tattoo across his forehead.

In the mating pen, the bull reached the cow. She put her right hand up to his face and touched his neck. BLUE-792 recoiled microscopically. Shanti doubted anyone else would have seen it. The outreached finger stumps tapped and stroked from the bull's neck to his shoulder. To anyone who didn't know how the Chosen communicated, it would have looked like she was shaking with fear. Shanti saw the gooseflesh rise in a wave all the way down the bull's left side.

Usually, the bulls turned their cow brides away from themselves and entered them from behind. It was quick and required less effort, leaving them more energy for the many other cows they would have to service during the brief mating season. WHITE-047 remained facing BLUE-792. They achieved something approaching an embrace, with the bull burying its face in the cow's neck. Shanti saw its pizzle, monstrously swollen and already dripping seed onto the straw, just before the bull lifted her up, pressed her back against the cold panels and did what he'd been bred to do. Shanti turned away, squeezing back tears, and left the barn.

***

Now, WHITE-047 was alone with her pain. It struck him both how human and how animal Maya had seemed in the same situation. WHITE-047 was sweating and panting, interspersing her breathing with longer, angrier sighs that had come out of Maya as grunts of frustration and screams of pain. He was glad not to have to hear those sounds again but he could tell from its expression what the cow was going through. There was nothing he could do to help the agonised creature he saw in the calving pen. She would be left to die if her birthing was unsuccessful. All expense was spared when it came to cattle; when they died, their flesh became profit.

The stockmen around WHITE-047's pen, seeing that she was still a long way from giving birth, moved on to check other cows in other pens in the barn. Shanti stayed. When the stockmen were out of sight in a parallel run of pens, he tapped his fingers on the horizontal bars of the calving pen. WHITE-047's head snapped around at him, eyes wide and disbelieving. Another spasm hit her. She crushed her eyes shut against the pain.

Shanti took hold of one of the lower bars and used it to steady himself while he squatted on his haunches. When her contraction had passed and

WHITE-047 opened her eyes, he tapped his fingertips on the bar again to get her attention. He looked from side to side, checking for the roving stockmen. The passages were clear.

'Like this,' he said, and bounced slightly on his heels before standing up and stepping well back from the bars.

'Understand?'

Another cramp coursed through her, eliciting more silent screams. When she'd recovered she rolled onto her knees and crawled to the bars of the calving pen gate and used them to help her stand. Shanti could see it was a struggle for her. She was no longer able to stand upright. She hooked her palms over a low bar, just as he had, and lowered herself into a deep squat with a hushed grunt of relief. Between her legs, her vulva swelled open. Moments later, the top of the calf's head began to appear.

Shanti nodded to himself. WHITE-047 was giving birth now; far too focussed to register him standing there. He walked away down the gritty passage between the calving pens and back towards the huge barn doors. Moments later he heard the only scream of the Chosen that was ever heard by MMP employees, that of a newborn calf. The stockmen would be coming now, coming to WHITE-047's pen to silence her calf for the rest of its life. He wondered whether it would be male or female.

Three

At ten to five in the morning, Greville Snipe stood in his crisp white cow-gown at the back entrance to the milking parlour waiting for his four dairy boys; Harrison, Maidwell, Roach and Parfitt. They must have hated their job at the dairy to turn up so close to clocking on time and to leave so soon after their duties were complete. They spent as little time in the milking parlour as they could and only ever did the bare minimum to keep the place running the way he wanted it.

He tapped his watch as if it would make his absent crew arrive more quickly. The MMP buses for the early shift arrived well in advance of start time, but he knew they'd be off in a crowd by the gates smoking and laughing with their mates from other parts of the plant. Maybe they were laughing at him. He was fairly sure they joked about him behind his back but what could he do?

Youngsters and the majority of low-level workers were lazy. Snipe had known this long before he was promoted to Dairy Supervisor. Subsequently, he'd devised standards well above what was required by management. When any of the dairy boys fell short of those standards, he knew that his procedures were still good enough to pass any inspection. Even so, he let them know how he felt about their shortcomings, sometimes threatening them with their jobs. They may have hated the Dairy but they'd never find as well paid a job anywhere else in the town and they all knew it.

He didn't believe he was a harsh supervisor. He'd known far worse in his early days at MMP. He liked to think that

Greville Snipe wasn't just about threats and bollockings; he was a man who tried to instil a sense of pride in the work that went on in the dairy. When he thought the Dairy boys had done well, and admittedly that was a rare occurrence indeed, he arranged bonuses for them in the form of extra milk, yoghurt, butter or cheese rations – things he knew they'd be thanked for again when they arrived home.

It was dark outside and the gas lamps were on. They illuminated circles of dirt all the way around the perimeter of the Magnus Meat Processing plant; all along the wide spaces between the pastures, the corrals, the barns, the outbuildings, the slaughterhouse and the dairy. He watched a couple of desultory moths circle and connect with the hot yellow bulbs again and again, believing that the light was a way out to somewhere when, in reality they were already free. Just like the Chosen, insects had stupid built into

20

them. Nevertheless, Snipe felt a brief stab of melancholy at the futility of their attempts. When their wings were singed beyond usefulness, the moths would fall to the damp dirt and die, their efforts purposeless and suicidal.

Footsteps thumped in the grimy soil, approaching. He checked his watch again. Three minutes to go. They were pushing it – hardly enough time to change and get out to the parlour before five.

'Come on, you bloody shirkers,' he shouted. 'Don't piss me about.' They skidded past him to the punch-card machine, clocked in and scrambled for the changing room. Red-faced, half giggling, half panicking. 'If any of you are even a fraction of a minute late onto the parlour floor, I'll take half an hour out of every wage packet. We're a team. We do not let the side down.'

With a minute to go, they sprinted out to the parlour and the stalls still buttoning their stained cow-gowns.

'And get those bloody uniforms washed!'

***

The lock-up garage was big enough for a small truck and a row of tools and storage boxes along each wall but it had been empty for years. It was made of concrete blocks and had no windows. The doors were wooden; painted a dull green like the others in the row and where the wood met the concrete floor it was damp and splintered. Icy draughts and dampness made it their home and even in the summer when the temperature outside was almost warm, the interior of the lock-up had a dark December heart. To enter was to shiver.

The other lock-ups in the row were doorless bothies to the miserable and the doomed. Too dangerous to sleep in, the transients did nothing more than shit there and move on before nightfall. It was a place where gangs brought rival captives and toyed with them throughout the long nights. It was far enough inside the Derelict Quarter, far enough from the nearest habitable houses that all screams went unheard. The sound of wood or glass or steel on flesh and bone might as well have exuded from some profound earthy pit.

There was no light in the lock-up and John Collins only went there at night. Sandwiched between the dirt and threat of it, he found a place to begin from. He took candles with him, set them up at the far end where he would sit on a high, backless stool and talk. In spite of the cold and the danger, in spite of the cramped space and the lack of light, people came to the lock-up to listen.

'In the flesh, as we sit here...as *people*,' he would sometimes say, 'we've all come from the same place, from the same beginning. That beginning is where we're all going back to sooner or later. That makes us all brothers and sisters. *All* of us. No one exists outside that simple truth. Can you see that much?'

If it was a new group, all first-timers, there'd be a silence then. Maybe one or two murmuring a faint 'yes'.

'I'm asking you an important question,' he'd say. 'So, I'm glad you're thinking about it before you answer. Can you see that we're all branches with the same root? Can you see that we're all brothers and sisters?'

There would be nodding, more yeses. It was a simple premise. Even the reluctant ones would shrug a silent I-guess-so.

John Collins would pause, take a sip of water, adjust the tattered grey scarf he always wore. Then he'd look back out at the six or seven rows of faces huddled, seated on the concrete. He'd look across each face and he'd know he'd seen some aspect of that face somewhere before and that he'd see other aspects of that face some time in the future. And there they sat, not recognising each other, fragments of a shattered self that had forgotten who it was.

He'd go to work on them again with whatever it took.

'Do you think your life is some kind of accident? Is it random? Nothing more than a grand mistake? Do you think our existence, the presence of intelligent humanity is nothing more than a casual coincidence?' He'd pause. 'Hands up if that's what you think.'

Sometimes there were hands. Usually not. To the hands he'd say, 'Why did you come here tonight? You've risked your reputation if you have one. You've risked your friends if you have any. You've risked your family's love. You've risked your life too.' A pause. 'You know what I think? I think your mind tells you that this life of yours is just a freak event in the lonely void of the wasteland and I think you've learned to believe your mind over the years. But I believe you've come here tonight because there's another part of you. A quieter aspect that whispers in your heart and never goes away. I think that's the part you're waking up to. That's the part you want to believe. Call it your soul. Call it your spirit. It doesn't matter. That's the part of you that makes you like all the rest of us. Spirit is where you come from and spirit is where you're going back to. That's what you know deep down to be true. But your mind wants to live in a safer world. Your mind wants footsteps on concrete and full stomachs and vodka. Your mind doesn't even want to consider what will happen when you die or what you were before you were born. But your heart yearns for that knowledge. It yearns for truth and that yearning is a torment.' A deep breath. A visible jet-stream of exhalation into the cold air. 'You can speak freely, my friend. And you need not speak at all if you don't wish to. The door's as open for you to leave as it was for you to enter. Speak freely, please. Tell me why you came.'

It was as if they were alone in the lock-up. One listener, one speaker. John Collins could make a person feel free just with his words, just with his smile, just with a look from his wounded, understanding eyes. They'd say:

'There's something wrong in the town. Something wrong with me.'

'I came because I feel trapped.'

'I feel bad about the way I've lived my life.'

'I want to change. I want to be better.'

'I'm sick. I heard you were a healer.'

It was amusing to him how few of them ever said they no longer wanted to eat flesh. Perhaps the willing ones would have said it, but the ones who were uncertain had never come as far as that in their minds for the first meeting. They were still unable to admit to themselves what it was they wanted from Prophet John Collins.

'If you thought this world and your life were an accident, that it was meaningless, you wouldn't have bothered to come would you?'

No one ever disagreed.

'It's because this life *isn't* meaningless; it's because we're all here for some special *purpose*; that's why we're all brothers and sisters to each other. When we die, it's natural that the special part of us goes back to where it came from, a place where we'll all be closer and freer than we ever were here.'

He'd let that idea float for a few moments. And then he'd ask the question again.

'Can you see that we're all brothers and sisters? Can you see that much?'

All of them would say yes. All of them would smile a little and the smiles were always awkward strangers on their faces. They would look from side to side at each other and the smiles would widen and find a home having wandered alone too long. It could be a fathom below freezing on a winter's midnight, breath fogging the air above their heads and John Collins would feel the warmth spreading out from all of them.

That was where it began.

Once a week, outside the lock-up on the littered and glass-strewn lot, there were no gang members divvying up the spoils of their battles, no rapes in the adjoining concrete cubes, no murders behind them, no suicides in the ruins beyond. Once a week, when John Collins was telling it, there was peace at the lock-ups.

Dark December peace.

***

The causes of mastitis were varied.

A teat cup removed before the vacuum was released might burst superficial capillaries allowing ever-present staphylococcus bacteria to enter the blood. A sudden backflow in the milk tubes could have a similar effect. Something as simple as incorrect sterilisation or cracked rubber in the teat cups. These problems had been legion before Greville Snipe was promoted to dairy supervisor. Since then, the incidence of mastitis had halved.

Mastitis was a common problem among the milkers. Some recovered from it and others did not. The priority was that milk should flow. If a little pus was drawn from a few teats, it was no big problem. Pasteurisation and homogenisation took care of it. The milk was safe and no one would ever realise it was anything other than the healthiest and most nourishing liquid a person could drink. Milk-drinking townsfolk knew better than to ask questions about how it was produced as long as it tasted good. So, the occasional dead white blood cell did make it into the stomachs of the population. But the milk was safe. It tasted great. And that was all that mattered.

Mastitis caused swelling of the udder and teat in the first instance. Passing milk would be accompanied by a more intense ache than the milking machines usually caused. As the days passed and the infection worsened, a discharge would begin to leak from the affected teat. Typically this discharge would contain some milk, some blood and some pus. Milking would continue regardless of the contamination. The increasing pain caused to the milker was not taken into account.

Sometimes, the teat would harden and crack like baked mud. Blood and pus would then flow freely. At this point, most milkers would be given a day or two of rest because the flow of their milk was retarded by the infection. This was their chance to recover if they were going to. A few did. Most didn't.

It was cheaper for Magnus to sell his milkers as meat than it was to treat them for the infection. Milkers whose mastitis worsened into fever were slaughtered, their meat sold for the most basic burger and sausage mince. In the long term, all milkers were headed for the grinder but those who made it through an episode of mastitis had a few more years of service to look forward to before they faced the bolt gun.

***

Richard Shanti watched the trucks grumble out of the packing department.

What had been living, what once was sacred, would now become the nourishment for thousands of townsfolk. Halves, hindquarters and forequarters being taken for further processing. Bloodless pink fillets, steaks, chops, ribs and roasting joints transported to butchers where they'd be arranged on sloping, glass-screened displays. Packets of mince, low-grade sausage and retrieved meat heading for the pie makers. There was no soul in the meat, no spirit. As far as Shanti was concerned, the sanctity of the flesh had died with its owners.

Where did that preciousness go, he wondered? Not with the meat in the trucks. Not to the tables of the townsfolk.

From time to time, the magnitude of what he was part of and the daily repugnance of it washed far into the hinterland of his awareness, into the exposed avenues and byways of his conscience. How could such violation occur in such great numbers? In those rare moments, he could almost comprehend what it was he contributed in terms of suffering and how that weighed against what little good he did.

On those days he took extra ballast in his pack.

***

Greville Snipe lived to work. It worried his mum.

'I've got no friends, no hobbies and no vices,' he would often boast to Ida Snipe as he slipped her a few extra groats and a free two-litre carton of milk. He visited his mum once a week for Sunday tea and always took her some of the 'bounties of his endeavour' to keep her happy.

'You should settle down with someone,' she would tell him as she twisted a greasy hanky between gnarled, quivering fingers; her face an atlas of concern.

'I couldn't be more settled,' he'd reply, annoyed that the good things he provided were never quite good enough. 'I've got a decent job, plenty of money. I've got my health,' *which is more than you've got,* he always wanted to add. 'And I'm happy as I am.'

Ida knew her boy worked hard.

'I'm proud of you,' she'd say, little tears at the corner of her eyes. 'You've always been a good boy. Good to me.' But who was going to look after him? He had no time to find the right woman. A man took a good bit of looking after. She knew that because of Greville's father, Anderton Snipe.

'One of those poorer girls from the northern quarter would be perfect for you. Quiet, obedient. Good cooks, I've heard. And they keep a tidy house too, you know.' She'd sigh to herself but loud enough for him to hear the wistfulness in it. 'I've got nothing against poor people, Greville. Just remember that.'

Visiting on a weekly basis, Greville found it hard to forget his mother's class-based forbearance. He told her he'd take a trip to the northern quarter and look into it.

There were things his mum didn't understand. Things he could never tell her.

Greville Snipe lived to work. His mum would have worried a lot more had she known why.

***

The numbers of the Chosen were vast; more than ten thousand. But their numbers fluctuated in response to the town's demand and also to diseases that occasionally afflicted them.

In warm weather, they roamed the fields to the far south west of the town in herds totalling many hundreds of head. Their pale bodies moved in swathes against the grass and mud. When it rained or if it was cold, they crammed into the huge, arch-shaped barns that had been there ever since the town began. The barns were ancient and rotting and there were holes in the roofs and in the walls. They gave only limited shelter and the Chosen pressed close to each other to stay warm.

Around the perimeters of the fields, there were wooden towers where stockmen could observe, count and keep the herds secure. Impenetrable hedges of blackthorn formed the borders of each field. Access gates were high and spiralled with barbed wire. The security measures were unnecessary, though. None of the Chosen had ever tried to break through a fence or a hedge in Abyrne's history.

Closest to the plant were the dairy herds that needed to make the daily trip for milking. They were kept corralled in the plant to be milked twice in the course of the day and then returned to their fields in the evenings.

The meat herds spent much of their time in the fields and barns. Herds made up of pregnant or nursing mothers and their calves stayed corralled in the plant longer term. When their calves were old enough and their rituals were complete, they would rejoin the main herds as heifers or steers. The Chosen that saw the fields most rarely were the bulls. They were kept penned and separate to prevent fighting and stayed within the plant most of their lives. Veal calves, once in their crates, never saw the fields or any other cattle again.

***

Anticipation made his heart beat so hard he could feel the throbbing in his neck. His face was hot and his balls ached.

His alarm went off at four in the morning but he never pressed the snooze button. He was washed and dressed within five minutes and tucking into a breakfast of steak and black pudding. He needed plenty of protein for such a long shift. Accompanying his breakfast, Greville Snipe drank boiled milk with three large sugars. Thus fuelled, he was ready for a day in the dairy.

Not for him the clammy, dread air of the slaughterhouse that thrummed all day with stark, final seconds of anticipation. Not for him the blue rubber aprons and knee-high rubber boots. Not for him the captive bolt gun, nor the hoisting chain, nor the double-handled bone cutters. Neither the long-bladed knife nor the saw. Snipe saw himself as a kind man. A humane worker in an inhumane industry.

There was no death in the dairy. There were no struggles, no kicking, no letting of blood. In his working world he breathed a quiet air. Not quite serene perhaps, but certainly not a condemned air. Not yet. In the dairy, the milkers were in the prime of life with years of production still before them. In that time they would eat well and sleep well and the promise of their certain dispatch was far away. Snipe cared for them as best he could. They were valuable and they were his responsibility.

By five o'clock he was checking the herd over before the first milking.

He strolled with pride through the milking parlour. The cows stood with their wrists shackled to their ankles by a long chain. This prevented them interfering with the equipment or resisting the attachment of teat cups to their udders. Snipe's team of four youths were quick and efficient because of his training. They ran from booth to booth and within minutes were able to connect a hundred and fifty cows to the machines. None of Snipe's team wanted to be there. If there had been any other job in the world they could have taken, they would have. It was not a time when people had many choices. The milking parlour, the cows, the machinery; all of it gave the youths the creeps. That was another reason they were so fast. Fast, but not careless. He'd trained that out of them.

They were young too, none of them over nineteen and they would, in time, come to understand and appreciate the importance of the job they were doing. They didn't know it but they were privileged and, unlike most jobs in the town, working in the milking parlour actually meant something. They were helping to provide for others.

Once the equipment was attached, the milking session was brief; only twenty minutes to harvest half of the day's yield. Then Snipe's lads passed through the parlour a second time removing teat cups and collecting them for sterilisation. Collected raw milk was then pumped into vats for pasteurisation and homogenisation. As those processes were fully automated, his boys could take a long break.

He then had a solid hour to pass through the milking parlour checking every cow in the herd. This was what raised his pulse.

There were four rows of forty individual milking stalls, the two centre rows were back to back. Between rows one and two and rows three and four were two broad concrete lanes with a gutter that ran down the centre of each. Many of the cows would urinate or defecate during milking. After they'd returned to pasture, the whole parlour would be hosed down a stall at a time. Snipe was used to the smell but his four lads wore their masks for the whole shift.

During his hour alone with the herd, Snipe inspected every cow in every stall. In a herd, they all looked alike, but it *was* possible to pick up on little distinguishing marks and individual behaviours. Snipe knew every cow by sight and number. He passed along the stalls, hands behind his back like a general inspecting his troops. In turn, every eye in the parlour watched his progress. As a dairyman, Snipe's interest was in a good milk yield and a healthy herd. He felt obliged to check the udders and teats of every cow.

In most cases, the initial check was a glance. Deflated udders with a ruddy rim around elongated teats was what he wanted to see. Healthy, spent udder tissue with a suction mark in the right place. But where he found the red rim too close to or overlapping the teat, he would pause to see if the suction had caused any damage. He would note the stall number and the number of the cow in a small white notebook that he carried in the outer pocket of his white cow-gown. Later he would have words with whichever team member possessed careless, rushed hands.

Officially, mastitis went untreated, excepting the antibiotic shots that every animal in every herd regularly received to keep them infection free. But Snipe ran a proud unit and he liked to do a little more for his milkers. Whenever he saw damaged, cracked or sore teats on his cows, he attended to them. In his trouser pocket at all times was a small jar of cream that his mother had used on his dry skin when he was a child. It smelled of honey and old leather and was called

Beauty Balm. In reality, it was a product aimed at women to keep their hands soft and smooth. Snipe had learned to use it for other things before he realised it could help soothe the udders of his milkers.

It caused him a very complicated feeling when he stopped to rub the Beauty Balm into the sore udders of one of the herd. His eyes would defocus a little and he would enter a righteous, delightful, guilty trance. He would look away from the face of the cow and concentrate on the feeling of the swollen udder beneath his gentle fingers. Sometimes a final dribble of milk would exude from the affected teat and Snipe would pause and look at the cow's face. Suffused with temptation, his penis painfully rigid and his testicles sharply aching, he would continue down the rows.

Four

Hema and Harsha were sick the next day.

Richard had left while it was still dark, every muscle on his emaciated frame standing proud as he hoisted the pack of bricks and sand onto his back. Maya watched him with anticipation, knowing that by the evening the pack would be full of something other than her husband's misplaced burden of guilt. She ate an apple for breakfast, not resenting it for once, and she sang a song she'd learned as a child while she prepared chopped fruit and porridge for the girls.

When she went upstairs to rouse them, she found them both in Harsha's bed, clinging to each other and shivering in their sleep. Sweat blackened their already-dark hair. It made her think of Richard, his temples dripping each night at the dinner table. She felt their brows. Her girls were burning up. Damn you, Richard, she thought. Their sweat was his sweat. Somehow he had passed his craziness into them. The craziness was damp on their foreheads.

She ran downstairs, pulled on a heavy coat and rushed out the door. She'd be exhausted by running for the doctor. Why couldn't they have lived nearer the town?

***

Snipe noticed the condition of WHITE-047's teats immediately. There was no broken skin and no cracking of the aureoles but they were too swollen – even minutes after milking – to be healthy. If he didn't do something about it now, it was almost a certainty that an infection would set in.

Snipe noticed certain cows in the dairy herd more than others but he had never been sure why that was. The ones he noticed were the ones he gave most care to. WHITE-047 was one of those cows and, as he looked at her now, he tried, as he often did, to work out why it was that some milkers were easier to look at than others.

She had the same stumps of fingers as all the others. Her big toes were missing like the rest of them. She made the same sighs and hisses. She limped because of her heel tag, but so did every Chosen in every herd. She was toothless and hairless and had the same hunched, weighed down posture that all the Chosen displayed. She was big in the hips – not all were shaped that way but most of them were – but there was something different about her shoulders. They were delicate somehow. Not the heavy-boned shoulders that milkers usually possessed. Ordinarily, weaker-looking stock was culled out of the herds to keep the offspring strong. WHITE-047 was slender at the top and that ought to have been noticed and taken care of. Perhaps it was the eyes that had saved her from a premature visit to the slaughterhouse. Her eyes were strong and, unlike almost every other cow in the herd, she risked making eye contact from time to time. That must have taken other stockmen's attention from her finely-boned shoulders. She was a lucky one. Or she had been until now.

Snipe approached the stall she was in but she didn't try to step away. Like many of them, she had come to trust him. Instead, she looked at him for a split second and then turned her head away. She tried to stamp one of her feet but all it did was clank the shackles.

'Easy there,' he said. 'Mr. Snipe's not going to hurt you.' He stepped into the stall with her as slowly and smoothly as he could. Cows were skittish and liable to hurt themselves if they felt threatened. He didn't need a damaged milker on his shift.

'Steady, girl. Steady now,' he breathed.

He was right beside her now. Even after the milking her udders were round and plump. She was younger than a lot of the others. It was another thing he often noticed, the ones with the fuller udders. His pulse pumped in his neck and a flush of heat rose to his cheeks. He reached for the Beauty Balm in his cow-gown pocket with trembling fingers.

***

The population was hungry. But that was no excuse.

And the ones that were starving – the ones that might really have needed the protein to survive – they rarely got it. Meat went to those who could afford it. *Life* went to those who could afford it and so it had always been.

Richard Shanti had blood on his hands. Unlike his co-workers he didn't deny it. He didn't pretend it was okay. While they absolved themselves with placatory readings from the Book of Giving or the Gut Psalter, he bore his guilt fully, at least in his own mind. He never spoke of his culpability to anyone. He did not share his horror at the part he played each day. Instead, he made himself suffer in every way he knew. In this manner he planned to punish himself for his wrongs while he was alive. Perhaps his next life might not be lived in a similar sort of hell to the one

he was employed to create every day of the working week. And if there was
no next life, some small justice would still have been served upon him.

His understanding of animals had been obvious from the outset. He
began his career as an untrained casual worker. They made him clean up
blood and off-cuts. Even then, he'd been drawn to the more agitated of
the Chosen, the ones that struggled and resisted. He wasn't authorised
to be anywhere near the chain but in his first week a young steer went
crazy in the crowd pens, halting the chain. Shanti walked straight over to
the panicking animal and calmed it in moments, delighting the stunner
who managed to recover a decent chain speed. Similar incidents happened
many times in those early days. Soon Magnus Meat Packers gave him a
permanent position: Shanti the pacifier, Shanti the whisperer, as he'd been
back then.

***

'Oi! What the hell do you think you're doing?'

Greville Snipe's roar echoed around the milking parlour. Roach and
Parfitt jolted inside their cow-gowns with the shock of it. They turned off
the high-pressure hoses and turned toward their boss. In the corner, against
the white tiled wall, WHITE-047 cowered, shivering; water running off
her reddened skin. Neither of the lads could look him in the eye.

Snipe approached with deliberate slowness and stealth letting them
know they were his prey. He lowered his voice to a whisper:

'I asked you a fucking QUESTION.' And screamed the last word.

'Look at me. LOOK AT ME.'

Weighted, their heads came up. Their eyes slid around, looked
everywhere but at him.

'You *should* be ashamed. Drop those nozzles – you've got no business
using them that way. What did you think you were doing?'

Roach and Parfitt glanced at each other but neither spoke. Behind
them, the sighing and hissing that came from WHITE-047 vibrated with
the uncontrolled tremoring of her muscles. Snipe looked from face to face
and then slapped Roach across the side of his head. The sound of the blow
reverberated in the silence. Roach's eyes blazed white but gravity overcame
his anger. He stared down at his feet.

'I'm going to ask you once more. I don't care who answers me. But I
want to know. I want to hear it from your lips. What do you think you
were doing?'

'I...' began Parfitt. 'Well we...she was dirty. Sir.'

'All cows are dirty. What was so special about this one?'

'She was...covered in shit, Mr. Snipe,' said Roach, finding his voice at last.

Perhaps, thought Snipe, he thinks I'm giving them an opportunity to make an excuse for their behaviour.

'Harrison and Maidwell aren't exactly intelligent,' said Snipe. 'But you two are probably the stupidest dairy boys I've ever had the misfortune of working with. I bet that cow's got more brains than the pair of you put together. Since when have you been stockmen?'

The two lads looked at each other again, not seeming to understand what they were meant to say.

'Dear Father of Abyrne, this is your last chance to speak to me before I report you to Mr. Magnus himself.'

'W...we're not stockmen, sir,' said Parfitt.

'So why are you doing a stockman's job? What makes you think you're qualified, eh?'

'We're not,' said Roach.

'Oh? So you do know what job you're supposed to be doing then? That's a fucking relief. For a moment there I thought you were trying to get promoted out of the dairy. You have no idea how much I'd have missed having you here.' He walked between them to WHITE-047. 'Stay where you are you two. I haven't finished with you yet.'

He opened the large wooden milking parlour doors and shooed WHITE-047 from her corner and out towards the feedlots. The cow hobbled, bent almost double. He called out to a stockman and pointed to the cow: 'Missing one?' The stockman nodded. Snipe nodded back and pulled the parlour doors closed again.

He gathered that the two idiot dairy boys had been talking to each other. Parfitt took the job of spokesman, seeing as Roach had already received a palming.

'Sir, we didn't mean anything by it. The cow was a mess so we tried to clean her up. It won't happen again.'

Snipe stared at them and then grinned in disbelief.

'You must think I'm a mushroom that grew in yesterday's cow-pat if you think I believe that rubbish. You two deliberately separated a cow from the herd and abused it with the high-pressure hoses. Hoses that are designed, as you're well aware, for cleaning encrusted shit off tiles, brick and concrete. What do you think that kind of jet does to an animal's body?

I'd be very surprised if that cow isn't damaged goods now. Might even have to be processed.'

'It's only water, sir. Couldn't have done it much harm,' said Roach.

Snipe smiled a different kind of smile.

'Do you know what Rory Magnus does to employees that abuse his cattle?'

The pair of them drained white.

'You're not going to report us are you, sir?' said Parfitt.

'You can't...I mean, we need this job. Our families need our help to survive.'

'You should have thought about that before you started damaging the herd.'

'Please, sir. We didn't damage the herd,' said Roach.

Snipe cupped an elbow in one hand and drummed the fingers of the other against his mouth.

'I'll give you a choice,' he said. 'A very simple choice. Either I send you over to the mansion now to report yourselves with a written note from me, or, you find out how *undamaging* it is to be on the other end of one of these.' He gestured to the stiff hoses at his feet.

'But, sir -'

'It's a simple choice, Roach. Even a shithead like you knows the right answer. Get those gowns off, the pair of you. Come on. And chuck your clothes in a pile over there.' Snipe bent down and picked up both hoses. 'Let's see if it's possible to wash off two severe cases of stupid.'

***

They were so much like animals that the townsfolk had forgotten what the Chosen were. Forgotten, or put it out of their minds. Shanti hadn't forgotten, though. Not when he worked with them every day, not when he listened to their harsh whispers and coded knocking on the walls.

Not when he looked into their eyes as he placed the captive bolt gun to their heads.

***

34

In the twilight, she saw him. The wire-tight tendons, the slick of sweat, the hammering of the pack against him, the never-straight legs, the penitent smile. Her eyes widened, the irises floating in pure white anger. She wanted to scream.

She confronted him as he threw cold water over himself in front of the old trough. Hands on hips, eyes luminous in the dusk she began with just two words.

'You promised.'

He couldn't look at her. The bloody coward. The weak-willed, pathetic coward.

'You don't care about anyone else except yourself, do you?'

He clenched his teeth. His ribs still heaved as his body recovered from the run.

'You can't manipulate me, Maya. It's wrong. It's dishonest.'

'When I simply ask you, nothing ever happens. This isn't about our morals, Richard Shanti. This is about raising a family. Caring for others.'

His temper snapped.

'There is nothing, *nothing*, caring about feeding meat to our children.'

Maya snorted her disgust.

'Really? Perhaps you can explain that to the doctor. Perhaps you can explain that to Hema and Harsha. And perhaps,' her voice broke and she half screamed, half cried at him, 'you can explain it to the Welfare when they come snooping into our lives next week.'

He grabbed the ragged old towel he used and ran past her into the house still dripping.

'What doctor? What's happened?'

She followed him up to the girls' bedroom where he stood beside their bunks, alternately resting a slim-fingered hand on each of their foreheads.

'They're on fire.'

She stood in the doorway shaking her head.

'What's wrong with them?' he asked.

'It's some kind of flu. Lots of kids have it at the moment.'

'But they haven't been in to the school this week.'

'That's what I told Doctor Fellows. He said the virus has a long incubation period. It's not uncommon.'

He turned his head towards her.

'Are they going to be all right?'

'They'll probably get over the virus, if that's what you mean. But there are going to be other problems now.'

35

He stood up and faced her.

'What do you mean?' he asked.

'The doctor was concerned that the girls were underweight.'

'No. No, Maya. We've talked about this. Why didn't you tell him that their weight is perfectly normal? I've told you it is a hundred times.'

Harsha tried to sit up. In the end she managed to stay up on one elbow.

'The doctor man had cold hands, Daddy. He said we're not eating enough poteem.'

'Lie down, sweetness,' said Richard,' You need to rest and then you'll feel better. Daddy's going to get you some protein.'

Maya signalled him to go downstairs and wait for her. She wiped the girls' heads with a damp cloth and kissed their hot cheeks saying, 'I'll be checking up on you. Use this broom handle to knock on the floor if you need me.'

In the kitchen, Richard stood with his palms resting on the counter as he stared into the darkness outside. He hung his head low and Maya saw his shoulders trembling. Her heart was hard.

'I can't believe it has to come to this before you start to care for your own children. They're too thin, Richard. We all are. And you, you're killing yourself with this running nonsense. No man can keep up the kind of punishment you give your body. Why must you treat us this way?'

The man who turned to face her was a tired old derelict. There was no flesh on his face, only hollow lines. His skin was pasty and blotched red from crying. If she hadn't seen him in the last ten years and then suddenly met him like this she wouldn't have recognised him.

'Because I care about you. I care about your *spirits*.'

'Richard, in this life, talk of the spirit is irrelevant. You have to care about our bodies. You have to look after us. If you don't, *spirit* is all that will remain.'

She watched his eyes. Dear Father, she thought, he really doesn't understand. He'd rather see us die for some inexplicable righteousness than live a healthy life.

'Richard, *please*. It's your duty as a husband and father to look after us, to provide for us. You could not be in a better position to do that. Most of the men you work with don't have the meat allowance that you have and yet you refuse to take advantage of it. Meanwhile, your family is starving.'

'You are *not* starving,' he whispered.

'Tell that to the Parson of the Welfare. She's coming on Monday evening. She'll be here for dinner and I expect there to be meat on this table. Otherwise I'm going to take the twins away myself. And I swear to you now, Richard Shanti, if that happens, you will never see any of us again.'

***

The second milking of the day was complete, the dairy boys had clocked out seconds after the shift had ended and Snipe was alone with his herd.

He tapped the jar of Beauty Balm in his cow-gown as he paced the rows. Most of the herd were back in the feedlots or pastures but those he was concerned about remained. WHITE

1260, WHITE 091, WHITE 7650 and several others looked in need of his ministrations. He gave his full attention to each one but he looked up often at a milking stall on the far side of the parlour where WHITE-047 was still chained. He was saving her until last. After what the dairy boys had done to her she would be traumatised. It could affect her yield or make her more prone to disease. Cows were far more sensitive to stress than management made allowances for.

He moved from cow to cow trying to maintain his soothing tones and movements but all the time he thought about WHITE-047 and her clear, shining eyes. He thought about the way looking at her made him feel. He'd unloaded all his anger onto Roach and Parfitt. They'd made it to the end of the shift but every move they'd made had been in agony. The hoses had bruised their pale skins and forced their closed eyes almost from their sockets. He'd played the jets over every part of them, making them move their hands from their crotches to their faces to protect themselves. He'd been one step ahead all the time. Water on their genitals would have been like a series of kicks. When they turned away from him he aimed at the backs of their heads where the pressure was almost enough to make them faint. Then the creases of their skinny arses where, no doubt, the jets of water would have forced their way within.

When he'd finished, their skin was red and raw from the rucking of the icy barrage. They'd cried and vomited and shat pale brown water as they ran away from him. He'd stood there trembling for several minutes unable to move or turn away from the place where WHITE-047 had stood before them. In the changing rooms he'd threatened them both with their jobs and told them he was docking a day's wages from their pay packets. Neither of them had spoken a word in response. He told them if they tried to take sick time, he'd report them.

37

There was a hiss from the cow he was working on and he realised he was massaging too vigorously.

'Hey, now, I'm sorry old girl. Here, how's this? Better?' He eased off the pressure, worked Beauty Balm more gently into the cow's swollen teats between his callused fingers. The hissing stopped.

One by one he led the cows out to join the rest of the herds. In time he was left alone with WHITE-047. His heartbeat quickened as he approached her and, for some reason he couldn't explain, his lower back ached. He swallowed again and again but his mouth and throat refused to moisten. He tried to ignore the stiffness of his crotch and the strange heat there.

Standing in front of the cow, he was once more amazed by the look of her. She was definitely different to all the others. But what was it? He looked and looked until it was a thoughtless stare. Only her nervous shuffling against the milking restraints broke his reverie.

Fortunately, the damage to her was superficial. They couldn't have had the jets on her for more than a couple of minutes when he'd caught them. He could see areas of redness where her skin was chafed by the high pressure and bruises beginning to flower on the strong curves of her thighs.

'It won't happen again, lass. Mr. Snipe promises you that. I've shown them the error of their ways. I've taught them some respect.'

He stepped into the stall with the cow and she backed away as far as the restraints allowed. Not her usual response.

Those stupid bastards.

'It's alright now. Mr. Snipe's not going to hurt you. Mr. Snipe's going to keep you healthy.'

His hands shaking, he brought out the jar of Beauty Balm and unscrewed the lid. He fingered out a larger scoop than he allowed the other cows, placed the jar on the partition, and split the lubricant evenly between his hands. Pressing close to the animal he stroked the greasy substance around its sore-looking teats. As he massaged, he entered a kind of trance. His pulse thrummed in his crotch.

'Beautiful, bounteous creature,' he crooned. 'Beautiful, beautiful girl. Mr. Snipe's going to make it all better.'

WHITE-047 cringed away from the touch but there was nowhere she could go. Snipe didn't even notice. Minutes passed and he felt a slow leakage in his underwear. He changed position to be closer to the cow, knocking the Beauty Balm from the edge of the stall with his elbow. It fell in slow motion, landed without sound, somehow remaining intact. He knelt to retrieve it and his face came close to the cow's bald vulva. A scent came from her, a singular note among many that made up the smell of the dairy herd. It was unique. Just like everything else about WHITE-047.

The smell affected him the way he imagined wives wanted perfume to affect their husbands. He paused, crouched on the concrete, his nose inches from the cow's skin, the Beauty Balm forgotten on the cold, wet floor. He breathed in the scent of the cow and it filled his mind. Some part of him snapped from its stratospheric tether and plummeted earthwards.

He dived for the cow's sex and pressed his face into it, licking, nuzzling and snuffling. The cow hissed but he didn't hear it. He was crying, his face wet with joy. He rose on trembling legs and looked at WHITE-047 as though seeing her for the first time but the look in her eyes was not the one he wanted to see. The look was one of knowing and disgust, of helplessness and hatred. The eyes were too cold. He turned her away from him. He unbuttoned his trousers and forced them down with shaking hands. He moved against her and the milking restraints tightened. She wasn't accepting him. Crazy now, he reached again for the Beauty Balm, plunged three fingers into the jar and slapped the wad of grease up between the cow's legs.

Half laughing, half crying he pushed into her once more and lost himself there totally. It was the only thrust he made. He convulsed and laid his head against her back still weeping tears he did not understand.

He never heard their footsteps. For a few moments he stayed close to her and then a strong contraction forced him from her. He reached down for his trousers, tucked his shirt in and turned around. They were all there: Harrison, Maidwell, Roach and Parfitt. All dressed in their town clothes. Legs apart. Arms folded. For once they weren't laughing.

Fearing a beating, Snipe began to babble.

'Listen, lads...this isn't what you think it is. I mean -'

'Shut up, Snipe,' said Roach. 'You're in some trouble.'

'There's an explanation, I can assure you. I -'

'You can explain it to Magnus.'

The crimson embarrassment faded from Snipe's face leaving it grey. The dairy boys didn't lift a finger to him. They turned away and left, their boots echoing off the damp concrete.

'Boys! Boys? Please don't do this. Please.' He sank to his knees with his hands outstretched to the deserted milking parlour. 'Pleeeease,' he begged.

But the dairy boys were gone.

Five

'We should pray,' said Parson Mary Simonson of the Welfare.

'Join hands with me, everyone.'

The girls, mostly recovered from their fevers, held hands easily with each other but the Parson was sitting between Hema and her father. The Parson reached out and grabbed Hema's fingers before she could pull away. A smile accompanied the unwanted grip. Maya took Harsha's small, hot hand in her left and reached the other reluctantly towards Richard. They had not touched for several days. It was his thumbless hand she found. She could see his bowed head from the edge of her vision. It was not bowed in piety but so that the Parson would not see his rage at her intrusion into their household. She saw his left hand take hold of the Parson's, saw the grip tighten.

'Such intensity, Mr. Shanti. How delightful.' Parson Mary Simonson composed herself, breathed deeply and settled her shoulders. 'Ah, yes. A couple of lines from the Gut Psalter seem particularly appropriate: Let us not reject Your gifts, Dear Father, nor take Your love for granted. Help us to have faith in Your mystery and may we never question Your ways.' She paused and sighed, not letting go. 'Bless this food, Dear Father, that we may do Your bidding gladly and with strength. We thank You for the gift of meat this day.'

She lifted her head and looked at each face around the table. All hands withdrew swiftly.

Maya had already served the plates. Each one was set before the members of her family and the Parson that had come to assess them. Maya's mouth watered, the children's faces were all anticipation now that their noses were full of the savoury scent from their plates. Maya tried not to look at Richard because she knew that he would be restraining his rising gorge long before a morsel passed his lips. If the Parson suspected that there was anything out of the ordinary in a good helping of meat, she would make her visits regular to be sure nothing was amiss. Everything had to appear normal or they risked losing the children. If Richard gave anything away he could be reported and lose his job. It was no secret that bad things happened to people who lost a job with Magnus Meat Processing. As far as Rory Magnus was concerned, you were either in or out. If you were out you weren't to be trusted. If Rory Magnus didn't trust you, life in the town wasn't worth living and you'd stop living it very soon.

'Please begin,' said the Parson but no one moved. She looked around the faces at the table again and then smiled.

'Well, that's very polite, I must say. Your family is a credit to you, Mr. Shanti.' She took up her knife and fork and stared into the rare griddled fillet that took up most of her plate. Lines blackened its surface and once the serrated edge of the knife was through the seared layer, it revealed the bloody flesh within. Watery red juices spread out on the plate as she sawed off a bite and forked it into her mouth. Maya watched her husband's jaw muscle ripple and clench. 'Mmm,' said the Parson, nodding in deep satisfaction. 'That is excellent steak, Mrs. Shanti. And, may I say, perfectly done.'

'Thank you,' said Maya. 'But it's really nothing to do with me. Richard has a top position at MMP. It comes with certain. . . advantages.'

'I understand. Extremely fortunate.' The Parson's words came out over half-chewed mouthfuls, the most polite way to talk at the table. 'But do you realise that there are townsfolk who can only afford meat once a week?'

Maya shook her head and then noticed the twins hadn't touched their food.

'Go on, girls,' she whispered.

They picked up their knives and forks and used them to tear at the meat. Maya had made sure it was thoroughly cooked. So cooked it was almost dry. The twins had problems cutting it up. Their knives and forks clattered against their plates drawing a stare from the Parson. Maya reached over and as swiftly as she could, cut their small steaks into manageable pieces while she blustered an excuse at the Parson.

'Still weak from the fever, poor things.'

She watched the Parson's eyes and decided that she was satisfied with the explanation. Thank the Lord, she thought, that Richard had brought home the best quality meat he could get his hands on. It seemed to be keeping the Parson happy. For the moment.

And the meat was truly delicious. Maya could not remember the last time she'd had any and the browned richness of it, the texture of it resisting her teeth, the nourishing juice of it flooded her mouth with saliva. It was close to impossible to eat it slowly.

'I wanted to ask you about that,' said the Parson.

Maya glanced at Richard. He still hadn't touched his food. She caught his eye, pleaded with him mentally not to let the family down. She telepathed to him in that split-second glance, one she prayed the Parson had not noticed, that if he didn't do his part, everything they'd made together would be finished forever. He picked up his knife and fork.

'Why do you think your girls are so skinny, Mrs. Shanti? Are they prone to this kind of illness? A healthy, well-nourished child shouldn't be getting sick, you know.'

Maya shrugged.

'Oh, I don't know,' she said. 'I don't want to tell you your job, Parson, but when I was a girl we were always coming down with something.'

It was the wrong thing to say and she regretted it almost before the sentence was out of her mouth. But it was too late to take it back and the Parson's face had lost any joviality that the steak had put there.

'When you were a girl, Mrs. Shanti, people didn't eat as well as they do now. Illness is not something to be taken lightly, as you would know if you read your Gut Psalter regularly. Illness is a matter to be taken very, very seriously indeed.'

Even at seven years of age the twins knew what 'serious' meant coming from the mouth of a Parson of the Welfare. They continued to eat their meals in silence.

Maya felt pale and cold inside. The Parson had stopped chewing her meat and was staring at her.

'I like a bit of gravy with my meat,' the Parson said. 'Adds a certain sloppiness. I like my meat sloppy. Shame,' she said, 'that there's no gravy.'

'I can easily make some,' Maya said. 'It won't take two minutes.'

Parson Mary Simonson smiled and thrust a dripping piece of flesh into her thin-lipped mouth.

'Not to worry, Mrs. Shanti. I'm almost finished now. I wouldn't want to put you to any trouble.'

'Oh, it's no trouble. No trouble at all. I just...didn't want to spoil the flavour of the meat. I'm...not a very good cook, you see.'

The Parson snorted.

'I think Mr. Shanti would agree with that. He hasn't touched his food.' She turned to Richard, appraising his lean features with what Maya took to be suspicion. 'I hope you're not feeling unwell, Mr. Shanti. Illness in the head of the family is not something that can be ignored.'

'I'm fine.'

He smiled at the Parson. It had been so long since she'd seen his face in that shape that Maya barely recognised the expression. She certainly didn't know that this was the smile he often cracked at work for his colleagues; the same smile that made him seem like a capable man who enjoyed his job. She thought it made him look insane. The Parson had seen the idiotic look he had. That was the end. They'd take the kids. Then they'd come and take him and that would be the end of her life as a respectable townsperson.

'It's been a custom in my family that we always let a guest finish their meal before we start our own,' he began. 'It's old-fashioned, I know. Going back to those very first days when Our Dear Father made the flesh honourable and sacred. The Shantis have been involved from the very beginning, you know. If it makes you feel uncomfortable, I will gladly join you before you finish your meal.'

The Parson was silent for too long. Maya knew whatever Richard had said was wrong and that the stupid look on his face had cemented their destiny. But she couldn't move, couldn't even kick him under the table to make him stop. She looked at the Parson's face. The woman had stopped chewing mid-mouthful and had yet to swallow. Finally she choked down the half-chewed lump on her tongue and said,

'I didn't realise, Mr. Shanti. I do hope you can forgive my behaviour. I assumed that...well, never mind. I'd be honoured to finish my meal before you begin yours. And after that I'll be able to make my report to Head Office. I can assure you it will be deemed entirely satisfactory.'

Richard performed a very small bow. Just a deep nod of the head really and the Parson finished her steak in silence.

Maya was stunned. The Shantis had been involved since *when*? The report would be entirely satisfactory? What had just happened? She had no way to tell. The Parson pushed her empty plate away and stood up.

'Wonderful food, Mrs. Shanti.' She cast her eye over the rest of the family and around the dining room and adjoining kitchen area nodding to herself. She removed a clipboard from a leather satchel at her feet and made a few marks on it with a red pencil and then said, 'Well, there we are. Everything's in order. I shall say thank you and bid you all good night. May the Father bless you and fill your stomachs.'

She was gone before Richard had put the blade of his steak knife to the meat on his plate. All that remained of her was a memory of her layered red robes. For several seconds everyone was silent. Then Maya said, 'Dear Father, Richard, what did you say to her? What on earth has happened?'

***

With four witnesses speaking against him and no one to defend his claims, Snipe's 'appearance' before Rory Magnus was brief. He spent most of the time looking at the cattle-hair rug on which he stood in the giant man's office. On the occasions he did glance up he saw a look on Magnus's face that he hadn't expected. The man was not outraged by the charges. He appeared almost amused as he smoked a small black cheroot and sipped vodka. From time to time he didn't even seem to be listening.

Snipe began to hope that what he'd done wasn't enough to bring the full weight of Magnus's might down upon him. Maybe they'd caught him on a good day. Maybe the rumours of Magnus's punishments were no more than idle talk to make the workforce toe the line. After ten minutes, Magnus dismissed the dairy boys and Snipe was left alone with the Meat Baron and his bodyguard.

When the sound of the boys' footsteps had receded down the stairs, Magnus spoke directly to Snipe for the first time.

'You'd be surprised how many cow fuckers I see in here, Snipe. Some of them like to fuck the veal calves, others prefer the steers. Doesn't matter to me what they do because when I find out, they never do it again.'

Snipe couldn't meet the man's glare. Magnus's dangerous joviality on top of his own shame was too much to bear.

'Sex has always been a risky business at the best of times. You never know what you'll catch off the scum that pass themselves off as women in this town. It's no wonder the cattle look better to some of my workers than their own wives and squeezes. I don't understand it, but I can see how it happens.

'Unfortunately, that doesn't make me any happier about the potential damage to, and disrespect for, my property. Every single beast in this town belongs to me and anyone that treats my beasts with anything other than respect is going to pay the price. What I can't comprehend is why my workers haven't got that into their tiny brains yet. It's not written down anywhere, but everyone knows the penalty for messing with my business.'

Magnus leaned back in his chair causing it to creak.

'I assume you've read The Book of Giving.'

Snipe was impelled to fill the silent void that followed the statement.

'Yes, Mr. Magnus.'

'You therefore know the punishment for 'lying down' with the Chosen, correct?'

'Yes, Mr. Magnus.'

Magnus pressed his lips together in a look that seemed to bring the matter to a close in his mind.

'In that case, I've nothing further to say to you. Bruno, arrange for Snipe's introduction to the herd. Have it done here as soon as you can find Cleaver. Make sure Snipe is processed immediately. I want nothing but sausage to remain by this evening.'

He poured himself another vodka.

Bruno grabbed Snipe by the back of the neck, his customary grip, and propelled him towards a curtain at the back of the study. Pulling it open revealed a door in the wooden panelling. Bruno opened it and pushed Snipe onto a dark staircase that led straight down.

'Oh, and Bruno, leave that open would you? I may pop down for a few minutes when Cleaver gets to work.'

***

Like many workers in the meat industry, Shanti was missing a digit. In his case it was the thumb of his right hand. Unlike the others, injured in the course of a day's meat processing, he had lost his in an accident of which he had no recollection. It had happened before he was even a year old and he had learned to cope without the use of it very well. It didn't hamper his use of the captive bolt gun at all.

As far as management were concerned, his dexterity was prized not because it was humane but because it meant more meat through the chutes each day. Shanti believed himself to be a kind, compassionate man and he dealt death as swiftly and painlessly as possible. He abhorred the thought of suffering in any creature but himself. What he saw each day was not a parade of mindless cattle, nor was it a queue of expressionless, animal faces. It was not lives he saw passing him by and winking out. No, that was too great a reality to take in. What Richard Shanti saw in the lines of Chosen that passed each day was a montage of eyes.

The eyes were luminous woodland green. The eyes were polished antique brown. The eyes were wise grey. The eyes were the blue of free skies and shattered sapphires. The eyes were ringed with the whites of pleading, whites of staring. The eyes were set in resolute white. Trapped in resigned white. Surrounded by the whiteness of death. The eyes spoke to him because the owners of the eyes could not.

Though he did not listen, he could not help but hear.

For calves of the Chosen, the various rituals performed that branded them cattle for the rest of their lives took place in their infancy and over several weeks. For Greville Snipe the process took less than an hour.

He had to wait while Cleaver finished his lunch. Bruno watched over him to make sure he didn't bolt when he saw the room they'd brought him to. Snipe had seen many of the procedures performed on young calves and had never given it much thought. Now he was in a windowless room where all these measures, and many others that usually occurred in the slaughterhouse and meat packing areas, could be carried out. The vibrating that began in his body was very different from the one he'd felt whilst conjoined with the object of his sin in the milking parlour. There was an unreliability in his bowels and bladder and in his knees. He could feel his patellae jumping like bait jerked on a line.

It had all happened so quickly that he couldn't make space for it in his mind. And yet, his body knew what was coming. It was preparing. He felt the cold in his feet and hands as his blood flow restricted itself to his core. His face felt cold and wet and there was a torsion of the muscles in his stomach. His thoughts fled wildly within the confines of his mind as his eyes fluttered across each of the areas in the room.

It was not clean. There were black, flaky areas on the floor that he knew could only be one thing. Similar stains covered the various straps, restraints and crude, slablike tables. The air in the room was stuck somehow. It smelled of animals and chemicals. The odour stung his eyes and nose.

Uppermost in his mind was the knowledge that this was a room where he would *not* die.

The clenching of his stomach became irresistible – his body still preparing itself – and he vomited a tubelike spray of greenish fluid. At this, Bruno kicked him away and he fell hard on his knees, unable to break his fall with his tied hands.

'Keep your filth away from me.'

Bruno kicked him again in the back of the thigh drawing a cry this time.

'Fucking useless piece of meat.'

A door opened at one end of the dim room and a switch was flicked. The place was filled with a cold, hard glare. Every piece of equipment seemed to become either black, white or silver. There was more to be seen too. Snipe saw the banks of instruments that no one had bothered to clean other than with the swipe of a rag. They hung from racks and lay in untidy rows on a bench; like tools in an uncared-for workshop. He heard Cleaver approach before he saw him through the stab of harsh light – steel-cleated boots on concrete – the sound of the slaughterhouse man arriving for work.

Cleaver stepped into view and wiped his hand down the front of his dark beard trying to remove the remains of his lunch. Snipe saw very clearly the scraps of grey meat and gelatine from a savoury pie. Cleaver looked right through him to Bruno.

'You hanging around for this or what?' Bruno shrugged.

'Do you need me?'

'Not unless you want to get that nice overcoat dirty.'

'Fine. The beast's all yours.'

'He's not a beast yet. He's still a man. Aren't you?'

He looked at Snipe for the first time. Appraising him as though he were already no more than a hindquarter.

'Not exactly a quality item, though, are you?' Snipe was unable to speak.

'Better leave us to it, Bruno. I'll have him ready in an hour or so.'

Bruno sauntered to the door without looking back. Snipe was a forgotten man and he knew it.

'Right you. Here's how we're going to do it. First, you need to void your tanks. That means number ones *and* twos – I don't want you messing on me when we're halfway through.'

While he talked, Cleaver prepared a long pole with a noose at the end of it and before Snipe could register what it was, the loop was around his neck. Cleaver pulled it tight then released Snipe's wrist shackles.

'Come on, this way.'

He hauled Snipe to a corner of the room where there was a rough hole in the concrete and told him to squat.

'Make it quick, I've got plenty more jobs to do before the day's out.'

Snipe couldn't have held it in if he'd tried. When he finished he felt empty not only of waste but of his organs. He was a hollow man.

Cleaver yanked him away from the latrine without letting him clean himself. That was when Snipe began to cry. His whole solar plexus shuddered until he couldn't tell if he was breathing in or out and the snot dribbled from his nose in bubbling rivulets. Cleaver didn't appear to notice.

On the far side of the room he kicked open a panel on the floor to reveal what looked like a giant sunken bath. It was filled with a thin white fluid. This was where the chemical smell originated. Without any kind of warning, Cleaver pulled Snipe into the bath. It was deep and though Snipe didn't sink naturally, he felt the pole forcing him down to the bottom of the trough. Within seconds, a burning began all over his body. He opened his mouth to scream and the chemical dip flooded in. He choked. Before he could take another breath, the noose was lifting him out at the other end of the trough and he was lying on the cold floor heaving and coughing. The noose loosened a little – Cleaver giving him a moment to recover.

It didn't last.

The pole hauled him to his feet. Though his stomach was empty he retched and retched trying to clear the fluid from his throat. When he opened his eyes he was half blinded. A white haze lay over everything. Even through this he could see the hair sliding off his body. Then the high-pressure hose was on him, its freezing jet welcome, at least for the first few seconds as it washed away the burn. But soon enough the jet was painful. Cleaver aimed it at every part of him, jerked him around to get the desired angles. Snipe shivered.

His hair, all of it, was gone.

***

Shanti watched the bull through a crack between the gate and hinge. It was on its side and curled tight like a giant baby. Amazing, he thought, how different they are asleep and awake. The bull's number was 792, stencilled onto a blue tag that pierced the flattened area of flesh between its Achilles tendon and anklebone. The tag bolts were made of stainless steel about half a centimetre thick. Removing them was impossible for the Chosen but a stockman could do it with a specially-made pair of pliers. The tags were attached to newborns around the time many of the other rituals were performed, whilst they were young enough to forget the pain. Once the piercing had healed, new numbers and colour codes could be attached as necessary depending on the animal's ultimate purpose.

BLUE-792 was a prize bull. His genes had created hundreds, possibly thousands, of calves over the years and some of his offspring, a very few, had become bulls too, siring even more calves to keep the herds going. Shanti recognised every one of BLUE-792's descendants. They weren't the beautiful cattle of the herds. They were the heavy-boned, hardy strain.

They were the ones that survived disease and the cold, regimented routine that was herd life. They were the ones that fulfilled their purpose. All of them shared his blue eyes and round face. Most of them had his swollen bulb of a nose. They were in the dairy herds, in the bullpens, in the veal enclosures and in the meat herds too. Only bulls and dairy cows would live as long as BLUE-792 and of those, only the very finest bulls would lead such a long and prosperous existence.

Shanti watched the bull sleep and wondered how many of its offspring he had already dispatched. So many times the access panel on the conveyor had opened and he would find himself looking into the eyes of BLUE-792 passed down one, or sometimes two, generations. And here was their predecessor, still alive. Still kicking, as the stockmen would say.

BLUE-792 stirred, causing the straw he was lying in to rustle. Shanti froze in position. If the bull knew it was being watched it could cause problems. Cattle that formed any kind of relationship with their human overlords tended to alter their behaviour patterns, to become unmanageable. Many words were synonymous with meat at MMP. 'Unmanageable' was one of them. Shanti liked watching this particular bull. He didn't want to find himself looking into its eyes as he pressed a pneumatic weapon to its head. Not yet. Not until BLUE-792's time was well and truly up.

The bull sat up, as though waking to a sudden loud noise. Shanti shrank back away from the crack and held his breath for a few moments. More scratching and rustling came from inside the pen as the bull raised itself heavily onto its legs. For a few seconds afterwards there was total silence. Shanti planned to back away quickly and noiselessly if he heard the bull come towards where he was standing. Instead he heard the swish of straw as BLUE-792 walked to the far end of its pen and began to tap its finger stumps on the wall. Shanti heard the whispered hissing and sighing coming from the bull's mouth. He wondered how many other Magnus Meat Processing employees had noticed the Chosen signalling each other this way. He doubted anyone had the time for observation. None of them took the same interest he did.

The not-quite-random taps and breaths continued and Shanti crept back towards the crack. Inside he saw BLUE-792 with one ear laid to the aluminium panels. There was a smile creasing its face. Perhaps it was comforted just to hear the response of other animals and know that it was not alone.

Nauseated and weakened by the chemicals in the dip, Snipe found himself barely able to struggle as Cleaver forced him towards one of the sarcophagus-shaped operating tables. The noose tightened, constricting Snipe's windpipe and cutting off most of the blood flow to and from his head. Just before he reached the table he blacked out.

It must have been part of Cleaver's method for handling his charges on his own. When Snipe came round, the hard lights came back into focus above him; he was spread-eagled on the slab. Cleaver was tightening a strap on his ankle. His other limbs were already secured but Cleaver appeared to want no movement at all to disrupt his work. A leather strap came over his chest and was pulled so taut he had to breathe from his solar plexus to get any air. Another was looped over the bones of his pelvis, another locked his knees flat. The final strap was for his head. He tried to fight this one because it would mean he could no longer see what was happening. He didn't want to look but it was the last modicum of control he possessed. He swung his head from side to side trying to evade Cleaver's grip and for a while he succeeded in preventing the last strap being fixed. It was only when Snipe felt a smooth section of timber slide under the back of his neck that he realised Cleaver wanted him to struggle so that he could arrange things according to his requirements.

With the block of wood there, his struggles were restricted but he didn't give up. The tip of a knife appeared large and distorted only millimetres from his right eye.

'You're going to make me late with all this fucking around. Blinding isn't part of the ritual,' breathed Cleaver. 'But I'd be happy to include it at your request.'

Snipe stopped moving.

'That's more like it.'

Cleaver drew a strap across his forehead and pulled it tight. Because of the block underneath his neck, Snipe's throat was extended and exposed as the broad loop of leather shortened against his brow. He could breathe but he could no longer swallow.

When Cleaver thrust the tip of a scalpel into his larynx, Snipe screamed for the first and last time. The sound was cut short.

***

50

Rory Magnus sat back in his chair with a creak so familiar he didn't notice it and put his booted feet on the scarred oak of his desk. He lit a cheroot from the previous one he'd been smoking and dropped the first one into his ashtray without bothering to crush it out.

From the door at the back of his study he could hear the faint sounds of struggling, the rush of bodily evacuations and inevitable dunking and wet thrashing. He'd heard it all a hundred, a thousand times, before and he never tired of it. This was how to rule the town. This was how to maintain high standards at the factory. This was how to command respect and destroy dissent.

The curtain by the door shifted in an air current and soon Magnus could smell shit and bile and the acidic tang of the dip. It was unusual in so far as there had been no words of pleading from the cow-poking dairyman. But soon, though. Any minute now there would be -

The scream.

The first incision was the easiest to abide but they all screamed. Every single one of them. And then the scream would cease as though someone had swept an axe down upon a block. *Efficient Mr. Cleaver.* He smiled.

And after the scream there was a different sound, just as intense. More so perhaps. A desperate sibilation that struggled to be heard. Magnus could imagine Snipe's lips moving as his words no longer came. The silent begging and the wordless hisses of transformation.

Deeper, more complete cuts would follow.

Magnus listened as if to a familiar duet played by unfamiliar musicians. He listened and it was good.

Six

It was dusty in the records offices. The further back through the years the Parson went, the dustier the filing boxes and the shelves around them became. The silence in there lay like dust also, strata of it pressing down and muffling the wood, the cardboard, the paper.

A records officer had stamped her Welfare pass; a flaky-skinned man with white hair curling out of his ears and nostrils, an air of ancient overuse about his faded green tank top and the worn edges of his collar. He had the smell of a man who lived alone. A records clerk assisted him. Between them they recorded all the births, deaths and marriages in the town and filed them in manila folders in brown boxes on racks of shelves.

Parson Mary Simonson's trip to the far end of the records office took her deep into territory where the dust had remained undisturbed for years, possibly decades. There was rarely a reason for anyone to go back there and very few Welfare workers had clearance in the first place. White-haired Whittaker, the records officer, and his clerk, Rawlins, were paid to keep accurate records not clean the place. It showed. Her feet scuffed trails in the dust and her robes swept the linoleum. She had to lift up her hems to keep from taking all the grime with her.

It was no different with the cardboard archive boxes. Disturbing them created clouds of irritating particles that made her choke and sneeze. Following the spasms of her airways, more clouds were created. She wanted to give up.

There was dust in her hair and in her eyes and ears. Dust all over her clothes. But by then she'd found the box containing surnames beginning with S in the year that she was curious about. There was no reason not to continue. She could satisfy her question and get out of there. Get away and get clean. She put her thick red sleeve across her nose and mouth and removed the lid from the archive box.

Inside, the manila folders became the brightest, newest things in the entire records hall. They almost glowed. Glad she'd persevered, she walked her fingers through to Shanti and pulled the file. Inside there was no birth entry as she'd expected. Instead, the record of the death of a child named Richard Arnold Shanti. The boy had suffocated during labour and was stillborn to his mother Elizabeth Mary Shanti.

She stood staring through the record card for several long moments, no longer taking in the information typed there. A little layer of the disturbed dust settled on the gleaming folders and when she returned the file to its proper position the dust was trapped there by her replacing the box lid.

***

A small delivery truck took Snipe back to the MMP factory. There was nowhere to sit and the space was not high enough for him to stand. These were the smallest of his discomforts.

The stumps of his fingers and the spaces where his thumbs had been were cauterised shut by Cleaver's white hot irons. If nothing else, the man had worked with tremendous speed, clipping digits at the knuckles and sealing them in seconds. The pain had been a revelation. Where his testicles had been, metal staples held the remains of his scrotum closed. Pinkish drool seeped from his mouth: he had no teeth left.

He could see the clear plasma that still welled at his finger-joints, and the drips of still warm blood that dropped from his crotch to the floor of the wagon. Staples also held closed the wound in his throat but that was the least painful of them all. The dirt from the bed of the truck was getting into the blackened ends where his big toes used to be and there was nothing he could do to prevent it.

The truck bounced over the barely-maintained country roads that led out to Magnus's plant, swerving to miss potholes and lurching over lumps and subsidence. Snipe was thrown against the walls and dashed to the floor many times and there was no way to stop himself without causing more agony.

The truck slowed and turned and he knew he had arrived at the main gate. He heard voices outside – the driver showing his card to the security guard. And then the truck moved on more slowly.

When the back doors opened he was looking into the slaughterhouse crowd pens. A ramp led from the truck to the slaughterhouse floor and a larger ramp led from there down into the pen. It was full of the Chosen, milling and jostling very gently, almost caressing as they swirled among each other.

Cattle. Cows. How swiftly we are made the same.

Some of them saw him and stopped moving. Soon the entire herd was still.

A burning electrical sting on his buttock sent Snipe stumbling down both ramps and he was amongst them. Their eyes took him in. Their noses testing the air he brought with him. Many of them shrank away. He saw their eyes differently now. These were eyes like his.

My God, what's behind them? What are they thinking?

It was impossible to tell.

He was frightened to move forward but gates closed behind him, forcing him on. He limped on incomplete feet to be among them but they parted whenever he came near and turned their backs to him. Hundreds of smooth bodies, fatter than his and somehow more beautiful. They stayed away from him, would not let him touch them. He looked at his own body and then looked at theirs. They were larger, more whole-looking even with their amputations. They were serene.

He heard the hissing, sighing sounds they made and it sounded like language in a way it never had before. He tried to speak to them but at the sound of his hissing, their faces became twisted and ugly as though he'd done no more than scratch a fork across a blackboard.

My name's Snipe. Greville Snipe. I work . . . I used to work in the dairy. I took care of the cows there. Perhaps you've heard of me.

They backed away, his whispers making no impression.

Dear Father, I am not even worthy of cattle. They will not accept me as their own. What am I Lord? What have I become?

The steel gates pressed against his back and he could not resist. The metal pushed him into the ranks of animals. Yet still they parted, none of them allowing closeness. He was alone among the Chosen for he was not Chosen.

Out of their ranks, a bull appeared. It dwarfed Snipe in height and width. As a dairyman he'd never been so close to one before. He knew their reputation though. Between the bull's legs a huge pizzle swung and below it the biggest pair of testicles Snipe had ever seen. The bull was layered with fat but the giant musculature was visible beneath it. It locked eyes with Snipe and he looked down and away. He wasn't even as alive as this creature now. The bull's bulk was terrifying, even through the pain of his trauma and injuries.

It gestured to Snipe with a flick of its enormous bald head. The meaning was clear.

Snipe edged forward and the cattle in the crowd pen opened before him. The bull stepped in behind, giving him no choice but to keep moving. His body, remembering only the intrusion of blades and the biting of clippers and the yanking of pliers, moved onward. He had no strength to turn and fight the bull and even if he had he no longer felt the self-worth it would take to stand firm. The crowd pen narrowed until it became a corridor and then a chute. He saw a cow step forwards into an alcove and then the alcove slid out of view. An empty one appeared in its place.

Snipe hesitated and turned. The bull was right behind him. Nowhere to go but forwards. He took a few more hesitant steps and stopped again, his body refusing to do what was required of it. The alcove disappeared and another took its place. And another.

A shout came from somewhere outside the pen.

'What the fuck's going on in that crowd pen? Get these fucking animals moving. That's two – no, wait – three misses in a row. Come on, lads, keep them moving.'

A new alcove appeared. The bull stepped forwards and pushed Snipe into it.

He saw the blood on the floor as the alcove began to move forwards leaving the bull and the crowd pen behind. A steel frame settled over him, locking him into a standing position and preventing him from turning his head. The alcove stopped with a jolt.

A small rectangular hatch slid open and he saw the face of a man he vaguely recognised from the staff canteen. The man's eyes were somehow blind. He lifted a gun to Snipe's forehead.

I am meat.

***

Jones was a new bolt gunner and it was an insult that he had to put up with empty restrainers. How was a guy supposed to get a bonus if the filers didn't do their job? The panel opened and finally he had a cow to whack. He glimpsed the eyes for a fraction of a second and thought they looked familiar.

'God is supre -'

He realised this one was not Chosen and cut the blessing short.

He pulled the trigger. The gun recoiled smoothly. Hiss. Clunk.

They all looked so similar.

Bob Torrance was incensed at the speed of the chain. Something was going on in the crowd pens but he couldn't tell what.

He bawled as he descended from his steel balcony:

'What's the problem?'

A stockman with a cattle prod shouted back from the pens:

'Delivery from Magnus, boss. It's taken care of now.' Torrance nodded to himself as he reached the factory floor.

Magnus's deliveries always fucked with the chain speed but there was nothing he could do about it. Tomorrow he'd move the new boy further along the chain and get Ice Pick back on the bolt gun to make up lost time. Every second counted. The demand for meat rose every day as the population of the town grew and it was up to Torrance to see they got what they needed. At least, that was what everyone believed. Torrance was paid to believe it too.

He marched past Jones to the bleeding station. There was always a backlog here. Between stunning and exsanguination cattle were hung by their ankles in loops of chain that hung from a giant steel runner. The runner was like a well-greased curtain rail suspended from the factory ceiling. The cattle swung upside down along this runner from one station to the next as they were broken down into food and by-products. The first port of call was the bleeding station.

The bleeder's job was to sever the neck of each cow from throat to neck-bone and push it along the runner. A broad trough caught the drainings from the Chosen and funnelled it into collecting vats. Later, the blood was used in making MMP black pudding. The delay between stunning and reaching the bleeding station sometimes resulted in the Chosen regaining consciousness before their throats were cut but there was no way around this. It had always been a weak area of the chain.

Of the seven Chosen that were hanging waiting for the bleeder's knife three were twitching. The movement reminded

Torrance of escape artists that hung upside down in strait-jackets and chains, trying to get free within a time limit. The cattle were going nowhere though. It was merely residual impulses travelling down the nerve pathways from brain to body and was a sign that death had occurred. It was when they started to breathe again – making their rhythmic hisses and sighs – that was the sign of the bolt gunner getting it wrong or sometimes just a particularly strong animal refusing to die quickly.

A fourth carcass shuddered and its ribcage expanded and contracted spastically. Torrance shrugged; it wouldn't last long after the knife. Looking more closely he saw the damage on the reviving animal. Its finger stumps were black and red and castration could only recently have been performed. The heel tag still trickled blood back towards its knee. So, this was the Magnus delivery. The thing, neither Chosen nor human, began to struggle by pumping its pelvis backwards and forwards. It nudged the stunned cattle on either side of it causing ripples through the bodies. The swaying caused the body to turn on its chain and Torrance saw the thing's face.

He knew the man, of course, though it was difficult to place him now that he was bald. The hole in his forehead had bled freely so there was a slick of gore drying both above and below it, making a mask of the face. Torrance thought back and remembered the rumours that had been coming out of the dairy for the last few weeks. Someone there had been getting a little too close to the milkers. Now he remembered. Greville Snipe; the best dairyman MMP had employed for years. Torrance shook his head to himself. What a shame the man had overstepped the boundaries. Devaluing stock was the stupidest, most dangerous thing anyone – MMP employee or otherwise – could do. It was suicidal. Snipe appeared to have found that out for himself. Well, almost; he wasn't quite finished yet.

Snipe's shocked eyes focussed on Torrance but the slow spiralling of the chain twisted his strange gaze away. The sound of runner bearings sliding in their housings brought Torrance back from his musings. The bleeder was pulling Snipe into position. Snipe hissed at the man – it was Burridge on the bleed this shift – and Burridge drew the knife across his muted throat. Torrance watched Snipe's eyes widen, white orbs surrounded by blackening blood, and the hissing became a bubbling. Burridge swung Snipe away to bleed out over the trough. There, the motorised section of the chain caught hold of his loop on the runner and hauled him, gently swinging, onward. By the time he reached the scalding vats that would loosen his skin for removal, he would be eight pints lighter.

His struggles continued.

Fascinated, Torrance forgot his inspection tour and followed Snipe's progress across the trough. What had begun as a gushing fountain was already slowing to a leak. Snipe's body was as pale now as the milk of the Chosen. Steam rose and bubbles burst on the boiling surface of the scalding vats. Snipe's eyes still swivelled in his head. The only place in his body that could possibly contain blood now would be his head. That, thought Torrance, was the only explanation for why Snipe was still alive. Could any creature – man, Chosen or otherwise – be so terrified of death that it would will itself to survive through all this? Snipe tried to bend away from the roiling water below him but there was no strength in his muscles.

The automated runner dropped him headlong into the vat. Torrance stepped back from the splash. Four seconds later, the runner drew his body up again, the skin now reddened and loose. Snipe's boiled eyes no longer moved in their sockets but here and there, his muscles twitched and jumped and Torrance knew it was no simple nerve impulse.

The wide wound in his neck had congealed in the water, the blood turning grey and gelatinous. Snipe's head flapped from the end of his body and the wound looked like the mouth of an inverted puppet.

Torrance had stopped walking.

Now it will be over. Now. Surely.

Snipe had reached the spinning blade that would remove his head. Torrance didn't care what kind of willpower the ex-dairyman had, when the steel slipped through the vertebrae of his neck that would be the end. Unusually, Torrance felt a wash of relief. He massaged his forehead with one rough hand and marched along the rest of the chain to make his hourly inspection.

He found it difficult to concentrate.

***

That night Parson Mary Simonson ate tripe to ease the pains in her stomach.

For a while they abated but less than an hour after her meal, the stabbing returned. She felt that the Father was punishing her for something but she could not understand what it was she had done, or not done, to deserve his ire. She followed the flesh codes as written in the sacred texts; she enforced Welfare upon as many in the town as her working days would allow. It hadn't been easy recently with rumours of a heretical messiah coming from every quarter. All this she did faithfully and still the Father sought to make her suffer. The pain in her stomach was a ball of jagged glass. Thrusting her fist deep into the flesh there seemed to quell it a little.

She lived alone, as all Parsons of the Welfare were required to do and so her evenings were her own to do with what she pleased. She liked it that way. Something about the idea of a man lounging in the house from night until morning and the incessant tug of noisy children made her uncomfortable. Better to be alone. Better to serve the Father in every moment that she was able.

That night, instead of embroidering, she sat down with her books and read the scriptures. Perhaps, she thought, I've been embroidering too much after work and not spending enough time meditating on the sacredness of the flesh. Perhaps that is the reason the Father gives me this pain.

She lit a small fire and pulled her hard wooden chair up close to it. On her lap she opened the Book of Giving and read aloud to herself from it:

'The Father sent his own children down to Earth so that we, his townsfolk, might eat. He made his children in his own image and laid down the commandments of the flesh so that we might be worthy of their sacrifice. Thus He commands us:

'Thou shalt eat of the flesh of my children. My children are your cattle. Break their bodies as your daily bread, take their blood as your wine. By sharing daily in this bounty shall you be united with me.

'Thou shalt keep my children silent by paring the reeds in their throats at the time of birth. Their silence is sacred and they must never speak the words of Heaven.

'Thou shalt keep my children from mischief by taking two bones from each finger in their first week.

'Thou shalt keep my children from wandering by taking the first two bones from the first toe of each foot in their second week.

'Thou shalt keep my children hairless by baptising them in the fragrant font.

'Thou shalt keep the mightiest male calves as bulls, that more strong children may be born.

'Thou shalt keep all other male calves chaste by castrating them in their ninth year.

'Thou shalt keep their mouths toothless.

'Thou shalt keep a sacred stock of male calves away from light and unmoving. These shall be my tenderest gift to you.

'Thou shalt drink the milk of the cows and from that milk make butter, yoghurt and cheese.

'Thou shalt allow all my sick children to return to their father but while they are in your care, thou shalt keep them from harm.

'I sacrifice my children for each of you that none shall ever be hungry. Their flesh is sacred. Thou shalt not dishonour me by wasting it.

'My children are divine. Thou shalt not lie down with them, neither taint their flesh with thine own.

'By eating of the sacred flesh of my children, may all mankind be one day sacred themselves and join me at my table. The suffering of my children is as nothing when compared to the suffering of mankind. They give themselves freely, knowing they return to me.

'Thou shalt, at the time of sacrifice, face my children East, that their souls may fly to the rising sun and so to me.

'My children are your medicine. To heal your eyes, eat their eyes. To heal your stomachs, eat their stomachs. To drive out madness, eat their brains. Heal yourselves; my children are your medicine.'

She sighed and pulled her chair closer to the guttering flames of the fire. There seemed to be no way to warm herself and she feared she was sickening with something. The reading she'd chosen for the evening gave her no comfort, certainly no answers to the conundrum of Richard Shanti. The child Richard Shanti had died and yet Richard Shanti the man was here in Abyrne. Alive and well, though painfully thin, and claiming ancestry to the old families. It was a bold statement to make. Not a risk he would have undertaken carelessly.

There were only two explanations that made sense. He'd either lied, thinking that she wouldn't be interested enough to check out his claims, or he really believed he was a Shanti from the first families. What was the truth? Surely he wasn't a stupid man. Quiet, certainly, but not stupid. There was too much knowledge behind those eyes of his. She didn't think he was deluded either. He had a wild look about him, the ascetic frame of a priest, but that was no reason to suspect he was delusional. No, she would bet anything that Richard Shanti believed he was the true son of Elizabeth and Reginald Shanti, that he had no idea anything else might be the case.

That cleared part of it up. But if he wasn't in the lineage, if he wasn't their son, then who was he? And was his identity an important factor in the Welfare of his children?

The centre of her gut twisted and she almost punched herself there to push back the pain. Without any warning at all, she was nauseous. No time to make it to the lavatory. She knelt before the fire and rucked the undigested contents of her stomach into the brass wood bucket next to the hearth. Seeing half-chewed stomach lining sticking to the logs and kindling made it all worse. She heaved and heaved, trying to force the spiky knot of pain from her own belly but once the meal she'd eaten was gone, dampening and tainting her wood supply, nothing was left inside her but a lump of thorns.

She forgot all about Richard Shanti.

Seven

'Let's play the dark game,' Hema said.

They were alone in the bedroom. Their mother had a visitor and didn't want to be disturbed. The girls didn't mind; they never got tired of each other.

'No,' said Harsha. 'It doesn't work any more. Let's make a new game.'

They knelt in front of a shabby chest and opened the lid. The toys in the toy box were old and battered, as was the box itself. It contained the playthings of children that had long since departed the world. The box was just big enough for one of the twins to fit into if they took out all the toys, but they were growing fast and the 'dark game' was one they played rarely now. For years, they'd taken it in turns to shut each other inside the box and sit on it, competing to see who could stay in there the longest. The stints of sitting alone on the lid or inside with the hard-sided darkness grew longer and longer until there wasn't enough time to both take a turn in one session. Their natural development had been the thing to make the game less of a challenge. It wasn't the same when your shoulder was pushing open the lid and letting the light in.

The box was wooden and handmade, probably by a well-meaning father with little skill. Each panel was covered, inside and out, with a layer of stapled-on curtain material. Inside, where items had been pulled out and put back in a thousand times, the faded drapery had torn and through it showed the plain pine boards that formed the floor and walls of the box. Some of them bore tiny holes where woodworm had tunnelled. The curtain material was silky with age and sometimes the girls spent a few minutes trying to stroke the wounds in the fabric closed for the comfort it brought to their fingertips.

The lid of the box was curtain-covered too, but the top side was cushioned with an ancient piece of quilting. The material that covered the padding, although worn, had never ripped. The maker of the box had been far-sighted enough to use a triple layer of old curtain there. Three brass hinges that still looked new secured the lid but the hinges were loose and, though their father had promised to tighten them, he was always too tired to remember. The box wasn't without its traps. It demanded an occasional sacrifice in the form of a cut from a rusty staple and it would, at times, impart a splinter to a careless hand.

61

The box smelled of things from a past they had never seen or known. Both Hema and Harsha associated the smell with play and risk and fantasy. Opening the toy box allowed it to breathe and when its sigh came out, the girls entered their magical world; a world that was never the same twice. There was an old wooden train set with pegs on its carriages where carved, painted soldiers stood to attention. A miniature dinner set. Nine silver thimbles they could use as dainty goblets. There was an old teddy bear with stitches where its eyes had been and more baldness than fur. A draughts board with missing pieces. A tin spinning top, its paint all worn away. There were old silk scarves of many colours, a Trilby hat and a Bowler. Deeply suffused in their leather bands, the hats bore the thick smell of trapped, greasy scalps; of strangers the twins only imagined. Dolls, dice, darts. A strange cube of black plastic with nine squares to each side and squeaky, twisting facets. Marbles rolled around at the bottom of the box.

'I know a game we could play,' said Harsha, picking out a plastic female doll with long blond hair. The doll wore a pink, red and white outfit: red beret, striped pink and white blouse. A red mini skirt and red high heels. She had a red plastic belt and a red plastic handbag. Harsha looked at her sister and they shared a moment of silent communication.

'We'll need Mama's scissors,' said Hema.

'You'll have to be very quiet.'

'She won't hear,' said Hema. 'She's too busy.'

She jumped to her feet in excitement and tiptoed to the door. Downstairs, all was quiet. She slipped along the hallway to the bathroom and took the nail scissors from the mug they shared with two emery boards and other implements for finger and toenail grooming. The scissors had curved blades but she was fairly sure they'd work. Keeping to the threadbare carpet, she approached their bedroom.

From downstairs she heard a noise; a chair moving, a cupboard being shut, something banging onto a counter? She couldn't be sure.

She stopped moving and listened hard. The silence was alive; like someone downstairs was listening for her, not the other way around.

Then other sounds came, too indistinct for her to hear properly. The chair again? A voice whispering? She didn't wait to find out. Even more carefully she crept the last few steps to the door, dodged inside and closed it tight and quiet behind her. She held the scissors up with a look of triumph and Harsha smiled back at her.

The game could begin.

They started by removing the doll's clothes.

***

There was so much you could tell about the townsfolk that came to the lock-up; so much you could tell about *people*. You only had to look.

John Collins watched them all as they slipped through the doors of the lock-up, eyes furtive or assured, guilty or hopeful.

What he saw affirmed his beliefs. People were animals of a kind, true, but they weren't cattle. They were individuals and they possessed beauty and divinity by the very fact of their existence.

He had been giving his talks in the lock-up every week for months now and some of the visitors had begun to use his teachings for themselves. They were different from the newcomers. Yes, they were a little thinner but they weren't starving by any means. They had the aura. Collins could see it. He wondered if anyone else could. His ability to sense light had increased ever since he'd changed his ways. He saw disciples of only nine or ten weeks as having a full-body halo of soft light, a kind of luminous mist that surrounded them at all times. No one else seemed to notice. Certainly not the newcomers. Perhaps the owners of the auras didn't even know they had them. It was a sign that what he was doing was right. Everything he did made him more certain of it.

One October night a different kind of seeker came through the lock-up doors. Collins knew immediately there was something unusual about him. The man was pale-skinned; almost a yellow tint to his face, and his hair was black, thick and curly. It came to his shoulders. He had a beard that was even coarser and darker but it couldn't hide the gauntness of the man's face. Nor could it shield the gentle calmness coming from the man's brown eyes. He wore an overcoat pulled up at the collars. It was a good quality garment – an unusual sight in any quarter of Abyrne – and Collins had guessed much, if not all, about the man before he'd taken a seat cross-legged on the concrete floor.

A profusion of hair was a fashion among the workers at MMP, whether dairymen, stockmen, herders or slaughtermen. Long hair set them apart from the smooth-skinned Chosen. A coat of such expense could only belong to a thief or someone who could afford it. Meat processors or employees of the Magnus household were the only people in the town with that kind of money. But the bony features, the suggestion of lean muscles and rope-like sinews beneath the coat were at odds with that. People that worked in Magnus's factories were well fed. They were fat on high-quality meat. The same went for the men and women directly employed by Magnus: the servants and maids and his small army of guards and enforcers. This man might have been powerful enough to be an enforcer. His eyes were haunted enough, but they were far too kind.

When the talk was over and Collins had told them all to leave for their own safety, the man with the gaunt face hidden by his mass of beard lingered behind. Two of Collins's longer-standing disciples, Staithe and Vigors, picked as guards because of their size, tried to send him home with firm words. He refused to leave. The doormen looked to Collins for guidance; they weren't in the habit of using force.

'He's fine. Let him stay a little longer. Make sure the rest of them have gone home and keep an eye out for anyone we can't trust.'

They left the lock-up and pushed the door shut behind them.

Collins, shaved bald, his neck well muffled, and the hirsute stranger in his heavy coat were left alone. Collins smiled to put him at his ease but for a few moments more the man said nothing. It was as though he was embarrassed.

'Forgive me,' he began finally. 'It's not that I don't believe you...'

'It's a lot to take in,' Collins said. 'For anyone. Especially true for you, I would imagine.'

The man took a step towards the door and then stopped.

'Do you know me?' he asked.

'No. Not really. But I think I've seen you. You run, don't you?'

The man nodded once.

'You look very...fit. A little thin perhaps.'

The whites of the stranger's eyes flashed and were serene again.

'I'm so sick of hearing the word 'thin',' he said. 'Can you really help me? I've done all I can on my own. Now the Welfare is involved and I don't know what's going to happen.'

Collins rubbed the back of his neck and sighed.

'I can help you but I can't stop the town's wheels from turning. If they're onto you, you have little choice but to do what they want you to do. You have family?'

'A wife. Two children. It's...difficult...at home right now.'

'I see. May I ask you what it is you do for a living?' The man winced at the question and lowered his head.

'I could never say it. Not to you, of all people. Not here in this place.'

'Look, it's alright. I think I know what you do. Because of that, because you want to be different, you're more welcome here than most. Someone like you...changing...well, that would be -'

'I've already changed, Mr. Collins. I'm not the same person

I was. You have...*no*...idea.'

Collins nodded, his eyes closed.

'You may think not but I couldn't be doing this if I didn't understand what people are going through. One has to have understanding first. I know you know what I'm talking about because you have that understanding. You've done your best to change and now you've come for the final piece that will help you to do it. I can help you. And I will. Do the exercises I've taught you and soon enough you'll see.'

'I don't want rituals. No more religion.'

'This is no religion. There is no dogma. There are no lies. Try it. If it doesn't work you can forget we ever met.'

'I don't see how that will help me.'

'No, of course not. So go and find out for yourself. If you need further guidance, come and attend again. I doubt you'll need to, though. A man like you should take to it immediately. You'll feel it. I know you will. And once I've helped you, perhaps you'll come back and help me.'

'Perhaps I'll do that. If I've still got a family. If I'm still alive.'

John Collins put out his hand. The man hesitated and then put out his own. They shook and Collins felt rather than saw the incompleteness of grip from the man's hand. He didn't see it because he'd noticed the faintest glimmer of light in the gaunt man's eyes.

***

The rising smoke and splattering of scalding fat caused mingled washes of hunger and revulsion. She turned the meat in the pan with heavy wooden tongs and pressed down on the slab of half-seared flesh to cook it faster. The force kept her hand still. No longer was it merely the pains in her stomach that caused Parson Mary Simonson concern.

Each morning she awoke to the nibbling in her stomach. That sensation of being devoured from the inside woke her throughout the night and acted as her alarm call come the dawn. Each new day was accompanied by nausea and dizziness the moment she swung her feet from the low, slim cot she slept in. It wasn't the grip of some week-long sickness that was doing the rounds; this early morning vertigo had been with her for months.

Breakfast was getting harder and harder to eat, but, as a Parson, she was required to eat three meals a day and each of them had to contain the flesh of the Chosen. For Parsons the eating of the flesh of the Chosen was a sacrament. To ordinary townsfolk, meat was simply a way to avoid starvation. The thing she required to heal her stomach was tripe but she found it too much of a struggle to chew and swallow first thing in the morning. Instead she had taken to frying a small chop or grilling some thin smoked cuts and accompanying them with a glass of milk.

It was in doing the cooking that she first discovered the new problem. She was unable to hold a pan or spatula steady. If she brought every ounce of her will to bear on her betraying hands, it seemed to control the vibration to a minor tremor but stop it completely she could not. In a matter of days, the trembling had spread to other parts of her body and now, waking this morning bilious and unbalanced, the very room was shuddering.

It took a few seconds to work out that it was her head trembling and not her surroundings. This was a sickening turn for the worse. No one ever talked about it in the Welfare offices or the Central Cathedral but the Shakes was very common among the Parsons of the Welfare. She'd seen many of them take to their beds with it and never stand up again. The Grand Bishop of the Welfare sometimes mentioned the 'burdens' that Parsons were duty bound to carry and she took that to mean the many illnesses that Parsons suffered from and the brevity of their careers. Few in the town lived past the age of fifty but for Parsons it was more like forty-five.

Parson Mary Simonson believed that it was the demands of the job that made Parsons prone to illness. Preaching the Book of Giving, short though it was, and maintaining moral standards among the townsfolk was increasingly difficult. There was more violence and aggression in the town every day, so the peacekeeping function of the Welfare became increasingly necessary. Every week now, she was compelled to use force to subdue townsfolk that had lost control and become unmanageable. In the past it had been possible to guide such offenders back into the fold. Nowadays, it was far more common that their status would be revoked and they would be driven out to the Magnus mansion before travelling on to the plant.

The Grand Bishop also mentioned, usually in the same speech as the one referring to 'burdens', that there were many blessings to weigh against the sufferings in a Parson's life. This too was true.

A Parson never went hungry. Provision of the flesh of the Chosen was paid for by the town's taxes. Parsons were noticed wherever they went and they had more power than any of the other townsfolk. They were more respected, for example, than the workers at the MMP plant and they were more educated. They had knowledge of medicine, law, faith – of course – and were imbued with divine powers. People feared them. It was good to be feared, for Abyrne was a dangerous place.

The fillet was cooked right through and burned dark brown on the outside. An accruing of fat on the inside of the pan ensured its charred crust was crisp with saltiness. She laid the still-sizzling meat on a plate, said a brief prayer, and cut into it. It was, as always, highest-quality produce hung for an appropriate number of days before being butchered for cuts. Most townsfolk got their meat in a hurry, causing the flavour to be less mature, but here again Parsons took the privilege and got the best. In the past, she'd only ever eaten her meat rare but since her illness began the desire to cook it through, and then to char it, had increased. Now she ate hard, blackened meat. It was still a struggle, though.

As she forked a piece into her mouth, the knife in her right hand juddered against the plate. She laid the knife down and was glad of the silence. As she chewed, she considered her course of action regarding Richard Shanti.

He was a man with a spotless record of work for MMP. His reputation for speed and efficiency was rumoured far beyond the factory floor. Townsfolk often blessed him as they blessed their meat, though she doubted he was aware of the fact. Shanti was so quiet and withdrawn she didn't believe he was aware of very much that went on outside his own head. She didn't like people like that. Too self-contained, too independent. Townsfolk should be accessible and predictable. They should be trustworthy. Richard Shanti did not strike her as possessing any of those qualities. He was an unknown. Unknowns were a threat to everyone.

But if she investigated him and was wrong to do so, or if it turned out the records in the archive were incorrect in some way – it wouldn't have been the first time – she could end up showing not only herself but also the whole of the Welfare in a very poor light. Did it matter that his name might not be Richard Shanti? He was an asset to the town. Did anyone need to know his true lineage?

She could easily drop the whole issue. She was sickening and the extra pressure would not help her. Did she need that? Was it really worth it or should she save her energy for maintaining high standards in her day-today labours? She couldn't make up her mind. Perhaps there was a quiet way of doing it, merely spending more time checking records and staying away from Shanti's family. They had two beautiful little girls with impeccable manners and just a hint of mischievousness. It would be a shame to shake up the family over speculations. No, she would wait. There was more she could do without mentioning anything to anyone. It just meant she would have to spend more time in the inch-thick dust of the records office. The idea almost appealed. She would be out of the way for a while, away from the harsh streets of Abyrne and its degenerating inhabitants.

Halfway through her steak a piece lodged deep in her throat – so far down it was almost in her stomach. She swallowed again, trying to produce saliva but the lump was fixed. She could breathe all right, there was no danger that she would choke, but this blockage was painful and seemed impossible to shift.

She reached for her glass of milk and brought the sweet liquid, its surface trembling, to her lips. She took a long, large gulp and waited for it to wash away the bolus of half-chewed meat. The milk slid easily down to the lump and stopped. It backed up into her mouth. She dived for the sink but didn't reach it.

She would fulfil her religious duty and eat three meals of Chosen flesh that day, as always, but she wasn't confident any of them would stay down.

***

Maya had no reason to feel guilty.

Getting a message to the factory had been the worst part. She'd felt bad about that for days. Well, for hours perhaps. Before and after she'd done it, at least. But what choice did she have? She'd asked herself the same question time upon time and ignored the answer just as often. None of it was a foregone conclusion. She wasn't setting out for betrayal. She was responding to necessity. She was managing a difficult situation – one that her husband was refusing to address.

He'd brought home meat on the night of the Parson's visit and it had been good meat. The best meat there was. There had been none since. Not the kilos he'd promised, not the backpack full of cuts and joints and chops and mince that they deserved, that he, as the man of the house, was duty-bound to provide. He'd weakened and reneged, become a victim of his pathetic obsessions once again.

What he'd said to the Parson had worried her too. He hadn't properly answered her about it afterwards. She had no knowledge of his connection to the first families or of his alleged understanding of the old customs. Whatever he'd said to Parson Mary Simonson had done the trick temporarily, but what if she decided to take things further? Maya wasn't going to let it go that far. She was a mother and she had duties she would not ignore, even if her husband ignored his. Dear Father, she thought, losing the children was what was at stake here; the end of their family and everything they had worked together to build. How could Richard care so little?

There was worse; if they were found to be wilfully negligent of the twins, and that seemed a provable point with the right evidence, they both stood to be tried and have their status as townsfolk revoked. There was no way back from a judgement like that.

So. No. There was no reason for guilt.

There was instead a reason to be happy, a reason to be hopeful about the future instead of terrified of it. On the counter in front of her, wrapped neatly in white paper, were packs of steak, links of sausage, and two huge joints that she could roast and then make soups and casseroles from. It was a large stack of parcels, mysterious gifts addressed to no one in particular.

They were all hers now.

She'd almost forgotten about the furtive, insistent movements behind her until her head banged gently on one of the cupboard doors. The movement stopped and she turned her head towards the stairs, listening. Was there a small footstep? She strained her ears into the early evening silence. There was nothing to hear. The movement began again. Soon she would cook the dinner.

Her mouth watered at the thought of it.

***

Whittaker, wisps of snowy hair sprouting from his ears and nose, looked very unhappy.

'What is it this time?'

His voice was wheezy, air passing over tuneless strings. Rawlins sneezed three times in a row.

'Same as before. Births. And deaths.'

'Something a little more recent, I hope,' said Whittaker, trying for a smile and missing. 'It took days for the dust to settle after your last visit.'

The Parson appraised him for a few moments. Whittaker stroked a tuft of his moustache and attempted to maintain the smile that wasn't quite on his face.

'Tell me, Whittaker, did you eat well last night?'

'Oh yes, very well indeed.'

'Might I enquire what you had?'

'Steak, Parson. The very best and tenderest steak.'

'And how old are you?'

'I'm fifty-one.'

She nodded slowly.

'Fifty-one years old. That's a rare age indeed.'

Believing he was being complimented, Whittaker's smile burst out from its hiding place. Long teeth, the colour of ancient ivory, leaned drunken.

'I put it to you, Whittaker, that were it not for your employment within the Welfare, you would have been dead long ago. I expect you to assist me in any way you can and be grateful that dust is the greatest of your torments. Otherwise, I may be persuaded that you are, in fact, *too* old to perform your duties here and I will recommend your immediate and unpaid dismissal.'

It was as though Whittaker and Rawlins had both woken from a deep slumber of many years' duration and had begun to see their surroundings for the first time. She smiled to see them trying to find something useful to do.

'Now, I shall be at the far end of the archives, the very dustiest part. Listen for my call, as I may need your help. Otherwise, be sure to send Rawlins down with a glass of milk from time to time.'

She went carefully, liking the dust no more than them. She lifted her hems and stepped over and onto the carpet of dead particles leaving the footprint of her heavy Welfare boots. Still the motes rose up in her passing and twisted like spirits in the air behind her.

It was the oldest records she wanted. Records from when the Welfare began. Records from the creation onwards. Most of the townsfolk believed the town had been created by God. A pure settlement commanded from the poisonous wasteland. Parson Mary Simonson was among them. As a Parson, it was her duty to instil in people the importance of the words in the Book of Giving and, though there were Parsons whose faith wasn't always apparent, she took this gospel for truth.

'In the beginning there was the promise and the promise was God. God filled the void with His presence. He commanded fire and fire arose in the void. From the fire He commanded the wasteland and the wasteland was so. But the wasteland was without life. From the wasteland God commanded the Town and he named it Abyrne. But the town was silent and empty and so God commanded the townsfolk that they might fill Abyrne with life and that they might dwell in the town forever. But the townsfolk hungered and their hunger filled God's heart with great sorrow. He commanded the Chosen that the townsfolk might never be hungry again. He commanded the grain fields that the Chosen might always be fatted. And thus was the town and all that is in it created and ever shall it be so.'

Simple words for God's simple townsfolk. She loved the words and knew the whole Book of Giving by heart. Even so, she still read from it as though the act of reading strengthened the message. Here in the office of records, she was accessing a time only a few generations before, when the first families of the townsfolk were brought into existence. They arrived with all their skills and tools and technology and began to live in the town in the way God required. They had the Book of Giving and they had their faith and that was all they needed. Very little had changed in the town since then.

She wanted to find the first Shantis and see what she could learn about them. Maybe there was a clue in previous generations to the enigma that was Richard Shanti. If not, she would search more recent records to see who else had been born around the same time. There was a good chance that Richard Shanti was who he said he was. Equally, he might be lying.

She was going to find out which, one way or another.

Eight

Maya stood at the bottom of the stairs and listened. The twins often played quietly together but the smell of food wafting up the stairs to their bedroom usually brought them down. She'd been cooking for half an hour and dinner was almost ready but there was no sign of the girls.

Their bedroom door was closed. They usually left it that way when they were playing and then begged her to leave it open at lights-out time. Maya could hear their small voices, a note of excitement in their whispers. But why were they whispering? And why did the door now seem closed so purposefully? She was probably imagining it but it felt like there was an invisible 'keep out' sign nailed to it.

Instead of calling them down to wash their hands before dinner, she began to climb the stairs. She trod to the outer edges of each step where there was less movement in the wood and therefore less noise. Reaching the landing, the stairs doubled back on themselves and continued upward. Maya was especially stealthy over the last few steps.

The voices of her daughters were louder now but still not distinct. She thought she heard the theatrical smacking of lips and the 'mmms' of someone enjoying cake. So, that was it. A dolly's tea party. No wonder they were so engrossed. She'd played the game herself as a child and remembered how utterly diverting it had been. Plump guests, furry guests, shiny guests, wooden guests, each eating and drinking their fill, each complimenting the hostess.

She turned the door handle as quietly as she could, hoping to glimpse their play. She wanted a moment in which she could return to their simple innocence and in doing so briefly turn away from the realities of the town and her life with Richard.

She had a moment, a very full moment, in which to take in the game before the girls came out of their trance-like absorption and realised she was standing there watching. It was a party all right. All the toys had been invited: the blind, balding bear, the toy soldiers, several dolls and even a rubber clown that smelled of chemicals – a toy they rarely played with.

The guests were sitting around a makeshift table formed by an upside-down biscuit tin with a white paper napkin forming the tablecloth. Each of the guests had a place laid for them at the table complete with tiny knives and forks, dinky plates and upturned thimble wine glasses. On each plate was a hollow portion of doll – an upper arm, a thigh, a calf, a foot, a hand. The torso had been cut into four slices like a small loaf. Hema and Harsha were 'sharing' them.

It was the attention to detail that stunned Maya. The girls had prepared the doll before butchering her for their distinguished guests. They'd cut as much of her hair off as they could. Maya could see how they'd removed two thirds of each finger on her tiny hands and clipped her thumbs off altogether. On the platters where feet were served, she saw that the big toe had been severed. The shaven head lay to one side but in the top 'slice' of the torso, she saw the neck and the puncture wound in the centre of it where they'd silenced the doll before slaughter.

'Hello, Mama,' said Harsha. 'Would you like to come to the party? We've made meat for everyone!'

***

The day that Magnus's boys came to get John Collins started out the same as any other since he'd fled to the Derelict Quarter.

He didn't need an alarm clock. Morning was the most important time and he could feel it coming even as he slept. It was as though the light had a voice. The voice sang to him and, while he was asleep, he understood the language but the moment he woke all he could remember were the joyful, wistful harmonies of a million voices singing as one.

Often the first thing he noticed was that he was crying. Sometimes it was ecstasy, a residue in the emotions of the sweetness of the lightsong. Mostly it was frustration that he could not understand the words with his conscious mind. That day, the tears were a memory of sublime melodies.

The flat he lived in was small. Since he'd left Marie and the boys he had no need for space. All he needed was light and a place to catch that light in the morning. He'd taken a small bag and walked across the town to the Derelict Quarter where anyone could move in and make a home without the need for leases or rental agreements. There was no power, no gas and no water and that had come to suit him fine.

He stopped turning up for work in the gas facility and received neither letters nor visits from the management because he'd already moved away. Marie didn't know where he was and couldn't pass anything on to him. This, too, was a suitable arrangement. The less they had to do with him the better. They'd be wise to forget him, say they never knew him. It happened in Abyrne. It happened a lot.

Knowing John Collins was going to be difficult. Being

John Collins was going to be worse.

He told no one where he was going. He was as good as lost.

Not going to work did strange things to time. He no longer knew what day it was. Not naming the day and not knowing the hour made time stretch. Sometimes a single afternoon would pass like a week. Or it would refuse to pass. Collins, with nothing important to do, would watch time from his balcony, watch the shifting grey skies and lose himself among shapes in the unbroken clouds.

Only two things punctuated his life; the arrival of dawn and the talks he gave that had started in the lock-up so many months before.

Bruno and his black-coated boys were still many hours from cornering him, binding him and taking him to the Magnus mansion in the parkland near the centre of town. He had no inkling of it, though he knew it was inevitable and might come at any time.

He let the tears stay on his face as he sat up from the bare mattress and swung his feet to the floor. The sun was still a long way from the horizon but he could sense the light in the centre of his head as a faint vibration. Naked, but for his scarf, he walked to the balcony, stepped through sliding doors from which the glass was long gone and spread his feet wider than his shoulders. He closed his eyes and raised his arms pushing the palms out in front of him as if gesturing something large to stop moving.

He breathed deep and slow. A warmth began in the skin of his hands at the mere promise of light on the horizon but it would be an hour or more before the sun came up. The world was no longer black, though. Light from far below the horizon seeped into the clouds. As the radiance grew he drew it from the atmosphere into his hands. The heat spread up his wrists. As the light below the horizon gathered, the vibration in the centre of his head, in the nucleus of his brain, increased.

The heat reached his chest and he breathed it downwards, deep into his abdomen. Led by the tidal rhythm of his breathing, his belly filled with light. There seemed no end to the amount it would hold; the light concentrated itself there, grew brighter. After standing and drawing in for a long time, he felt the power from the sun increase exponentially. Everything blasted white and the store of light in his abdomen released, flowing out to every part of his body, filling his organs, energising his limbs. Daybreak. As much light as he could take.

He let his hands down and placed them over his lower abdomen, holding in the warmth and nourishment. Opening his eyes he saw the outer dawn, a pale arrival cloaked by clouds that never left the town alone.

It was another dull day outside, but inside John Collins the sun blazed through clear skies. He gave silent thanks and stepped into the flat to exercise.

Once fed by the light there seemed to be nothing that could tire him. He performed dozens of squat thrusts and star jumps – exercises he remembered from the Physical Education classes he used to hate at school. He started out with ordinary press-ups and then did them one arm at a time, pumping out fifty with no noticeable strain. Hanging from a doorframe he did pull-ups as though he weighed no more than a bag of sugar. There was a delight in being able to make his body work so hard without ever exhausting its energy.

He had lost weight, of course. People thought he was starving and often brought food to the lock-up for him – bread they'd made, some vegetables they'd grown. They were the ones who didn't yet understand. The ones who didn't believe. Once they'd realised the truth of his message, they didn't bring any more gifts. So, there was no fat on him and the minimum of muscle. But John Collins was not malnourished. Nor was he hungry. He was lean and his eyes shone like solar fragments.

John Collins believed that when enough of the townsfolk lived the way he did, people like Rory Magnus would have to find new ways to make their money.

***

Each day at dawn Richard Shanti practised the exercises he'd learned from John Collins. It was difficult not to criticise himself for being so easily taken in but his desire was greater than his scepticism. Within a couple of weeks, he began to feel something changing in his body. The exhaustion that he felt throughout most of every day – brought on by the constant punishment he gave himself – began to lighten. The difference was so small he attributed it to a change of mood rather than something physical.

It was in those moments just before sleep and immediately after waking that he noticed it. Instead of plummeting into sleep the moment he lay down, he would feel his body and mind relax and release. Then he would sleep. Before dawn he woke a little earlier than routine dictated and felt an eagerness for something he couldn't define. The dread of his slaughterhouse duties plagued him as badly as ever but there was something more in his consciousness now than that simple trepidation. By the time he had risen, these tiny alterations in him were mostly forgotten.

But the time came when he could not ignore the difference in himself and he began to take the exercises more seriously.

Maya was occasionally feeding meat to the girls, sometimes in front of him and other times not, depending on her mood. Generally, though, since the Parson's visit, she had been more easy-going about things and less accusatory about his way of life. He didn't want the girls eating flesh but he knew that if he tried to prevent it, Maya would leave him and take the girls with her. He had no doubt that she would do it. Her singleness of purpose frightened him at times. She was like a wild animal protecting her offspring, fighting for them, hunting for them, defending the lair. He tried not to think about what Maya might be capable of if pushed to her limits. Since she had found a way of procuring meat for Hema and Harsha – no doubt wasting his wages in one of Abyrne's butchers – she no longer used her body to inveigle him. Now that he had a tiny reserve of energy, he wished that she would. He wished, simply, that she would love him.

With work taking up so much of his thoughts and the running off of his misdeeds filling most of his free time, it was easy not to think about how things were at home. Sometimes, though, he couldn't stop himself wondering about the 'life' he had outside Magnus Meat Processing. He worked and he punished himself and he slept. He hardly saw his wife or his daughters and when he did, they treated him as an outsider in their home; a tolerated stranger.

However, it was the thing he tried hardest not to think about and endeavoured most seriously to atone for that most haunted Shanti's waking and sleeping hours: the lives of the Chosen. Abyrne was an aberration, he was certain of it. Somewhere along its history, the town had lost its way. The Book of Giving, the Gut Psalter, the control of the town by the Welfare and Rory Magnus – all this was a sinister misunderstanding of how things ought to be. What the alternative was, he didn't know. He only knew that the town and everything about it was wrong.

But there was nowhere else to go. The wasteland surrounded the town and there was nothing out there. It stretched uncharted miles in every direction. Nothing could survive except within the confines of Abyrne. Hardest of all for Shanti, harder to bear than the misguided respect he was shown at work because of his skills, was the knowledge that there was no one he could talk to about how he felt. Maya would report him and make good on her promise to separate him from his family forever. To her it would be crazy talk to question a single aspect of how the town was run; the kind of talk that would put them all at risk of the might of the Welfare.

She was right to fear them. The Welfare had the power to revoke status. When you ceased to be 'townsfolk' you became meat. The only possibility left to you was to run to the Derelict Quarter and hide. But out there, there was nothing. Nothing to eat, no running water or sewers, no power lines. Just blocks and blocks of crumbling, abandoned buildings and heaps of rubble. The Derelict Quarter was as unforgiving as the wasteland.

It was no secret that starving vagrants lived in the Derelict Quarter – people who had run there from the Welfare or from Rory Magnus. Were they fortunate to have made it to a place where they would die slowly of disease and malnourishment? Shanti didn't think so. Better to meet the quick fate on the other end of his bolt gun and be released. He'd seen them fed into the crowd pens a hundred times or more, faced them through the access panel when he stunned them. Without exception they'd been begging for the end by then. He had faith that, with him dispatching them, his compassionate eyes would be the last thing they ever saw. The Derelict Quarter was no option for anyone. Besides, even if it came to that, Maya would never agree to go with him. He'd be cut off from his family and the loneliness would probably be enough to kill him.

No way out of his life that he could see. Sentenced to murder or dismember the Chosen every day of his life; that was his fate. No other way forward.

Except for the teachings of John Collins, Shanti's life was empty of hope. And so, before the sun rose each morning, he did as the quiet man had shown him.

Day by day, he changed.

* * *

'Don't hurt him, Bruno, you bloody lout. I don't want him distracted. I want him focussed on what's going to happen when he gets downstairs.'

Rory Magnus sat back in his swivelling, reclining chair and lit a small black cheroot. The links of gold on his broad wrist reflected yellow firelight, as did the gold lighter when he snapped it shut and dropped it onto his desk. He was freckled and massive. His mane was ginger, white at the temples and sideburns, his beard overgrown. There was a constant tension in his face and the tendons of his neck, a barely contained urge to leap forwards, to be first out of the blocks, to hammer someone with his fists, to place a kiss or clap a shoulder. No one could predict what the tension implied, only that it implied action.

Ten feet away on an intricately woven rug were two younger men. One wore a long black coat over the machinery of his muscles. He was the size of a door. His dark hair was permanently greasy and dandruff salted his parting and shoulders. The other man was naked and kneeling on the rug. His hands were secured behind his back with a leather strap, his head forced down by his captor.

Magnus looked at him in silence for a long time. Then he took another puff on his cheroot and exhaled two streams of smoke from his nose.

'How long have you been preaching your bullshit now, Collins? A year? Two?'

The kneeling man didn't respond.

'What's it achieved, eh? Anybody really listened to you in that time? Anybody "changed their ways"?' He made more smoke. 'Let go of him, will you, Bruno? I can't see his bloody face.'

Bruno released his grip. The naked man's eyes met his and held the connection. The look took his attention from the scar above Collins's weedy sternum. The eyes of a man with nothing left to lose. Magnus had seen this kind of bravado before.

It never lasted.

'Didn't your parents teach you any manners, son? It's rude to stare.'

Collins, kneeling exposed and helpless, didn't speak. He didn't look away.

Rory Magnus inspected his cheroot, rolled it between thick fingers and nodded to himself at the quality. Perhaps the nod signalled some inner decision. He let a thin stream of ochre mist exude from the corner of his mouth.

'I'm going to let you keep your eyes, Collins. Until you've watched everything we do.' He paused to lend his words weight. 'Then I'll have them cut from your head and pickled. I'll keep the jar right here on my desk. That way you can give me your lover's gaze forever.'

Words were the first weapons for breaking a man. Sometimes they did the job long before the knives. He watched Collins's face for traces of fear. A flicker of his attention, tremors around the eye muscles and lips. Tears. Sweat. There was nothing. He shrugged inwardly.

First there would be reasoning, man to man: slow-down-and-let's-be-sensible-here bargaining. Magnus didn't make deals when deals were already done. Pleading then: mentions of the widowed wife and orphaned children, all the things left undone in life, just one more sunrise with the loved ones. Rory Magnus's fatherly response: 'Don't worry, I'll take care of them', was never misinterpreted. Tears then: 'Please, Mr. Magnus, please. I know I made a mistake – a huge mistake – but I don't deserve this. Not *this*.' A shrug in response, an I-don't-give-a-rancid-kidney-about-you shrug. Followed by his businesslike defence: 'I can't be seen to let people mess with Rory Magnus. I can't afford to look weak.' Anger of course: 'Fuck you, Magnus, and fuck your children forever. I'll see you in hell, I swear it. I'll come back and haunt you to your dying day.' Blah-de-blah. But Magnus would end up fucking *their* children if the mood took him, saw his victims in hell long before they died and had never seen a single ghost. When the anger was all gone, they wept and blubbered like children. Hot-faced, red-cheeked, snotty-lipped babies.

Magnus knew a little psychology. Dying was a process that everyone had to go through. Rage, denial, acceptance – he understood the general idea. And it was true to a degree. People with the canker had time to work it all through at leisure. People in Magnus's basement didn't have that kind of opportunity. But they did come to terms with death. Almost all of them. What they couldn't handle, what none of them had ever handled was the pain of their systematic destruction. The unmaking of their bodies with knives while they yet lived. They all broke in the end.

All of them.

Even Prophet John Collins here on the rug, so defiant in these first moments, would do the same.

***

There were Shantis all the way back to the creation of the town but it quickly became clear from reading the records of their births, marriages and deaths that she was going to find little of any bearing on Richard Shanti. She followed his bloodline from seven generations to the present. Everything was in order except for the death of the child named Richard Shanti. But if Richard Shanti's records were false in any way, if he did not possess true status as one of the townsfolk, then every generation that followed him must also have no status. The beautiful twin girls, children any family in the town would be proud of, and even his wife, because she'd taken his name; they would all face his fate.

She found herself not wanting that because she had been so fond of the girls. Maya Shanti she could take or leave; she was like so many of the women of the town and the Parson could smell the deceit on her. Mere deceitfulness was not enough to cause loss of status, however. Being the wife to a non-townsfolk bloodline, a defrauder of the Welfare and abuser of the faith on the other hand was the thing that would finish her and her daughters.

Richard Shanti held for her a certain respect and fascination. He was a man whose work kept the town of Abyrne alive. He was an MMP legend. The Parson did not consider herself without sympathy for the Chosen; while it was a divine privilege to give flesh in the name of the Lord, she realised that the Chosen suffered in order to do so. Men like Richard Shanti understood the Chosen the way most could not. Because of this he reduced their suffering and, at the very same time, provided the high chain speeds that supported the town. She truly did not want to find this man lacking in such a fundamental aspect.

It was a matter of religious duty, however, and she would see it through.

Rawlins brought her a glass of milk and though she'd seen him step with due care along the central walkway of the archives, there was a gritty film of grey particles on the surface of the milk by the time he arrived. She thanked him anyway. The milk relieved the pain in her stomach for moments only. She would have asked for another if the thought of drinking it didn't make her feel so nauseous. The quivering of her fingers made the dust rise from the old record boxes and files no matter what she did.

The Shanti files exhausted from creation to present day, she went to Richard Shanti's file, checked the year of his birth and his recorded, if not actual, death and began to scan the files of every child born that year. Her plan was to cross-reference with orphaned children and look for possible switches. She was certain now, that if there was an infraction, it was down to someone taking the dead child's place rather than an incorrect entry. The adult Richard Shanti was someone else's child and had been taken in by the Shanti family.

All that remained was to find out whose child he was.

***

'Don't you know anything about evolution, Collins? I thought you were educated.' A wet, lippy suck on the cheroot. A swill of clear, fragrant vodka. 'Food chains. Natural selection. Survival of the fittest. It all makes sense, you know. More than this religious crap the Welfare put about. The strongest, smartest animal is at the top of the pile. Take this situation here; the hunter catches its prey. The hunter eats the prey. The hunter survives.

The bloodline of the weaker animal is thus removed from the equation. Surely even you can understand that.'

Collins didn't respond. He looked into Magnus's eyes. There was silence in the room but each man heard the sound of breathing in their own head; Magnus's harsh and loud. He was used to it and it seemed normal. Black-coated Bruno's breath was rapid and shallow, his adrenaline high, impatience making his heart beat fast. He shifted his weight from foot to foot wanting violence, wanting dismissal, wanting anything other than this silence. John Collins could hear his breath but it was a distant thing, not like the waves on a beach; slower, like tides. He controlled it and everything else became calm.

After a couple of minutes, Magnus laughed. Bruno's bunched shoulders dropped an inch or two. Collins continued to stare.

'Your problem is that you still think you're my equal. Bollock-naked and on your knees, you still believe your life means something, don't you? You're finished, Collins. You may not know it yet but your life is over right now. You have no more significance in this world.'

Collins's voice came in some perfect nano-pause when neither Magnus nor Bruno were completely focussed. It made them both jump. His composed tones didn't belong in the room. Magnus recovered himself first; in time to take the words in:

'It isn't of any concern to me,' he said, 'but my life is significant and will continue to be so, long after I die.' He kept his eyes on Magnus. 'You, on the other hand, while you may be remembered as an aberration, are already nothing more than a walking, talking carcass of fat and meat.'

Magnus's face heated up but he kept himself quiet. It wouldn't do to let either of these men see him rattled. Instead of shouting, instead of mashing Collins's pathetic testicles in his fist and putting out his cheroot in the scrawny man's eye, he forced a chuckle. He finished his vodka and dropped the cheroot into the damp dregs where it hissed and died. He stood up and his full height became clear. He was a giant.

Two metres of bulk and muscle. He had a paunch, but his chest was enormous and his arms bulged beneath his suit. His thighs were like the trunks of small trees and his neck was as wide as his head. Bruno felt the physical threat rolling off him in pulses and wanted to step backwards. He stayed where he was.

Magnus walked around to the front of his desk which already stood on a plinth. To keep eye contact, Collins had to stretch his neck upwards. The movement was enough to cause Bruno to respond. He pushed Collins's head down until he was bowing before the Meat Baron.

'You're a far weaker man than I,' said Collins towards the rug.

'I could snap your neck with one hand,' said Magnus.

'You could do anything you want to me while I'm tied up like this. Anyone could. That tells me that you're afraid. I wonder why that is, Magnus. Why would a man as well put together as you be afraid of a thin little man like me? It's because you're frail inside. Your will is frail. Your mind is frail.'

Bruno looked down and away, embarrassed; scared of what would come next.

'You talk of the strong surviving but you could never fight a man like me and win, Magnus. You don't understand what it takes to be truly strong. True, I'm an easy catch for your gang of thugs. I can't deal with the numbers. But one-on-one you wouldn't have a chance against me. You know this and that is why I'm kneeling naked and bound on your carpet instead of talking to you man to man. You're afraid of me.'

Magnus knew what Collins was up to. He was the cleverest and the bravest yet. Or maybe just the stupidest. He considered his options. He could take Collins downstairs now and finish him at leisure; one piece at a time. Hell, he could play his ace; cut off and eat Collins's genitals while he watched. But he wanted to prove to Collins who was the stronger man.

Make him admit it before he finished him off. No, it didn't really matter what Collins thought once he was gone. And Magnus knew who the stronger of them was without having to prove it. But Bruno was here. If Magnus left it like this, there was a chance that Bruno would mention it outside the office. Strength was everything but the rumour of strength and ruthlessness was even more important. If people outside thought Magnus was letting people get away with insulting him, it would be the thin end of the wedge.

No. This was an opportunity to burn his supremacy into the minds of all those who thought to undermine him in the town. He'd bring in some of the others and humiliate Collins in front of them all before he took the wretch downstairs into his private abattoir. But there was plenty of time for that.

'So you want to fight me, is that it?' Collins said nothing.

'Let go of him, Bruno.'

The heavy hand released his neck again. Collins raised his head and met Magnus's gaze with steady eyes.

'When a weak man and a strong man come to blows, it's not a fight,' said Collins. 'It's annihilation.'

Magnus pressed his lips together. He was meant to be a serious man, a man not easily amused. But he couldn't help it.

He chuckled. He snorted. He laughed. Soon Bruno was laughing too.

Seeing the misplaced smile on Collins's face made him laugh harder. It took several minutes to get control of himself. After a few final, disbelieving chortles he said, 'You're a fucking piece of shit, Collins. You'll get your come-uppance. Right after I thrash the smile off your face forever.' He chuckled again. 'But there are a few more things I wanted to talk to you about first. That's why you're still up here and not...downstairs.'

***

'I don't want to see you playing games like this again, understand me?'

'Why, Mama?' asked Hema, 'It's just pretending.'

'Your father wouldn't like it. Besides, girls, what makes you think you can go cutting up your toys like this? Where do you think you'll get another doll?'

'We can make one,' said Harsha. 'We make dollies at school all the time.'

'Not like this one. These smooth-skinned ones are hard to find and they're expensive too. I won't be getting you another.'

'Can we play the meat game if daddy's not here?'

Maya stood with her arms folded and looked from one pretty face to the other. She could see no harm in them at all. She'd told them their father wouldn't approve and that was an understatement. If he caught them playing the 'meat game' it might turn the tables; instead of her leaving, he might kick them out. The excuse she'd given wasn't really anything to do with Richard though. Watching her own children play at butchering and serving up the Chosen turned her stomach. It made her feel uneasy.

It was particularly true today when, instead of blowing south east, the prevailing wind had reversed and smells from her husband's workplace were carried back towards the town, back past their house. This was the second time she'd found the girls serving 'meat' to their toys and she wanted it to stop. If not, she wanted not to see it. Ever.

'I'll make you a deal. You can play the meat game. But you must never get caught doing it – either by me or your father. That means it's a secret game. You never talk about it to anyone. All right?'

83

The twins looked at each other and made no attempt to hide their delight at the idea of a secret game. It was even better than the original.

They both nodded as if pulled by the same strings.

'All right, Mama.'

Nine

'What have you been telling the townsfolk, Collins?' No hesitation.

'The truth.'

Magnus closed his eyes for a count of ten.

'You're not making things any better for yourself by being a clever dicky. What *exactly* have you told them?'

'I've told them that they don't have to eat meat to survive.' This much Magnus knew. Reports had been coming in about Prophet John for months. He hadn't believed them at first. No one could talk such nonsense for more than a few days without being laughed bleeding into a gutter somewhere. But the rumours and stories had persisted and Magnus had sent out his feelers. People came back telling him about the lock-up meetings, how they were full every week, how word was spreading around the town that meat, the very basis of all life, was not necessary in the diet. Even then, Magnus couldn't believe it was a serious problem. So there was a lunatic spreading cow shit about what people should and shouldn't eat. So what? No one was going to fall for that kind of idiocy.

But they did. In substantial numbers.

For the first time in MMP's history, in the history of Abyrne, supplies of meat had been greater than the demand for it. A few cuts of meat went unsold in butchers' shops around the town. A few cuts of meat browned, greyed and spoiled. Magnus had never known the like of it. Steaks rotting in their displays while poor people all over the town starved.

What were these non-eaters of meat eating instead? The vegetables and grains that the town farmers grew and sold were poor quality at best. A few people grew their own food, albeit reluctantly, to supplement their diets. What they really *craved* was meat. Meat would keep them strong for work. Meat would help their children survive to adulthood. The ability to afford and eat meat gave you status; it meant that you weren't meat yourself. It meant that you were above cattle. The townsfolk ate meat to stay human. For someone to come along and tell them they didn't need meat, that eating it was *wrong*; it was the most outrageous and insulting thing Magnus had ever heard. And some of the townsfolk were swallowing it the way they'd swallowed mince and stew the previous week.

John Collins was responsible for all of it. John Collins was going to pay.

The rumours were unbelievable but they were true. Magnus had to accept it as a fact when orders from butchers and other meat processors went down. He didn't want the workers at MMP to know, so he kept the chain speeds high, told his managers that demand was climbing just as it always had. And then he sent unmarked vans with loads of un-saleable meat to be dumped out near the wasteland where no one could see or smell it.

The rumours carried a supernatural element too. If the idea of not eating meat was lunatic and unbelievable, the other aspect of the rumours was suicidal. How sophisticated people could believe in such self-destructive lies, he had no idea. But it revealed people's nature. People were weak. People were stupid. People were gullible. People were corruptible. Upon such truths he had built his empire.

Now that the man was here, before he beat him to a pulp of blood and bones in the pointless fight he was picking, and before he carved him up, he wanted to know what muck Collins had been spreading.

Maybe, he thought, maybe I'll make his a *public* slaughter. The first Abyrne has ever seen. He smiled. The idea made him feel a lot better. It would be the kind of execution that no one would ever forget. The kind of drawn-out death that people would write down and tell their children about. Collins would be the meat on his table for weeks and Magnus would be feared for eternity.

People would eat meat gladly. Obediently. The way they were supposed to.

***

From time to time Shanti passed through the herd of new mothers to check on the progress of WHITE-047 and her new calf. The calf was male and as stock from BLUE-792 there was a good chance it would become a bull and avoid the meat herd. Shanti was quietly delighted about this. It almost fitted with his fantasy of the calf growing up as a child. The reality, of course, was that the young bull would face all the same mutilations as any other young male except for castration. However, instead of being taken for slaughter when it reached maturity, the new bull might have years of successful mating to prolong its life. It was the best any of the Chosen could expect and Shanti was glad for that tiny mercy.

The mothers and calves were kept together until the calves could be safely separated and given ordinary feed. The mothers would then rejoin whichever herd they had come from, assuming they were still healthy enough following calving. WHITE-047's calf would be raised in a separate bull enclosure. Other male calves would enter the meat herds to be matured and fattened for slaughter as soon as possible. Female calves would join the regular herds to become milkers or breeding stock for a few seasons before entering the crowd pens themselves.

The shortest-lived of all, barring those born weak or sick, were the veal calves. These young males would be chosen randomly from the newborns and taken away to a warehouse full of small, darkened crates. Here they would be fed a special mix of feed and their movement would be restricted by the dimensions of their enclosure. Prolonged darkness ensured that by the time they were old enough for slaughter, they were practically blind. The veal calves were kept in crates allowing them enough room to sit or lie down but never to stand to their full height. Very soon, each veal calf learned that standing up was a waste of effort and from then on they would remain seated or reclined. When they reached maturity, still much younger than any other cattle, they were taken for slaughter on canvas stretchers because they didn't have the strength to walk.

Veal slaughter took place in a smaller facility but with very low chain speeds owing to the rarity of the stock. It was one aspect of MMP processing that he had never been involved in and had no wish to be. Fortunately, his skills were required in the main slaughterhouse where the pressure of maintaining high chain speeds was a constant consideration.

As the weeks passed, Shanti watched WHITE-047 and her calf 's progress. The calf looked strong and fed ravenously from its mother. One by one the rituals of the Chosen were performed on the calf and its kind. Their fingers were docked, their big toes were removed, they were dipped. Teeth were extracted as they appeared, to be pulled again when adult teeth arrived. At each new procedure, the mothers became agitated and the sound of sighing and hissing grew loud in the pens and feed lots. Calves were taken by the stockmen and returned minutes later, altered by their tools. The time came for tagging and Shanti watched carefully to see what WHITE-047's calf would become.

He passed by one day and saw WHITE-047 cradling her calf to her udders and rocking it. The calf was sighing and sucking alternately. Its chest hauled in huge gasps and released long hisses that Shanti knew would have been screams if it still had a voice box. Tears and milk smeared its blotched red face. A thin rivulet of blood still dripped from its right heel and there, finally, Shanti saw its fate sealed by a steel bolt and a coloured tag.

WHITE-047 saw him watching but did not turn away. Unusually, the cow met his gaze from among the hundreds of others. She inclined her head fractionally. Shanti checked for stockmen that might be watching before he returned the gesture as subtly as he could. He smiled in spite of the obvious pain her calf was suffering and he thought he saw her lips change shape too.

The tag was bright blue. Not faded and cracked like its father's. Its number was 793.

***

'We shouldn't. Not now.'

'I've brought you everything you asked for. And more. Look.'

Maya looked into the bag, saw the wrapped shapes of chops and black pudding. There were other things too. Hand-raised pies and still warm pasties. Saliva flowed beneath her tongue.

'The girls will be home from school soon.'

'How soon?'

'Any moment.'

'Don't you want the meat? I know plenty of people who do.'

Fear of malnourishment yanked her like a fishhook. Now that she was plumping the girls up, seeing the rosiness of their cheeks, it was difficult – no, it was impossible – to entertain thoughts of them losing weight again. She must keep them well. That was her task. It was her duty. The only thing a mother could give in the world was love and nourishment to her children and she wasn't going to allow anything to prevent her. She loved them. They came before everything else. No matter what the cost.

Torrance had her pushed up against the sink, her back to the window where she watched for her family to return each day. His breath smelled of half-digested steak and diseased gums. His teeth were broken or discoloured and kissing him was almost enough to make her vomit. He moved closer, pushing cracked lips out through his greasy beard and the stink of his stomach and mouth filled her nose.

But she didn't have to kiss him. She only had to satisfy him. The quicker she did that, the sooner he would leave. Before he made contact she sank to her knees on the kitchen floor and unbuttoned his trousers. She reached in, found the panel in his underwear and guided his penis through it. Already he was gasping. Before she took it in her mouth she studied it briefly. There wasn't much to it. In its way, it was very much like a fat, short sausage. The only difference was the musky hair that surrounded it and the hole in its end. Anything was better than kissing him though.

88

Anything at all.

'Keep your eyes open and let me know if you see them coming. They mustn't know. And they must never see me like this.'

Torrance pushed his penis into her face without answering. It fit easily inside her mouth. Even though he thrust with all his strength it never reached the back of her throat. There was very little she had to do, seeing as he wanted to be in command. So she let him pump away at her face and kept her mouth open for him. The worst part was the way her head banged back against the kitchen cupboards.

It was a small price to pay.

***

When it came right down to it, a bull's life was a lot easier than a stockman's.

It was easier than the life of most of the townsfolk of Abyrne. Aside from the quarterly mating flurry, which obviously exhausted the bulls – the stockmen joked about how they'd like a reason to be similarly worn out – there was little else for them to do but feed and rest. Shanti made a point of stopping by BLUE-792's enclosure regularly, especially in the lunch break when there was likely to be no one else around.

At first he'd hidden from the bull, not letting it know that he was observing it. As the number of visits increased, Shanti let the bull glimpse him through the cracks in his panelled pen. Sometimes he whispered to the bull:

'I've seen your son. He's beautiful.' Or:

'He's going to be a bull. A special one, just like you.'

Did BLUE-792 understand him? The Chosen listened daily to the chatter and banter and shouts of the stockmen. Maybe they could interpret some of the words even though they couldn't speak. Shanti didn't care one way or the other. He wanted to let the bull know that he thought about him. That he watched him. That he cared.

These were ideas and feelings he could never share with anyone if he wanted to stay alive and keep his job. He knew he should have been frightened to have such notions but he wasn't.

That was what really scared him.

Occasionally, when BLUE-792 was resting, Shanti would tap a soft beat on the panels. He would peer through a crack or even stand in plain view on the outside of the enclosure's gate. The bull watched him but that was all.

***

The morning was an agonised parade of last-second glances.

Placing the muzzle swiftly and correctly required unbreakable concentration. The sound of breached crania and pressure-shocked brain tissue was blotted out by the noise of the bolt gun. Its air supply hose looped up behind Shanti like a black viper draped from the ceiling. The pneumatic snake fired its pointed tongue every time Shanti touched its trigger. Its bite was deadly.

'Ice Pick! Chain speed, please!'

Shanti could hear the delight in Torrance's voice. It was because Torrance knew that Ice Pick Rick Shanti was annihilating the Chosen like a machine.

'One thirty-one, sir.'

'Outstanding, Rick. You know how to make an old stockman very happy. No one's going hungry in Abyrne when you're on the stun. And, hey, don't let this conversation slow you down.'

He didn't.

At the same time he knew that sooner or later he would slow down and that it had nothing to do with anything Bob Torrance said.

Snatches of their language had come to him. He didn't understand how exactly, only that it must have been the same way he picked up language from his own family as he grew up – because he needed to know it.

In front of him the access panel slid open and he shared a split second of eye contact with the Chosen before him.

'God is supreme. The flesh is sacred.'

He placed the bolt gun to the centre of its forehead, pulled the trigger.

Hiss, clunk. The light in the eyes of the Chosen went out. He hit the completion button. The access panel slid shut.

It was intuitive perhaps that the beginning of each message would be some kind of greeting or possibly the name of the Chosen 'speaking' and that the end of each communication would be some kind of farewell. That wasn't enough of an explanation for how he'd picked it up so easily, though. Shanti thought he knew the meaning of taps and breaths because they were so familiar.

On a subliminal level he heard the sounds every day. All the stockmen did. Therefore, in some way, the sounds the Chosen made must have become, at the very least, a ubiquitous part of MMP life. Such sounds would have been prevalent in every part of the factory, penetrating the

90

unconscious mind of every worker. Shanti surmised that it would only take a little extra effort to begin interpreting the sounds and rhythms the Chosen made, translating them into the language of the townsfolk. He had worked there for ten years. It was no wonder that, once he'd decided it was language the Chosen were using and not just random noise, he'd come to understand it so quickly.

The panel opened. New eyes. The same eyes. Eyes he'd seen a hundred thousand times. Their colours differed, their bloodlines varied. He knew them all. He loved the Chosen in a way he could not communicate.

'God is supreme. The flesh is sacred.' Hiss, clunk.

Hit the button.

He thought about the language all the time, trying hard in his waking hours to make connections between groups and types of taps and the accompanying hisses and sighs. It was at night, however, that the real leaps came to him. He would dream that BLUE-792 was signalling to him and then speaking the meaning of each phrase. In the morning Shanti would remember every nuance and he would run harder to work, keen to test his new knowledge.

Eyes. Beautiful eyes.

'...supreme...sacred.' Hiss, clunk.

Red button.

It took only a few days of this for his excitement to turn to a deeper dread of the plant than before. He could not unlearn what the Chosen were saying to each other. The meanings of many pattered exchanges became clearer and Shanti found himself heartsick over what he heard. Manning the bolt gun, what everyone loved him for, had become a new nightmare. Far worse than before.

'...supreme.'

Hiss, clunk.

'...sacred.' Hiss, clunk. *Sacred*.

Hiss, clunk.

One by one he dropped the Chosen, sent them to the bleeding station knowing none would recover consciousness on his shift. His part was done and done well. But he heard them now in every part of the plant. There was very little he no longer understood about the nature of the Chosen. They were noble in a way that few in Abyrne could ever understand. Except John Collins and his followers.

In the crowd pens that led to the restrainer they spoke a prayer to each other. Shanti now heard the prayer hundreds of times a day:

91

Hhaah, Ssuuh. Your time comes. Surely it comes. May you go forward into your time with great dignity. May you hold your head up before the deft ones and welcome their shining points and blades. May your nightfall be complete before they take what you go to give. We who give, we who are certain to follow, salute you. On a far tomorrow we will see you with new eyes. We will see you in a land where pain is not even a memory, where what we go to give will not be asked for again. Hah, suh. Surely your time comes. Give what you have to give, give it freely. We who give salute you for we are certain to follow. Haah, suuh. For all our times come.

Looking into their eyes, pulling the trigger of the bolt gun became harder and harder to do. The gun itself seemed heavier than before, a gun made of lead. He believed he'd been a man of peace all these years. Doling out the inevitable with true compassion and skill. Never allowing a morsel of meat to pass his lips. But here he was, performing his duty still and fully conscious now of what it meant. Here he was listening to the gentle Chosen prepare for their premature, violent deaths with the grace of saints. No Parson of the Welfare could come close to their purity of heart. The townsfolk did not begin to understand the manner of evil that ruled Abyrne. The town was rotten, and everyone in it, save just a few, were the worms that fed on its foulness.

Shanti knew he was the rottenest worm of them all. He was the stun man, the bolt gunner, the stockman every MMP worker respected for his death-dealing talent. Shanti was the killer that made the way the town worked possible.

Everything began and ended with him.

Ten

'What else have you filled their heads with?'

'I haven't bothered with their heads. It's their spirits I've communicated with. The townsfolk are hungry, Magnus, but not for the tainted meat you provide. They're hungry for truth and righteousness. They want their spirits to overflow with joy. They want freedom. Not a line of products you'll never be able to supply.'

'The more shit you talk to me, the more pleasure I'm going to take in dismembering you, son. You have to be the cheekiest bastard I've ever met, but it's not your bollocks talking. I could respect a man with some bollocks. No, you're talking this way to me because you're not right in the head. No freak is going to ruin my business. No psycho is going to twist the minds of the people in this town. But I'm curious about what I've been hearing from my people. They've been telling me stranger stuff than you've told me. Maybe you're too scared to tell me your secrets. Maybe you think I'll steal them.'

Collins laughed. Raucous, delighted guffaws. Laughter too big for a man of his diminutive frame.

'Shut up, Collins or I'll cancel this fight you want and we'll start taking you apart right now.'

Collins blinked the tears of laughter away as best he could and said, 'You've got all the power, Magnus. You start on me whenever you want. I'll miss knocking your teeth down your throat, though.'

Shit, thought Magnus, I'm going to start thinking that people talking to me like this is normal if I'm not careful. The sooner we get this over with the better. This bloke's doing my fucking brain in and we can't have that. No, no, no.

'Get on with it, son. Tell me about what you're eating these days.'

'There's no point. You wouldn't understand it. Not even the simplest principles.'

'I don't want to fucking understand it, Collins. I just want to hear it from your mouth. I just want to know that I've been receiving my information correctly.'

Collins shrugged.

'I live on God. It's as simple as that. There's really no other way to explain it. It looks like breathing and taking in light but really what I'm doing is eating God.'

Collins's eye contact softened. It disturbed Magnus. No one had ever looked at him that way before. What was it, sympathy? Empathy? Compassion?

'I wish you could experience it, Mr. Magnus.'

So, now he's all deference, thought Magnus. What kind of nutter is this bloke?

'There's no experience like it in the world. I know it would change the way you felt about everything if you just gave it a try. That's the beauty of it. Anyone, anyone at all, can do it. It's so simple. It's the reason I'm not afraid of you. The reason I'm not afraid to die.'

Magnus took his time composing an answer. There was a lot to say about the man's views. A lot of roads a thinking man's mind could go down. Magnus didn't like to think too much. He preferred action. Action was the measure of a man. So far, Collins was all chat. His bizarre mission in the lock-up was chat and everything that had taken place between them in the office was chat. The difference between them was that Magnus had taken action. He'd sent his boys to find Collins and he'd brought him here. When their tête-à-tête was complete, Magnus would follow through on all his threats, make deeds of his words. Right now, even Collins's challenge for a fight was no more than words and Magnus was fairly sure the man was merely trying to buy himself some time.

For all the rubbish coming out of Collins's mouth however, there was something about him that didn't seem mad, so much as misdirectedly inspired. A man like Collins, if he'd had his way, could have changed people's minds about almost anything. Magnus was glad he'd stopped him now rather than waiting until he had some kind of revolution on his hands. Collins had something. It wasn't simple insanity. Some of his words had penetrated Magnus's defences. Right now he was considering them. Something of the man on his knees in front of him had lodged in his mind.

Magnus's mind was strong, though. No one, not Collins, not anyone, was going to steamroller their way into his head and change his thinking. And yet . . . there was something here. There was something inside this man that he wanted to communicate with. Magnus wanted to talk. He was strong enough to talk just a little longer and not be swayed. There was something worth pursuing, just to put his curiosity to bed. Then he could carve Collins up and forget about him forever.

'It's a good thing I'm not a religious man,' Magnus said. 'Or I might have to point out you're blaspheming. You contradict everything I know of the Book of Giving. The Father gave us His children to feast upon. He didn't instruct us to try and eat *Him* directly.'

'God is the only food there is. The only flesh. The only nourishment.'

Magnus shook his head, disappointed.

'Don't do this, Collins. Not to me. Don't make yourself sound like the Parsons of the Welfare with their psychodrivel. Don't preach to me like I'm some kind of idiot.' Magnus sat down on the step in front of his titanic desk so that he was on a similar level to his prisoner. 'I personally don't believe a single word in the Gut Psalter or any other holy book. I'm not a stupid man. I know that keeping Parsons on the prowl is important. I know that keeping order is important. I know that rules are important and I know religion has a part to play. But I don't give a shit about any of it and you ought to know that. The fact that I encourage readings from the Book of Giving in my stockyard and processing plants is merely a sign that I want things to be maintained, to run smoothly. The religion of the Welfare is an aid to business. Business comes before anything else in the world. Before love, before men and long before God.' He stretched his neck from side to side easing the tension out of it. He was relaxing. 'But what you've said to me is interesting. Interesting enough for me to want to understand a little more.'

He watched to see if Collins would relax too. He was sure that his generosity regarding Collins's final moments of life would be well received. But Collins, if he felt any relief at knowing he had a few more minutes of life, showed no outward sign of it.

'Tell me about eating God, Collins.'

'What do you want to know?'

'I want to understand what it means, if it means anything at all. I want to know how to do it.'

He saw Collins shake his head to himself, close his eyes momentarily.

'What is it?'

'I can't show *you*. You of all people, who destroy the Chosen by their hundreds every day in the pursuit of wealth and dominance. Why should I tell you about any of it?'

'Maybe I'll change. Maybe you'll convert me.'

Collins glanced sharply at him. Then his face melted and he laughed. Magnus laughed with him; loud, deep laughter. Bruno shifted, uncomfortable in his skin. Magnus ignored him.

The strange, too-loud laughter died quickly.

'Do you really want to know?' asked Collins, 'Or are you just humouring me?' His eyes found Magnus's again, in a way that bypassed all authority. 'Because I'm ready for the end right now. We don't have to go through all this talking. I've said it a thousand times to as many people and, of all of them, you're the least likely to take it on board. Any of it. Perhaps it would be more meaningful – for both of us – to proceed with my slaughter.'

'Don't you want your final scrap any more?'

'It isn't that important. I only wanted to prove a point to you. In the end, whether I make that point or not probably won't make much difference. I've already made all the difference I'm going to make.'

'We'll do it all before the end, Collins, my old son. We'll do it all. For now, I want to know all about it. I want to know what you've been telling everyone.'

Collins's eyes closed, breaking the invisible beam that joined him to Magnus with such disrespect for their difference in station. Magnus took the moment to shake off the effect of the stare. He wanted to hear this but he had to stay strong. Not let this fractured messiah too far into his mind. He watched Collins and his over-dramatic pause before beginning his sermon. The man didn't seem to be breathing. Magnus looked closer, watched his tent pole ribs and his sunken solar plexus for the rise and fall of respiration. There was nothing. So, he can hold his breath for a while, thought Magnus, so fucking what?

Collins opened his eyes.

'The first thing you need to know is that it's all lies. The town, the book, the Welfare. It's nonsense. It's like the corsets and girdles and make-up and hairspray that make a plain woman seem beautiful. Artful strokes with eyeliner and mascara to enhance a drab gaze, hot air and combs to tease lank hair into fullness, foundation and blusher to bring health and prominence to pale, sunken cheeks. Pencil and lipstick to shape and accentuate thin, passionless lips. Bone-ribbed underwear to make a figure where before there was shapeless dough. Tight bras to push up sagging breasts, pads to make small breasts larger. High heels to lengthen legs. Perfume to mask bodily odours, mouthwash to cover bad breath. Take it all away and what you are left with is this town: stripped of its shroud of lies; naked, ugly and rank.'

'You seem to know the women of Abyrne very well, I must say,' said Magnus, laughing. 'I've had hundreds of them over the years and many match your description, I was disappointed to discover.'

'They all use cosmetics that originate from Magnus Meat Products. You're part of the lie too.'

Collins had a sense of humour sometimes and sometimes he didn't. Magnus couldn't work it out. He laughed at the prospect of his own death and pissed on Magnus's light-hearted asides. He wasn't going to be any fun until it was time to get physical.

'Keep going,' said Magnus.

'If you go back to the start of all this -'

'Wait, Collins.' Magnus held up both hands. He didn't want Bruno hearing what he thought was going to be said. 'Bruno, untie him. Get him a chair and a blanket or something.'

'Sir?'

'Then wait downstairs in the hall until I call for you.'

'But what if -'

'Now, Bruno. Just do it.'

The big man leaned down to release Collins's bonds.

'I'm fine as I am,' said Collins. 'I don't need anything.'

'You're mine now, son, and you'll do as you're bloody told.' Bruno left the room and returned with a moth-eaten blanket.

'Is that the best you can do?' demanded Magnus.

'I'm sorry, sir, I thought -'

'Piss off, Bruno. But don't go far.'

When they were alone in his study, Magnus drew a straight-backed wooden chair over from the other side of the room and placed it beside Collins.

'Make yourself comfortable,' he said. 'Don't get used to it, though.'

Collins, blanket wrapped around his middle, sat cross-legged on the chair with his hands in his lap. Magnus shook his head. The man was like rubber.

'There are some things no one else should hear,' said Magnus.

'Believe me, Mr. Magnus, enough people have heard this already. Heard it, believed it and acted upon it. The town is changing. The world is changing.'

'I doubt that. Not because of some skinny Mary-boy like you. You've held your secret little meetings and probably bent the minds of a few weak townsfolk but the rest of them, the rest of us, will forget your words and move on. By the time I've eaten my fill of you, sucked the marrow from your bones, shat you out over the next few weeks, you'll be history. The kind no one remembers.'

'The writing of history is important, it's true. Written history – written anything – is what people tend to believe and remember. Whether it's lies or truth doesn't appear to matter much.'

'You're not as stupid as I thought.'

'I'm the stupidest man you'll ever meet,' said Collins. 'I've followed the calling of some tiny inner voice that tells me what is right. I've allowed myself to be railroaded into a premature and unpleasant death because of that voice. A voice that no one else can hear or prove exists. Even I can't prove it. But I'll tell you something, Mr. Magnus, being this stupid feels good. You see me as a man throwing his life away over some small point in a forgettable argument but, to me, it's the most liberating, joy-creating thing I could have done with my life.' Collins laughed to himself in a wave of private astonishment and continued, 'I mean, I'm sitting here and I *know* what's going to happen to me. I know what's going to happen to you and to the town too. You, Mr. Magnus, you know nothing of this. And even though I sit here and I tell you it willingly and against my better judgement, even though I give you the means, perhaps, to prevent it by forewarning you, you will not listen to me and you will not understand. That's destiny's work. I can say what I like to you, betray every nuance of my mission and you'll still make the mistakes you were fated to make.' Collins laughed again. 'You have no idea how happy it all makes me. Even the promise of the knives and the bone cutters. I give myself joyfully to set others free. You could join them if you wanted to but I don't believe you will.'

Magnus was unimpressed but he admired the man's strength. His delivery wasn't bad either. Perhaps Collins, despite his wasted body and his lack of respect, was a worthy adversary after all. All the better. In defeating him, Magnus would become that much stronger. That was why he had lasted all these years as the head of MMP and as the head of the town. He took his strength from the vanquished and grew in power each time.

He reached into his jacket pocket and pulled out a slim silver case. Prising it open with his butcher's fingers, he removed a dainty cheroot, engulfed it with his teeth and lips and lit it from a candle that burned on the desk. Even the tallow of the candle was made from the rendered fat of those he had disposed of, those he had eaten, thereby removing their bloodline forever. The flavour of liquorice and burnt leaves filled his mouth and he drew it into his lungs before exhaling a cloud towards Collins.

'Carry on, son,' he said, 'I'm going to enjoy this.'

'You know, Mr. Magnus, it doesn't matter whether people remember me or not. By the time I'm dead, I'll have done all I ever needed to do to change things in this town. There won't be any need to write it down for posterity. There won't even be any need for me to be talked about as some kind of legend -'

'Failed legend,' said Magnus, wagging a sausage finger in reprimand.

'Failed or otherwise. What I've done matters right now. For today. In the future it won't have any relevance. The point I want to make about history is an important one because it explains everything about the way the townsfolk live. The Book of Giving is a lie. How's that for blasphemy?'

Magnus chuckled.

'You talk about destiny. If I hadn't got to you first, the Welfare wouldn't have been far behind. You can't go around talking like this and expect another birthday.'

'I know. But we all have our parts to play. I'm happy with mine.'

Whatever, thought Magnus to himself. Talk it up while you've got the chance, son. You won't be so happy when I cut your play parts *off*.

'The Book of Giving was written by men. Men lie. Men want the world and their God to be a certain way and so they write their lies accordingly and call it the word of God. The townsfolk have altogether too much belief in the written word. I'm here to change that. You have to take all the books away and see what's left. You have to ask yourself what's right and wrong inside yourself. Then the world will start to work the way it's meant to.'

'Yeah?' Magnus was unimpressed. 'Well, so what, Collins? What do I care about books anyway? The Book of Giving serves my purposes. It makes my business indispensable to everyone. In turn, I support the Welfare – on a monthly basis and very handsomely. Sometimes I take out the trash for them, like I will with you. Everybody's happy. Everything works.'

'Yes, but everything is wrong. The Welfare is wrong. What they tell the townsfolk is wrong and what you do is wrong. It's hard for me to believe, sometimes, just how far from simple righteousness and decency we've wandered. You cannot kill your own folk, Mr. Magnus. And you certainly can't live off their flesh. It's the very purest wrong there is.'

Magnus raised placatory palms.

'Collins, Collins. Calm down, son. They're not our 'own folk', as you put it. From the point of view of the townsfolk and the Welfare they're the Father's sacred children and they're His gift to us. They keep us nourished and strong to do the Father's will. You and I both know that's as much bullshit. And as far as I'm concerned, they're just animals. They exist purely for our benefit.'

Collins was pale. It was the first time Magnus had seen a serious expression touch the man's face. So, this is the nub of it, he thought, this is what touches Collins's pain centres.

'You can't tell me you've never eaten a nice bloody steak or a few sausages at breakfast time. A bit of pâté on your toast?'

Collins put his head down, chewed his words back.

'Come on, Collins. Confess, old son. Tell your uncle Magnus everything.'

Collins looked up, crying.

'When I was a kid, I ate meat all the time. My mother wanted me to grow up strong and healthy. Like everyone else she believed that meat was the only way to ensure that.'

'Ah, well, if it was your mother that made you do it...I mean, you can't possibly be held responsible. You were just a little boy, after all. Not old enough to know any better. I'm being unfair. I couldn't possibly expect you to account for the fact that you willingly ate the flesh of the Chosen for several years of your life. Could I now? I could never expect you to take the burden upon your shoulders. All that suffering, the captivity, the squalor, the exploitation. You were just one of tens of thousands eating the meat, so of course it wasn't down to you. I couldn't blame a little innocent boy for all that. That would be...excessive. Don't you agree?'

Collins's tears seemed to have evaporated. The colour and equilibrium had returned to his face. Magnus was disappointed.

'I'll pay the price,' said Collins. 'And like I've said before to thousands of people, I'll pay it gladly. I ate meat for decades, Mr. Magnus, if you really want to know. I ate it long after I left home. But I never stopped thinking about where it came from. At the back of my mind, the idea that there might be something wrong with the way we got our food never left me alone. We learnt about the Chosen, God's sacred gift to us, when we were at school. The similarity between them and us seemed obvious but the teachers and the Parsons always played upon the differences – the lack of hair, the deformed hands and feet, the inability to communicate with us or each other. But I always had my doubts. I'm pretty sure that everyone does at some point before burying the doubts under the words of the Book forever. I started to think about what the fields and the processing plant must really be like. Of course, it's hard; in fact it's almost impossible to get any information about what really happens to the Chosen. No such information is available. To start with, I had to imagine everything.

'The first thing I realised was that to make meat, you actually have to kill something. I can't imagine why it took me so long to work out that one simple thing. You have to raise this living thing, feed it, breed it, fatten it. Then you have to find a way of killing it and cutting it up. I wondered about that for a long, long time. How do you kill something? Do you use a knife? Do you hit it with a club? Shoot it? All this I had to investigate purely in my imagination.

'I took a job in the gas plant where excrement and intestines from the Chosen arrived by the truckload. After a few weeks I realised just how many living things must be dying each day to produce that volume of waste and off-cuts for conversion into usable methane. I tried to do the numbers in my head but I couldn't. It made me sick, Mr. Magnus. It made me vomit to think of the amount of dead there must have been, and still are, whose shit and guts are powering parts of the town with electricity.

'And then, one day, I got talking to a drunk in the Derelict Quarter. Turned out he was an ex-meatpacker. He told me what really happens at MMP. He told me everything there was to know about how you run your 'business', Mr. Magnus. That was the day I set out to find another way.'

Cheroot smoke drifted between the two men, connecting them somehow. Magnus listened without expression.

'The first thing I did was stop eating meat. It wasn't easy. There's so little else to eat in the town. Most of the grain we produce goes to feed the Chosen. There are vegetables to be had, but the butchers sell them as decoration for meat. A couple of green beans and a small potato with your steak, a leaf of cabbage beside your chop, onions with your liver, some parsley to garnish a pie. Getting enough vegetables to make a meal was a struggle, especially with Parsons of the Welfare watching all the time. It took months to collect enough seeds and sets to start my own garden. But there are sources, places you can go. You'd be surprised just how many townsfolk enjoy vegetables more than they do meat, Mr. Magnus. Even though they would never admit it in polite company, possibly not even to members of their own family, but they are out there. And there are vegetarians too, people who have disappeared from the habitable quarters and gone to the derelict parts of the town to live out the rest of their lives without a single MMP item in their diet. They're quiet, reclusive folk, Mr. Magnus, people like me. But they have a simple joy. You can see it in their eyes. It's like they exude a sense of relief, as though the sacrifice they made in dropping out was worth it.

'They welcomed me, those people. The real folk of this town. They're the ones that have begun to see through the Book of Giving's precepts.'

Hmm, thought Magnus. I'll enjoy extracting the locations out of you before you die. A smile almost touched his lips but Collins didn't seem to notice.

'Among them was a very old man. There was no way to verify it but he told me he was a hundred and eleven years old. The average life expectancy of a male in Abyrne is, what, forty-five? Fifty?'

Magnus shrugged but said nothing.

'I've never met anyone else, man or woman, that made it to sixty, have you? There's one simple reason. Meat causes illness. Flesh of the Chosen is toxic. Removing it from the diet ensures a longer, healthier life. Imagine living twice as long as we do now, Mr. Magnus. Simply by removing one ingredient from our diets.'

Magnus blew smoke and replied:

'Look, Collins, just tell the bloody story. Don't try to give me your spooky sales pitch alongside it. I am the producer, the processor, the distributor *and* the salesman. You are merely the product. If there's any selling to be done, I'll do it. To put it another way, I'm the butcher and you're the meat. You'd do well to remember that.'

'You wanted to know the details and I'm giving them to you. Taking meat out of your diet is the most natural way to extend your life.'

'It hasn't extended yours,' laughed Magnus.

Collins conceded the point with an inclination of his head and continued.

'This old man had learned a lot over his years of exile. Trying to survive without meat was harder when he started out. He spent a lot of time close to starvation. The fasting was unintentional, but he found that it brought him a good deal of wisdom and knowledge. He discovered that refraining not only from eating meat, but from eating anything at all, changed the workings of his mind and gave him access to different levels of consciousness.'

'You mean he went mad with hunger,' said Magnus, enjoying each interruption.

'Of course you'll see it that way. You don't know any better and how could you? But ignorance is no substitute for experience, Mr. Magnus. It's no match for hard-won knowledge. I'm sure you'd agree with me on that.'

'No one has ever spoken to me the way you have today, Collins. When I've finished with you, it'll be a cast iron guarantee that no one ever does again. A little 'history' about you might actually serve my purposes. I'll suggest to the Welfare that they write your story down in the Book of Giving so that no one ever forgets. Hell, they can put me in it too. I'll be a ruthless king and you'll be my flawed subject. The tale will exist forever more, as a parable for the foolish, explaining what happens when you disrespect those who hold the reins of power.'

'It'll make just as good fiction as the rest of the Book does.'

'Finish your story, Collins, and make it quick. I'm getting restless.'

'There's not much more to tell. The old man -'

'What was his name, this old man?'

'It's not important.'

'It's important to me.'

'The man is dead now, Mr. Magnus. He can do no harm.'

'Starvation, was it?'

'Hardly. He passed away peacefully as he slept. He was a hundred and seventeen years old.'

'I want the man's name.'

'No.'

Magnus gritted his teeth.

'You're going to wish you died in your sleep, Collins,' he said.

Collins nodded.

'I know.'

For a moment Magnus thought Collins looked frightened. No, it wasn't that satisfying. It was resignation. Acceptance. The man was just too bloody relaxed. Suddenly it occurred to Magnus that there might be a real reason for such equanimity. Did Collins have a *plan*? Could it be that he had some group of skinny vegetarian activists on his side, people ready to fight and die for their leader like the guards and enforcers in Magnus's employ? It was too outrageous. But perhaps it was true. It certainly explained a lot about Collins's behaviour. Maybe there was some signal he was going to give to his empty-bellied followers. Something to do with the fight he was trying to engineer. Magnus was forced to reconsider Collins's stature. He wasn't telling him everything and he'd never intended to. What if Collins had *allowed* himself to be caught so easily for exactly this reason?

Magnus tried to keep his face even and unmoved. If there was a mob waiting in ambush outside the mansion, he'd need to bring them down before they had the opportunity to use his lack of preparation. Shit, how could he have been so stupid? He'd underestimated his enemy. It was the first and last time that would ever happen – he promised himself that right then. Never again. No more convivial chats. No more discussions. Collins would be the last. But there was just a little more he wanted to know.

He picked up a small brass bell from his desktop and shook it between his fat fingers. The noise from it was clear and piercing. Seconds later there were thumping footsteps on the stairs, louder along the hallway outside and Bruno burst into the room panting.

'Everything all right, sir?'

'Fine, Bruno. Absolutely fine. I wonder, would you mind closing the curtains for me?'

'Sir?'

'The curtains, Bruno. It's getting dark and I don't like the curtains open after six o'clock.'

'But, surely, Juster -'

'Juster will be preparing the dining table at this moment. Close the bloody curtains.'

'Right.' Bruno ran to each of the three windows and drew the thick dusty drapery closed. 'Anything else, sir?'

'Yes. Come here.'

Bruno approached and stepped up to Magnus's chair. Magnus beckoned him closer, gesturing for secrecy. Bruno leaned his ear down to Magnus's lips and nodded as he took his orders.

'And Bruno,' whispered Magnus. 'As quietly as you can, son.'

Bruno nodded again and left the room without even looking at Collins.

'Something wrong?' asked Collins.

'Only for you, old son. Only for you. Why don't you finish your tale?'

Eleven

His mind could hide his new knowledge but his body couldn't. It got harder bleeding the Chosen, gutting them, quartering or boning them out. But he could disguise that because he was further along the chain and the killing was done. On the stun, though, it was impossible to disguise his misgivings. It didn't show in his face or his demeanour or in the things he said to his co-workers but it showed and it was impossible to do anything about it. The familiar shout from Torrance's steel balcony made Shanti want to disappear.

'Chain speed, please.'

He kept his voice even.

'One eighteen, sir.'

Torrance must have thought he'd misheard.

'Say again, please, Ice Pick.'

'One eighteen.'

In the pause he could hear Torrance thinking. The next yell was aimed at the filers moving the Chosen through the crowd pens.

'You men, keep those cattle moving. Rick's standing here with no heads to break.'

One of them yelled back:

'Everything's moving fine over here, sir. Got a good steady stream.'

'Ice Pick, what's the problem?'

'No problem, sir.'

'Why aren't we turning 'em over quicker?'

'I thought we were. I'll get us back up to one thirty in just a few minutes.'

Torrance didn't shout any more, so Shanti hoped he was satisfied. Something in the man's silence worried him, though. It wasn't just the low chain speed – that happened to everyone once in a while. An off day was an off day. But Torrance had been looking at him recently. Not looking at him strangely but looking at him *more*. Noticing him. Watching him. Maybe he already knew something. If he did, Shanti knew his days at MMP were coming to an end.

He ground his teeth down upon each other. The access panel opened. He didn't hesitate. By the end of his shift they were working at one twenty-eight. Good enough to keep Torrance off his back, but only just.

'It's very simple. The old man had plenty of time to think about food and survival as a loner in the Derelict Quarter. He realised that, in theory, cutting a vegetable and eating it was not so different from eating meat. Either way, you ended the life of the thing you wanted to devour. Unlike the meat-eating folk in the town, he could look with new eyes. He was prepared to think about things differently. He wondered if there might be a way for folk to survive without causing harm to any other living thing. He experimented with prayer, meditation, and exercise and came up with a basic system for nourishing the body using only light and breath.'

'Wait a minute,' said Magnus. 'You're telling me that this man ignored everything written in the Book of Giving but that he still prayed? Who the hell to?'

'It's not the writings in a book that prove or disprove the existence of a higher power. It's our deep experience of the world that informs us of such things. In this town there are believers and disbelievers that have no interest in the writings of the Book.'

'Do you believe in a higher power?'

'Isn't it obvious?'

Magnus had to think about that.

'It isn't as obvious as you might think. You've come here and spouted so much nonsense that it's hard to define anything about you. Except that you are highly motivated and a bit of a head case. You say you eat God, and I suppose that means you believe there is one. It hardly appears to signify your respect for such a being however.'

'I apologise for not being clearer. One is sometimes . . . so overwhelmed by truth that one forgets to speak it. In answer to your question, yes, I believe in a higher power and I respect it beyond all other things. It feeds me, it nourishes me, it . . . supports me. It shows me a path every single day of my life.'

'The old man, you said he survived on light and air. But you say you live on God. How is that possible? What does it mean?'

'Perhaps you have an image of me munching my way through a fragment of divinity. But it isn't like that. You see, the first thing you have to do is give yourself completely to God. That act, if genuine, is a sacrifice of great value. You can't imagine what it means at the moment, Mr. Magnus, but it is within all of us to have that understanding and for each and every one of us to make that very sacrifice. The result is that

God gives you everything you will ever need. It's as plain as that. My daily nourishment involves a routine that is some combination of prayer, calmness of mind and gentle movement of the body, but, unlike the old man, I took it all a step further. I sacrificed myself to the Creator and in return the Creator has given me everything. Absolutely everything.'

Magnus crushed out another cheroot, his lips downturned in judgement and scepticism.

'He hasn't given you freedom though, has He?' said Magnus.

'He hasn't delivered you from the hands of your enemy. And

He hasn't saved you from slaughter. You'll pardon my ignorance if I don't see your hands overflowing with His gifts.'

'The value of things changes when you live in the care of the Creator. The things you're talking about have no value to me. The Creator might give them to me or He might not. It doesn't matter because He has already filled my life up. I am content and rich beyond your imagining.'

Magnus nodded and stood up. He stretched his massive arms behind his back and audibly cracked a few joints into place before walking over to Collins.

'I'm surprised, you know,' he said in a matter-of-fact tone. 'You've really made me think about things differently. I thought you were just some lunatic that had enough energy to fool the stupid people of this town. But you're a lot more than that, Collins. You're intelligent. You're passionate. And you're dangerous. You've taught me a lesson about myself and you have, against all the odds, changed my mind about what I'm going to do with you.'

He looked at Collins's face, still so placid and open. The man was listening but he didn't seem to have taken in that Magnus might be hinting about some kind of leniency, some kind of arrangement. He wasn't, but it annoyed him that it didn't seem to matter to Collins one way or the other. The man's face was lean, serene and bright. Magnus smashed one hammer of a fist straight into it and felt the nose break and flatten beneath his knuckles with minimal damage to himself. The chair sailed over backwards spilling Collins onto the floor and separating him from the old blanket. Magnus expected him to lie there and check himself over before begging not to be hit again.

Collins's naked body rippled and tightened as he rolled over backwards with the momentum of the spill. He was on his feet and half crouched ready to defend himself before Magnus had finished inspecting his knuckles.

It was a short walk from the office of records back to the main cluster of Welfare buildings but the way she felt, it was an effort to return. Why they hadn't located the archives nearer the rest of the Welfare offices and Central Cathedral she couldn't understand. She pulled her gowns closer around her, struggling to get warm again after hours of studying records. It was hard to tell now whether she was shivering with cold or because of her sickness. Her stomach kept up its jagged griping; worsened, she felt, by her frustration.

The records had revealed nothing of any use to the investigation. There had been two hundred births in the town the year that the baby Richard Shanti died. Of those, thirty were stillborn. Twelve mothers died in childbirth. Of the surviving children, only eight – a very few – were orphaned by poverty, calamity or neglect. It had been a good year for the population. However, each of the orphans was accounted for in the records and nothing seemed out of place. There was certainly no connection between any of them and the Shanti line.

Right now Parson Mary Simonson planned to obtain eight warrants, one for each of the orphans, and visit each of them to be certain nothing underhand was going on.

But first, an audience with the Grand Bishop of the Welfare.

The steps that led up to Central Cathedral were fifty yards broad at the base, narrowing as they neared the tall entrance. Sixty steps. She waited at the bottom composing herself, gathering breath, and then began the ascent. Her muscles complained, her chest laboured, cold was replaced by a sudden prickly sweat. Three times she stopped. Parsons passed up and down to her left and right. None helped.

On gaining the cavernous main entrance, she rested again with her back to the ornate stone of the pointed arch rising high above her. The great wooden doors had long ago rotted beyond use and been removed. Now the Cathedral's entrance yawned like a huge toothless mouth whilst the Parsons scuttled in and out of the darkness beyond.

She queued outside the Grand Bishop's chambers with many other Parsons of varying rank. Most of them spent no more than a couple of minutes inside and so the queue moved swiftly. Just before it was her turn to go in, her stomach twisted and tightened around its hub of spikes and she put a fist there to control it. Sweat broke again, not long dried from her trek up the steps.

The spasm was still in control when the Grand Bishop's door opened and her name was called from within.

She hid it as best she could, knelt before him and kissed his hand.

'Mary,' he said. 'It's good to see you.'

It was good to see him too, as far as looking went, but the reason she was there made seeing him no good at all.

'And you,' she managed.

She raised her head to look at him and saw the man that had inspired her into the Welfare years before.

'You may rise now, Mary.'

He was looking at her with concern. She must have been kneeling there for longer than she thought. She tried to stand and understood why she hadn't already – it was a task even to lift her own weight. Seeing her struggle, the Bishop offered her his hand again and this time she took it and used it to haul herself upright. She smiled but she knew he could see past it.

'Why don't we sit for a while,' he said.

'What about all the others?'

'They can wait. That's what the queue's for.'

Instead of sitting behind his desk and keeping her on the opposite side, he walked her over to the fireplace where a few sticks were almost burnt out. Still, the warmth was what she needed; it eased the pain off a little to be so comforted. They sat facing each other on straight-backed wooden chairs in which the woven straw seats had been replaced by rough planks.

'I've been keeping watch over you in my way,' he said after they'd been quiet for a few moments. 'I'm told you're not yourself these last few weeks.'

It was months but she didn't bother to correct him.

'I need...guidance,' she said.

'Whatever I can give, I give gladly.'

'There's a...not a problem exactly, but an issue with someone who is a great server of the town. I am not sure how to proceed. If I pursue the issue, there's a chance I'll discover an irregularity.'

'How serious an irregularity?'

'Serious enough to revoke status.'

'I see.'

'My concern is that the individual in question, judging by his exemplary service to us all, is entirely unaware that the irregularity exists. Even if my concerns turn out to be justified, this individual may have no knowledge that his very existence is…blasphemous. My question is: do I allow this situation to exist and hope that no one else ever discovers it or do I take my investigations further and risk destroying a man who, in his own mind, is entirely without fault?'

The Grand Bishop's face didn't change outwardly but she could see that her question had caused him to access some deeper part of himself. His eyes still made contact with hers but were focussed somewhere else, somewhere far beyond his chambers.

'What does your heart tell you?'

'My heart tells me that if a wrong has been perpetrated, it was by someone other than this individual. If he has no knowledge of what has gone before, then he is as innocent as he believes himself to be.'

'And what does your God tell you?'

'My God tells me that only townsfolk may feast upon the Chosen. Only townsfolk may undertake the husbandry of the Chosen. Regardless of this individual's impression of himself, my God tells me that if he is not one of us, then his status must be revoked. He must face the truth and all it brings with it.'

The Grand Bishop nodded very slightly and smiled to himself. Then the elsewhere-focussed stare returned to his face. He remained silent for some time.

'Sometimes the heart and God are in accordance and sometimes they are not.' He wasn't looking at her when he said this but she knew what he was referring to. 'As you know, I have always based my decisions upon what God dictates. Because of that I look back on my life without regret.' He let his eyes meet hers. Somehow, he suffered his own inner barbs. She thought she could see dampness around his eyes.

'*Without* regret, Mary. And I know without question that I am saved. That I go on to glory. Adhering to the will of God makes life so much simpler. It relieves us of complexity. It makes suffering unnecessary.'

She sat in silence letting his words cover her as they had so many times throughout the years. She knew this was what he would say even though she'd hoped he would say otherwise. It was no different from before. His response in all matters came down to the simple acceptance of God's law as laid down in the Book of Giving. She found it both disappointing and reassuring to discover that he had not changed. That he would never change.

'Thank you, Your Grace.'

He seemed to become suddenly aware of the long line of Parsons waiting outside his door. He stood and helped her to her feet. She wanted to ask for help in the other matter, the matter of her illness but she knew that his answer would centre around the idea of selfless service at the expense of one's own Welfare. That was what being a Parson of the Welfare was all about. Maybe he knew she wanted more from him or maybe he just took pity on her. Or could it be that despite the words he said, some part of him would have liked very much the complexity and suffering of acting against God's will? Whatever was the case, she did not expect what came next.

'I'll make sure your dutiful rations contain something particularly sacred and nourishing from now on. I'm sure it will make you feel a lot better.'

She went to kneel and kiss his hand but he stopped her.

'That's really not necessary, Mary. Go and get some rest now. Start again tomorrow.'

She smiled and left.

***

Torrance watched the group of four workers exiting the dairy while he smoked a cigarette against the back wall of the slaughterhouse.

Beside him a truck had backed into a loading bay, its engine idling. He could hear the wet sound of vats being emptied into the stainless steel compartments of the wagon and the rumbling thud as hollow units filled with valuable flesh.

'Hey, boys!'

He held up a packet of smokes as he beckoned them. They changed course and approached.

'What's the rush?' he asked when they were close enough.

'Got something better to do than milk cows?'

'No, sir,' said Harrison. 'We were just...'

'It's all right, there's no need to explain. I get out of here as quick as the next man when my shift's over. There's more to life than MMP, am I right?'

They nodded, relaxed a little.

'Here, smoke with me.'

Torrance offered the pack around. They hesitated and then all reached out together. He flicked a match and four heads leaned in to draw on the flame.

'Thanks, sir.'

Torrance nodded. Respect was right and proper. They had

it for him but not for their previous boss. That too, was right and proper.

'How are things in the dairy now?'

'A lot better without that freak Snipe,' said Roach. The others looked at him and then at Torrance. Roach realised he'd gone too far and looked down at his feet wishing he didn't have such a big mouth.

'You're right,' said Torrance. 'Snipe was a freak of the lowest order. Not fit to work here, not fit to be townsfolk. You know what happened to him, right?'

They shrugged.

'Status revoked,' said Maidwell.

'That's correct. And you all understand what that means, don't you?'

They nodded but he could tell they were still too young to fully understand. They knew but they didn't really get it.

'If you're not townsfolk, you're meat, boys. It's as simple as that. Let me show you something.'

He walked over to the truck in the nearby bay and they followed. They could now see the gas logo on the doors and the nature of the cargo. One by one, vats of intestines were being up-ended into the wagon's open sections. Shiny ropes of pale pink, grey, white and blue innards avalanched from each vat. Stomachs, pancreases and gall bladders went with them. The natural twists and turns in the loops of large and small intestine made them look like links of strangely-coloured sausage. There was something intimate and sexual about the way the intestines glistened and coiled around each other as they tumbled down.

'That's the power for the town right there. Those of us lucky enough to have electricity – this is where it comes from. Snipe, your old boss, is in there somewhere and that's entirely fitting. He did something unforgivable by God and by Magnus. Now he's going to give of himself to feed the townsfolk, light their stoves and power our trucks. He's going to make sure the plant has power to keep processing the Chosen. One way or another we all make that contribution, boys. Best to make it the right way. Know what I mean?'

Parfitt was as pale as the spent organs slopping into the truck but the others were accepting, if a little grim-faced. They all nodded and said 'Yes, sir.'

'Well that's fine.' Torrance crushed out the cigarette under his boot. 'And now that you've all been working here a few months, I think it's time you enjoyed a little extra-curricular activity. Be at Dino's tonight at ten o'clock.'

Harrison was about to protest but Torrance didn't give him the chance. 'Don't be late.'

***

It wasn't what Magnus had expected.

Collins moved like a cat. Not a startled animal. A very lean, confident and deliberate cat. The claret ran from both of his nostrils but Collins hadn't even bothered to swipe the back of his hand across his face to see the extent of it. Instead, he breathed, far too slowly for Magnus's liking, and the occasional blood bubble filled and burst above his upper lip, sending a brief scarlet mist into the warm air of the study.

His eyes were mesmeric – a full border of white surrounding each iris – and he seemed not to stare so much as allow everything in. Magnus had the feeling that Collins could even see behind himself. The odds, so screamingly in Magnus's favour only seconds before, now seemed a little closer than he wanted to believe. Smooth and steady as a surgeon, he reached his right hand under his jacket and extracted the cosh he kept in a sling under his left arm. It was the head and first eight inches of a humerus, the marrow replaced with lead – everyone called it the 'no-brainer'. The bone was polished to a pale yellow gleam and delicately monogrammed, R.M. It wouldn't hurt to tip the scales further in his favour and Magnus didn't want to use a blade on the man. Not yet awhile.

Collins's eyes didn't flicker when the no-brainer came into view.

Now he held the cosh, Magnus felt happier to approach Collins. He'd beat him like an expert now, rupture a muscle here and there, crack a few ribs and a facial bone or two but nothing that would spoil Cleaver's work. Nothing that would prevent Collins from feeling every parting of his skin, every tear in his flesh, every snap of his ligaments and tendons and every crack of his separating bones and joints.

The overturned chair lay between them. Magnus would have to kick it out of the way before he could lay another finger on Collins. He stepped forward a pace gauging Collins's response. Still nothing. Not a twitch of a muscle. Not a flicker of his eye. Magnus hefted his boot-clad right foot at the chair and sent it spinning away from them towards the wall. The way between them was now open. Magnus raised the no-brainer and advanced.

***

Of the orphans adopted that year, two were already dead. The others knew nothing about the Shanti family. Nor did they know anything about other orphans who might not have been accounted for. Those surviving were as ignorant and uninterested in her questions as the worst townsfolk could be. She reflected that perhaps orphans shouldn't be adopted, losing status instead to be taken out to the plant. It would keep the numbers of worthless townsfolk to a minimum. Abyrne already overflowed with the ignorant. Ignorant of their religion; ignorant of their protectors, the Welfare; ignorant of everything it took to keep the town going.

Turning up nothing but dead ends, she made a final trip to the office of records. Whittaker and Rawlins rose from their seats whenever they saw her now and glasses of milk came without her needing to ask.

She was having a few good days. The trembling in her body had eased off and the pain in her stomach had also receded. She put it down to the Grand Bishop's kind request for veal in her dutiful rations. She now ate it every day, usually at breakfast, and found it much easier to keep down.

There was a trail worn through the dust where she had passed up and down the centre of the archives to reach the shelves of boxes. Having bid Whittaker and Rawlins a more cheery good afternoon than was normal for her, she went straight to the original record box that she'd first checked and took it down again. In it she found the details of the dead boy, Richard Shanti, killed by his own umbilicus as he was born. She then found, on looking more carefully, that Richard Shanti had an older brother named Reginald Arnold Shanti. This brother had been stillborn. The Shanti line had not been destined to continue, no matter how noble a name it had been when the town was first created out of the ash of the wasteland.

Two tragic pregnancies. Two dead boys. Dead on their first day in the world.

What would that do to a mother? What would it do to a father who wanted his line to extend and flourish? Surely they would have to admit to themselves that their lineage was finished. Once they'd accepted that, what would they do? Taking orphaned children would benefit the children by making them townsfolk and saving them from the plant or from a

114

life as fugitives in The Derelict Quarter, but it would do nothing for the bloodline.

So what did it mean that *two* boys were dead? Was there another man out there in the town with a noble name who was not what he believed he was?

She went to check the records of the parents again to see what more she could discover.

***

Bruno sprinted into the study, knocking the door open with a violent shove as he passed through. The door connected with the inner wall and the handle gouged plaster from the wall.

'Stay back,' shouted Magnus.

Bruno noticed his boss was careful not to take his gaze from Collins's face. The eye contact between them had become compulsory. A glance away at the wrong moment and either man might take advantage.

'Me and Mr. Godhungry here are about to get a little better acquainted,' continued Magnus. 'I don't want any interruptions.'

Bruno looked at Collins's bloody nose and mouth, saw again how starved he looked and remembered how easy it had been to bring him in. He noticed the shining piece of human ivory in his boss's right hand and relaxed a little. The no-brainer was legend in the town, a weapon feared by everyone.

The noise of the toppled chair and sprawling body had been loud downstairs. Bruno had thought for one panicked moment that it might have been Magnus who had been overpowered. Now he realised how stupid that was, how needlessly paranoid. Magnus only needed a curtain of men around him to stop knives and rocks and spears. Magnus didn't need any kind of bodyguard when it was man-to-man like this. He had the physique of a heavyweight boxer and speed utterly at odds with his bulky gut and chest. He'd seen Magnus take dozens of men over the years. This fight with Prophet John would be meat and drink to him. If they got too close for blows to be struck, Magnus's sheer weight and power dwarfed Collins. The thin man had no chance.

He'd called in an extra shift of enforcers to check out the grounds of the mansion. There was no trace of any accomplices out there, no ambush of starving townsfolk, no heretical raiding party. The mansion was entirely secure. Collins was a man alone in the very worst situation. Magnus would bludgeon him with great skill and care, leaving him intact for an execution that promised to be the bloodiest the town had ever seen.

He compared them now; the pale wraith of a man – by his own admission an abstainer from meat and underfed for months – with his crazy-sounding words and blasphemies, and his only strength coming from the intensity of his eyes. He was crouched, almost cowering. He faced a giant, the man Bruno had worked and killed for ever since he was a teenager brought in off the streets. Magnus looked bigger than the largest bull; his shoulders and chest always pressing out from his suits, as though he might burst his tailoring. And Magnus was a full man; full of rage, full of hunger and passion, full of the lifeblood and flesh of every man that had crossed him since he took his place as Abyrne's Meat Baron.

He put Bruno in mind of some kind of ogre made human. His rust-coloured hair, thinning but still long, hung far beyond his collar. His beard was so full you could only guess at the shape of his mouth beneath it and the whiskers spread so far up his face they speckled his cheek bones. His shoulders were two arcs of muscle and his hands were as large as shovels. Hunger must have made Collins rotten in the brain. Only a total nutter would go looking for a fight with a man like Magnus.

'That means, depart, Bruno.'

Bruno was reluctant to leave them alone. It wasn't for fear of his boss's welfare; he merely wanted to see this mismatch play out to its inevitable consequence. He wanted to see Collins beaten and humiliated before they gave him to Cleaver to dissect at leisure. It would be a slaughter no one would ever forget.

Bruno backed out of the room and kept the image of the two fighters in his mind. On one side, the ruddy bear of a man that ran the town of Abyrne. On the other, the whippet-bodied ascetic, soon to perish.

It was a shame he had to miss it.

Twelve

Magnus knew there was no perfect moment now that he'd taken first blood. It was time to use his muscle.

He leapt forward, aiming to catch Collins with an outstretched arm, depending on which way he dived. Collins didn't move. Magnus had time to grin to himself as he put out both arms to engulf his opponent in a full body tackle. Collins would be crushed by it. At the last possible instant, Collins sidestepped and he flew right past. The lunge became a dive and Magnus crashed to the floor. The rug of woven hair did little to cushion the impact. And Collins, the sneaky little bastard, was now behind him.

He squat-thrusted himself upright like a drill sergeant showing his men how it was done. Before Collins could make another move, Magnus was facing him, no advantage lost. Right-handed, he swung the no-brainer at Collins's jaw hoping to knock him out in one swipe. Again he believed he was going to connect and again, when it seemed too late to be possible, Collins moved a few inches outside the arc. Magnus, unable to stop the momentum of his bone-cosh, followed through clumsily, once more leaving a flank open to Collins for dangerous moments. He spun back using the circular movement to try for the other side of Collins's face with a backhand strike. Collins shifted his head and the blow missed. He seemed to melt in the face of each onslaught. Magnus didn't like the calm look on his hollowed face.

'I thought you wanted a bloody fight. Now you're the shrinking violet. What's it to be, Collins?'

Collins, so passionately expressive before, said nothing. Magnus saw his eyes taking in every nuance of movement he made. He tried a couple of feinted jabs with his left fist but Collins knew they weren't going to connect and stayed absolutely still. His passivity was taking the fire out of Magnus, replacing it with childish frustration. They weren't fighting like men. They were playing tag.

Magnus eyed his opponent. His only satisfaction in that moment was knowing without doubt how all this was going to end. Collins didn't stand any kind of chance at all. The serenity of the man was disquieting to him, though, and for a few seconds, he almost made the decision to call Bruno back in and bring Collins's little performance of agility to a close. Safer to have him bound and moved into the town centre for public torture and execution by slow dismemberment and ablation. Take him out and let Cleaver have him and everything would return to normal – better than normal – with nothing left of Collins save a bloody and shocking memory in the minds of the townsfolk. Enough to remind them who ran Abyrne and forget all ideas of abstinence from God's divine gift: meat.

What am I thinking? The man hasn't had a proper meal for months. Anyone as light as that would move with a bit of speed. When I catch him, he's finished. If he doesn't want to be caught, I'll get Bruno on the job. Either way, this is my contest for the taking. By God, it'll feel good to break a few of his bones.

Magnus swiped with confidence; Collins dodged again. The big man swung so hard that he lost his balance. He saw the disbelief in Collins's eyes; an opportunity he couldn't have dreamed up. Magnus felt something like a sharp stone hitting his Adam's apple square on – Collins's bony elbow, the closest part of his body. By the time it had happened it was too late to respond.

The no-brainer dropped from Magnus's limp fingers. His left hand went to his throat. He could neither breathe nor swallow. The blockage there felt as hard as the stone of a plum. He tried to call for Bruno but was unable to make any sound. Words of fury and fear backed up in his mind but he could not speak them. He was suffocating while Collins looked on. He was vulnerable to any attack and yet Collins hadn't moved.

This is it. The skinny bastard's going to stand there and watch me die.

'Perhaps now you'll take me a little more seriously,' said

Collins.

Magnus could see Collins could barely believe his luck. He put his hands out to steady himself on something but there was nothing there. He sank to his knees, finally attempting to massage his throat with his fat fingers. It didn't do anything except hurt more. Collins smiled and Magnus saw real relief there, a dispersal of tension.

'Still, I'm glad we met.'

Collins stepped out of view towards the window and Magnus's vision became black and starry.

***

Dino's was a stockman's shift-end paradise.

It was loud and smoky and served harsh grain vodka to loosen the minds and muscles of all MMP workers whether slaughtermen, dairymen or herders. The place was sawdust rough because of its clientele. However, their high wages and standing in the town made it difficult for others without the right connections to get in. Many of Abyrne's unattached ladies came to Dino's to look for a solvent husband. They were any age from sixteen to forty and some of them had been waiting that entire span of years. Stockmen called them spent milkers. They never gave up their search, though. It was that or die of hopelessness.

A band played danceable jigs with fiddle, guitar, whistle and a couple of rattling drums. The music had a stretched, laboured sound to it but it made the workers jump and twitch nevertheless. Musical instruments were hard to come by in Abyrne. Live, well-played music was even rarer. Within an hour of the shift end, most of the patrons were dancing, kicking up dirt or slamming their vodka. The rest were watching the floor for openings. Stockmen looked for a healthy young woman – another rarity – and the women looked for stockmen of any kind.

The dairy boys made sure to arrive before the Cathedral clock struck the hour. They didn't know what patience Torrance would have with tardiness, even outside the plant. None of them wanted to find out.

They walked through the front doors with several minutes to spare, having showed their MMP cards to the massive doormen who didn't recognise them. Inside they blinked at the smoke, the clamour of laughter and shouting, the cloud rising over the enormous dance floor. No one noticed them.

Unsure what to do, they followed Parfitt when he began to shoulder his way to the bar. Each of them felt like kids on the first day at school, nervous about what to expect, afraid of danger, excited at the possibilities. It was the final part of growing up and they were glad Torrance had 'invited' them.

Parfitt would have liked more time to view the minor selection of drinks behind the bar before ordering – none of them had drunk anything before – but one of the many barmen had already seen him. He didn't try to speak over the commotion, he merely gave an upward flick of his head, signalling that he knew they were waiting and what did they want? Parfitt had to make a decision and picked a label he liked the look of.

'Four bullwhips,' he shouted.

'Where's your bloody manners?'

Something wrong with the way the words sounded. Parfitt reddened anyway. No choice.

'Please.'

The barman grinned. All his upper and lower front teeth were missing. He turned away and spilled the vodka into four bullet-shaped shooters.

He placed them on the bar. The dairy boys reached out but he held up his hand.

'A few words of advice to you, lads. If you want to drink in Dino's, you've got to behave like stockmen – that means give respect and you'll get it right back. Don't ever come in here thinking you're better than anyone else. Understand?'

They turned to one another and every pair of eyes said *Do we really have to take this?* No one knew the answer and it wasn't worth risking a fight on their first visit. They might want to make a habit of it after all. Parfitt was thinking in particular about the surfeit of women in the bar.

Angry but contained, they all nodded.

'Good lads. That'll be a groat for the drinks.'

'How much?' said Parfitt, disbelieving.

The barman heaved a long-suffering sigh.

'Listen, you pick the most expensive drink, you've got to pay for it, right? All booze is made by the grain bosses. All vodka is equally piss-like and the price makes little difference. Next time go for Prods.'

The barman gave a final smile, more of a taunt than a pleasantry, and wandered away to other customers. Roach slapped a hand onto Parfitt's shoulder.

'Forget it, mate. Let's enjoy ourselves.'

He held his glass up and the others did likewise.

'To the Chosen. Long may they give us their flesh.' And together:

'To the Chosen.'

They threw back the shots with a toss of their heads, the way everyone else did, and all of them regretted it. It tore each throat all the way to the stomach making their gorges rise and their eyes leak. Saliva flooded Parfitt's mouth as he tried not to vomit. After a few moments he got himself under control. They caught each other's eyes, saw each other's faces and then they were laughing. The laughter felt good. The tension evaporated and they leaned back against the bar to survey their new territory.

Parfitt lost himself for a while in all the activity, let it wash over him, envelop him. This was what their work was all about. They worked the Chosen and gave the fruit of their labours to the people of Abyrne. They were paid well for their skill and appreciated for it too. Stockmen were respected members of every district and every quarter. Here in Dino's their efforts came full circle, they drank, they relaxed, they danced and the women came looking for them. He smiled at no one in particular. Life was suddenly very good. The job made sense to him.

He was turning to Roach to tell him it was his round when a hand rested on his shoulder.

Turning he saw the well-built hulk that was Bob Torrance, his eyes watery with vodka and laughs.

'This way lads. Come and join us.'

***

John Collins ran naked from shadow to shadow through the streets of the town and gave thanks for the darkness. There wasn't enough gas in Abyrne to provide street lighting for all the districts and once he was away from the Magnus mansion it was easy to cling to walls, to pad silently down narrow alleys, to be part of the darkness. He was calm. He'd slipped past Magnus's guards without any need for conflict. They were brutish and insensitive to the subtleties of movement and though he'd passed within a metre of some of them, they never knew he was there.

He'd been ready to die in Magnus's study. Ready to let the Meat Baron do worse to him than he did to any of the Chosen. The fight. What had been the point of that? Somewhere along the way Collins had changed his mind. He needed to get the measure of Magnus and survive a little longer. His message had not yet been fully received and there was so much more he believed he could do. Had he become fearful in that study? Allowed the thought of his public dismemberment and humiliation to extend his mission – his life? He believed he'd acted for the good of all but he doubted himself too.

This was new terrain. He'd been so sure of everything for so long and now this. Maybe he'd needed to place himself in such danger to force the next part of his mission up from his subconscious. After all, none of his activities had ever been planned. They began as promptings that became inner commands he could not ignore; notions that became inspirations that became obsessions.

It was cold out on Abyrne's streets but he didn't feel it the way others in the town would. He merely released some of the light concentrated inside him.

Each dwelling he passed was old and in need of repair, even in the wealthier quarters. There weren't enough materials to fix everything. Slowly the town was dying but no one realised it. Even the Welfare, even Magnus and the grain bosses that supplied him believed Abyrne would continue forever and that there would always be enough for everyone to eat. But the wasteland was growing, or to put it more realistically, the town was shrinking. Every year the wasteland encroached a little further into the arable acreage of the grain bosses and every year they pushed their fields a little further into the Derelict Quarter and ploughed up land that had once supported tower blocks and houses. The Derelict Quarter was huge but the encroachment couldn't go on forever. Townsfolk needed to realise that there had to be another way. The words in the Book of Giving and the Gut Psalter were not only wrong and evil. They were suicidal.

Collins's job wasn't finished. That was why he'd challenged Magnus. He had more to tell his followers, more folk yet to convert. He couldn't just tell them; he needed to *steer* them away from the warped traditions of the town. They needed to know what to do for the future and he was the only one who could educate them. So, no, it was not cowardice that had made him fight to survive the encounter with the Meat Baron. It was sacrifice. It was necessity.

Every house exuded the smell of grilled, fried, roasted or boiled meat. Cuts of the Chosen on every table in every household that could afford it. All the money went back to Magnus or the Welfare. The only other players in the game were the grain bosses that farmed cereals on the north-west perimeter of the town. Magnus bought almost all the grain they produced to feed the Chosen. To this basic ingredient he added a mush of ground bone and unusable off-cuts. Collins wasn't sure but he felt the Chosen must have known they daily ate the flesh of their own brothers and sisters as part of their raising for slaughter. To Collins this was one of the worst evils of the town.

Trucks filled with spare bone-meal from the Chosen travelled daily out to the grain bosses who stored it until it was time to fertilise their fields. Without the nitrogenous material, the crops would fail and the Chosen would starve. Meat production would cease. This put the grain bosses in a strong position; if they wanted to squeeze Magnus for the price of grain, they could do it by threatening to reduce supply. Magnus, on the other hand, could not bargain with his truck loads of waste because, by not supplying them, he would only hurt himself in the long run. By the same token, the grain bosses would never squeeze Magnus too hard; if they did, the whole town would be in danger of starvation and the cyclical economy between meat and cereals would collapse. So Magnus and the grain bosses waltzed with each other year in, year out, never completely trusting, never completely ruthless.

Now that Collins had escaped, Magnus would send his men out into the Derelict Quarter to look for him. He had to warn everyone that they would be in danger. Humiliated and furious by now, the Meat Baron would go to any lengths to find Collins and bring him in. There was no one he wouldn't hurt to achieve it. But Collins would get the word out that night. And there were many places he could go where Magnus would never know to look.

***

Torrance had a tray of drinks and he led the boys, the crowd opening miraculously for him, to a table away from the small stage where the band was playing. The music and shouting was less of a roar but the floor still shook with the impact of hundreds of drunken boots.

They recognised some of the other men at the table but didn't know their names. Torrance introduced the dairy boys to his coterie but didn't introduce them back. Parfitt assumed this was all part of some unspoken hierarchy that they would, by osmosis, come to understand. Also at the table were a few women – definitely not girls, some of them looked old enough to have been mothers to all the dairy boys – not the most attractive in the room but not the worst looking either. Parfitt decided after another vodka that he didn't much care what they looked like. He and his mates were out for the night and they had ladies with them. The possibilities multiplied accordingly.

The older stockmen ignored the dairy boys and even Torrance paid them only a few passing words when he wasn't busy laughing with his crew or slapping one of the women on the arse. More rounds arrived and the detached sense of freedom that had first hit Parfitt deepened along with his sense of well-being. Harrison, Roach and Maidwell were all laughing now, shouting along with every other stockman in the room as though they'd been regulars at Dino's for years. Parfitt felt melancholic suddenly to discover this spectator inside him. He wanted to laugh along with the rest of them, slap a backside if the impulse took him, tell a joke or dance in the sawdust.

'Boys,' shouted Torrance. 'Time we were moving.'

Parfitt, snatched from his mental balcony, blinked. His ears filled with sound again.

'What?' he shouted. 'Where are we going?'

He wanted to stay. Of all the things the evening might offer he realised it was the ladies he was interested in. He didn't care how old they were.

'You'll see,' shouted Torrance. 'The night is yet young in Abyrne and plentiful the sights for its eyes. Even young eyes like yours. Come on.'

Torrance's crew stood and Parfitt and his friends followed. He was surprised that he was unsteady on his feet but it didn't worry him. He felt elated. As they walked out to the back entrance, he staggered into several stockmen. No one gave him a second glance. Outside, the night air was chill. It didn't stop him reeling.

Everyone piled into one of the MMP buses that took workers to and from the plant.

'How did you get hold of this?' he asked Torrance.

'I've earned my privileges.' Parfitt didn't understand.

Once the bus was rolling with Torrance at the wheel, the ladies moved from seat to seat and, for the first time that evening, one of them talked to him. She was thin, too thin really, and her streaked hair hung in greasy strands below her shoulders. She smelled of the perfume and creams that MMP made from the oils rendered from the Chosen. It didn't smell bad exactly, but it reminded him of work and he didn't like that. She sat beside him, oppressively close.

'I haven't seen you before.'

Her voice was low; smoke and crushed glass.

'First time we've been to Dino's,' he said. There was no point lying.

'What do you do?'

'I milk the cows.' He gestured behind to his friends. 'We all do.'

'No gore and guts, then. No chop and slice.'

'Not our department.'

'Ha. Very good. I think I like you...'

'James.'

'I'll call you Jimmy. Does your mother call you Jimmy?' Parfitt shrugged but didn't answer. His mother was long dead.

'You must like working in the dairy. Seeing all those titties all day long.'

It was like ice in his brain. He sobered immediately, all suspicion. Was Torrance testing them? Was that what this evening was all about?

'That's blasphemous,' he said. 'They're udders. I wonder what your Parson would say if he knew you spoke of the Chosen this way.'

She didn't look frightened at the thought that he might tell someone, but it did stop her stupid chattering.

'It was just a joke, Jimmy.'

For a while they sat in silence but she didn't pull away from him. The bus lumbered over the broken roads and she fell against him often. He liked it but tried to concentrate on working out where they were going. It was tough; he'd already lost his bearings. It seemed like they were heading for the Derelict Quarter.

Someone had brought a bottle of vodka and it was passing from row to row. The woman took a big swallow and grabbed Parfitt to kiss him. As she did, she let the vodka dribble from her mouth into his. The kiss made him drunker and the moment of alert watchfulness passed. She handed the bottle forward to Torrance who took a swig and passed it back. She gave Parfitt another vodka kiss before passing the bottle back again. He heard laughter and raucous cooing behind him. Some of the lads were getting lucky with the other ladies and some weren't. There weren't enough to go around.

When the bus stopped, no one wanted to disembark. It was warm and comfortable; the perfect place to continue their embraces. Torrance had to shout at them, even his crew. They staggered from the bus onto a dark, cracked pavement. There were no streetlights this far from the town centre. Parfitt could barely see his feet until Torrance brought out a gas lamp.

'This way.'

They followed, some arm in arm, others alone. Parfitt's woman – she still hadn't told him her name – stumbled and he held on to her easily. She weighed very little and, as he'd discovered on the bus, she had tiny 'titties'. He suspected jealousy had prompted her comment about the cows' udders and not some signal from Torrance to sound him out. He didn't care what her tits were like though. She was warm-bodied and willing and he hoped that by the end of the evening she would provide something more than alcoholic kisses and clothed explorations of her wiry body.

***

Torrance led them over a rubble-strewn pathway between derelict buildings and high-rise blocks. The ground was black and nothing grew, neither grass nor weed. They came to an opening in the concrete with a broken wall on three of its sides. Torrance held his lamp forward: steps descended into blackness.

Intrigued, Parfitt didn't hesitate to follow. The woman's grip tightened on him not because of the steepness of the steps, he felt, but because she was excited, anticipating something. Her heels clicked and echoed on the concrete stairs. They seemed very loud out there in all the silent blackness.

Parfitt became aware of muffled voices ahead. It could have been roaring. Torrance stopped, seemingly at a wall, and kicked it three times quickly and twice slowly. Huge sliding steel doors had been painted to look like concrete. Slowly but silently, the doors rolled open on well-greased runners. Sound rushed out at them. Cheering, jeering, drunken laughter. The sounds at Dino's had been sounds of pure merriment and release, these sound were different, they had an edge of illicit expectation. Torrance spoke to the men guarding the door but Parfitt couldn't hear what was said over the noise of the crowd. The guards parted and all of them stepped in.

The corridor reminded Parfitt of the chutes and crushes used for guiding the Chosen in the slaughterhouse. As they progressed, the noise grew. A yellowy light from many gas lamps lit an opening at the far end. They passed into a vast rectangular space, a subterranean stadium. It must have held almost a thousand people but it wasn't full. Even so, the noise of shouting spectators was overpowering. Torrance took them to a row of stalls at the very front. People looked at him and made space immediately.

The woman squeezed next to Parfitt on the splintery wooden bench and put her arm round him. He ignored her. In the centre of the stadium was an arena upon which all the lamps were concentrated. The shouts of the audience reached a crescendo. On the ground in the centre of the arena were two bulls but Parfitt had never seen them like this. On their wrists and ankles they wore heavy cloth bands that sparkled – resin-tacky hemp dipped into broken glass. The bulls had been fighting each other; that was obvious from the amount of blood on each of them and still glistening on the concrete floor. As they could not hold weapons, these ankle and wristbands must have been the next best thing. They had no protection.

One bull, as big as any he'd seen in the plant, lay on the floor on its back. It was trying to get up but didn't have the strength. The other bull stood over it, lungs pumping like bellows. Its pale skin was slick with sweat and blood from hundreds of scratches and deeper incisions. Parfitt wished the two bulls could roar and scream at each other but, like all the Chosen, they could not even speak. Their hissing was inaudible over the taunts of the crowd.

With nothing further to fear from its downed opponent, the dominant bull looked up and around at the faces that watched him from the safety of the tiers of stalls. Parfitt couldn't bear the look in the creature's eyes as it faced its next challenge. The crowd wanted blood and it had given them that. Now they wanted death. Their chanting found a rhythm. It was easy to make out the simple, brutal words.

'Kill it, kill it, kill it . . .'

Some silent acknowledgement passed between the bulls, Parfitt was sure of it, before the winner stepped behind the bested bull's head and raised its right foot. Parfitt couldn't comprehend how it could succeed in killing its rival unless – The bull brought its heel down on the other's forehead, lifted it and brought it down again. The sound made Parfitt queasy – bone on bone against concrete. The beaten bull was still alive, still breathing, its eyes were still open. Again the stomp. And again. And finally the knocking of heel bone on skull became a splitting and a crushing and the supine bull breathed no longer. A cheer went up, the people in the crowd lost all control, shaking their fists, punching the air, turning to embrace each other and jump up and down in the cramped stalls.

The winning bull held up its triumphant arms. Parfitt could see it did so because it knew that was what the crowd wanted, not because it felt the glory of its achievement. It turned slowly on the spot to receive the adoration and hysteria of the spectators. Blood dripped from cuts, ran from its mouth and nose. Its legs trembled. Four handlers came out with hotshots and nooses but the bull made no attempt to evade them. It was led from the arena. Another team of men dragged out the body of the defeated by the ankles. The corpse left a wide smear of fresh blood and brain tissue as they hauled it away.

Parfitt was jolted from his shock by Torrance's meaty hand clapping him on the shoulder.

'There you go, boy. Now *that's* entertainment.'

Someone passed the vodka bottle and Parfitt drank deep, drunk enough now to ignore the burning of his oesophagus as the liquid fire swept down. He passed it on. He felt the woman squirming beside him, saw the leer of lascivious enjoyment on her face. She squeezed closer, sat on his lap and ground against him. The noise of the stadium retreated and Parfitt re-entered the small, safe world inside his mind. There were more fights that night, more slaps on the back, fiercer attention from the woman. He found himself responding – smiling, nodding, kissing, groping at the correct moments, but he was very far away.

At some point in the evening, it must have been very late, the woman took his hand and dragged him away from the stalls. She took him to a toilet where the plumbing wasn't working, pushed him into a free stall and shut the door behind her. Kneeling in front of him she said words he didn't really hear and put his penis in her mouth. The vodka – or was it the blood? – had numbed every part of him. He couldn't even make his face smile at her lack of success. There was nothing she could do to make him hard. Eventually she stood up, twisted-faced and nasty. Her knees were wet – with piss he assumed. Stupid bitch.

The vomit came in a single long bark and joined the other fluids on the floor. He wiped his mouth and she was gone.

The world came back to his numb ears and he went to find Torrance.

Thirteen

Magnus watched the surface of his vodka rippling in its glass.

He tried to remember the first time he'd noticed that his hand wasn't dead steady but he couldn't pinpoint it. Recently, that was for sure. It made him angry and he set the glass down on his desk. In his other hand a roughly rolled cheroot vibrated. The ash dropped from it onto the hide-bound desktop. He stamped out the cheroot in frustration and then lit another one straight away. Sometimes vodka soothed the tremors, he took a large, burning swill and bit it down. His throat was swollen and swallowing anything other than liquids was still painful. He'd been eating nothing but soup for a week. Holding his hands out, he scanned the fingers for movement. The jitter was still there.

All this had started with that sneaky, skinny bastard, Collins.

All the threats, all the promises he'd made about the pain he was going to inflict and the runt had tricked him and beaten him in his own house.

I must be going soft in the bloody head.

It was not the first time the notion had occurred. In the weeks leading up to the 'capture' of Prophet John Collins, Magnus had experienced problems concentrating. Especially trying were the production/demand figures. He could read them easily enough but he found interpreting them more and more troublesome. The figures proved something was amiss and had been for several months – the meat surplus was increasing. It had to be something to do with Collins. But far worse than this for Magnus, who couldn't help but attract most of the money in the town, was that his ability to come up with a strategy for increasing the demand was practically non-existent.

He couldn't concentrate for more than a few minutes at a time. The span was shortening. So was his memory. Over the years Magnus had faced many rivals and every kind of man from the wily to the ferocious, hand-to-hand and in business. None of it scared him as much as what was happening to him now. He couldn't blame Collins for cursing him with an illness – he didn't believe that kind of rubbish, just as he didn't believe a word in the Book of Giving – but he knew whatever was ailing him had accelerated ever since he woke up from the throat jab that had floored him. Perhaps it was his illness that had permitted the attack.

No one talked about it much, especially not the Welfare, but the Shakes was a common illness in every district of Abyrne. There were many remedies, the majority of them based on by-products from his plant, but what good they did he couldn't determine. Veal was particularly sought after for the Shakes. No one ever seemed to recover, though. The illness progressed gradually over years or swiftly within months, reducing its victims to quivering, man-shaped lumps of gelatine. They lost the ability to look after themselves – to eat, dress or shit without help. Eventually, they had no say in whether they held their shit in or not. Then they laid down to die. Some opted to have their throats cut or hanged themselves long before it ever reached that stage.

Magnus supposed he would have to do the same. Unless...unless it wasn't the Shakes. It was just possible that he had a low-grade fever – they too went round the town with some regularity. If that was all it was, he'd beat it and be his old self again.

He took another swallow of vodka grimacing more at the pain in his throat than the heat of the alcohol. Collins would pay with the most exquisite torture Cleaver could devise. He would ensure the process took days to complete – long enough that parts of Collins would be rotting and rat-eaten while he still lived to see it.

He checked his hands again. The tremor had subsided.

Good. Bloody good. I've got the flu and I'm going to beat it. I'm getting better already. I'll see Collins in white-eyed agony by the end of the week.

He leaned back in his chair.

'Bruno!'

The door opened and his greasy-haired aide stepped in.

'Mr. Magnus?'

'Get the cook to bring me three veal cutlets. I want them rare. I want them bloody. Still hissing. Understand?'

'Absolutely, Mr. Magnus.'

'And get him to cut them up like he would for a baby. I don't want to bloody choke.'

Bruno nodded and turned to leave.

'Wait. I want some action too. Three maids. Straight after I eat. Tell them...tell them I need my wash. All right?'

'Of course.'

'Good. Now, fuck off.'

Alone again, Magnus felt better.

Three steaks. Three maids. Followed by a nice long rest. And tomorrow I'll be my old self again.

A frown passed across his face.

Bugger it. Forgot the most important thing.

'Bruno, get back here.'

He heard footsteps on the staircase as Bruno returned, not having reached either the kitchens or the maids' quarters. He heard Bruno pause outside his door and smiled. Nice to know that the man wanted to compose himself before entering.

Bruno reappeared showing no sign of breathlessness or disarray.

'Yes, Mr. Magnus.'

'Tell me what's going on out there. Have you found him yet?'

'We've got teams of two patrolling the border of the Derelict Quarter, watching the comings and goings for anything strange. Every now and again we take a random traveller between the two areas and remind them why the Derelict Quarter is so dangerous. Want to send out the right kind of message.

'We've got people inside the Derelict Quarter too. They keep their eyes open. There have been several sightings and they seem to centre round a particular area on the far side of the tower blocks. There's a rumour he's underground and has others with him. We're not sure of numbers and we're not sure of his exact hiding place. But we're getting closer every day. It's only a matter of time before we send in a decent-sized force and root him out. Him and his so-called followers. Then you can do what you like with them. With *him*.'

Magnus stared out of the window.

'It's not bloody quick enough, Bruno. I don't want to wait another day. Another hour. Another minute.'

'We're doing everything we can, Mr. Magnus.'

'I know that, Bruno. Just do more of it. Otherwise, it's going to look very bad on your CV.'

Magnus lit a new cheroot from the one he was smoking and crushed the first one out. His eyes defocused. He didn't notice Bruno studying his hand as he smoked.

'Will there be anything else, Mr. Magnus?'

'No. But hurry up with that veal. I'm fucking starving.'

***

The more he understood of the Chosen and their language, the longer each day at the plant became.

But Torrance – usually his greatest supporter and protector when other stockmen were ridiculing his refusal to use the MMP buses and his insistence on wearing a backpack that must have weighed the same as a stunned cow – had changed. Instead of watching him work with his usual air of pride and pleasure, now Torrance's eye had become critical and overbearing. It was like he was waiting for Shanti to make a mistake; willing him to. There was something else about Torrance's manner that disturbed Shanti, a kind of mocking disrespect.

Torrance and Shanti stood on the steel balcony that overlooked the many stations on the MMP chain. Torrance leant on the railings only half surveying the activity on the plant floor. When he spoke, he didn't turn and address Shanti face to face. The words went into the void above the ceaseless slaughter just loud enough for the two of them to hear.

'Your stun rate's dropping, Rick. Are you sick?'

'No, sir. I'm fine.'

'You're not fine. *It's* not fine. I've got the speeds for the last month logged right here.' He lifted a clipboard from the railing but didn't turn. 'Want to see them?'

'No.'

'I didn't think you would. Because you know what they'll show, don't you?'

'Yes.'

Torrance was silent. He looked out across the factory floor but didn't seem to see it.

His pause was filled with the sounds of the plant: the sighs and hisses of the Chosen milling in the crowd pens, the hollow knock of struggling knees and elbows on buckling metal panels, the pneumatic stamping of the bolt gun, the rattle of chains, the harsh breath of the scalding vats, the succulent drawing of blades through warm flesh, bearings in the high runners like curtains being closed, the snap of severed joints, the thump of body parts onto rubber conveyors, workers sharpening knives on endlessly rotating whetstones. The sounds of men using steel to transmute life into meat.

'Why don't you take some time off?'

Shanti couldn't imagine anything better but he couldn't allow Torrance to discover as much. It was difficult to make himself sound shocked, offended by the suggestion.

'I don't want to, sir. There's no need.'

'There is a need, regardless of what you think you want, Rick.' Now Torrance turned to him and Shanti didn't care for his expression. 'I can't allow chain speeds to drop when demand for the flesh of the Chosen is so high. Besides, we have standards to maintain. We can't be seen to do a poor job. But very specifically, we can't let someone like you, the Ice Pick, be seen to lose his way. You're a legend around here, Rick. An inspiration to the other workers regardless of your habits – we all get by the best way we know how. I've got no choice but to take you off the stun while your rate of efficiency is still relatively high. That way you'll be remembered for the good things you've done here. I wouldn't want it any other way.'

'What are you saying, sir? Are you...firing me?'

'No, Rick. I wouldn't do that to you. You're one of the best stockmen I've ever seen. You're a credit to MMP and I want to keep it that way. What I'm suggesting is that we gradually transfer you off the high-pressure jobs and on to something less stressful. God knows, I've seen plenty of stunners lose it over the years, Rick. I wouldn't want to see that happen to you.'

'What *is* going to happen?'

'I'm going to move you to other areas of the plant and keep moving you until we find you a new niche where you're as comfortable as you've been here in the main slaughterhouse all these years.'

Shanti was amazed by his reactions. Despite having hated the job since the first day and now having come to a new understanding that filled each working moment with revulsion, he found himself hurt, upset, rejected. He was being reduced from the man he had been to a smaller man, a lower man. There were tears in his eyes.

'My God, Robert...I...I just can't believe what you're telling me.'

He searched Torrance's face and thought he saw something there, something that showed Torrance *did* care what happened to him. Was it pity? A kind of sufferance?

'Rick, listen. If it was anyone else, anyone else at all, I'd be sending them home to look for a new job. You're different. You belong here among the herds, working your magic on them and, in time, we'll find you a position you'll fill as well as you have your position in the slaughterhouse. I'm saving your life, here, Rick. I wouldn't keep another man on if he was in your position. Do you understand what I'm telling you?'

Shanti nodded, his throat too swollen to speak.

'I'm sending you home for a couple of days' rest. No arguments. It's official. My report will say you haven't been well. When you come back, I'm going to reassign you. We'll find you a better job.'

Shanti looked at his boss with undisguised anguish. Tears bled into his beard and were lost there. Torrance's face hardened.

'Just go home. Now.'

***

Between the two daily milking sessions, after they spray-cleaned the walls and floors, there was plenty of time for the dairy boys to sit around, play cards and smoke. Conversation inevitably turned to their first night out on the town.

'Betty's got a serious fixation with my cock,' said Roach. They'd heard his tale about a dozen times. Maidwell cut it short.

'That's not what she told me, Roach. After you passed out, she told me she was looking for a man with a real weapon.'

Roach was scarlet.

'I...I did not pass out.'

'Do you remember puking all over the back seat of the bus?'

'No,' said Roach, indignant.

'That's because you passed out.'

Roach looked at Harrison and Parfitt, then back to Maidwell. They all nodded.

'Aw, shit.'

'Don't worry about it, Roach. Everyone was sick. We just managed not to get it all over the work's transport. The girls were nice enough to give it a sluicing out but the bus still stinks. Everyone's calling you Retch now.'

'Fuck off.'

'Cool name,' said Maidwell.

Parfitt grinned but didn't speak. The night out with Torrance was still troubling him. He didn't think he was the only one. None of them had mentioned the bullfights and he didn't believe it was just because they were illegal.

'Anyway,' said Maidwell. 'The point is that I was able to give Betty what she wanted. She's . . . an energetic lady.'

Harrison: 'She's no lady.'

Roach slid down in his seat and pretended to scrutinise his hand of cards. He'd come so close with Betty and then blown it. He couldn't help himself, though. He had to find out.

'So, uh...did you fuck her?'

'Course I fucked her. I was doing you a favour. I merely gave her what you couldn't provide. The least a mate can do, eh?'

Everyone chuckled. Roach reddened again.

'Are you...you know, will you see her again?'

'God, no. What for?'

'Well, I just thought you might...I don't know – '

'Listen, Roach, I've got no reason in the world to see Betty a second time.'

'Don't you want to do her again?' asked Harrison. He was merely voicing what they were all thinking.

'No need. When Jeff Maidwell fucks a woman, she stays fucked.'

Parfitt left the three of them, even Roach, doubled over with laughter and went outside to smoke a cigarette.

He'd had it lit for a few seconds when he saw Bob Torrance striding over to him from the slaughter block. He stopped leaning on the wall and straightened up. Torrance raised a hand in greeting.

'How you doing, Parfitt?'

'All right. You?'

'Nothing a bolt gun couldn't put right. Listen, I've got a job for you. You'll get very decent overtime.'

'What is it?'

'Don't worry about that. Just meet me by loading bay when the shift's over. Wear some overalls and be ready to do some proper work for a change.' Torrance flashed a humourless grin, exposing brown teeth, and slapped Parfitt on the shoulder. 'Don't mention it to anyone, understand?'

Parfitt had no choice but to nod.

'Good man. See you tonight.'

Torrance walked away and disappeared back into the slaughter block. The rest of Parfitt's cigarette tasted awful.

Fourteen

For the first time in many years, Richard Shanti walked home. He still wore the sand and brick-filled pack but he didn't have the will to move any faster than a heavy-footed trudge. It took a lot longer; familiar landmarks he normally passed between in seconds took minutes to go by. When he reached the short drive of his out-of-the-way house, his legs felt wearier than on any arrival home in his life.

He saw Maya's face in the window, concerned that he was home early. Already wondering why he wasn't running and what it meant. He didn't think she had any real concern for him. All she worried about was getting enough meat and staying a cut above the other women in the town. Her concerns meant nothing to him now. He realised that he didn't love Maya any more. Perhaps this was the first opportunity he'd had both the time and energy to consider it.

Her face in the window was a cheap copy of what it ought to be. *There should be a woman there who loves me or there should be no face at all.* He walked past the window to the back of the house, shrugged off his pack and didn't bother to wash himself off at the trough.

In the kitchen he smelled meat. She'd been cooking it for weeks now, more and more it seemed. The greasy taint of it smothered the kitchen curtains and adhered to the damp, flaky paint on the walls. He could smell it in her hair and clothes without going anywhere near her. She was sweating it, meat juice running from her pores, as she worked over the cooker preparing the family meal. She had raw meat on her hands and with those hands she was touching the vegetables he would later eat, rinsing his rice with the same unclean fingers.

He could tell she wasn't sure whether to reprimand him for his early return from the plant or give him sympathy over whatever his problem was. She was deciding whether to care about him or not. That wasn't love.

'What happened?' she asked eventually. On another day he might have believed it was a question of concern.

'Where are the girls?'

'They're still at school.' She dried her hands on a towel and approached him. 'What's going on, Richard?'

'I'd like to see them when they come in. Wake me up, would you?'

He walked away from her to the bedroom.

'Darling, I asked you a question.'

136

'Don't disturb me until they get back. I'm exhausted.'

In the bedroom he didn't bother to change out of his running gear. He lay down diagonally across the bed and pulled a corner of the coverlet over himself as far as it would come. He could hear the confused silence in the kitchen while Maya considered whether to be angry with him or be safe and let him sleep. He knew she wouldn't disturb him. She didn't have the right.

He closed his eyes. All he saw were the faces of Chosen passing before him. Passive, loving eyes that did not even accuse. They spoke to him. *Hhah, sssuuh. We know you. You are the one who blesses us with darkness before we give of ourselves. You are the compassionate one, the releaser.*

He thought back over the years and the eyes that had passed before him. The souls. He knew what he had done. There was no way to atone for it. No punishment in this world that could repay him for his evils. In some unimaginable eternity, he would relive the death of generations of Chosen. He knew it was true.

Sleep would not come.

***

He saw mutilation. Skin punctured. Skulls breached. Blood wasted on floors and steel tabletops. The decisive *thunk* of cleavers through joints. The deft trimming of fat with long, fine blades. Chops and fillets tossed onto moving belts – separated from carcasses so swiftly the meat was still war m and steaming. Rainbows of viscera sorted into types by bloodstained hands. Drooping livers. Turgid kidneys. Fibrous hearts. He saw raw bones, obstinate nubs of flesh and ligament still attached, pale blue cartilage shiny with lubricant. Bones cooking in vats of simmering water, grey scum and pools of melted fat floating on the surface. He was paralysed. A panel opened in front of his eyes. He looked out from the restrainer, saw the bolt gun placed against his head, Torrance behind it smiling through his filthy beard.

'There is no God. There is only meat.'

Hiss-

-*click*.

Hema and Harsha opened the door. He'd been in some weird half-doze, his unconscious mind believing the MMP plant as real as his own bedroom, his own home. He swallowed down the half-formed scream in his throat.

'Hello, sweet peas.'

The twins stayed in the doorway.

'Why aren't you at work, daddy?'

He almost smiled. Kids had no time for subtlety. The dream faded quickly and he was glad.

'Mr. Torrance gave me a couple of days off because I'm tired. I came straight home and went to bed.'

It appeared to be enough of an explanation. The girls edged closer to the bed.

'Are you allowed to go running?' asked Hema.

'I can do whatever I want now that I'm at home.'

'But won't it make you more tired?' asked Harsha.

'Yes. It will make me tired. And that's why...' he pulled the coverlet tighter around him, '. . . I'm going to stay right here in bed for as long as I like.'

This elicited a small giggle from both of them and, though they still seemed wary – or was it shy? – they approached the bed twisting from side to side and knotting their fingers as though he couldn't possibly notice them getting closer.

'Papa?'

'Yeeeeees?'

'Will you tell us a story tonight?'

In the past he'd made time for stories before bed but over the last couple of years the routine had slipped. All his family habits had. He rarely saw the girls.

'That depends.'

'On what?' They both asked.

'Well,' he said, feigning a long, broad yawn and snuggling further into the bed. 'It depends on whether I wake up in time.'

'Wake up in time for bed time?' asked Hema.

'Mmm hm.'

Harsha said, 'But why don't you get up now and then go back to bed after you've told us our story?'

Shanti yawned again. It went on for a very long time.

'I can't possibly get up now. I'm exhausted. Mr. Torrance has told me to rest and that's what I have to do.'

'Do you have to do everything Mr. Torrance says?'

'Absolutely everything. He's my boss.'

The girls seemed to like the sound of all that power.

'Papa?'

'Yes, girls.'

'Please don't sleep too long. Please come and tell us a story before bed.'

He stroked his beard as though lost in decision-making.

'Tell you what,' he said. 'I'll tell you a story if you come and give your papa a nice big cuddle.'

Without hesitation, they leapt onto the bed and squeezed him tight. They weighed a lot more than he remembered. *All that meat.* He squeezed them back and then patted their backsides.

'Right. That'll do. You're crushing the life out of your poor old man.' He pushed them off the bed, glad to see they were reluctant to leave. 'Go on, off you go now. See you at bed time for a quick story.'

'Not a quick one. A long one.'

'We'll see.'

'Papaaaa.'

'The longer you stay here, the shorter the story.' Defeated, at least temporarily, they left him and shut the door.

The sweetness of their visit, and the renewed contact after what felt like years, quickly passed. All he could think about was the girls being pushed into the crowd pens, prodded towards the chute and restrainer. Entering the chain live and leaving it in anonymous pieces. He took the image down into sleep.

***

Parfitt dawdled getting changed out of his cow-gown and stayed back after the other dairy boys had clocked out.

It was drizzling as he made his way across the yards in his green overalls to stand near the loading bay. He felt uncomfortable loitering there on his own, dressed for work when everyone else was heading home. No one saw him though. The plant cleared swiftly at the end of each day. Everyone rushed for the buses and crammed in. The convoy then ferried them all back to their homes in Abyrne. A skeleton crew stayed behind at night to watch the herds and discourage break-ins. Not that any townsfolk would be crazy enough to break into MMP. As base as the townsfolk were, none of them would go looking for such a swift revocation of status and such a terrible end to their lives.

He was about to smoke a cigarette but then put away the packet. Spots of rain dappled his green work-wear. He slipped inside the loading bay. He'd never known the place so quiet. Usually, the sounds of the slaughterhouse could be heard from all around the plant. Now there was nothing but the tapping of a chain that swung somewhere beyond sight. The crowd pens were empty for the night; the herds of the Chosen out in the fields, corralled or penned in other areas until morning.

But the smell of the place was exactly the same. He was used to the smell of the Chosen's waste. It lingered over the whole plant. Here in the slaughterhouse, it was worse, as though in their fear, they shat and pissed out every toxin and hormone in their bodies. The result was almost chemically abrasive to the nose. Their blood had its own smell too. No one would have sensed it from a simple cut or when the Chosen were ritually docked during calfhood. However, released by the hundreds of gallons – eight or more pints from each carcass – the stuff stank. Hygiene was a buzzword in the slaughterhouse more so than anywhere, but blood, like water, flowed and sprayed and found cracks to seep into. No amount of scrubbing and pressure-hosing found all of it. And though the sawdust was regularly swept out and replaced, the blood of the Chosen was bound into the concrete floors. The intestines of the Chosen were full of the slop they ate in various stages of digestion. They were full of raw gas, the sharp tang of bile and decomposition. The vaguely uric scent of kidneys lay below it, the ripe aroma of plump spleens and fatty livers, the ingredients of meat and offal pies and delicious pâtés. Standing in the empty loading bay, Parfitt found it hard to be excited about pâté even though he was ready for his dinner. The least offensive smell in the slaughterhouse was that of the butcher shop, of healthy meat parted from the still-warm bones it once held upright.

The sound of an engine jolted him into alertness. He put his head around the loading-bay door and saw a truck approaching from beyond the dairy. Whoever was driving it flashed the headlights once. Without conviction he half held up his hand in response. The truck arced outside the bay and then reversed in. The engine died and the door opened. Torrance stepped down from the cab. Parfitt recognised the two men with him; they'd been among the crew at Dino's.

'Right. Let's get this done and get home.'

Torrance's men knew exactly what they were doing and hauled themselves up onto the loading dock. They ran into the gloom of the factory and Parfitt heard the sound of trolley wheels returning.

'Get a bloody move on, Parfitt. I could eat a whole hind-quarter right now. If we don't get home soon, I may be forced to eat my wife.'

Torrance's grin was humourless, his eyes shafts leading somewhere Parfitt didn't want to visit. He climbed up to the loading dock in time to see the two men, each pushing a trolley filled with meat.

'You'll see where they are,' said one of them. 'Right by the end of the chain.'

They would have been hard to miss even if he hadn't been looking for them. There were twenty trolleys, maybe more. They weren't just full, they were piled high with cuts of meat. Parfitt tried to gauge how many Chosen it would have taken to fill the trolleys. When he took hold of his first trolley he saw it wasn't a calculation based on simply chopping them up and dumping them in. These were good cuts of meat – chops, joints and steaks. The trolleys must have held between two and three hundred head in total.

Parfitt put his back into shoving it along. When he reached the truck, low rails caught hooks on the base of the trolley so that when he pushed, it tipped into the truck. An avalanche of meat slid into the back. Parfitt hauled on the trolley rope bringing it upright again. Dragging it with him, he went to retrieve the next.

With three of them shifting trolleys, emptying them all took less than ten minutes. Torrance looked on, smoking. Parfitt felt very much the focus of his attention. He worked accordingly but he was terrified. Moments earlier he'd been musing on how insane it would be for someone to break into MMP – for whatever reason. Now, here he was helping Torrance and his henchmen steal an entire truckload of quality cuts. No wonder Torrance had promised him 'very decent overtime'. If they were caught, they'd join the Chosen in the crowd pens just as Greville Snipe had done and with exactly the same amount of sympathy.

The loading done, the four of them squeezed along the seat in the cab and Torrance passed out smokes. Parfitt took one but his hands gave away his state of mind.

'Bit young for the Shakes, aren't you, Parfitt?' There was no point trying to hide it.

'I'm nervous, sir. Never thought I'd be...nicking meat.' Torrance put the truck into gear and moved off. His men chuckled amongst themselves and Parfitt's unease grew. He began to suspect he'd been chosen not because Torrance liked him or felt he could rely on him. At the end of this after-hours job they were going to let him take the fall.

Eventually, though, Torrance let him off the hook. At least a little.

'We're not nicking it, son.'

'What are we doing then?'

'You'll see soon enough.'

They reached the front gates where, strangely, there was no one in the security guard's box. Instead of turning left towards town, Torrance pulled out and went right. Parfitt had never been this way before. Never even looked in this direction. Beyond the MMP plant there was very little more land before the wasteland began.

It was dusk now. Almost directly behind them the sun was falling to earth behind Abyrne. Ahead of them, all was shadow but Torrance left the truck's lights off. The road quickly deteriorated and he slowed down to negotiate the ruts and potholes assailing the suspension. Then the road ended and all Parfitt could see were two wheel ruts that led into the darkness.

To their right there were more tyre marks. Torrance stopped the truck and reversed it into these tracks.

'Better get out and guide me in,' he said.

Parfitt waited for one of the men that knew what they were doing to climb over him to the door.

'I'm talking to you, Parfitt. Get a bloody move on. I don't want to be out here a second longer than necessary.'

Parfitt opened the door and jumped to the ground. He walked to the back of the truck where he could see tracks continuing. At the end of the tracks the ground fell away. He stood on the rear driver's side corner and signalled for Torrance to reverse. As the truck came towards him, he stepped back too. The tracks ended. Beyond them was a precipice deep enough to lose a truck in forever.

He held up both hands.

'Whoa!'

The truck's brakes whined and it juddered to a stop. Torrance shouted out from the cab:

'Spring those catches and stand clear, Parfitt.'

Parfitt did as he was told. The back panel of the truck, hinged at the top, was now free to open. Hydraulics hissed and the bed of the truck began to rise. Parfitt looked into the crater-like abyss falling away behind the truck but he already knew what it contained. The smell, a hundred times more rank than any smell in the slaughterhouse, rose up all around them. In the belly of the pit, rotted the butchered remains of thousands of the Chosen.

The truckload they'd taken from the slaughterhouse slid down the steep incline to join its own kind in jumbled decomposition.

'Make sure it's empty, son.'

Parfitt reached into the back of the truck to clear the flesh that had lodged in corners or stuck to the panels. Not all of it was within reach. He walked back to the cab as Torrance let the truck's bed descend to the horizontal.

'I'm going to need a -'

Before he reached the cab a broom was passed out. He took it, leapt up and swept out the final obstinate cuts. Torrance revved the engine, impatient to leave. For once Parfitt felt the same eagerness. He ran to his door and climbed up. The broom was deposited behind the seat. They drove back to the plant in silence.

Torrance parked up.

'Get changed and I'll give you a lift into town,' he said. It was dark by then and a long walk. Parfitt didn't have much choice.

He met them by the gate, this time Torrance was driving a smaller shuttle bus. Parfitt sat at the back. It was no surprise that Torrance drove them straight to Dino's.

'Quick cleansing of the palate,' said Torrance.

'I'd better get home for my dinner,' said Parfitt.

'You'll have a drink first, son.'

***

Being a weeknight, it was quieter in Dino's but there were still plenty of stockmen drinking up their high wages.

Torrance bought the round. The barman nodded his recognition to Parfitt and the four of them went to sit at the same table they'd used the first time.

'Parfitt, this is Stonebank and Haynes.' They shook hands.

Torrance:

'To the blood of the Chosen. Long may it nourish the town.'

Everyone raised their glasses and drank acid.

There was an expectant silence. Parfitt knew they were waiting for his questions.

'What have we just done?'

'We've done two things. We've cleared the surplus and we've followed orders.'

Parfitt was incredulous.

'Surplus?'

'Keep your voice down,' snapped Torrance. 'You work for a very efficient organisation. MMP are so good at what they do,' he gestured around the table. '*We* are so good at what we do, that the Chosen are breeding at peak rates and production is the highest it's ever been. In order to stop the price of meat going down, we have to dispose of some of it from time to time.'

Parfitt tried to take it in. As far as he knew, there were plenty of townsfolk on the verge of starvation precisely because meat was at such a premium. Torrance had to be wrong. Or lying.

'There's a meat shortage, Mr. Torrance. We're struggling to provide enough.'

'Not true,' said Torrance. 'Not true at all. We're talking about economics. We're talking about business. People may not be able to buy meat but that's not because we can't provide it. MMP thrives – our wages are so good – because of the price of meat.'

Haynes, who, Parfitt realised, must have heard this very conversation a hundred times, left the table to buy another round.

'But, surely if Magnus dropped the price of meat then more people would buy it, therefore increasing turnover.'

Torrance nodded.

'You're a smart lad, Parfitt. In a way, you're right. That probably would be the outcome of a drop in prices. However, the whole situation turns on people's attitudes. If people think that meat is costly, they respect it and those who can afford it. If anyone could buy it, it wouldn't have the same *perceived* value even if Magnus could still turn the same profit. Do you see?'

Parfitt nodded. He did understand. He just didn't understand the point of it.

'What have the Welfare to say about this? Surely God's word is that the Chosen are here for all of us, not just those wealthy enough to afford their flesh.'

'Abyrne's business and its religion, as you'll discover, are strange bedfellows. They tolerate each other because without each other neither would survive.'

Haynes returned with vodka. They swallowed once. It wasn't worth sipping.

'I think we all need some dinner. Want a ride home, Parfitt?'

'No thanks, sir. I can walk it from here.'

'Fine. You'd better come out to the shuttle and collect your pay first, though. After which, you'll be well worth robbing.'

Fifteen

'Once upon a time,' said Shanti, 'there were two brothers named Peter and James.

'Peter and James were the poorest children in the whole town and they lived in a place where all the houses were smashed and broken with no doors or windows to keep out the cold and no roof to keep out the rain. They were very thin because there was so little to eat. Sometimes they ate the weeds that grew through the cracks in the broken pavements. Sometimes they ate the leaves and nuts from the few trees that grew in their district. Sometimes, if they were feeling brave, they sneaked into the wealthy districts and found bread that had been thrown away by folks that were already full up. Sometimes they stole apples from rich people's trees.

'Peter and James had no mother and no father and no friends. They'd lived alone for as long as they could remember and all they had in the world was each other. At night, especially in the winter, Peter and James snuggled up close together to stay warm and keep from feeling lonely.

'One day Peter said to James, "I'm tired of being lonely and hungry and having no friends."

"Me too," said James. "Why don't we see if we can find somewhere better to live?"

'So, the two of them decided to explore the broken-down district where they had lived all their lives. They couldn't go into the nice parts of town because the people there, even though they were rich and fat, would have tried to catch them and eat them. Instead they searched through the tumbled-down old houses and empty streets for something better than they had.

'They searched for a week and found nothing but more deserted, wrecked places.

'They searched for two weeks and found no more food than they already had.

'They searched for three weeks and found no one else they could talk to.

'Then they sat down beside a ruined road and cried, holding on to each other because they were so, so sad, so, so hungry and so, so lonely that they didn't think they could go on.

'It was just then that a strange tiny creature appeared in front of their faces. It was buzzing and flying in little spirals and looked like a tiny person with flashing wings. The boys were so amazed that they both stopped crying. And then, even stranger, the hovering little person spoke to them. It had a very loud voice for such a teeny thing. "Why are you crying, silly boys?" it said. "You've barely started looking yet. Search for another week just a little further on and I promise you will find something to make you both very happy." The little flying person zipped and bobbed as though it was very excited. "But," it said, looking suddenly very serious, "make sure you watch out for the Furry Man. If he catches you, he'll roast you alive and then eat your ears and your eyes and your noses before he starts munching on your bellies."

'Peter and James shivered with fear at the sound of it. They were so weak they didn't think they could search a single step further. And if they met this Furry Man, they didn't think they had the strength to run away from him.

'Embarrassed because he'd never spoken to a little flying person before and not really sure what to say, Peter said, "Excuse me, but we're only little and very, very thin. All we eat are weeds and leaves and nuts and old bread, you see. Sometimes we...we...get an apple or two. Look," he said, pointing at his and James's arms, "we're no stronger than old twigs."

'The little flying person scratched its weeny head. "How much do you want to be happy?"

"Oh, very much," said James. "Are you hungry?" it asked. "We're starving," said Peter. "Are you lonely?" it asked.

"We're the loneliest boys that ever there were."

"Well then," said the little flying person. "Keep in mind all the things you're looking for and that will make you stronger than old twigs."

"Really?" asked Peter. "Truly?" asked James.

"Yes," said the little flying person. "Much, much stronger."

'And with that, the little flying person zapped and zoomed in three speedy circles and disappeared.

'Peter and James looked at each other with wide eyes. "Did we really see a little flying person?" asked Peter.

"I think so," said James. And he added, "Did it really talk to us?"

"Yes," said Peter, "I think it really did."

'Both the boys were smiling because the little flying person had made them feel so much better. It was a strange little creature but it had been kind to them. No one had ever been kind to them before.

'They searched around for some weeds to give them a little strength for the next part of their journey and found a big clump growing nearby. It seemed very fortunate. They ate the bitter weeds but were glad for them. Soon they were searching again.

'They wandered through parts of the broken district they'd never seen before and knew nothing about. After six more days they were exhausted again but the landscape around them had begun to change. There were fewer buildings and the ones they found were not so broken as the ones they'd left behind. Some of them still had roofs and some even had windows and doors. Peter and James searched inside these houses but they never found anything to make them happy, nothing to fill their bellies and no one to talk to.

'They began to think they'd dreamed up that little flying person and all its advice. Worse, they started to believe that maybe they'd just got so hungry they'd imagined it.

'Then a mist came down, all swirly and white like the coat-tails of an army of ghosts. They found themselves in front of what seemed like the very last house in the broken district. Beyond it there was nothing. They saw a large pile of bones by the front door. The bones were smooth and picked absolutely clean. Some of the bones looked like they must have belonged to little boys exactly like Peter and James.

'They both thought that maybe the little flying person was the friend of the Furry Man and that it had told them to come here so that the Furry Man could share two more lost little boys with it.

'They started to back away from the house when the front door opened and a huge figure lumbered out into the mist. He was a giant; much bigger than a normal man and twice as wide too. Long, thick, shaggy red hair covered his hands and feet and face and hung down from his head to his hips. He wore only a pair of ragged trousers that stopped below his knees and a waistcoat with no buttons. It looked like he'd left the same clothes on for a hundred years and just grown out of them.

'Little boys, thought Peter and James, must be very fattening.

'The Furry Man saw them and roared, "AAAARRRGGGH! SUPPERTIME!"

'He ran down his garden path with his arms stretched wide ready to grab a boy in each hand.

"Run," cried Peter and both the boys turned on their heels and sprinted away as fast as they could. The mist was thick and it was hard to see where they were going. They held hands because they didn't want to lose each other and it slowed them down. Meanwhile, the Furry Man, running on legs like tree trunks, took steps four times the size of theirs. He caught up with them very quickly. His two enormous arms reached out to grab the skinny boys.

"Now I've got you little morsels. Now I've got my SUPPER!"

"Let go of my hand," said James. "It's our only chance." "No," cried Peter. "What if I never find you again?" "Think of all the things we're looking for and you'll find me."

'The Furry Man's hands came whooshing at them. James let go of Peter's hand and ran into the fog. The hand missed him. Peter ran the opposite way. The other hand missed him.

'The Furry Man couldn't decide which one to chase and while he was thinking about it, they both disappeared.

"ARRRRGGGGHHH!" shouted the Furry Man. "NO SUPPER! AAAAARRRRGGGGH!"

'Well, the Furry Man stood there for a long time sniffing the fog. Then he decided that one trail smelled juicier than the other so he turned and went the way Peter had run, following his big nose through the thick mist.

'Separated now, the two boys could hear the Furry Man's huge feet stomping over the rubble as he came looking for them. Every step made the ground shake.

'James tiptoed as quietly as he could but he couldn't see more than a few feet ahead and had no idea which direction he was going in. Peter did exactly the same thing. Both of the boys were more lonely now than they'd ever been and certainly more frightened. They were so scared they thought the Furry Man might be able to hear the pounding of their hearts through the mist and that he'd follow the noise until he caught them.

'James stumbled on a broken brick and fell down. His hands met nothing but air as he fell. The ground hit his chest and knocked all the wind out of him. His head and arms were hanging into space. He found himself looking down into a black pit so deep it seemed to have no bottom. One step further and he'd have tumbled into the pit never to see Peter again.

'But the Furry Man heard James fall and he changed direction to follow. Peter heard too. He wanted to call out and see if his brother was all right – to make sure that it hadn't been the sound of the Furry Man catching hold of him. But Peter dared not make a sound. Instead, he too ran towards the spot where he thought he'd heard the noise.

'Then he heard the sound of heavy footsteps behind him. Somehow he'd managed to come between the Furry Man and his brother. Now the

Furry Man was chasing him as they both ran towards James. Peter risked a glance over his shoulder and saw long red hair in the mist. The Furry Man was right behind him, his huge arms held out in front to catch him.

'There was no need now to be quiet so Peter screamed for his brother, "James! Where are you?"

"This way!" called James. "Quickly, Peter, I can hear the Furry Man coming!"

"He's right behind me!" called Peter. "I don't think I can get away."

"Yes, Peter. Yes, you can. Keep thinking of all the things we're searching for. I'll think of them too. When you're near enough I'm going to tell you to do something and you must do it the very best you can. OK?"

"I will, James. I'll do it the very best I can."

'Peter could hear the Furry Man snorting behind him. He could smell the smell of dead little boys in the Furry Man's stomach. He thought of all the things that he and his brother had been searching for and ran as fast as he could. But Peter hadn't eaten anything for a long time and his legs were tired and heavy. He started to believe that he was going to end up eaten by the Furry Man. Just then a crack appeared in the mist and from somewhere very high above a thin shaft of light penetrated. As Peter ran through the light he felt all his strength return. He pushed a little harder and felt the Furry Man's hand swish through the air behind him. It just missed him.

'And then he heard James's voice very loud and very near, "Jump, Peter, jump as far and as fast as you can."

'So Peter jumped with all the strength he had left and he took off into the air.

'He looked down and saw that he was over a black hole that seemed to go on forever. James had told him to jump to his death. But Peter didn't give up even then. He thought about what it would be like to be with his brother somewhere safe and for them both to be happy. He thought about it as hard as he could.

'The next thing he knew, James had caught him in his arms. He was standing on the other side of the black pit.

'They both looked back and saw the Furry Man rumbling through the mist. He saw them too. Two lovely, tasty little boys ready to roast alive on a spit.

"AAAARRRRGHH! SUPPER!" shouted the Furry Man as he got closer and closer.

'And then, very suddenly indeed, the Furry Man dropped out of sight.

'They heard him falling for a long, long time because he shouted all the way down.

"AAAARRRRGHHH..."

'They never heard the Furry Man hit the bottom.

'Well, Peter and James were so pleased to see each other again and know they were safe that they both sat down and cried happy tears. And then they both lay down, snuggled close and fell asleep because they were so, so tired.

'When they woke up the mist had gone and in the distance they could see the house where the Furry Man had lived. They went to have a look at it. Outside, the pile of bones of all the little boys that the Furry Man had eaten had gone.

'They walked into the house and it was dusty and quiet as though no one had lived there for many, many years. All the rooms were empty. They walked all the way through the house and then they found another door at the back. They opened the door and found themselves looking at something that neither of them had ever seen before.

'It was a garden. In the garden were many trees and all the trees were heavy with different kinds of fruit. All around the garden there were wild plants growing with flowers of every colour and even colours the boys had never seen before. Stranger even than that, they saw many little flying people that buzzed and flickered from one flower to another collecting nectar.

'But the best things they saw were all the little boys the Furry Man had eaten. Not only that, there were little girls too, all restored, just the way they'd been before he'd caught them. And now the Furry Man would never chase or eat any of them again and Peter and James would never ever be lonely or hungry or sad. Not then and not ever.'

Usually his stories put the girls to sleep long before he finished them but tonight he'd glanced at them from time to time. They were intent, wide-eyed and very far from sleep. Telling the story the way he had was a risk. If Maya had been listening she'd have put a stop to it long before the end; the story verged on blasphemy for so many reasons. But the more of it he made up the more sense it seemed to make to him and the more obviously the tale unfolded in his mind. He found a kind of rhythm in the telling of it and the rhythm carried him through to the end.

Now the girls sat staring at him, each clutching a doll to their chests, their faces intense. He could almost hear the questions before they came. He didn't know how he was going to answer them.

'Why didn't the boys have a mama and papa?' asked Hema.

'I think their mama and papa had died and left them all alone in the world.'

'Does that really happen?' asked Harsha.

'Yes. Sometimes it happens. When a child is left with no parents or if the parents are too poor to keep the child and have to give it away, the child is called an orphan.'

'Are there orphans in Abyrne?' asked Hema.

That was a tough one. He decided to turn it around.

'Have you seen any?' he asked. They shook their heads.

'None in your school?'

'No,' they both said.

'I guess that's your answer then.'

The girls looked at each other and appeared to agree on the next question without exchanging a word. Hema asked it.

'What about the Furry Man and the little flying people, papa? Are they real?'

'What do you think?' Hema considered.

'Just because we haven't seen them, it doesn't mean they aren't there, does it? Maybe they're hiding.'

He smiled.

'Maybe they are.'

'The Furry Man wouldn't come to our house would he, papa?' asked Harsha.

He hadn't set out to be cruel. That wasn't the point. At least the idea of the Furry Man took their attention away from the more dangerous themes of the tale.

'I don't think the Furry Man would ever come here. Too far for him to walk. I wouldn't worry about it. Now that's enough chatter for one night. If you're very good, I might tell you another one tomorrow night. But you'll have to go to sleep right now with no complaining or there'll be no stories at all. Come on, into your bunk Harsha.'

They'd both been on the bottom bunk for the story. Now that it was over it was time for Harsha to get back into her own. Reluctantly, she scooted past her sister and climbed the ladder. Shanti gave her a kiss on the forehead and gave another to Hema.

'I'll leave the door open a crack for light, but I don't want to hear a single noise. If I do, no more stories, all right?'

'All right, papa,' they sang.

152

'Good. Now you two sleep tight.'

He left them alone then but an hour later was back to check on them before he went to bed himself. Harsha was back down in the lower bunk and they were snuggled together as tight as two clingy monkeys. He wasn't about to wake them just to separate them. He watched them sleeping for a few moments and then crept away.

***

From his deserted tower block, Collins could signal for his closest aides, Staithe and Vigors. He lit a gas lamp and took it out to the small cold balcony where the changed wind was smearing the town with the rotten smells from Magnus Meat Processing. He placed the lamp on the balustrade for a count of sixty seconds, knowing at least one of them would be watching. Then he took the lamp inside and sat down on the cushionless sofa.

It was less than ten minutes before the gentle series of coded taps came at his front door. He pulled back the hinged steel bar – the only locking mechanism that still worked – and opened the door. Both of them stepped past him. They sat on the floor in front of his sofa. The lamp gave out a feeble yellow light. He hated to use anything that required gas but, whilst he was perfectly capable in the dark, he had to provide something for Staithe and Vigors.

'We didn't think you'd come back,' said Staithe. He was a burly man but he had a tissue-paper heart. Collins could hear the relief in his voice.

'I didn't think I would, either. But there's more to do. I had to.'

'What happened?' asked Vigors.

'Magnus played into my hands. He's not going to let it go lightly. You've got to get word to everyone to hide or prepare for visits from MMP thugs. Anyone connected with me is at risk. Make sure they all know never to go back to the lock-up. I mean ever. We're past that now.'

'What will we do?'

'First, we're going to disappear.' Collins leaned back and looked from Vigors to Staithe. 'And then we're going to make life difficult for Magnus.'

'And the Welfare? They won't be far behind him.' Collins nodded.

'I know. They'll have their part to play.'

They were silent for a while, Staithe mesmerised by the gas lamp's hiss and waxy light while he mulled it all over. Vigors's face was less readable. It was hard enough to guess whether she was male or female in full daylight and here in the gloom her face was a domino blank. She was the first to speak.

'There's no going back from this.'

'No,' said Collins. 'A lot of people are going to get hurt. Make sure everyone that comes does so voluntarily. They must be free to choose.'

Sixteen

It was difficult to know how to tell them his plan. Would they still trust him then? Have faith in him?

He hadn't seen this far ahead at the start; hadn't understood what was required until after he'd met Magnus and seen what kind of man he was. It was not enough that he martyr himself at the hands of the Meat Baron for all to see. It would change nothing. All it would achieve was silence; a silence that needed to be filled by Collins's voice. His was the voice of truth, the voice of sanity.

He'd brought his followers this far and he had no choice but to tell them exactly what he believed should come next. It wasn't going to be easy. They waited. He considered. They were used to his silences.

Collins ran his hands over the smooth dome of his head. It should have been stubbly with new growth but since the last time he'd shaved it, no more hair had come through. The same was true of his face. He ought to have had at least a few days of beard but his cheeks were as smooth as the inside of his wrists. He thought it might be the shock of his interview with Magnus – more apparent in his body than in his mind – but that didn't fit. He was calmer and more resolved now than he had been during his kidnap and he'd been ready for death even then.

Their den amid the rubble and decay of the Derelict Quarter was squalid but tidy. By night they cleared it of debris, swept and cleaned as best they could. Furnishings had been smuggled in by every member of his following. They made it deep, their hiding place, risking entombment if the ageing supports and arches ever gave way. Here and there in the tunnels, there had already been cave-ins but Collins reassured them that they were from the time before Abyrne became what it was now.

Outside their circles, to discuss the idea of a time before the town was blasphemy. According to the Book of Giving, Abyrne appeared out of the wasteland at God's behest. Before that there had been nothing but blasted, blackened land incapable of life.

They all sat there with him now, waiting for him to speak.

These were his people, the renewed souls of the town, their essences forged by the exercises he'd taught them. They were stronger now – eating vegetable matter occasionally or, in the case of the more advanced, eating nothing at all – than they'd ever been dining on the flesh of the Chosen. They numbered thirty. Thirty pure souls out of the thousands in the town.

He lifted his eyes and looked out across their faces.

'When I look at you, I see what is possible. In a short time, less than two years, there are this many of us willing not only to change the way we live because we know what is right, but also to leave those dear to us and risk everything for the future.'

He looked around at the walls that encased them. But for the gas lamps they would have been in a darkness more complete than any night out on the streets of the town. Three levels below the Derelict Quarter there was no light.

'It's ironic that we who subsist on light and air are forced to live where the sun cannot penetrate and where the air could not be more lifeless. Everything we do now is in the nature of a sacrifice. That's what I need to talk to you about.

'As recently as a week ago, I believed my public execution at the hands of Magnus and his butchers would be the event that pushed the town into seeing how wrong its ways have been all these years. I believed that those of you here, and the others who have heard my message in the lock-up, would spread the word and that, in time, a revolution would quietly end the need for meat in Abyrne. That done, the Meat Baron would be finished forever and the Welfare would collapse.

'I've seen Magnus now. Spoken to him. Crossed swords, so to speak. And I can tell you that I've been naïve and foolish to think that we'd done enough. We have not. We have only just begun to change things.'

Collins looked into his outstretched palms, made fists and opened them again. He held them up to his following.

'I wish I could tell you the future. I can't. I've been wrong about it once already. I see now that all I can do is plan carefully and hope each of you still wishes to help me. I reiterate now, before saying anything more, that every one of you is free. You always will be. I ask nothing of you that you are not willing to do. You may back out at any time and no less will be thought of you. Each of you has achieved far more than I believed possible when I started out. You have made yourselves pure. What I ask of you goes against everything I stand for but I ask it because I am certain that there is no other way.

'We must stand against Magnus and his men. We must take the message to them in a form they understand. In the first instance, that form will not be mere words. I think you all know what I'm trying to say.

'Evil rules Abyrne through Magnus and the Welfare as surely as human blood flows in the veins of the Chosen. Nothing we say, no example we

156

give, will ever change Magnus's need for power or the Welfare's need for control through its twisted religion. We must do what no one has yet been prepared to do.

'We have to fight them.'

Collins looked from face to face, anxious that the more he spoke the further from their ship of unity he was drifting. None of their faces showed any expression. Their new way of living allowed them to master most of their free-floating emotions and to keep their minds very clear. So they were thinking now, evaluating his words. And, he was certain, readying themselves for separation from his cause. He nodded inwardly. They were free. He meant that. If he had to walk back and fight Magnus alone, he would do it without a single bad feeling over the actions of his followers. Truly, they had changed Abyrne already.

There was silence in the underground chamber, but for the hiss of gas lamps. Collins felt there was more he ought to say, that he could be more specific before he asked them to take up arms, give them an outline of how he envisaged their campaign. He was about to speak when Vigors stood up.

'I will fight,' she said.

Staithe rose at almost the same moment.

'I will fight,' he said.

One by one they stood and echoed the simple words and when the echoes were silenced, not one was left sitting.

***

The puny fire crackled in the grate but it was a luxury only a few in the town could afford. There wasn't much land left where trees grew and where they did, they didn't flourish. Only the Welfare could decree when a tree was to be felled and townsfolk caught damaging trees or stealing branches

- windfall or otherwise – faced heavy fines or forced labour. Much of the wood used for burning was scavenged from deserted buildings but these days it was increasingly difficult to find.

The fire gave out little warmth or cheer but the Grand

Bishop never resented its meagreness.

'You and I have got a very big fucking problem, Bish.' What he resented was the behaviour of his visitor. The way he moved and spoke, the man's very presence rankled. The Grand Bishop shifted in his chair.

'The way I understand it,' he replied, 'the entire town has 'a very big fucking problem'.'

His visitor shrugged, fluffed his ginger beard with the fingers of one hand while he dragged on a cheroot in the other.

'This town and the people in it have no significance for me. Except,' and here Magnus pointed his two ochre-stained smoking fingers at the Grand Bishop, 'for those that eat meat, my employees and the Chosen. Those people make this world go around. They make your world go round too, Bish. But most of the townsfolk are as stupid as the meat they eat. If it weren't for their groats buying my produce, I'd just as soon turn them into cheap pies.'

'Yes, I can see how you care for those around you. And yet you've come all the way here to discuss the matter with me in person. It's most unusual, considering you normally send a runner with your 'requests'.' The Grand Bishop appeared to muse for a few seconds. 'Heavens, it must be five years since I last saw you, Rory.'

He watched the pressure building inside Magnus knowing there was nothing the man could do to him. They would needle each other until the matter was resolved and a plan formulated. It would have been quicker and simpler to cooperate but Magnus didn't work that way.

'Sales are dropping,' said Magnus.

The Grand Bishop decided not to hear. Instead he stared into the fire, piously distracted.

'Hmm?'

'We're dumping tons of meat each week. Demand is slumping.'

The Grand Bishop raised his eyebrows but continued to stare into the fire.

'Slumping, you say? Well, well.'

Out of the corner of his eye he could see Magnus swelling in his chair. The man already engulfed it, barely able to keep both buttocks on board.

'The townsfolk,' said Magnus through clenched teeth, 'are not eating as much meat as they used to.'

Looking bored and slightly annoyed, the Grand Bishop hauled his gaze away from the fire.

'That, Rory, sounds to me like *your* 'very big fucking problem', not mine.'

Magnus stood up, tipping his chair over.

'That nutter John Collins is spouting blasphemies to all who'll listen, Bish. He's telling them they don't need to eat meat. He's telling them .

158

. .' The Grand Bishop noticed now the vibration that seemed to affect Magnus's whole body and inwardly he smiled. He'd seen Magnus angry before – Magnus was always angry about something – but he never shook with rage. This was something new. Perhaps the man wasn't going to be such a nuisance for much longer. 'He's telling them that they don't need to eat anything at all. Some of them believe him, Bish. The man's a disaster.'

'Sit down, Rory.'

'I'll do no such th-'

The Grand Bishop held up a calming hand.

'Just sit down and listen to me for a second. John Collins is a lunatic. That much I grant you. But what he's saying is so outlandish that he destroys himself with his own message. Surely, you don't believe what he's telling them.'

'Of course I fucking don't believe it.'

'So what makes you think that what he says will make any difference? We've got to look at the long term here, Rory. The man will have his moment and when the people realise that not eating meat and not eating at all leads to weakness and ultimately death, they'll realise how stupid they've been. Collins's time will be over.'

'But he's already made a difference. People are listening to him and acting on what he says. Doesn't it bother you that he's a blasphemous heretic?'

The Grand Bishop let his eyes find Magnus's.

'He wouldn't be the first one I've had dealings with, Rory.' Magnus sat down. It looked as though he did it because he was tired rather than because he'd regained his composure.

'But he's making a mockery of the Welfare.'

'We'll survive. And when his downfall comes, we'll be sure to capitalise on it.'

Magnus's shoulders slumped. He took a new cheroot from a case and lit it from the one he was finishing. He flicked the spent one at the fire but missed. Sighing, the Grand Bishop stood up and scraped the butt out with his boot.

'I want your Parsons to help my men find him.'

'And why should I authorise that?'

'I'm not making this up, Bish. I've met this man. I've...we came to blows.'

This time the Grand Bishop's eyebrows raised in genuine interest.

'Indeed?'

'Yes. Indeed. He's a strong man. And I don't mean purely physically. He has a will, Bish. You know what I'm talking about. He sees through lies. He fears nothing.'

The Grand Bishop was silent for a long time. He'd thought long about how to deal with Collins, taken a lot of advice and information from his scouts and spies around the town. He was more than aware of the threat the man posed but he wasn't about to share that with Magnus. Especially now that Magnus looked so weak.

'I'm sorry, Rory. I understand your concerns, I really do. And I can see how important it is that your business runs profitably. But I have our faith to consider and the spiritual welfare of the town. I cannot be seen to form an open alliance with MMP -'

'For fuck's sake, Bish, it would be clandestine. We're not going to advertise it.'

'We wouldn't need to. Word gets around, Rory, you know that. I can't afford to let the townsfolk think the Welfare sees John Collins as a threat. I must be seen only to deride the man for the charlatan he is.'

'Is that your final word on this?'

'It is.'

Magnus stood. With difficulty, the Grand Bishop was delighted to observe.

'Support for Parsons entering dangerous areas of the town may no longer be available, Bish. I'll be experiencing some manpower deficiencies in the near future as I try to take care of a problem the Welfare should be dealing with. But with you as an example, I'm sure your representatives know how to look after themselves, don't they?'

He didn't wait for a reply.

When the door had closed, the Grand Bishop permitted himself a smile. Welfare had been cowed by Magnus Meat Processing for far too long. Now Magnus himself was sick and things were going to change in the town. The Grand Bishop's best Parsons were already searching for Collins. Reports suggested they were very close to finding him and his gang of starveling followers. Welfare would root out Collins for the whole town to see. Welfare would show the town what happened to people who didn't eat the flesh of the Chosen as instructed by God. And then Welfare would reassert religious control over the production of meat, and harmony and piety would return to the town.

***

160

Each morning before dawn they rose as if pulled by an invisible tide and ascended the many stairs and broken escalators that brought them to the surface. He led them and they moved silently. The night after their council, the silence was loaded, resolved.

Collins believed they were deep enough in the Derelict Quarter that the Welfare would not come looking for them but he couldn't be certain of it. However, there was nothing Magnus wouldn't do to find him. His scouts and spies would be abroad in the town like cockroaches picking over people's leavings.

So they were quiet and careful in the early aura. To stay strong they had no choice but to emerge at this precise time each day and perform the rites and exercise that Collins had shown them. It was their most vulnerable time.

That said, Collins knew that they were strong and sensitive in ways that the townsfolk weren't. All their senses were clear and sharp. They had intuition that could warn of many things, not merely danger. As dark as it was when they first stood among the monolithic outlines of ruined buildings, Collins could 'see' all of them by the auric signature that their bodies exuded.

On this morning, Collins felt something that had been growing in him for some time. He felt not so much an individual or a leader but rather that all his followers were connected. It was a physical sensation like magnetism in the blood. When they walked together he felt their movements like a force in his guts – approaching, a little push against him: departing, a little pull – and the connection was never broken. The more they breathed together and swallowed light, the stronger the sensation became.

It led him to believe that not only were they stronger as individuals but that as a group their power was exponentially greater.

They stood facing east where a dusty grey light sprouted. Collins stood at their head. Together they drew in the dawn and when the sun cleared the dirty horizon, they were filled with warmth. As one they concentrated the light in their bellies.

Collins had never seen himself as a general. He didn't *want* to fight. Fighting would bring bloodshed and death. It was wrong to use the forces he was trying to eschew in order to defeat those same forces. However, he knew there was no other way. In the silence of the morning they charged themselves.

Soon after sunrise, they slipped back underground, each taking a concentrated gutful of sunlight with them, their muscles and sinews tightened and invigorated by the exercise.

In the dark, John Collins plotted and each of his followers grew stronger.

Seventeen

Richard Shanti's father had been a stockman too. He'd worked on the chain in the days before Magnus took control of the plant and the Chosen. Back then the Welfare had more control over the way meat was provided. Visits by the Grand Bishop and Parsons to the plant had been frequent and the air of sanctity around the rearing and slaughter of the Chosen was far greater. These days it seemed as though Magnus left the religious doctrines out of his working practices, merely paying lip service to them whilst trading ritual practices for higher chain speeds. It had become a production line.

Parson Mary Simonson doubted the correct prayers were spoken at the moment of stunning and exsanguination. In Shanti's father's time, those prayers were every stockman's mantra from clocking on to knocking off. She wondered if the pious-seeming Richard Shanti remembered his prayers at work. Welfare inspections of MMP practices happened so rarely these days it was impossible to tell.

She rifled through the cards that recorded Albert Shanti's life. Like his son he'd been an exemplary stunner – caring, efficient and quick. Still, back then the chain speeds had rarely reached ninety per hour. So much had changed in just a generation. She checked for irregularities in his behaviour, interventions by Welfare at any time and found that there was a file showing some Welfare involvement. She checked the dates. It was around the time of Elizabeth Shanti's second tragic pregnancy that the Welfare had visited. Reports of screaming and fighting in the Shanti house – a property nearer the town centre where neighbours could listen in.

It could have been a grudge – someone making trouble for Shanti by telling tales and bringing the suspicion of the Welfare down on him. She couldn't rule that out. Or it might have been genuine unpleasantness between a childless couple with no more chances.

Further reports to the Welfare were made by the plant when Albert Shanti's stun performance dipped. No visit was made, as it was the province of the then Meat Baron, Greg Santos, to deal with employees in his own way. But other reports were made – not by Albert's superiors but by other workers in the plant – of inappropriate behaviour. It was stated in the records that he had been seen spending his lunch hours watching cows nurse their newborn calves. Parson Mary Simonson's heart went out to the man as she imagined what it must have been like to lose two children and see so much life being brought into the world where he worked.

And then there was a final report.

At least there was space for another report, a dated card divider with an incident number, but there was nothing in the file. No actual record of whatever it was Albert Shanti had done. The incident number was coded with a 'C' which meant whatever it described had occurred in the plant and was related to the Chosen. The Parson shook her head in disbelief. Someone had tampered with Welfare files. She'd never come across such a thing. Never even heard of it.

It had to be a mistake. Likely hers. She hadn't been concentrating and had either dropped or moved the file along with the others. She checked through every entry in Albert Shanti's record box then checked it again. Then she checked each inserted card to be sure there weren't two sticking together. The more she looked the more it became clear that something was amiss. Interfering with Welfare files was suicidal.

Utter madness. She stood back and got her breathing under control. It wasn't possible. She *had* to be wrong.

A final check turned up nothing.

'Whittaker!'

The old man arrived with surprising speed, churning up dust devils in his wake and not seeming to notice at first.

'Yes, Parson?'

'Look at this file box, would you? Find me the report C:127:42.'

She handed him the box and leaned against a bank of shelves as she watched his ratlike fingers scurry through the cards. The pain in her stomach swelled like a sphere of teeth. She clutched herself.

Whittaker made a tiny mew of disappointment and flicked through the record box again. The Parson's legs weakened beneath her, the muscles in her thighs quivered and she began to sink down.

'It's not here,' announced Whittaker. 'But that can't b-' She looked up at him from the dirty floor, her head leaning to one side and saliva dribbling onto her shoulder. She wanted to move, to talk to him, but her body wouldn't obey.

'Parson? Whatever's the matter?'

Whittaker closed the box and placed the file carefully back in its place on its shelf. She noticed how reverently he handled the records and felt bad for ever having been unkind to him. Only when the box was in position did he kneel beside her and try to help her up. He looked genuinely worried. None of his pulling or hauling did any good for her. She could neither move nor speak.

'Rawlins,' he shouted. 'Get some help for the Parson. Get Doctor Fellows.'

It was only then, as he waited with her, that the old man's body remembered its allergy. He began to sneeze.

***

Shanti awoke in blackness long before dawn. It was too early to practise gathering the light but he felt agitated and enlivened. Maya was deep in slumber beside him, turned away as had become her habit. Silently, he rose and dressed, put on his long coat and walked out to the darkness through the back door. The wind had changed again. Instead of blowing the evils of the MMP plant towards the town, now the smells drifted out into the wasteland where there was no one to smell anything. He breathed deeply, grateful for the clarity of the air. Something pulled at him. Hard to define the feeling – a faint tugging in his stomach, an urge to move. He had nothing else to worry about, no work to go to, at least for today. Normally he would run, today walking would be the alternative.

He left the house behind, thinking only of his daughters sleeping so tightly curled in the lower bunk. At first the pace was leisurely and his steps cautious in the dark. But he'd run these roads so many times that he wasn't too afraid of falling into the gorse or a patch of nettles. When he reached the main road where he usually turned left to run to the plant, he turned right and set off for the centre of the town.

From time to time there were potholes and uneven areas of road but, not really noticing, he negotiated them without a stumble. Soon he was passing the first houses of the town proper – most folk didn't like to live as close as he did to the wasteland. A pavement became available, albeit cracked and subsiding in many places, so he stepped onto it from the road.

To his right and a little behind him, a faint light was born. It quickened his step. The houses became closer together and smaller. The smells of habitation – sewage, cooking, spent gas – grew stronger. It was still early and no one was awake except insomniacs, lovers and the sick. He liked it that way and hoped to be through the centre of town before the townsfolk began their business for the day.

On his left, he passed the stone gateposts and black iron gates that marked the front entrance to Magnus's mansion, its extensive grounds walled off and guarded but set very near the centre of Abyrne. Where the property ended, he turned left and walked past the Central Cathedral, a dark Gothic beast, frozen in the light of the approaching dawn. Beside it were the many offices of the Welfare and further along on the right most of the central businesses – butchers, flesh apothecaries, religious shops and various craftsmen.

He passed them all, turned right onto Black Street and walked out past the worst of the inhabited houses in the town. This was where the poorest of the townsfolk lived, barely scraping enough money together to buy a single cut of meat each week. If these people listened to Collins, many of the town's problems would evaporate.

Black Street ended suddenly, as though a cleaver had swung down through it, removing the far section. Beyond it there was no more road, no pavement and for a long way, no buildings left standing.

Shanti stepped over the break in the street like a man stepping out of prison. For most townsfolk, entering the Derelict Quarter meant their lives in the town had been ruined and that they'd never return. He'd have to be careful to go home under the protection of darkness to avoid starting rumours. Magnus had spies everywhere and one never knew when a Parson of the Welfare might step out from an alley and enquire after your business.

Stepping over broken bricks and concrete and avoiding the spokes of steel that rose and twisted from the debris brought a smile to Shanti's face. He stepped lightly, following all the time the encouragement of an unseen pull.

He passed many houses that were only half-ruined and sometimes had a sense of people living there, even though he saw no evidence of it. Further into the Quarter, the monolithic shadows of high-rise buildings towered in the dawn. Many of them were unsafe even to walk near because of falling masonry but others were more stable. None, however, had windows, any form of power supply or water from the town. They never had. Rumour implied that Collins – Prophet John as so many had come to call him – lived in one of the tower blocks but Shanti didn't believe that was still true. To survive, Collins would have to keep moving.

He passed the familiar lock-ups – a strangely untouched part of the Derelict Quarter. It was down in a deep hollow and a road, in surprisingly good condition, led down in a spiral to the row of concrete units. Shanti picked up the pace; the lock-ups were nowhere to go alone, especially now that Collins had disappeared and the meetings had stopped.

It was only beyond the lock-ups that he began to question why he'd risked coming to the Derelict Quarter at all. Being seen here could affect his status. It was crazy when his job at MMP was already on sandy foundations.

He had been called. That was it.

Something had reached out to him and he was following the prompt. There was only one thing he would find out here among the ruins that could not be considered part of the town. Instead of pretending he didn't know what it was, he began to look for it. He concentrated on the drawing sensation in his belly and felt it strengthen in response.

Ahead were more shattered terraces of what had once been houses. He walked towards them. Sick-looking weeds grew occasionally from cracks and rents in the grim landscape. The earth below held little or no nourishment and the weeds appeared to survive on light, air and tenacity.

He passed between the remains of houses, crossed what once had been a street and passed through more houses on the other side. Beyond them the destruction appeared total. He merely wandered between unrecognisable piles of mortar, tile, brick and block, every hillock of wreckage thick with grey dust and grit. Here and there rusted steel or char red wood frameworks rose like broken fingers reaching towards the sky. The damage stretched out to the horizon.

A few feet in front of him, the ground dropped away at a shallow angle for a few paces. He slid in the debris as he scrambled down. Looking back he could see nothing of the town centre from this depression in the land. Only the very tips of some of the tower blocks were still visible. He moved on feeling safer now that he was less likely to be observed.

The sun had been up for several minutes but there was nothing it could do to make this part of Abyrne cheerier. All it did was lighten the grey all around him. The ruin seemed to go on forever.

He stopped walking.

What's out here? What could possibly exist in all this destruction and decay? Am I crazy walking out here like this? What's wrong with me?

He looked down at his long black coat. The lower half of it was grey now with the dust of the Derelict Quarter. He'd snagged it on some sharp protrusion and there was a tear in the back of it.

The landscape is changing me. Making me like it. All it takes is a few minutes and it's taking me over. I have to get home. For the girls. They're all that matters now.

167

He turned back towards the slope and began to walk back, panic moving his feet.

Then he saw the opening.

It was a very definite thing. Not some accident of the shifting rubble. It was several yards to the left of where he'd slithered down the incline. Coming down the slope he hadn't noticed it. It was a broad hole, once perfectly rectangular but now bitten and ragged like everything else out here. He walked towards it and the opening grew, more of it becoming visible as he approached. This had been some kind of entrance way.

When he stood on its threshold all he could see beyond was darkness descending. A few steps were visible leading downwards. That was all.

***

Moments before, it had seemed that no environment could be worse than the Derelict Quarter. Now there was nothing worse than darkness. He tried not to think about it.

To guide himself, he ran his hand along the wall and felt with his feet to make sure there were more steps and that the ground didn't disappear into a drop. Every few steps he turned around, reassured himself that he could still see the light from the entrance and that he would keep going deeper while that light was still visible.

The Derelict Quarter. He realised now, as he tried not to think about what he was walking into, that the name was completely wrong. The area covered by the tumbledown buildings and tracts of formless demolition was vast. The part he'd seen was larger by far than the town centre and many of the other districts put together. It stretched into the distance for what must have been several miles. He'd seen near the horizon something that looked like a ladder on its side and he tried to guess what it might have been. Not a bridge exactly but something similar. It would have been enormous if he were closer to it. Perhaps some kind of walkway or road built through the air. But for what purpose he couldn't imagine.

He felt for the next step with his right foot but there was no next step. He'd reached a level floor. The sole of his boot crunched over the grit. The sound echoed. The space around him was large then. What must it have been? He put his back to the wall and edged along it. This way he could still see the sliver of light where he'd entered. A few sideways paces and the entrance itself disappeared from view. Still, he could see the glow coming from it. Just a few paces further and then he'd go back.

The sensation in his guts intensified. Maybe it was because the darkness had made him concentrate on what he could feel rather than what he could see. The feeling drew him deeper into the black space.

Shanti stopped.

The light from the entrance was now very faint indeed. He felt very far from familiar, safe things. The darkness became aware all around him. It was alive. There was something down there with him, coming towards him out of the depths. He couldn't see it but he could -

- *feel* many hands taking hold of him, pressing him into the wall so that he could not move. By the time he tried to struggle, he was pinned. He felt the warmth of faces in the darkness, the breath of others. And then the tones of a familiar voice.

'Glad you could join us.'

***

They led him across an open space and down more steps. This happened three times. They left the light far behind. Some insane corner of his mind fantasised that they were taking him to a new world. Somewhere down in all this darkness there would be a door and that door would open into a better place, a place without slaughter and violence.

It was the fear making him think that way, he reasoned. After all, he had no idea what they were going to do. He had discovered their secret place. They might wish to prevent that secret from ever being known.

No one spoke and he didn't try to make use of their silence to beg for mercy or plead his innocence. Instinct told him to keep quiet. There were several of them; he could tell by the footsteps in front and behind. He considered trying to tear from their arms and run away but he'd only end up hurting himself. They seemed to know the way to walk without putting a foot wrong. He'd probably run straight into a wall or break his legs on unseen stairs. There was nothing to do but go along with them.

They came to a halt in a space that had no echo. The arms let go of him. Many footsteps retreated but he sensed he wasn't completely alone.

'Why don't you sit down?' suggested the voice.

Shanti felt around and below himself for something to sit on. There was nothing there.

'Sorry,' said the voice as if the person speaking had forgotten to provide milk with tea. 'Just a second.'

In the dark, Shanti heard a hiss and smelled the familiar odour of gas. A match flared and the lamp lit up the room. He was standing opposite a smiling John Collins.

'Welcome to our temporary new home.'

Shanti looked around in the yellow gloom. They were in some kind of small office or storeroom cleared of all furniture except for a cot on the floor and some blankets folded into makeshift cushions. Collins gestured towards one and Shanti sat down.

***

Richard Shanti didn't run the next day either. He rose again when he sensed the sun ascending toward the horizon and went outside with a new sense of purpose. An hour later he returned when the sun was well up. Maya rose and woke the girls, made their breakfast of grilled steak.

He assumed they all ate meat every day now. It had gone on long enough that he had begun to appreciate the irony of it rather than shouldering the guilt for them. There was another way to live and in time he would show them. First he had to prove it to himself. As a vegetarian he was halfway there already. The next step ought to be easy for him.

He'd usually left for work by the time his wife and the girls were up, having made breakfast for himself. Maya seemed to resent his presence. When she spoke, her tone was grudging.

'Do you want food? I'll make you some rice gruel.'

'I'm fine.'

He watched Hema and Harsha sawing through slabs of steak and forking lumps of grilled meat into their mouths. They chewed hungrily and efficiently. In just a few weeks they'd been transformed into carnivores by the determination of his wife. The steaks oozed clear juice tainted brown onto their white plates. At least she cooked them all the way through. Or maybe she'd done that because he was here watching them.

It didn't matter.

Finally, after so many years of hopeless wrestling with the implications of his job and the sickening realities of the town, there was a new hope for him, for the girls; something beyond his imaginings, beyond what seemed possible.

It could be the answer to everything. A chance to start again. To atone. Never in his life could he have believed this might come to him and yet, now that the time was near, it seemed predestined. It was everything he could have voiced in petition but never knew how to say.

'I'm going to go back to work today.'

'I thought Bob told you to take more time than this.' He didn't reply for a few moments.

'Mr. Torrance'll know when he sees me that I'm ready to start back. He's an experienced judge of character.'

'If he's so experienced, he must have given you the time off for a reason.'

'True. But he'll be pleased to have me.'

She shrugged like she suddenly didn't care and busied herself at the kitchen sink. He watched her back. There was language in the movement and he thought he understood it now like never before in their fifteen years of marriage. He knew what people's bodies said, what the bodies of the Chosen said. Maybe he'd never allowed himself to read her before.

As far as he was concerned, she could eat all the meat she wanted and live in ignorance of the suffering she perpetuated. But the twins were a different matter.

When the time came, they were the ones he'd look out for.

***

Veal.

Torrance couldn't have given him a worse job. Shanti hoped he'd picked it because it represented a reduction in pace and pressure and not because Torrance knew what was troubling him.

The veal yard was a self-contained building, smaller than the dairy and the slaughterhouse. Once veal calves arrived and were installed, they remained there until they weighed enough to be slaughtered, which also took place on the premises. Even the butchering was performed on site giving Magnus total control over veal quality.

This meant the calves, secured for years in their darkened crates, could hear the sound of their own kind being killed every day of their lives. They used similar sounds to communicate but their language differed from the rest of the herd because they were isolated and had created words for things only they experienced.

Shanti didn't understand all of it and he was glad. There was so much innocence to their communication, so much acceptance of their end that it broke his heart to listen. The older calves, usually the respected teachers among them, would become frightened as they neared their time and then

171

the hisses and taps would become a kind of harmonised prayer to give them strength and courage. The dusky halls of the veal yard throbbed with their muted rhythms and Shanti was nauseated.

Torrance, knowingly or not, had given him the job of stunning the calves. The frequency was entirely different from the slaughterhouse. There was no chain speed – no chain even. They killed no more than eight or ten calves a day which meant one every hour or so. Shanti had plenty of time to think about what he was going to do to them.

They took each ready calf from its crate and laid it on a stretcher. None of them had the musculature necessary to stand straight or walk. They could barely support the weight of their own heads. The only strength they had was in the four short fingers of each hand, fingers that had become their tongues. Because the calves were kept in near blackness every day, the lights in the veal yard were always dimmed. Even so it must have been like looking directly at the sun for them. Two stockmen would haul them out onto the sawdust and then roll them onto a stretcher, face up. The calves would struggle to hide their half-blind eyes. The low hissing and tapping would increase all around the yard as the stockmen ferried the helpless calves to Shanti.

All it took to stop the calves struggling to protect their head or wriggle away was a couple of weighted belts laid over their arms and legs.

One thing was the same: The bolt gun.

Same design. Same recoil. Same noise.

A wedge on either side of the head was enough to stop the calves from shaking Shanti's target. He was fairly certain that after only a few seconds in the light they could still not see. Therefore they could not see him. This was scant consolation because he could see them. He could look into their eyes as he killed them. All he saw were the curious, trusting eyes of children.

He couldn't stand there thinking about what he had to do. He couldn't allow the other stockmen to interpret his hesitancy as a sign of fear or weakness. Nor could he allow the calves to suffer the torment of anticipation a second longer than necessary. All the same, every muscle in his body resisted his mind's programming to apply the pneumatic gun to the centre of the forehead and pull the trigger. But he did it for the sake of speeding the little ones on their way and for the sake of saving his own skin a little longer.

'God is supreme. The flesh is sacred.' Hiss. Clunk.

Immediate rolling of the eyes to show pure white. A tension tightening up their soft, fatty bodies followed by the spastic jerks of confused, dying muscles working against each other. Then stillness. And with it relief.

At least for Shanti.

But it didn't stop then. One calf an hour meant that Shanti accompanied the calf on its journey from wholeness and life into dismemberment and disembowelment. His stockmen hauled them up by their ankles and Shanti bled them with a sure, single stroke of steel across their voiceless throats; between the juvenile Adam's apple and chin, straight back to the neck bones. A single small vat collected the blood for very holy Welfare rituals.

Shanti walked the hoisted, bled calves down to the scalding vats to remove their skin. He pulled their bodies on motor-less runners, assisted in the skinning, beheaded them by hand, helped to gut them, quarter them and bone them out. Shanti even knew how to create the most prized veal cuts from either side of the lumbar vertebrae. Other stockmen dealt with the hands, feet and heads. He let them sort the offal themselves too. But he was still with the calves when there was nothing left but bones to one side and fresh cuts to the other.

All the while, the veal yard was filled with low percussion on steel panels and harsh, muffled breathing as row upon row of calves fed, grew, waited their turn. He could hear them.

He learned their tongue.

We are soft for their points and edges, they said. *We yield before them and we give ourselves. We are brothers through walls, brothers in darkness, prized above all others.*

Then one might speak alone: *Brothers, I feel the fear that we all will one day feel. Surely my time comes. Strengthen me, brothers, for I go to give.*

And all would reply: *Brother you go to give and truly we go with you. For, in time, we shall all go. We are with you brother. Trust those we serve for they will give you swift release. We have all heard it come, the end.*

A sharp hiss here followed by an abrupt tap mimicking the noise of the bolt gun.

Then a shivering, faltering beat upon the panels as stumps of fingers imitated the nerve shudders of the brain-shocked calves. A soft scraping to mark the sound of chains hoisting a body, a *HHHaaa*, signifying the sweep of the bleeder's blade. Incomplete digits pattering first the gush and then the dwindling trickle of blood from the calf's neck wound.

173

And so it went. Their trusting acceptance of their situation and their deep commitment to each other's emotional safety in all matters. They used their language to touch each other because their hands and arms could not.

We are with you. Here we are.

They said that so often.

None of it escaped him. He lived in the world of the Chosen veal calves while the stockmen around him lived in the world of the plant, their workaday jobs, their top wages and their families.

Vile.

Every last one of the meat-eating townsfolk was ignorant, vicious filth. They were the ones who should be slaughtered – at two hundred an hour, if only that were possible.

Yes, and Bob Torrance should be first in line.

***

At three in the morning by the town bell they moved, silent as shadows, yet full of light.

He took them all with him, wanting their numbers to be worth more than their might. He knew the best place to enter the facility's grounds, far from the main gates where the truckloads of stinking intestines arrived for processing. They slipped through the badly-maintained fences and he led them from one station to another, fairly certain which would be manned at night and which would not. They padded between storage tanks and chimneys, under wormlike ducts and around the edges of industrial blocks.

Where they found men, they silenced them with non-lethal blows. The control room demanded more skill as they were forced to enter single file. The followers were strong, the struggle brief. When the operators lay quiet, John Collins cut the power.

In the yards of the facility they took what tools they could find – wrenches, axes, cutters, screwdrivers and hammers and wreaked as much chaos as they could. Metal on metal made more noise than flesh on flesh. Time was short. He made sure he voided the stored gas tanks and cut every power line. They moved the unconscious operators out to the safety of the main gates, set a fire in the control room and left.

They were back in the depths of the Derelict Quarter with dawn yet to break when the first tanks exploded.

When she first regained consciousness she didn't understand where she was. Why was she lying on a cot in a bare room with stained white walls? What was the last thing she could remember? *Who* she was – even that presented a problem.

Slowly, it came back.

The rows and rows of shelves and stacks of cardboard boxes, the smell of dusty decay, the feeling that there was something important she needed to find. This filmy recollection was interrupted by anxiety. Why didn't she recognise this room? How had she come to be here? Her mind had lost its flexibility, pathways of memory hit sharp corners or dead ends. She started to remember and then found herself back at the beginning.

Here, in this dirty white room.

Each trip into memory brought her a little closer, though. She was a Parson. Parson Mary Simonson. She was investigating something.

Someone.

'Damn it.'

It wouldn't come.

She was surprised to find that the mere effort of trying to think had caused a sweat to break on her upper lip, under her arms. Her face felt hot.

She tried to sit up but her head was a weight her neck barely supported. She managed to get a small way up and tried to use her elbows to push up further. The attempt made her triceps shudder with strain. Halfway up she was overcome with dizziness. Her elbows slid from under her and she collapsed back. Nausea followed the dizziness. The bed inverted itself. She gripped the thin, damp mattress with shaking hands. Over it turned until she was upside down, the ceiling the floor. She did not fall but she felt she would at any moment. She cried out, a gasp of desperation.

'Someone...'

In her belly, in the depths of her stomach, something swelled; as cold and spiked as the head of a mace. The pain expanded out of her control. She cried out again – anguish.

The door – she hadn't even noticed there was one – opened. A man walked across what was now the ceiling without falling off. He sat beside her on the upside down chair. She stared, the ivory white around her irises marbled with bloody cracks.

'It's good to see you back with us.' She could not speak.

'How are you feeling now?'

Was he blind, she wondered? Could he not see the claws her fingers had become? Could he not see the sweat, icy on her face? Noises in her throat were not words.

'Don't worry,' said the man. She thought he seemed familiar.

'I'm getting something good for you. Something very special. We'll get you right. Oh, yes indeed, we'll fix you.'

She knew him: the doctor. A word formed.

'Where...'

A soft, strengthless hand patted hers.

'Well, my dear, someone must think very highly of you. You're in the Grand Bishop's personal infirmary. I'm sure he'll be along to visit you very soon.'

Slowly, the bed slid from the inverse to the vertical and finally to the horizontal. The unclenching mailed fist in her stomach closed again leaving her some space to breathe. The vertigo receded and with it the bloated nausea. She took several deep breaths and then her eyes were able to swivel.

'What happened?'

'You collapsed. Among the archives. Kicked up a little dust storm all of your own.'

'How long have I...'

'A couple of days now. I wish I could tell you you hadn't missed much.'

After a few moments she took his inference.

'What do you mean?'

'Well, I think I'll let the Grand Bishop fill you in on that. I know he'll be along in just a minute.' The doctor reached down beside the bed and brought up a small glass and a finely-crafted white bowl. 'First of all, we need to get some healing done. Here, drink this.'

He held out the glass to her but she made no motion to sit up.

'Let me help you.'

He slipped one hand beneath her head and eased it forward. With the other he tipped the glass towards her lips.

''tis it?'

'Never mind that, just drink it.'

She sipped and gagged.

'Hold it down! Don't dare waste it!' he commanded. 'That's precious stuff. Here, have some more.'

'No.'

'Do as you're told. Drink it.'

Sip by sip he had her take the whole glass. The liquid had an evil tint of bronzy yellow mingled with a filthy green hue. It was syrupy in texture.

'No smell,' she said. 'No taste.'

The doctor frowned, took the glass and sniffed it. She saw him turn his head away as though slapped and thought she caught him trying to swallow something back. Turning back to her, he was pale.

'You can't smell that?'

'No,' she said.

'It's a symptom of your sickness, I'm afraid. Not to worry.' He put the glass down and took up the white bowl. With a tainted silver spoon he lifted up some porridgy mass and pushed it home. She chewed, unnecessarily, and then swallowed.

'Good?'

She managed a facial shrug. He continued to feed her the remedy until the little bowl was empty.

'Well done. That'll give you some strength. We'll have you up and about before too long, I'm quite sure of that.'

The doctor sat back, smiling at his good work.

'Are you going to tell me what my medicines are?' He puffed up in his seat.

'Certainly. These are medicaments of my own devising based on the tenets of the Book of Giving. For your stomach ailment – with a liver involvement, if I'm not very much mistaken, I have prescribed the finest, freshest calf's bile in a suspension of the very purest veal calf's urine. For your Shakes, and I'm very sorry to tell you that the Shakes *is* my official diagnosis, I have dosed you with pulped brain – calf's again, naturally, as that is the very healthiest there is.' He leaned forward and lowered his voice. 'Not to mention the fact that the Grand Bishop himself has insisted on providing your care, therefore putting the very best remedies at our disposal.' He patted her arm with his limp hand. 'You rest up, Parson. We'll get you right. Oh, yes.'

Eighteen

Barney Bernard sat on the hard chair. He was unable to find a comfortable position and shifted every few seconds. A large man stood beside each of his shoulders. He was in the one room he'd never wanted to see, a room most people were glad they'd only ever heard about.

Opposite him sat Rory Magnus. He wanted answers.

'Don't tell me you don't know what happened. You're the night shift manager. Explain it to me.'

'Mr. Magnus, I...I can't explain what I didn't see.'

'Then tell me what you did see.'

Bernard tried again to make sense of what little he remembered. He closed his eyes as he spoke.

'It was after three. I remember the bell tolling. Nothing was amiss. Carter and Lee were at their stations. Then,' Bernard's face corrugated with the effort of recollection. 'Then I heard something behind me and swivelled on the chair to –'

'Did the others hear it? Did they turn around?' A sweaty pause.

'I don't remember. I can't –'

'Never mind, keep going. You heard something and turned.'

'Yes, it was the sound of the door opening and I remember thinking, "Who the hell could that be?" Then they were in the control room with us. Like they belonged there. Not scared or rushing but calm. Purposeful. I...' Bernard wasn't sure he should mention the next part. The thought had crossed his mind at the time that perhaps they *were* meant to be there. Some kind of surprise inspection sprung by Magnus. Maybe that moment of hesitation might have been enough for the three of them to defend themselves and the facility, at least to have put up some kind of fight. Better not to mention it. '...Yes, I stood up to challenge them. Don't remember what I said or even if I managed to get the words out. That's it. That's all there is.'

'And your staff will corroborate this, will they, Bernard?'

'I can't vouch for that, Mr. Magnus. I have no idea if they'll remember more or less than I do. However, up to that precise moment, I would say yes. I would say they'd concur with my recollection of events.'

Magnus made a few notes with an unsteady hand and sat back in his chair. He ran the fingers of both hands through his ginger mane and then rubbed them over his face as though he might open his eyes to a better reality. Apparently it didn't work. He sat forward again.

'Bernard, last night you were responsible for my gas facility and for the supply of electricity to the town. Do you have any understanding of the destruction that has befallen Abyrne during your watch? Because if you do, you don't seem very worried about it.'

'Mr. Magnus, I am truly sorry for what happened. In fact, I'm devastated by it. But I'm an engineer not a soldier. I make sure the facility supplies electricity throughout the night and I hand over that responsibility in the morning. I'm not trained in security measures or combat. None of my men are armed. No one has ever threatened the gas facility because everyone in the town depends on it. No one saw this coming. So, while it happened on my night shift, I was never – nor would I ever have been – equipped to deal with the situation.'

Magnus smiled and nodded.

'I see, Bernard. So now it's my fucking fault, is it?'

'Sir, I'm not suggesting th-'

'Yes you bloody are. You're saying that if I was better prepared none of this might have happened.'

Magnus stood up from his chair.

'Mr. Magnus, I -'

'Shut up, you festering piece of shit. Your job just went up in flames. Forever.'

'Please, Mr. Magnus. At least allow me to help with th-'

'Take him downstairs, Bruno. The back stairs.' Bruno laid a heavy hand on Bernard's shoulder.

'Shall I fetch Cleaver, Sir?'

'No, you shan't. I'm going to do this myself. Bring the rest of the factory's night shift down, though. I want them to understand what happens to incompetent employees.'

***

The next time she opened her eyes it was to wake from sleep, not return from the blackness of collapse. She remembered everything. At least, she hoped she did.

There was a soft tap on the door. She didn't have time to call out permission and someone was entering. He smiled at her, his eyes full of concern. Was there regret there too, she wondered?

'How are you feeling, Mary?'

'Better.'

'That is good news. That old quack must be as good as he says he is.'

She didn't want to throw the Grand Bishop's kindness back in his face but she thought the doctor was useless. A misguided fool. She understood her situation now.

'Bishop...I don't think there's much time and -'

'Nonsense, Mary, you're going to be fine.'

His hands when he took hers were strong and warm and truly comforting. The hands of the man she should have known so much more of, so much more intimately than this.

'I'm dying. You know it and so does Fellows. The only question left now is how long it's going to take.'

'Mary, please. Don't talk like -'

'Bishop, my dear Grand Bishop, you have to listen to me now. If you don't, I may never have the chance to say this and make any sense.'

The Grand Bishop sighed.

'All right. Tell me.'

'You remember, don't you, the matter I came to speak with you about?'

'Of course.'

'I investigated further.'

'And what did you find?'

'Well, there's the problem. Officially, nothing. Or less than nothing.'

'I don't understand.'

'No. Of course not. I checked these files to find the appropriate history. What I discovered was that one file, an incident report, of all things, was missing.'

'What was the incident number?'

'I don't remember. I'm going to remember less and less as the days go by, so you must remember this for me.'

She squeezed his hand and he squeezed back.

'I will, Mary. I promise.'

'I don't even know if this is important or not. And if it is important, I don't really understand why. But you must know it and you must find out what it means. I've had a strange feeling about this right from the beginning. There's something wrong about him.'

'About who?'

'Richard Shanti.'

'The Ice Pick?'

'Yes. He's not who he says he is.'

'I don't follow you.'

'He isn't townsfolk.'

'He has no rightful status? How do you know?'

'I don't know how I know. It's just something about him that isn't right. Him and his daughters too.'

'To revoke the status of a man like that...well, you must know how bad that would be for people's perceptions.'

She nodded.

'I do. I understand fully. But I have this sense of dread, Your Grace. Of something terrible to befall Abyrne and all its townsfolk. Whatever it is has something to do with Richard Shanti.'

The Grand Bishop sat back for a few moments as if deciding something. She watched him carefully.

'I wasn't sure whether to worry you with this in your condition but as things stand, well...I think you ought to know. The town no longer has power. Someone destroyed the gas facility. All our gas reserves are gone.'

'Dear Father. Who was it?'

'It could only be John Collins. Even Magnus isn't insane enough to go to war with Welfare in quite such a self-destructive way. Though, he too seems to be...'

'Be what?'

'He's not himself. The power of his position has corrupted him.'

There was something he wasn't telling her but she didn't push for it.

'What will you do?'

'Well, I haven't told Magnus of course, but every available Parson is out searching the Derelict Quarter for Prophet John and his hideout. We have to find him before Magnus does and make this a religious crusade. The lack of power might even work in our favour to re-establish the supremacy of the Welfare and cause the townsfolk to put God before everything else as we all did in the old days.'

She closed her eyes for a moment and prayed for restoration of the old ways, for the Meat Baron to be a man who respected the Welfare, the Grand Bishop and his God. With a pious man watching over the herds of the Chosen, all things would be different. One question troubled her still.

'How is it possible for records to be taken from the archive? I've never heard of such a thing. Have you?'

'Well,' the Grand Bishop let go of her hand and massaged some tension from his own neck. 'Seeing as we're revealing hidden things today, I'll tell you. As far as I know, it's only happened once. No one knows which record was taken – it was only a rumour, you see. But, as you must be aware, the only person who would be able to take a record and dispose of it would be a Parson. There was such a Parson a long time ago. He was old when I was a novice. His name was Pilkins.'

'What happened to him?'

'He disappeared.'

'Where to? Why?'

'No one really knows. He was investigating something, as you have been, and found facts he couldn't deal with. He should have gone to the Grand Bishop of the time but he didn't. He fled into the Derelict Quarter to live out his life beyond God's care and without the comforts of the Book of Giving. As far as I know he died out there. No one ever saw him again.'

'Do you think it could have been the record I'm looking for that he took?'

'It's the only thing that fits.'

'But we'll never know what that incident was, will we?'

'No. I don't see how we can ever know that.'

The Parson took his hand and squeezed it with what little strength she had.

'You must find Shanti. Bring him in. Find him and make sure he's kept out of trouble. Don't let him disappear like Collins.'

'I'll do what I can.'

***

As Magnus stood over Barney Bernard's body, he was panting. The man had not been reduced to the level of the Chosen in the normal way. He was, however, dead.

Magnus had made Bruno strap Bernard down without even dipping him first. While Bruno collected the survivors of the night shift that hadn't been killed by the blasts and fire,

Magnus paced up and down, his rage gathering, muttering to himself.

'No one's fucking listening to me. No one's got any respect any more. This is fucking Magnus. This is THE Magnus of the town. Magnus *is* the fucking town. Not the fucking Welfare. Not the fucking workers. Not the fucking Chosen. Abyrne is my town. I am the town. This fucking town is Magnus now. Fuck it. Fuck the Book of Giving. Fuck the Gut Psalter. Fuck the wanking, pissing Bish and his poncy pissing Parsons.'

A sweat broke on his forehead. He shook his head as if to clear it. His beard and hair scattered rancid droplets. The night shift arrived, bound into a chain. Awkwardly, they descended the stairs followed by Bruno and two other guards. When they saw the state Magnus was in they backed up against the wall. Magnus grabbed a larynx splitter off the rack of tools. It was no more than a scalpel, tiny in his meaty fist.

He held it up like the tip of a finger and walked along the line of gas workers.

'Poncy pissing Parsons. Poncy pissing workers.' He shook the knife in their faces. 'A poncy pissing town. That's what this place is. And you...' He pointed at each of them. 'You fucking, useless, scum-eating shirkers. You're the worst of the lot.'

He plunged the scalpel into the nearest man's eye. The scream filled the basement chamber. The other workers went pale. Bernard's piss pattered loudly from the slab to the floor. The wounded man held his breached socket, trying to hold in the jelly-meat of his eye. He screamed louder the more he understood his wound. There'd been a crunch of bone. Magnus had pierced not only the orbit but the bony socket itself. The man still lived, in the knowledge that Magnus had pierced through to his brain.

'SHUT UP,' screamed Magnus. 'SHUT UP SHUT UP SHUT UP.'

He plunged the scalpel into the man's face again and again until he sank to the floor taking the next man with him and the next man in the line halfway. Still the worker screamed. Each stab was a punch with a small blade at the end of it, not doing enough damage to kill, only enough to hurt him and cut him deep.

'SHUT UP. SHUT UP.'

Magnus aimed his blows into the man's neck and soon inflicted the right kind of damage.

Through red bubbles the man found words.

'Stop it. You're killing me.'

But Magnus only stabbed him faster and harder, aiming around his hands and between his fingers every time the man tried to protect himself. He kept stabbing long after the man had stopped moving and pleading. And all the time his mouth ran off his frustrations.

'Useless, useless, useless. Look at you. Not even good enough for meat, are you, eh? I could have hired women that would have done a better job than you. I will not let this town go under. I will not let that...that freak do this to me. I'm Magnus. I'm the fucking Meat Baron. I run this fucking place.'

He left the scalpel protruding from the man's other eye and straightened up. From the tool rack he selected the largest cleaver and hefted its weight in his hand. He walked up to the line of tied workers.

'What was this man's name?' No one spoke.

'Bruno? His name please.'

'Uh, that would be...Lee, sir.'

'Yeah? Well, Lee had it the easy way.' He walked over to the slab where Bernard lay. The man wiggled beneath the leather straps and farted wetly. 'Now, Bernard here was in charge of my gas facility last night when it was infiltrated and destroyed. This town may not have electricity for many years to come as a result. We may never be able to fix it. And all the gas we stored there for running trucks and keeping the chains running at MMP and all the other things we use it for, all that reserve is gone. And it's Bernard's fault. The Welfare states that such an infringement is cause for immediate revocation of status. But I say fuck that. Fuck the Welfare. This man's not good enough to feed this town. I wouldn't touch the primest cut off his filthy bones. And nor will anyone else. Because I will...

He raised the cleaver and brought it down.

'NOT.'

He hoisted it up, bloody. Slammed it down.

'TOLERATE.'

He worked it free, lifted it, hammered it down.

'USELESS.' And again.

'PISSING.' Again.

'SCABBY.' Up. Down.

Words. Insults. Metal parting flesh, chewing bone. And on.

And. On.

Which was why, as Magnus stood over Bernard's body, he was panting.

Nineteen

Sometimes Bruno studied his own hands to see if they were trembling. He did this now as he stood outside Magnus's bathroom. He was sure he could see some kind of vibration, at least in the very tips of his fingers, but he knew he could have been imagining it – morbidly willing it upon himself. So many townsfolk had the Shakes these days. If it wasn't his imagination then it was...better not to think about it.

From inside the bathroom he could hear splashing and Magnus's curses interspersed by giggles and cries of pain from his two maids. He'd gone in there to remove the blood that had dried onto his hands and hair and beard. By the sound of it, now that he was clean, he'd found other things to do in the bath.

Bruno had been standing there waiting for a long time. He'd come to announce an important visitor – still waiting in the downstairs drawing room – and Magnus had said he'd be right out. Bruno had never minded waiting in the past but these days he found it harder and harder to stand or sit and do nothing while Magnus did whatever it was he did behind closed doors. A change was coming; Bruno could sense it in everything that was taking place.

Magnus's gruntings seemed to reach their conclusion. Bruno knocked on the door again.

'Sir, he's still down there.'

'All bloody right, Bruno. I'm coming.'

The door was unbolted from inside and the two maids left, both of them avoiding Bruno's eyes and one of them still crying. A few moments later Magnus appeared in his dressing-gown and slippers with his long hair dark and dripping. He wore a towel around his shoulders to catch the water.

Magnus started to shuffle along the hallway and Bruno followed. From behind, Bruno was able to study his master a little. The man had shrunk unless he was imagining that too. He looked unsteady on his feet and Bruno was sure it wasn't due to his bath-time fun.

'What does he want anyway?' asked Magnus.

'I don't know, sir. Says it's important. Said you'd want to know about it.'

Magnus descended the stair using the banister for support. Bruno had never seen him do that before. Bruno followed until they were in the downstairs hall.

'Do you still need me, sir?'

'No, Bruno. You piss off for a game of cards or whatever. I'll call when I want you.'

Bruno turned to walk away. When he heard the door of the drawing room close behind Magnus, he crept back and stood with his ear to the wood. Magnus was no more polite with the doctor than he was with anyone else.

'What's so bloody important it can't wait until tomorrow, eh, Fellows?'

There was a pause and Bruno imagined Doctor Fellows taking in what he saw of Magnus and making an on-the-spot diagnosis. He'd realise there was no need to take offence at Magnus's manner because soon enough his primary services would be required. For now, though, this was all about Fellows's secondary function.

'Quite a lot, Magnus. Quite the sort of thing that absolutely cannot wait until tomorrow.'

'I'll believe that when I hear it.'

The doctor cleared his throat. Hesitation? Embarrassment?

'I'm trebling my fee for this.'

Magnus let out a genuine laugh.

'Treble? For the hearsay of a quack?'

'I want them delivered to my chambers tonight.' Someone sat heavily in a chair making it creak. Bruno guessed it was Magnus; his legs betraying him.

'I don't think Bob Torrance is going to like losing three bullocks in a single day, Doc.'

'Take it or leave it, Magnus. This information is going to save or destroy you depending only on whether you hear it or not.'

'Tell me why I shouldn't take you round the back and cut the information out of you.'

'Because it'll be the last time you'll ever use me and I know for a fact you've got no one else in a trusted position like mine.'

Bruno could hear the slight tremor in the doctor's voice. He must have had something pretty solid to be bargaining like this with Magnus. Or perhaps he sensed Magnus's weakness. His approaching downfall. He heard a sigh from Magnus.

'All right, Doc, you can have your toys but only if, at the end of our meeting, I feel satisfied that what you've told me is worth it.'

Bruno heard the other man take a seat.

'I've been doing a nursing job over at the Cathedral.' There was excitement in Magnus's too-quick response.

'The Grand Bishop?'

'No, Magnus, not him. Give me a chance. There's a Parson he must think rather highly of.'

'Oh, yes? Male or female?'

'Female.'

'Hm. That's a surprise.'

'She's got the Shakes and the canker. Serious case. She won't last much longer. Anyway, the Grand Bishop called me in specially and told me to spare no expense in treating her sickness. Turns out she's been doing some kind of investigation and she's found some irregularities. An incident record is missing from the archive. To listen to them it sounds like it must be a serious infringement.'

Bruno heard the sound of a cheroot being lit which was a sign that Magnus was already losing patience with the doctor's story. Might mean his boss would have reason for a second bath.

'I trust all this waffle is leading somewhere juicy, Doc.'

'I'm getting to it. The individual the Parson was investigating is one of your top men. Richard Shanti. Ice Pick Rick. His whole family, in fact, going back through generations.'

'They've been a great line of stockmen. So what?'

'So, whoever made that record disappear from his father's file was covering up a crime or the allusion to a crime so serious that no one could ever be allowed to read it or hear of it. It's of such concern to the Welfare that they're going to bring Shanti in for questioning.'

'They can't do that. He's my best stunner. With the power down we need him now more than ever.'

'Magnus.'

'What?'

'They're comparing him to Prophet John. John Col-'

'I know who you're bloody talking about,' Magnus shouted.

'What's the connection?'

'I don't know. But they don't know either. Whatever information Shanti has, you need to get it before they do. And you've got better access to him so it shouldn't be too difficult.'

There was a silence in the room that Bruno couldn't decipher. He considered moving away from the door and down to his quarters but he couldn't let it go like this.

'I'm not really sure this is worth three bullocks, Doc.'

'I'm not finished. I've saved the best part.'

'Get on with it.'

'The Grand Bishop has every Parson he can spare out searching for Prophet John. He intends to get to him before you and make an example of him. A religious example, if you know what I mean. He wants to use the destruction of Prophet John to re-establish religious control over the town. He wants you, and the Meat Barons of the future to be the lapdogs of the Welfare like it was in the old days.'

Bruno had heard enough to know that Magnus might explode out of the room at any moment. He slipped away down the hall.

Behind him he heard the rants and screams of his master. The man sounded more like an animal every day.

***

Parson Mary Simonson was dying and she knew it very well.

In the small white convalescent room, she sat up in the cot and leaned her head back against the whitewashed wall. The Grand Bishop had been extremely kind. In the end she felt his reasons were more of a salve to his own guilt than they were out of compassion for her. Still, she was grateful for his care.

Doctor Fellows had come to see her at least twice a day and she had taken his meals and remedies patiently, though not without nausea. She knew the doctor meant well but she also knew that she was beyond his powers to heal. She could have lain comfortably there – comfortable, were it not for the pain in her abdomen and the jitters that now rattled inside her very bones – and let death come for her in its own time but that was not how she wanted it to end. One last time she wanted to be outside, about the town, anywhere but in that room.

There had been a lot of time to think while she'd lain there, sleeping, dreaming, imagining. She thought a lot about Parson Pilkins and what kind of man he might have been. She thought too about what it was he had discovered that was so dangerous or offensive or secret that he had removed it from the archives. But she had no access to records or witnesses or any other source of information and so she merely lay there and wondered.

Her mind scouted where her body could not. She imagined. She let herself fly above the landscape of all she knew to look for patterns on the

188

ground. She swooped and upturned artefacts of memory. In facing her own death, she thought about the deaths of others, of all deaths. Her inner wanderings took her to unexpected grottos of peace and caverns of terror. She considered the nature of truth for the first time and was crushed by how little she knew.

The time had come for her to make one more journey, this time in the real world. She would walk the streets of Abyrne and where her feet led her she would finish her life. She felt certain that she might find one tiny truth out there that would comfort her on her way.

She swung her legs out of the bed.

It was hard. Harder than she'd expected and for a moment she thought about lying back and forgetting all this nonsense in her head, all this diseased madness, and sleeping her life away to the end. But the moment passed and her bare feet touched the cold, gritty stone floor. She examined her legs beneath her bed-shift. They were thin and wasted. Her arms were the same. But her stomach was bulging and firm. She was pregnant with disease. On standing, she had to reach for the wall with both hands and lean there for several minutes until the whirling of the world and the whiteness across her vision receded.

Finally, she found her robes and gowns in the small wood-wormed closet and dressed. She put on her Parson's boots, laced them loosely for she did not have the strength to do more, and slipped away from the room and the Cathedral. Her small footsteps took her away from the centre of the town, away from the dirty, scrawny townsfolk.

She found herself on the road out to Richard Shanti's house.

***

Trucks brought the men to work as usual but when they arrived it was chaos. Without power there were still plenty of jobs that could be done but no one was sure how to organise it. The electricity occasionally went out in the town but it never, *ever*, went off at MMP.

Even Torrance was stumped. He stood in a circle of worried men.

'We can move the carcasses along by hand from station to station, I suppose. But skinning's going to be harder.'

'Fucking understatement,' said one of the skinners.

'What's the word from Magnus?' asked someone else.

'Well, it's two words in fact,' said Torrance. 'Keep working.'

'How're we going to stun them?' asked Haynes.

'Right,' said another. 'We can't just haul 'em up and slit their throats. It's against the teachings.'

Torrance had that one covered.

'We'll do it by hand. Lump hammer and steel peg. Same effect exactly. A little more elbow grease.'

There were shrugs around the group. Most of them weren't stunning so they didn't mind one way or the other.

Then there was general chatter among them.

'Did you see the explosions?'

'No. Heard them, though.'

'They say it can't be fixed.'

'I heard that too. We might be working manually forever more.'

'I'll take a pay rise for that.'

'Yeah right. Magnus'll cut your bollocks off and eat 'em in front of you first.'

Laughter.

'Did you hear what he did to the gas crew?' The laughter died away.

Torrance filled the gap.

'Let's make sure nothing like that ever happens here at MMP, right lads?'

Everyone voiced agreement.

'What about the dairy, Boss?' It was Parfitt asking. 'We can't milk them without the equipment running.'

'Only one option,' said Torrance. 'You'll have to put calves on most of them until we think of something else. Meanwhile, do as many as you can by hand.'

'By hand? Isn't that a sacrilege?'

'Forget the teachings for now, people need their milk.' Parfitt looked dismayed.

'Don't worry, lad. You'll work it out. And, all of you, don't slack off because of this. It's no excuse. Just remember Magnus's words: *keep working.*'

***

Torrance watched the black bus turn into the main gate and park. It was full of black-coated figures. Only one of them disembarked. He recognised Bruno, Magnus's top dogsbody, striding across the plant's forecourt. Stockmen moved out of his way.

'Somewhere we can talk?' asked Bruno when he reached Torrance.

Torrance shrugged.

'This way.'

He led Bruno into the slaughterhouse and up the stairs to his observation balcony. There was a small office up there with a desk and two chairs, glass windows all around.

Torrance parked himself at the desk.

'Have a seat, Bruno.'

'No thanks. I've got a message for you from Mr. Magnus. He says keep this place running no matter what it takes. Hire more men if you have to and he'll budget for it.'

'It's not as simple as that.'

'Mr. Magnus believes it is.'

'We don't need more men, Bruno. We need electricity and gas. Then the men we've got can work as fast as Magnus wants. We've only got one chain in the slaughterhouse and that chain goes as fast as we can stun cattle. It won't go any faster no matter how many men you put on the job.'

'He doesn't want to hear this, Torrance, believe me.'

'I'm sure he doesn't. But someone has to understand what goes on up here and it ought to be him. I will do everything in my power to keep the plant working as efficiently as possible until Mr. Magnus gets the power back on.'

Bruno shook his head.

'I can't see that happening any time soon. It's going to take years to fix the gas power station. We're not even sure we *can* fix it.'

'What? Why not?'

'We're short of the right kind of materials for a start. Mainly it's a lack of knowledge. The maintenance engineers are going to have to learn how to put it all back together. They're starting almost from scratch. When the Father created the town, I don't think he was expecting a bunch of heretics to blow bits of it up.'

Torrance was quiet while he considered the implications of running the plant forever without electricity. It was possible but it would take a lot of doing. If Magnus demanded the same efficiency as before, they'd have to create more chains working manually in the slaughterhouse. They'd have to take men on for milking. If they couldn't create gas from waste, none of the herds would move in trucks any more. Men would be hauling carts of meat into the town. Everything would change. Torrance felt the first naggings of doubt about the order of things, the first tugs of fear over the future.

Bruno interrupted his thoughts.

'We've got to make sure that something similar doesn't happen up here.'

'You think they're going to attack the plant? Why would they do that? It's suicide.'

'From what I've seen, this lot have death wishes. I've seen . . .'

'What?'

'Doesn't matter. This guy Collins that leads them, he's crazy. There's nothing he won't try. That's why I've brought some of our boys up here. They're going to keep an eye on your perimeters. Especially at night. Make sure you look after them, right?'

'I'll let the stockmen know.' Torrance rubbed a hand over his mouth and beard. 'You really think they'll try something?'

'I don't know but we're not leaving it to chance.'

'I should arm the stockmen.'

'Too right. Get them bladed up, Torrance. This place has got to stay on track or the town's in big trouble.'

Bruno turned to leave.

'Wait. What about the Welfare? Have they sent word? They must have an answer to all of this. They should send out the Parsons and seize this Collins man.'

'I don't know what the Grand Bishop's response has been to the destruction of the power station but I know that Magnus has already asked Welfare for help and that they weren't very cooperative. Him and the Grand Bishop...they don't get on.'

'Fuck me, Bruno. Two men with a disagreement is no reason to let the town be overrun by lunatics.'

'That's what I've been thinking.'

'There must be something else we can do.'

'If I think of anything, I'll let you know. No reason why we can't work together.'

Torrance nodded. No reason at all.

Twenty

They didn't knock.

She heard footsteps, glimpsed dark figures passing the kitchen window and hadn't even the time to be frightened when they walked through the back door. They entered as though into their own mother's house and threw themselves down on kitchen or living-room chairs. So nonchalant, she half believed they were meant to be there – friends of her husband – and he would follow them in at any moment.

He didn't.

One of the men, his hair long, black and greasy, couldn't be still. He paced around the open-plan ground floor picking things up, half inspecting them, putting them down. It was as though she didn't exist. She found her voice and began to speak but the restless one held up his hand to silence her without even looking her way.

'Where are the children?' he asked.

It was easier now to stay silent than to talk. She didn't answer.

The greasy-haired one gestured with his head to two of the others and they slipped upstairs.

'No.' She ran towards them, still holding a wet dishrag.

'Wait. Please just tell me why you're here. You're not Welfare. What do you want?'

The leader grinned through bad teeth.

'How do you know we're not Welfare?'

'You're not...Parsons.'

'We could be...undercover Parsons.'

The others laughed.

'You can't take them away. We've done nothing wrong.'

'Denials. Without an accusation even being made. I smell a guilty conscience.'

'I swear to you, we're good townsfolk. We live by the Book.'

'Oh? And what book would that be?'

She could see how her confusion amused them. Why would they toy with her this way?

'The Book of Giving, of course.'

'Sounds a bit old-fashioned to me. Bit...dated. Sounds like the sort of book we could burn and no one would miss it.' The two men descended the stairs, each carrying one of her daughters.

'Ahh. Soon have the whole family together, won't we?' The girls and their bearers were smiling.

'Please.' She dropped the rag and took hold of the man's hands. 'Please don't take them away. I told you, we do things right in this family.'

The man smiled in genuine amusement.

'I'm sure you do, Mrs. Shanti.' He removed his hands from hers. 'But I'm really not interested in how piously you run your household. I'm merely here to extend you an invitation from my employer, Mr. Rory Magnus. He's requested the pleasure of your company.'

'But I...I mean we...this is something to do with Richard, isn't it? What has he done? Tell me what he's done.'

'Mrs. Shanti, I don't know what you mean. All I know is that you and your daughters *and* Mr. Shanti are all required to be the guests of Mr. Magnus.'

'Required? I -'

'He's very particular about who he invites. I'd say you were all very honoured. Wouldn't you, boys?'

There were nods all around the room.

Hema and Harsha could hardly contain their excitement.

'We're all going to go for a ride in the big black bus, Mummy. We're going to see the biggest house in the town.' Maya knew she had a choice about how she handled their captors. If she struggled, protested and begged it would frighten the girls. If she went meekly, calmly, at least they would be shielded for a little longer.

'Well, in that case, I'd better put my best shoes on.'

***

Torrance tapped a pencil against a chipped mug in his office. Shanti watched his face for clues, for any sign of what the man was really thinking. There was nothing there but veils. What he said after his long silence was unexpected.

'We have to reduce the herds.'

'Reduce?'

'It amounts to a cull, really. Management of numbers.'

'But why? It'll result in a reduced yield. More people going hungry.'

Torrance shook his head. He had the look of a teacher trying to explain something to a small child.

'No one goes hungry because of a lack of meat, Rick.'

'There isn't enough to go around as it is...Bob.'

If the familiarity annoyed Torrance he showed no sign of it.

'It's true, that's what people think. But that's just what Magnus wants townsfolk to believe. It keeps the price high, funnels the town's wealth in a very particular direction.'

'I don't understand.'

Torrance appeared to make some kind of mental decision.

'Look, Rick, I like you. You're a good man. A great asset to MMP. So I'm going to tell you something. But first you have to swear to me that nothing I say will be repeated. To anyone. Ever.'

'I'm not sure I want to be party to that kind of information.'

'It's too late for thinking about what you want. We have to start thinking about our jobs and our futures. I'm going to need men like you to help me manage the changes. Men I know I can rely on to do their jobs properly.'

Torrance stood up to tell it. Shanti listened in pale shock. Hundreds of Chosen slaughtered for nothing. Flesh dumped by the ton on the borders of the wasteland. Townsfolk starving in the midst of a glut. And now this.

'The thing is, with the power plant shut down indefinitely, there's no way we can maintain previous yields. Cattle will age past their prime and be useless to anyone. Less money coming in will mean fewer jobs or, at the very least, pay cuts across the board. Everything will have to be done by hand, without power – at least until we can build up gas reserves again, but that could take years. The trucks won't run, the chain motor won't run, the milking machines won't run. There'll be no more automation. Not for a long time. Instead of slaughtering the steers, we have to start thinking about reducing the numbers of fertile cows and getting rid of most, if not all, of the bulls. That will halt the growth of the herds. We have to cull the milkers too. There's just no way we can service them all. So, starting tomorrow, I want you to round up the oldest dairy cows and the oldest bulls. Bring them in for slaughter.'

Shanti waited. It didn't seem as though Torrance was finished with him. Torrance sat back down and continued to flick the pencil against the cup.

'Will there be anything else?' Torrance looked up.

'Isn't that enough?' Shanti shrugged.

'I...'

But there was nothing else to say. He turned and left. Behind him he could sense Torrance's expression. Something like a smile.

***

He had the children taken straight to the maids to be looked after while he spoke to their mother.

They ushered her into the drawing room – a more fitting place to meet than his study – where he was lounging, still in dressing-gown and slippers, and medicating himself with a large vodka. He dismissed Bruno and the boys and poured her a measure.

'I don't drink,' she said as he passed her the heavy crystal tumbler.

He smiled.

'You do now.' He gestured towards one of the sofas. 'Make yourself comfortable, Mrs. Shanti. May I call you Maya?' He waited neither for her to sit nor reply but sat down once more in his own armchair and put his feet up. The silk dressing-gown slipped a little, revealing one lumpy, trunk-like thigh. He made no effort to cover himself up. 'I suppose you know why you're here?' No reason not to start testing her straight away. They were all short of time.

He looked her over. Long, dark, straight hair, a nicely curved figure – only a little spoilt by childbirth. Better than most in the town. Her face was too angular though, the eyes too focussed. He got the sense of a woman who manipulated but without any real intelligence. There was an underlying tension there too, some kind of frustration rarely addressed.

'No, I don't,' she said. 'I don't know anything.'

Too much protestation already; her words proving his assessment.

'But surely you can guess. Isn't it obvious?'

'Mr. Magnus, we're a God-fearing family. We abide by the laws of the town. I have no idea why you've brought us here.'

Time to stop circling and pounce.

'Your husband, Maya. Richard. We believe he's not quite the man he purports to be. Has he been behaving strangely at home? Have you noticed...deviances?'

Her fingers tightened on the crystal tumbler just enough for the knuckles to whiten a shade. Her initially firm stare now skittered around the objects in the room. A little colour came to her cheeks before draining and leaving her pale. Excellent. There was dirt here somewhere.

'He's been...working very hard. Too hard.'

Magnus's vodka hand started to shake. He rested it on his thigh, took the glass in his other hand and drank.

'I don't think he's been quite as dedicated as you might believe. Tell me, have you ever known him to go anywhere else other than work? Does he have friends? Does he ever drink at Dino's?'

'Richard is not a drinking man. He's not a gregarious sort, Mr. Magnus. As far as I know, he's never done anything but come home after a day at work and collapse in exhaustion.' Ah, so there it was. Shanti didn't give out what a wife required, he was one of those rare, sexless automatons that did nothing but sleep and work. Great for MMP. Useless to his wife. Yes, Magnus could see the strain in her neck muscles, sensed the hunger in her crotch. She would want it hard and rough. She would welcome pain. How happy he would be to oblige.

When they'd concluded their business, of course. Not before.

***

Shanti visited the dairy and watched the dairymen struggling to milk the few cows they had in there by hand. It was obvious from the look of the cows that the process was more painful than the machines. Cows that had been milked had red udders with fingerprint-shaped bruises already appearing. He looked for WHITE-047 but she wasn't there.

Behind the milking parlour, the rest of the dairy herd were corralled with their calves, allowed to nurse them to prevent their udders from over-distending. He spotted WHITE-047 at the back of the herd against the cracked brick wall. There was no way he could get to her without others in the herd noticing. A couple of stockmen patrolled lazily, waiting to send the next few cows into the dairy. The whole plant was on a go-slow.

Shanti put his hands in his overall pockets and put his head down as he walked towards the bull barn. It didn't really matter if he was noticed but he wanted to feel anonymous nevertheless. In the barn there were no stockmen. All the pens were locked and secure and with more hands needed elsewhere, the bulls had been partially abandoned. He walked the rows until he saw BLUE-792's familiar bulk through a gate slat. Using his fingertips and rasps that he'd practised thousands of times when alone, he beat the steel panel softly, breathed the secret language of the Chosen.

This time, when he'd finished, there was a long reply.

***

It was unusual to come home in the evening and find no light coming from the house. He was accustomed to seeing the glow of firelight and candles at the very least. Of course, with the power down, Maya would be making do with what they had and that would mean trying to stretch every stick of tallow and every fallen branch.

As he stepped past the kitchen, he expected to see the flicker of a single wick burning but there was nothing. It was still too early for the girls to be in bed; too early even for dinner to have been served. Perhaps Maya was working out how to cook her filthy meat over the flames of an open fire.

Stopping at the back door, he listened. No sound from inside.

Nothing.

Instead he noticed his own heartbeat and realised he was afraid.

He opened the door silently, knowing exactly how to twist the handle and pull the door towards the hinges to avoid any sound. Pushing the door wide allowed a little of the final light of dusk to show him the deserted kitchen and living-room. He stood just inside the door for a long time listening for breathing, watching for the slightest movement. There was nothing.

When he was satisfied the downstairs was deserted, he checked upstairs. The house was empty.

So. She'd taken them away, just as she'd promised she would.

He ground his teeth together as his anger rose up. That tainted woman assuming charge of his precious girls. She was the one who deserved slaughter. She was the one who should experience death at the hands of MMP stockmen.

In the gloom, something almost glowed on the dining table. A white rectangle. A letter.

He reached for it but it was too dark to see any writing.

In the kitchen he fumbled for matches, lit a stick of tallow.

It was worse than he'd expected:

Mr. Rory Magnus kindly asks that you join your family at his mansion at your earliest convenience. Tardiness will not be well received.

His hands shook. Melted fat dripped onto the table.

His pupils constricted in the candle flame. There was a noise at the back door. The flame whipped out in a draught. He saw not faces, but shapes, figures, steal into the room with speed and purpose. He dropped the letter.

They took him.

***

198

The back door had been left open and she walked in without knocking or calling out. It was clear there was no one inside. The Shanti place was silent and still. The house seemed to be listening to her.

She found the note from Magnus and was too jaded to despair. What did it matter that Magnus got to Shanti before the Welfare? What did it matter that the town fell into the hands of a Meat Baron or even those of the insane John Collins?

Her indifference astonished her. All these years of piety and adherence, all these years of service. Where was God now that she was dying? Where was God when lunatics threatened to take over Abyrne? She listened. If God heard her questions, He made no answer.

Weakened, she sat at the table where they had eaten the night she'd inspected the house. The children had pushed their food around on their plates before eating. Shanti himself had not touched the food until she'd left the table. Only Maya ate with gusto. Had Shanti even touched his meat that night? Quite suddenly, she was certain he had not; that he had not eaten the flesh of the Chosen for some considerable time. He was thin, yes, but he looked far fitter and healthier than most in the town. Could that really be attributed to his bizarre running habits or was there more to it? According to the Book of Giving, no townsperson could survive without the nourishment of the Chosen. Now, such folk were abroad in the town in numbers. Collins and his acolytes. Shanti too probably. How could God explain this?

God did not explain.

When she thought about it, had God ever truly spoken to her? Had He ever answered a single prayer? Had He appeared in the form of signs or portents? Had He shown himself in the shapes of the clouds? Had His presence ever given her comfort on the decades of nights she'd spent alone and chaste?

Dear Father, surely this is not the time to doubt You. Not when I approach the threshold of the next world. Not when my soul is about to fly to You. Perhaps this was the Lord's greatest test of her, the final examination of her faith. Perhaps everyone faced this test at the end.

She felt an emptiness within herself. She had always expected to be filled by the divine light of the Lord's spirit. She had saved this cold space for Him ever since she'd entered the Welfare as a novice. The hearth within was swept and clean, the wood lay ready in the grate, the chimney was clear.

199

Fill me up with Your flame, Lord, for I need no other nourishment now. I shall not eat again nor wake from my next sleep. I come to You. Place Your gentle fire within me.

Many hours passed in the kitchen and Parson Mary Simonson sat unmoving with her hands folded on the table in prayer. The light moved across the room indistinctly through the clouds but she sensed the day growing old and the approaching twilight. There was nothing inside her. Not the merest spark of the Lord's presence.

Instead the foetal canker in her guts stirred as if turning in a womb. It unclenched, at least that was how it felt to her, and the points and blades of its body wounded her from within. She had swallowed a baby fashioned from splintered bone and broken glass and the baby was growing, trying to get out. Nausea accompanied the churning, expanding pain in her abdomen. The trembling returned to every part of her body and as she sat, she was unable to keep even her head from shaking side to side.

Was this, then, her answer? The absence of God?

Or was it worse than that? Was their town's God a God of cruelty? A God whose mission was to inflict pain on His creations?

She could sit no longer. Before the darkness came she wanted to move on. There was one last place to search for answers. Then she would rest and gladly.

***

Since the blast at the gas plant, the roads had become very still. What little gas was left was being reserved for emergencies only. No trucks grumbled back and forth from the meat packing plant to the town.

As she walked, the Parson's numbed senses seemed to clear for a while. A wind got up and, out here, much nearer than she normally came to the fields of the Chosen and to the plant, the smell was very strong. So many odours combining on the cold air. She tried to isolate each one. Faeces was the most recognisable and it smelled no different to the stink that arose from the town's sewers. Almost as strong was the smell of rot and decay, the smell that came off meat left too long to be edible, the smell of flesh breaking down. There were living smells too. Sweat from the Chosen; not unlike that she might smell from a group of workers on a hot day. With all this came the aroma of fresh blood and the thick odour of the butcher's shop, of cleaved, hanging meat, of ground meat, of cutlets and chops, of steaks and raw sausage. These were the smells that had once caused her mouth to water; the smells of her daily dutiful intake.

Now those smells only added to her deep nausea. Despite the weakness of her knees and the strain in her legs, she walked on. She pushed through the pain inside her as though through a high wind, leaning forwards slightly. Like a starving woman climbing a steep hill into a gale. She kept her head down. She did not imagine that there would be a return journey.

The road was broken, the hawthorn hedges bulging and jagged. From time to time a spike would catch her gowns and the jerk on the material would be enough to stop her. Resuming the walk was harder each time. Finally, realising that there was unlikely to be a passing truck, she stepped into the middle of the road to walk and only had to watch for ruts and cracks in the blacktop.

***

She reached the gates at dusk.

In the security man's box there were three men, not one. Two of Magnus's personal guards accompanied the gatekeeper.

She stopped at the window. The black-coated guards stood up behind the gate man. He slid the window open and stuck his head out.

'Bit late for an inspection, isn't it, Parson?'

'These are dangerous times,' she said. 'Never too late to be vigilant. Can you arrange an escort for me?'

The Gate man shook his head.

'We're fully occupied, Parson. All hands we can spare are on the task.' He flicked his eyes towards the guards standing behind him and tried to make himself sound grateful. 'Magnus has sent a shift of extras to keep watch while we work but I can't assign them to you.'

Parson Mary Simonson hadn't wanted an escort; she'd merely asked out of politeness and to comply with protocol. Parsons were entitled to go anywhere they wanted, most especially around the MMP plant, but it had been a long time since they'd actually felt welcome to do so.

'I'll make my appraisal alone then.'

A cloud of weakness hit her and she went momentarily blind. She reached out a hand and it found the wall of the security man's box. Slowly the fog lifted and the faint retreated.

'You alright, Parson?'

She was surprised to see the security man looking genuinely concerned.

'Fine. It's . . . been a long shift, that's all.'

'I can get some food sent out to you – we can do that much.'

She wondered if she looked as pale as she felt at the thought of it.

'That won't be necessary, but thank you all the same.'

She walked around the closed gate and towards the nearest building. She could feel the eyes of Magnus's men on her back but she was unafraid.

Twenty-one

Maya Shanti was a little too willing for Magnus's liking. He preferred women who fought. Women who struggled and cried out before giving in to him. The problem was she wanted it too bloody much. Her husband had neglected her for far too long.

She slept now, naked beside him in his huge bed. Magnus couldn't sleep. The sex hadn't been enough for him and there were other things on his mind. Shanti hadn't responded yet. Why hadn't he come? Didn't the man care about his family? It could be argued that he didn't care much about his wife judging by her willingness to betray him. But what about the twins? Didn't he worry about what might happen to his two beautiful little girls? The thought was enough to make his groin tingle and his cock stir.

He pulled the cord for the maids. Far off in the mansion a bell rang.

He slipped from the bed making sure not to wake Maya. It would be better if it was a surprise. He crept to the bedroom door and waited outside for his maids. Two of them came, still rubbing the sleep out of their eyes. They were used to his demands, however, ready to be of service day or night. It was their duty.

He jerked his thumb towards the bedroom.

'Go in there and tie her up. Gag her and blindfold her. Do what you want with her. Enjoy yourselves. When she looks like she's stopped having fun, you come and get me. Then we'll all take our time. I think I could go on until morning. Tomorrow we'll start on the twins.'

He sauntered to the lavatory, pulled down his pyjama bottoms, sat down on the toilet and lit a cheroot. The smoke couldn't mask the scent of his filth.

'What a fucking stink,' he said.

***

She toured the plant in silence. The closeness of her own end made it a cathedral of nightmares.

In the dairy, the men struggled to milk the cows. Extra restraints were necessary now that automation was no longer available. When things didn't go well, the dairymen brutalised the cows. In the past such a treatment of the Chosen would have been a serious offence. Now, no one seemed to care. Even her presence in the various barns and houses of the MMP plant didn't affect the workers. In the past, they'd have made sure to follow religious procedure to the letter whilst observed by Welfare.

In the veal yard, calves were dragged instead of carried. The barn was filled with a pulsing rhythm of fingers and sharp breaths. The slaughtermen proceeded straight to the slitting of the calves' throats without stunning. When she challenged one of the workers about this he merely said:

'They're practically dead anyway.'

'But you're not following the code of the Gut Psalter.' The man shrugged.

'Townsfolk need to eat. We have to supply them. It's all about efficiency and now that there's no power, we've had to cut a few corners. But believe me, Parson, it's for everyone's benefit.'

She'd left them to it, unable to watch.

In the main slaughterhouse, conditions were slightly better but not by much. The crowd pens were still being used to hold cattle until their turn for slaughter arrived. However, the machinery that had propelled them into the single file chute and then the restraining box was unusable.

Now, the Chosen were led from the crowd pens directly to the bleeding station and the hoists. They would see the mess made by the blood of their own kind as well as seeing the bodies being swung manually along the runners to each successive station. This was unheard of. Six men would hold each of the Chosen down and two would administer the bolt. Without the pneumatic gun, the bolt was now a pointed chisel with a lump hammer to back it up. Some procedures did conform to the old ways. The slaughter men would lay the creature with its feet facing the west – the setting sun – and the man with the hammer would speak the blessing:

'God is supreme. The flesh is sacred.' Then he would stun the animal.

Unused to the unwieldy equipment, the stunner mis-hit the chisel at least once for every four he got right. She saw one poor animal receive three successive hammerings before the bolt did its work properly. The atmosphere in the crowd pens was different to anything she'd encountered before. The Chosen milled and jostled like an angry crowd. They seemed half-terrified and half-enraged by what awaited them. In the past she'd never seen them anything but passive and accepting. It was as though they too had ceased to believe in the surety of their masters' hands. They sensed more than just a worsening of their conditions. They sensed a crack in the perfection of those that husbanded them.

Further sickened, she escaped to the bullpens where no slaughter was taking place. In the past she had always taken a little pleasure in watching the huge males swagger around their pens or sleep in the straw or eat their meals as though they'd starved for a whole month. In the barn where the bullpens were, there was only one stockman in evidence. He looked young and nervous. Many of the pens were empty when in fact the whole barn should have been full.

'Where are the rest of them?' she asked, thinking that they'd been put out to pasture or else were being prepared for mating.

The timid stockman looked embarrassed. Obviously he knew the answer he gave was a bad one.

'They're slaughtering them.'

'What? All of them?'

'Yeah. I mean, not at the same time, but they'll all be gone in the next few days.'

She looked through a crack in a panelled gate and saw a bull tagged as BLUE-792. This particular bull was like royalty. His stock was the best and his reputation had spread far beyond the walls of MMP.

'Even this one?'

'Yep. Even BLUE-792. Hard to believe really.'

'But why, for God's sake? Where are the next generation going to come from?'

'Torrance has got it all worked out. We're culling now because we'll never have the capacity to process as many as we used to. The herds'd grow out of control. What we'll do next is raise a new generation of bulls from existing stock but not as many as we've got now. If the gas plant ever gets back to working again, we can always increase the numbers then. For the moment, though, we've got to stop reproduction or at least slow it down.'

The Parson eyed the bull and it eyed her back. This was something strange. No Chosen, bull, steer or heifer ever made eye contact. The bull looked away. Immediately she knew she'd imagined it. Imagined the look of mistrust and hatred on the face of an animal that had always been well treated; better treated perhaps than any other Chosen in the town's history. And not only mistrust, but something else. Dissent. It wasn't possible and she put it from her mind.

It was dark outside and much colder too but she couldn't bear to be indoors a moment longer. Pulling her red cloak around her she walked across the yard and down towards the fields and outbuildings where most of the Chosen spent each night. Somehow, she believed she'd be more at ease there than among her own kind.

Twenty-two

When the light came, it was through a window too small for a man to crawl through, even a man as thin as Richard Shanti.

He sat with his back to a wall and as the grey light grew in strength he saw that all the walls were white. Dirty white. There were stains too; rusty-looking smears and splatters easy to recognise. The room was bare in every other respect. No chair, no bed, no basin. The door was ancient wood, shaped in a pointed arch, its patina worn away by neglect. There was no handle on the inside, just an old metal plate housing the lock.

He could think only of Hema and Harsha and what Magnus was doing to them. What he might already have done. His heart was filled with the urge to destroy the man, to revoke his status one knuckle, one deliberate slice at a time. He was horrified by the violence within himself yet welcomed it too. It might be the only strength he could use to fight back.

They hadn't hurt him yet, not really. His handling had been rough and they'd put a hood over his head before they threw him in the back of the truck. It must have been important to bring him in quickly otherwise they wouldn't have wasted the fuel. How much they knew and what were they willing to do to find out the rest he could only guess at. It was better not to think about it. Anger would be stronger than fear; that was the emotion he should nurture.

Footsteps along the hall outside. The rattle of one key being selected from many. The lock releasing.

The door opened.

In it was framed a man in velvet robes. He had a long, thinning beard of white and not much hair left on his head. On his fingers were many gold rings and mounted in them opulent gems. Shanti tried to conceal his puzzlement.

'Do you know me?' asked the robed man.

'Of course...Your Grace.'

'Then you know why you're here.'

Shanti cast around. Nothing came to him. He shook his head.

'Think about it. Why would an exemplary man like Richard Shanti, the Ice Pick, be brought to the gaol chambers of Central Cathedral?'

'I don't know.'

'Well, it's very simple.' The Grand Bishop stepped into the room. Behind him were two Parsons and the gaoler with his bunch of keys. The two Parsons followed him in. The gaoler pulled the door shut and locked it again. 'And yet, it's very complex.'

Shanti had not stood up when the door opened and now the urge to do so was strong. The presence of the two Parsons, both bulky men beneath their robes, persuaded him to stay seated. No need to upset them. Additionally, he sensed he might not be in quite as much danger as he'd imagined.

'You were visited by Parson Mary Simonson, were you not?'

'Yes.'

'She had some doubts about the way you cared for your daughters.'

'I think we put those doubts out of her mind.'

'Perhaps. However, you aroused others.'

The Grand Bishop was waiting for a response. Shanti didn't give him one. He had to find out how much they knew. Finally he said, 'What others?'

'You're too *good*, Shanti. You're not typical of the townsfolk. Parson Mary Simonson felt she had to find out more about you. More about your family and where you came from. Your line goes back to the creation. Did you know that?'

'I mentioned it to her, I believe. The Shantis are an old family.'

The Grand Bishop glanced up at the window. He seemed impatient, agitated. He turned and looked directly at Shanti.

'You're not who you say you are.'

Shanti couldn't help but smile. Did they think he was some kind of spy?

'Who am I then?'

'That's what we want to find out.'

Shanti thought it over quickly. They didn't seem to know much about him. They didn't seem to know much about anything. Now they were accusing him of some kind of fraud. Meanwhile, his family – his daughters – were in the hands of the most dangerous man in Abyrne. He had to do something.

'When your men came to collect me last night, I was reading a note that had been left on my table. No doubt you'll have noticed how quiet the house was. Magnus has my family, Your Grace, and he means them harm. He's threatened their safety if I don't go to meet him.'

'Magnus has your wife and daughters now?'

'Yes. I thought your Parsons were his men. I thought this was his mansion.'

The Grand Bishop's expression turned from curiosity to anger.

'Magnus wants you at his house?'

'That's what the note said.'

'Why? Why does he want to talk to you?'

'I wish I knew. All I care about is getting my daughters away from him. He's not to be trusted.'

'Ha.' The Grand Bishop snorted. 'Trusted? The man's a cockroach.'

The Grand Bishop stroked his beard and turned away. Shanti could see an opening here. Magnus was the Grand Bishop's enemy and that might just make Richard Shanti the Grand Bishop's friend.

'Let me go to them,' he said. 'Let me find out what it is Magnus wants. I'll find a way to get that information to you. All that matters is getting my family away from him. Promise me you'll protect them and I'll find out as much as I can. Magnus can have me as long as they are safe.'

'I can't guarantee anyone's safety in the town any more. Things have gone too far. And I can't let you out of here now that I have you. You may be far more dangerous to me than Magnus whether you admit it or not. The fact remains that we have to find out who you are. Because one thing is absolutely certain. You are not Richard Shanti. Richard Shanti died twenty-eight years ago.'

***

The maids took Maya away when he'd worn himself out. They took away the sheets, soiled with smears of her blood and vomit, and replaced them so that he could sleep. They bathed him and he shook as though frightened, though they knew that he was not. They put him in his clean bed and pulled the covers over him and even in his sleep he shook, his head trembling on the pillows.

***

'What do you know about John Collins?'

'Only what I've heard. People say he's some sort of Messiah.'

'Have you met him?'

'No.'

'I think you're lying.'

Shanti was a useless liar and he knew it. The Grand Bishop, on the other hand, must have been an astute judge of individuals after all his years of dealing with the town's transgressors and ministering to his flock. There was no way to hide from the Grand Bishop's questions or the way his eyes read the secret signals that Shanti couldn't prevent his body from creating. But there was no way he could tell the truth now. Not until they tore it from him.

They *would* do so and it was only a matter of time. He would break and tell them everything he knew. He was not a strong man, there was no point pretending. He would take it as far as he could.

'I don't know him.'

The Grand Bishop looked up and out of the small window as if there was something out there more significant than a patch of cloud-obscured sky.

'I notice you're...how shall we say...a man of slight frame. But you're not a poor man in this town. You don't have the excuse of not being able to afford the flesh that God provides.'

'I'm a runner. I run many miles every day. It keeps me thin.'

'Emaciated, I'd have said.'

Shanti didn't respond. The Grand Bishop continued.

'I've heard it said that John Collins is similarly light of build. Do you suppose that's just a coincidence?'

'There are a lot of thin townsfolk.'

'None of them have the kind of job you have, Shanti. Or the kind of job Collins had before he strayed from us. So I ask you again, why are you and he so . . . undernourished?'

'All I know is that I burn off my fat every day. Collins I can't speak for.'

The Grand Bishop glanced at his two Parsons and sighed.

'Very soon I'm going to run out of patience and pleasant conversation.'

'Very soon Rory Magnus is going to mutilate my family.

He may already have done so. I don't care about Collins or your questions. I don't care that you say I'm not the man I think I am. All I care about is them. Help me to save them and I'll do anything, tell you anything you want. But not right now. Let me go to them. Give me a chance to save them, I'm begging you.'

'If I let you go, Magnus is going to ask you the exact same questions I'm asking and for the exact same reasons. He's going to do to your family what he wants to do whether he's satisfied with what you tell him or not. You can't save them or yourself just by getting out of this room.'

'No, but I can at least try. And they'll know that when it mattered most, I didn't abandon them. For God's sake, show some mercy.'

'Tell me where Collins and his followers are hiding and

I'll let you go.'

'I can't do that.'

'Then your family is lost. I'm sorry.'

Shanti let his head drop into his hands in misery and desperation. He was out of options. When he looked up his face was wet, his eyes red.

'He's in the Derelict Quarter –'

'Tell me something I don't know, Shanti, or I'll kill your daughters myself.'

'Let me finish. It's a long way in. Maybe a couple of miles. Beyond the blocks the ground slopes down, away from the town. At the bottom of that slope, somewhere near the centre of it, there's an opening. It leads down into tunnels. That's where they are. I couldn't see where they took me. All I know is it's deep – three levels down.'

The Grand Bishop seemed shocked to hear it. Not because they were there. To Shanti it seemed he was shocked that there were places in Abyrne he knew nothing about, realms where he had no authority.

'How many of them are there?'

Shanti completed his betrayal.

'Twenty-five, maybe thirty at most. Some women among them.'

The Grand Bishop laughed.

'Thirty? John Collins thinks he can take control of Abyrne with thirty starveling cave-dwellers? I can't wait for the Parsons to shut him down.' He nodded to his two companions. 'Take your best out there and finish this for me right now. Bring Collins back to me alive.'

'What about this one?'

'We're going to let him go to Magnus. He can't do any harm now. By the time Magnus gets the information out of him this nonsense with Collins will be over. We'll show the town what happens to blasphemers. I think it's time we put the Welfare back in charge of the Chosen and make their sacrifice to us a thing of Divinity once again.'

The two Parsons left.

The Grand Bishop looked into Shanti's eyes.

'If you live through this – whether you save the lives of your family or not – I'm going to find out the truth about you, Richard Shanti. For better or for worse. You are one individual I will not allow to run to the Derelict Quarter to live out their days in exile. I will find you no matter where you go.' He looked back out of the window, perhaps finding nothing in the clouds. 'Get going. Make your sacrifice. But be ready for me when you're done.'

Without the pack to drag him down, Shanti sprinted.

He flew.

***

The Parsons were a hundred in number. They fanned out across the broken landscape of the Derelict Quarter like monks wearing robes of blood. Soon the hems of their raiment were grey with the dust of destruction. From every right hand hung a polished femur, each one engraved with a passage from the Book of Giving. They made ideal clubs; lightweight but strong and slightly flexible. The broadened end where the knee joint would once have been, acted as a natural haft that prevented the bone slipping out of the wielder's hand. The hip end of the bone was part club, part blunt hook. The Parsons used them to trip, to block and to bludgeon and these Parsons were the best the Welfare possessed.

They walked warily, eyes flicking, heads scanning from side to side. The Derelict Quarter was a place the Parsons hated and feared. Here Abyrne ended and became a no man's land where fugitives went to eke out their days in starved deprivation. What was safe and pious and lawful became wild and unpredictable. The Derelict Quarter was wrong. They all felt its malignancy to their core.

From time to time, one of them would stumble on the jagged, unforgiving rubble. The sudden sound would make them all stop and spin towards the noise. Nervous guts rumbled. Damp palms left smudges on red velvet.

Parson James Jessup was the youngest and arguably the strongest of all of them. Beside his fear he felt a deep instinct to deal out pain and punishment to the Godless ones they'd been sent to find. Only Collins needed to return alive. The rest they could do what they wanted with. His excitement brought the taste of iron into his mouth and he savoured it. This was God's iron that ran in his blood, in his very saliva. It would be his strength and with it he would cast the Godless down forever.

He walked near the front of the group so that, when the ambush came, he was one of the last to be aware of it. When he turned, his Parson brothers were already falling like the red leaves of autumn. Among them moved what appeared to be the shadows of slender men and women. They were dressed in rags; the sleeves and trouser legs tattered by the shard-like corners and projections that lay all around.

Parsons turned and hefted their femur-clubs in time-worn arcs: diagonally down, hooked from right to left and back, sweeping uppercuts. None of the blows landed. Cassocks billowed as the

Parsons collapsed to the wounding ground.

***

They stopped him before he reached the front door. Men in long coats ran out from both sides of the driveway to tackle him. There was no need, he was giving himself to them. He made no attempt to resist.

'I'm Richard Shanti,' he said. 'Magnus wants to see me.' Inside the mansion, one man holding each of his arms as they marched him, Shanti's breathing quickly returned to normal. Only his heart didn't completely settle into its usually slow rhythm but not because he wasn't fit. He'd come for his daughters.

The men took him upstairs to the study but it was empty. They waited.

Somewhere else in the house there was crying. He recognised the voices. *No, no, no.*

'Where the hell is Magnus?' he shouted into the face of the man to his left.

The man smiled.

'Busy.'

'I need to see him. He needs to see me. Now.'

'When he's finished, he'll come. Maybe.'

What the hell was he going to do? The beast was with his girls. What had he already done?

'Listen. You tell him I know where John Collins is. Tell him I know where Prophet John and his people are hiding.'

'You can tell him yourself when he's ready.'

'No. You have to tell him now. Believe me, this is something he wants to know. He won't want to be kept waiting a moment too long.'

'Like I said, you can tell him yourself.'

'Fine.' Shanti filled his lungs and began to shout. 'Magnus! MAGNUS! I know where Collins is. I can lead you to him right now.'

The grip on his arms tightened.

'Pipe down, Shanti.' He screamed louder.

'MAGNUS! DO YOU HEAR ME? I KNOW WHERE HE IS. I'LL TAKE YOU THERE.'

212

The two men slammed Shanti back against the wall. A picture dropped to the floor shattering glass onto the floorboards and rug. Shanti felt the tip of a blade pierce the skin of his throat. He swallowed and the blade sank a little deeper.

'Now you shut up Mr. Ice Pick or I'm going to cut you a new smile.'

No choice.

There were heavy footsteps in the hallway and the study door burst open.

'What the fuck is going on in here?' Magnus wore only his dressing-gown, still wrapping it around himself, his sexual arousal obvious beneath it. He took in the scene. 'Who smashed this picture?'

The guards looked at each other.

'It's this one, Mr. Magnus. He's been misbehaving.'

'Who allowed him to do that, I wonder?' Neither guard replied.

'Did I hear you correctly, Shanti? Did you say you could take us to Collins's hideout?'

'Yes. I can take you straight there.'

'Why don't you just tell us where it is and we'll go?'

'I suppose I could do that but I've only been there once. I think there'd be a better chance of sending your men to the right place if I retraced my steps.'

'Like any stockman worth his wages, I know bullshit when I smell it. You're lying to me.'

'No. I'm not lying. If you want me to tell you the way, I will. But the Grand Bishop's best Parsons are on their way out there right now. If you want your men to beat them to it, I suggest you allow me to go along.'

'Fuck. Fuck it. You filthy fucking...how do they know where he is?'

Shanti shrugged. He noticed the way Magnus's body shook. It wasn't just anger. Even his head seemed to wobble.

'I told them.'

'I don't believe I'm hearing this. You told the Grand Bishop where that skinny lunatic is hiding with his skinny lunatic pals?'

'I had no choice.'

'Death's going to be too good for your wife and daughters, Shanti. Far too good.'

'If I hadn't told them, I wouldn't be here giving you the same information, Mr. Magnus. I haven't told them the best route. There's a chance they'll get a little lost along the way. I've bought you some time and you're standing here wasting it. Do you want Collins for yourself or not?'

'No one talks to me that way, Shanti.'

'If I lead your men to the hideout successfully and you take Collins, I want your guarantee that you won't harm my family.'

Magnus snorted.

'Harm? You haven't got a fucking clue.'

'I'm serious. If you want to stay in control of the town, time's running out. Promise me you won't hurt them.'

'I believe my invitation to you was quite specific, Shanti. You're late. Very late. And I don't like to be disrespected.'

'What have you done to them?'

'Oh, I haven't had a chance to get started. Not properly. Not yet.'

Shanti thought about the crying and the erection that still beat beneath Magnus's robe.

'Let me see them.'

'No. I'll tell you this much, though. Your wife is a natural convert to cuckoldry. There's nothing she won't do for her

family. You should be very proud.'

'My girls. What about my girls?'

'Ah. Now they're a very different story of course. A real revelation to me. I've never had the pleasure of twins before, though I've seen plenty their age. And much younger. Let's just say that I've been very gently introducing them to the duties of womanhood.'

Nausea and rage rose up inside Shanti. He felt what little control he had slipping away.

'Please. Let me see them.'

'No. But I'll tell you what. If you and my men come back with John Collins before the Parsons get him, I give you my word I won't touch any of your family again. But you must both return or I'll do whatever I want with them. And it won't take days or weeks, it'll be years. Pleasure for me and whatever they can salvage from it. Understand, Shanti? You bring him back. You bring John Collins back to me alive. Then and only then will your family be safe.' His erection had subsided. He adjusted the dressing-gown around his shoulders and smoothed it over his paunch. 'I have to say, I'm a little disappointed to have been interrupted but,' he spread his palms wide, 'business before pleasure, eh? That's what sorts the winners from the losers in this world.'

Magnus walked to the study door and shouted downstairs.

'Bruno! Take everyone you can spare and get down to the Derelict Quarter. Shanti here is going to take you to see our old friend. Make

214

sure they both come back alive. If you run into the Parsons out there,' he considered for a moment, 'take them down. All of them.'

He turned back into the study.

'I believe you mentioned something about running out of time, Shanti.'

And then Shanti was sprinting again. Behind him came Magnus's burly guards, black coat-tails snapping at their heels.

***

After what felt like far too long but what could only have been a few seconds, Parson James Jessup ran into the fray. His brothers were struggling to recover from the shock of the attack. They had no cohesion or formation. They needed a centre.

'On me!' he shouted.

The other Parsons seemed to awaken at his call and realise the extent of their jeopardy. They fell towards him; their ranks thickened and gained strength. Their training surfaced and they timed their blows as a unit. The Godless attackers – Parson James Jessup could only assume that these were Collins's followers and that Collins was among them – pursued them.

The onslaught did not falter but it slowed. The Parsons ceased to fall as often but Parson James Jessup gauged that they had already lost thirty men. That left seventy against the thirty in opposition. It should still have been easy odds but it was not. He moved to the edge of their circle and took the place of a fallen comrade. It was not obvious what had brought the man down. No dark patch on his robes suggested a wound beneath them. No marks on his head or face showed the landing of a blow. But Parson James Jessup had seen men fall many times and he was certain his brother was dead. Most certain.

He found himself facing the Godless tramp that had felled him.

He swung his club in anger, a curve that was swift and heavy. It would stave in the woman's head when it made contact. But when the bone reached its target, the woman was no longer in its path. He couldn't see how she had managed to move. Thinking he'd misjudged the distance, he swung back in the natural opposite direction calculating for his mistake. This time he saw that she moved not when she saw the blow coming but somehow just before, almost at the moment he thought of it. Any moment now her attack would come and he was wasting energy on roundhouse swings that made him look like a brawler in Dino's at the end of a Saturday night.

He feinted. She dodged, and, knowing exactly where she would go, he used the club in a thrusting motion. It made contact with her solar plexus – exactly as he'd planned. She was already moving away from the blow, though, and it connected without the weight he'd hoped. As he recovered his balance she was back in his face again and he could see the calm exultation in her expression. The certainty of purpose and utter absence of fear. And this, more than any speed she'd shown, was what shook his belief.

Behind him he heard the cries of shock and frustration as the other Parsons faced the same agility, the same self-assuredness and he knew that they would die.

All of them. Swiftly.

Without mercy.

And yet, without malice.

It made him think of the Chosen.

Twenty-three

He had to slow down so that Magnus's men could keep up with him.

The stamping of dozens of pairs of boots echoed off the cracked pavements of Abyrne's streets as the black-coated army passed through. All the men loped, beefy and bulky. Shanti ran at the front of them like a whippet before a pack of wolves. Townsfolk shrank into doorways, peeped from windows and pressed themselves back against damp brick walls as the mobsters ran by. Magnus's men, upholding their pride, pretended the running wasn't affecting them as they clattered through the streets, but when they reached the fringe of the Derelict Quarter they let their faces show the pain. None of them was as fit as Shanti. Not by miles.

In the shattered, abandoned districts of the Derelict Quarter, while Shanti still ran lightly over every obstacle, the others stumbled and lumbered.

'...Wait,' shouted Bruno. 'Stop...a moment...damn you.' Shanti glanced over his shoulder and slowed a little.

'What is it?'

'Take a look...we're exhausted.'

Behind Bruno the Magnus contingent, allegedly among his best men, were strung out like a caravan of refugees. Even Shanti could see they were easy prey.

He stopped and Bruno caught up to him. The big man couldn't regain his breath. By ones and twos the others joined them. It took several minutes for the last man, shorter and fatter than all the others, to arrive. All around him the Meat Baron's men sat or lay down on the churned debris.

'Let's go,' said Shanti.

There were ill-tempered shouts of protest.

'Let them rest,' said Bruno.

'For how long?'

'As long as it takes for them to be ready for a scrap. We can't lead them into battle in this state.'

'No. They've rested enough. We have to move now.'

'Who the fuck put him in charge?' someone shouted.

'Here,' said the last man in, still struggling to breathe. 'Let's tie his ankles together so he can't run. Use my tie.'

'Let's just go back and say we couldn't find anything. Magnus'll off this one and his family and it'll be business as usual.'

The grumbling increased in volume.

'Shut up, all of you,' shouted Bruno. 'You've got five more minutes to rest and then we move on. Save your breath.'

Shanti was aghast.

'Five minutes? It's too long.'

'It's what I'm giving them.'

'Bruno, I'm begging you. You know what he's doing to my family. To my girls. Please.'

Bruno sat down on a tilted slab of concrete and ran his hands through the oily mess of his hair.

'You brought all this on yourself, you know, Shanti. Acting weird with the Chosen, this running crap you do every day, not eating the flesh. Torrance told me all about you. If it wasn't for your usefulness in the plant, your status would have been revoked a long time ago.' Bruno rummaged in his coat pockets and brought out tobacco and papers. He proceeded to roll a ragged cigarette. 'I'll tell you something about my boss, Shanti. When he gets an idea into his head, he can't get it out until he's made it happen. The moment he thought about taking your family, they died. Right in that instant. He's not going to keep any promise he's made to you. He's going to use you, use your wife and daughters, and then he'll kill you. All of you.' He lit the cigarette and took a long pull. It seemed to calm his breathing instantly but Shanti noticed that his fingers trembled as he smoked.

'I'll tell you something else. I'm going to make sure he sees his plan through to the end. I can't wait to see you gone. You don't belong in this town.'

Shanti turned away and looked out into the Derelict Quarter. Ruination stretched to the horizon. Perhaps it extended far beyond. He was one man against many and he was leading his worst enemies to the hideout of Abyrne's saviour. Not only was John Collins his ally, he had also become a friend. They believed in the same things, held the same dreams dear. Was he really going to sacrifice the man to save his children from Magnus? How many more children, hundreds of thousands more, had been killed already in the pursuit of meat and the assuaging of the town's deep hunger? Collins's death would be a far worse sacrifice to make than his daughters'. Collins's end would signal an end to hope. Shanti knew it, could not deny it. But things were in motion now that he could not stop. Without his guidance, Bruno might be too slow. He might not even find Collins. It was his girls who needed him.

When he skipped away from Bruno, leapt a few chunks of broken concrete and tore off back towards the town, none of the men stood up to chase him.

'Fuck it,' said Bruno.

'What do we do?' asked the fat straggler. Bruno checked his watch.

'We finish our break and then we go find Collins.'

'What about him?'

Shanti was already a small figure against the backdrop of rubble.

'There's more people at the mansion. Enough to take care of him.'

'Magnus is going to be raging.'

'True. But he'll be even worse if we don't finish what we came out here to do.' Bruno stood up with a grunt. 'Come on you lot, on your feet. Let's get this job done.'

'How will we know where to find Collins now?'

'I've got a feeling about where he is. Just a hunch really, but I think there's a good chance he'll be there. At the back of the arena, where they train the fighting bulls, there's a breach in the wall that leads to a lot more caverns and tunnels. If I'm right and we keep heading out this way, the way Shanti's been leading us, I think we'll find the place where those tunnels come out. If we don't, we'll go to the bullring and do it the other way round. Can't go wrong.'

He slapped the shorter man on the shoulder and led them all deeper into the ruins.

***

Magnus grunted and sweated and shook in his frustrated desire for them. He didn't need to use force with these little ones. That was too easy. With children it was always words that were his weapons. He sat on the wooden coffer at the end of his huge bed, his dressing-gown open to reveal his hairy, plump gut and the tumescence below it.

By the window, as far from the bed as they could get, Hema and Harsha held onto each other, their small fingers clenched painfully over each other's skin. The first part of his game had gone well. Cajoling and chastising them, he had persuaded them to remove their dresses and under-things. It had taken only a few minutes. Now his captives trembled in misery like sallow, cornered prey.

'Good little girls *love* lollies. Are you good little girls?' Confused, they neither nodded nor shook their heads.

Perhaps their tears flowed a little more freely, and the clear mucus from their snivelling noses. Lubricant!

How he ached for the game to progress.

'Lovely, lolly-loving, luscious little girls. My lolly-licking lovelies. Doesn't it look tasty?'

This time both girls shook their heads.

Magnus roared out delighted laughter.

'Well, now,' he said. 'You must both be bad girls in that case.' He paused to light a cheroot. There was plenty of time.

'And you know what happens to bad girls in this house, don't you?'

They didn't move. They didn't want to know.

They were right not to. He loved each moment of their terror.

The cheroot twitched between his fingers but he didn't even notice any more. His head vibrated as though he was repeatedly shaking it – 'no' – in the tiniest movements.

Their little solar plexuses quivered as they tried not to let out their sobs. Their lips were sucked in and out by their hitched breathing.

'In this house,' he said. 'I eat bad girls. I chop them up while they're still begging me to stop and then I eat them. Raw. By the handful.' He made the motions of chopping and picking up and chewing and wiping his mouth on his sleeve.

'Mmm. Delicious. Lovely, luscious, tender little girls. My . . . FAVOURITE!'

At his shout they started back against the glass of the window. It rattled in its old frame. And then the sobs came out loud and long and he pressed home the advantage.

'SHUT UP THE PAIR OF YOU. Shut your nasty little gobs or I'll cut you up and eat you right now.'

They clasped their hands over each other's mouths to stifle the sobs.

'Now then, who wants a lolly?'

Like wan Siamese twins they approached him. Like calves.

He licked his lips.

***

Luck, or rather misfortune, brought them to the opening Shanti had told them about. Reluctantly, they'd pressed on past the tower blocks and out further than any of them had been before. In the distance they saw the giant outline of structures built into the air. All of them, even Bruno, were belittled by the vastness of the ruination. They could see no end to it. By comparison the town behind them seemed small.

They reached a place where the rubble sloped down away from them. Fanning out along the ridge, they picked careful steps downward. Several of the men lost their footing and slid despite the extra care. One of them fell a lot further than the rest.

Someone shouted, 'Shit!'

Bruno looked in the man's direction.

'What is it?'

'Andrews has disappeared.'

Bruno clambered across the slope towards him. The hysterical outburst annoyed him. It was a sign the men were on edge. Not thinking right.

'He hasn't disappeared, you idiot. He's probably fallen down.' Bruno neared the spot. 'Where was he?'

The man pointed.

'Just over there. He -'

At that moment Bruno found the place. The rubble was so uniform it hid the contours from casual glances. Even scanning the ground, he'd missed it. And there it was: a dirty great hole in the slope the size of five doorways. He missed his footing and slid towards it. A piece of rusted steel reinforcement saved him from following Andrews down. He grasped it and pulled himself to a safer position.

'Take me as your marker,' he shouted. 'And get to the bottom of the slope. There's a way in right here.'

Once the men were moving he called out to Andrews several times. Andrews didn't answer. Losing a man before the action began was bad but he was glad that they weren't going to have to go in via the bullring. This way would lead them straight to their objective.

At the bottom of the slope he joined his men; all of them dustier than ever and many with torn coats and trouser legs. The landscape did not yield. Before them was the entrance to the tunnels. Steps led down into darkness but they'd come prepared. Several of the men carried gas lanterns, items soon to be a thing of the past.

He split his men into seven groups of ten, each with three lanterns. Every man let a short-bladed machete slip down from inside his sleeve. Thongs kept the knives attached to their wrists in case a handle slipped in a sweaty palm. Each knife was a foot in length and ended flat, as though cleanly snapped. This was the Meat Baron's enforcers' weapon, a blade for slashing, cutting and chopping.

Two or three groups at a time, they descended into the darkness.

The first thing they found was Andrews. His eyes were still open but it was no wonder he hadn't called back. He'd fallen headlong and landed on his neck. The impact had snapped it and he lay like a discarded toy, legs and arms at ridiculous angles.

'Straighten him up, will you?'

Bruno said a few words over Andrews and they all continued downward.

The spaces below the earth were enormous. The bullring was nothing by comparison. Light from their lanterns didn't penetrate to the highest ceilings. Then they'd find themselves in long tunnels with the tubed ceilings only a few feet overhead. Similar tunnels with shiny metal steps led them down at steep angles further into the ground.

Bruno sensed panic in some of them. He could smell their sweat and its soured edge of fear. Without looking, he could sense the tightness in the tendons of their machete-holding wrists. Down here in the bowels of an unknown part of Abyrne, a blade was all they had for comfort and for strength. He knew because his own tendons were just as taut.

The air was stale but not as still as it should have been. Someone had been down there before them or was still there. The air was stirred up somehow – there was dust in it. What should have been undisturbed was not.

On descending to the third level, with some of the men beginning to reach their limit, Bruno began to see signs of habitation; blankets arranged into seats and bedding; symbols drawn on to walls in charcoal; footsteps in the dust. He wanted to give the men more orders now that they were there. At least give them encouragement, tell them to keep their nerve just a little longer because they almost had their man. He dared not raise his voice to speak though – the less they did to give away their approach the better.

How long had Collins and his people lived down here? What had they eaten and how had they survived? There was no sign of anything other than their drawings and makeshift cots.

In the whole place they found only one gas lantern. It was in a dead-ended room where many blankets had been arranged as seats in rows. At the far end there was a space and then room for a single floor-level seat. A preacher and his followers. This was where they had been. This really was Collins's hideout.

Bruno turned swiftly and exited the chapel-like room expecting an attack from behind them. Nothing came. There was no one else down there with them.

'We've missed them,' he said to the shadowed circle of faces around him. 'Time to go and look elsewhere.'

He felt the relief wash through the group. None of them wanted to fight down here, to risk dying in the dark. Like hunched crows, they followed him back to the light.

***

They stood in front of him, hesitating, their faces the purest misery.

His cock jutted, blunt and stupid. A silvery bead appeared at its tip and they took a step back.

'Sweet lolly juice, just for little girls.'

They were almost his now, at the beginning of a journey in which he'd be their guide and tormentor. They would become his favourite maids, these two. He could already tell he wanted to keep them around for a long time to come. Train them, educate them, twist them to his will.

Hema reached out her hand and he smiled, his heart missing a single blessed beat.

Outside there was noise. Footsteps running in the downstairs hall and then thumping on the stairs. He heard the shouts of men and a struggle. Someone fell down the stairs yelling. The yell was cut short. The struggle continued and the voices came nearer. He recognised the voice of one of his men and another voice that should not have been in the house.

'Fuck it all,' he said, standing up. The girls ran back to the window.

He wrapped his dressing-gown around himself as best he could and went to the door. He turned and pointed a fat finger at the girls.

'You two stay where you are or I'll suck out your eyeballs. Understand?'

They said nothing. They only stood and trembled. One of them was pissing herself. Whoever made him miss that little treat was going to pay a heavy price. He tore the door open and stepped out into the upstairs hallway.

'What the fuck is going on in this house? I want some fucking peace and -' He saw who was there. 'What are you doing back here, you freak?'

At the top of the stairs, Richard Shanti was struggling with two of Magnus's men. They couldn't control him. Instead of fighting them he was dragging them along the upstairs hallway. At the bottom of the stairs a third guard lay silent and unmoving.

Seeing the trouble his men were having restraining the intruder, Magnus strode along the hall to his study and slipped inside. He returned with something hanging from his right hand and walked towards the affray. Shanti was elbowing, kneeing, jumping and twisting. Despite his diminutive size next to the two guards, he'd broken one of their noses and was almost free. When he saw Magnus so close, a new frenzy of energy took him. He broke the grip of one guard and lunged. Magnus raised his right hand and brought it down once, hard. There was a dull crack and Shanti fell. The Guard let him drop onto his face.

Magnus stared at his men through bloodshot eyes. The no-brainer hung beside him.

'Why is it,' he said, 'that if I want a job done, I end up having to do it myself?' He didn't expect an answer and didn't get one. 'Lock Shanti up until I'm ready to see him.' He looked over the banister at the motionless guard. 'Who's that down there?'

'Juster, sir.'

'If he's dead, bury him. No, wait. Juster you say? I've always liked the look of that man's arse. Get Cleaver to cut me some rump steaks. Then you can bury him. And do a proper job this time or I'll have your bollocks.'

Magnus turned and walked back towards the bedroom. He was weary and the urge to finish with the girls had slipped from him.

'Sir?'

Magnus stopped.

'What the hell is it?'

'What if Juster's not dead? Should we fetch the doctor?' He turned back to them.

'If Juster let Shanti get the better of him, he's as good as dead. You get Cleaver to fix him for me one way or the other.'

In his room he sat down on the coffer, exhausted. There was no sign of the girls in front of the window. He stood and glanced around the room. Cursing himself for leaving the door open, he flicked up the bedcovers and checked under the bed. Nothing. Likewise in the cupboards. He rang for the maids and heard them sprint up the stairs. His unpredictability and savage moods had worsened, even he was aware of it, and now everyone around him was not merely quick to respond but strained as well. Two maids appeared at the door looking drawn and tense.

'My baby love-bitches have run off somewhere. They can't go very far. I want you girls to search the house top to bottom. Get everyone else to check the grounds. But keep all the outer doors locked. At worst, they'll end up back at home and we'll round them up there. I don't think they'll go far away from mummy and daddy.'

The maids entered the bedroom and proceeded to check under the bed and in the cupboards.

'Not in here, you stupid pair of twats. I've already checked. Now, I'm going to get some sleep and I don't want to be disturbed until I wake up or Bruno gets back with Collins. Go on, fuck off, the pair of you.'

He collapsed back into the bed and covered himself up. The door clicked shut and he was unconscious.

Twenty-four

He'd managed to suppress all emotions of panic on the journey out and then down into the tunnels. Returning was different, assailed by misgivings. Why wasn't Collins where he was supposed to be? That was what worried him most.

Returning empty-handed to Magnus was the other thing that concerned him. Over the past few weeks – ever since the encounter with Collins and the blackout he'd suffered at the emaciated man's hand – Magnus's behaviour had worsened. He'd always been a man that ruled by violence. Everyone knew it and that was how he kept Abyrne in such an efficient stranglehold. But since the incident with Collins, Magnus had turned nasty even by Bruno's standards. It had become hard to respect him.

It was obvious to everyone that Magnus was sick with the Shakes. Now was the time when a man like Collins really could wrest control from the ailing Meat Baron. If that happened, who knew what the future would hold for Bruno or the town?

Bruno had been Magnus's personal bodyguard and the leader of his army of guards and enforcers for seven years. Magnus trusted him and he trusted Magnus. He didn't always like the way his boss treated him, but at the end of each day he knew that he could not have been in a safer position – other than being Meat Baron himself.

Now, all that had changed. Magnus was sick enough and crazy enough to destroy any of his employees including his most trusted. When Bruno returned to the mansion without Collins and a man down for no good reason, Magnus was going to get very upset. For the first time in his career, Bruno was thinking about a change of allegiance. But to whom? The Welfare? He could never live that kind of life. He hated prayers and churches and rituals. He couldn't see himself abstaining from sex or anything else for the sake of a God he neither understood nor believed in. Who did that leave? The lunatic prophet, John Collins, with his half-starved crew of zealots?

There was nowhere else to go – except perhaps the grain bosses. Would they trust him, considering where he'd worked and the things he'd already done to keep power from their hands? He doubted it.

The blizzard of questions and fears assailed him as he led his men back across the Derelict Quarter. By now, most of them had fallen or stumbled badly enough to bruise or cut themselves on the uneven ground. They were tired from the running and let down by the unfulfilled adrenaline rush in the tunnels. If they were attacked now, he wasn't sure he could even rely on them to hold their ranks.

Before they reached the tower blocks he saw a flash of red. In the next step it was gone behind broken masonry. He crested a small rise and saw it again. Beyond it there was more red. It was the gowns of Parsons he was seeing. At first he thought it was an ambush as all the figures were lying down. Then he noticed the discarded or dropped femur clubs and knew it could not be that. Closing on them cautiously he saw that every cassock was no more than that – just the shell of a Parson. The uniforms had been removed and laid out on the ground. They'd been arranged, and carefully so.

What the hell is this?

His men saw the uniforms too and tensed.

Then they were among the red gowns of the Welfare, positioned with care and imagination to look as though they'd fallen in battle. Whose trickery was this? The Welfare, pretending to have been attacked by some other force? John

Collins leaving a message for him and his men?

For several minutes, Bruno believed it was some kind of a set up. He walked among the gowns and inspected them.

'What's going on, sir?'

Bruno held a gown in one hand and a femur club in the other.

'I don't know.'

If there'd been a battle, most of the clubs should have had fresh bloodstains on them. There was nothing. Had there even been a battle? Or was it simply that the Parsons had never landed a single blow? Bruno remembered how one starving peck of a man had bested the giant that was his boss and he knew to his core what was going on. This skirmish, if such it could be classed, had taken place long before they'd even stepped into the Derelict Quarter. Collins and his followers had hidden it from them until they were ready to let it be seen. That was why there'd been no one in the tunnels.

They were busy elsewhere.

'This is nothing more than a message,' he said. And to himself he added: *and a warning.* 'We've got to get back to the mansion. Right now.'

He dropped the relics of the skirmish and began to run. He hoped Collins and his people couldn't run like Richard Shanti.

The girls lay in total darkness, their small thin bodies pressed tight together. They dared not speak but instead whispered, little more than a silent breath, into each other's ears from time to time. As terrified as they were of the moment when they were discovered and the light blasted in to reveal them, they felt a sense of security in the cramped blackness.

In the past, there'd only ever been one of them enclosed like this when they played the dark game and it had always been a competition. Now, they faced the cramped confinement together, tighter than they'd ever been squeezed and staying brave for longer than ever before. If they wanted to win this time, they'd have to work as a team.

It was impossible in the darkness to tell how much time had passed. It seemed like hours but they knew it might only have been minutes since the shouting and wrenching of doors and the stomping, running footsteps of people searching for them. That had been the worst time, knowing that they might be exposed at any moment and listening, listening, listening for the faintest sign that their captors might be coming closer rather than getting further away.

And then there'd been a growling sound. At first they thought it was the hairy man coming back to get them but the growling sound stayed where it was, rising and falling rhythmically. Snoring. They could still hear it now. They whispered for a long time about whether they could creep out of their hiding place without being seen or caught. Back and forth went the barely-breathed discussion until they made up their minds. They had to wait. Only when they heard the snoring stop and footsteps walking away, only when the room was silent again would that be their moment.

They had agreed what would happen next. It was very simple. They would run out of the house and into the grounds where the trees and bushes would hide them. And every time they hid and people didn't find them, they would run to another bush and then another until they reached home. Home would be safe. And mama and papa would come home and love them again.

In utter blackness, they squeezed each other tight.

'Soon,' breathed Hema to Harsha.

'Soon,' replied her sister.

The cell in the mansion was far worse than the one the
Welfare had provided.

He awoke to pain in many parts of his body and the smell of shit and urine. He tried to sit up and smacked his forehead against hard wood. Stars spread across his darkened vision. His head was exploding. He lay back and felt with his hands. The cell was more like a coffin than a room. It was about two feet deep, seven feet long – so he was able to stretch to his full body length – and about three feet wide. Whatever he did, there would be no way to stand.

He imagined the pressure sores that would erupt on the bony areas of his body while he waited for Magnus to do him in. Perhaps Magnus was so incensed at all that he'd done that his end – removal from the box, at least – might come swiftly. In the next moment he was ashamed that his first thoughts were of himself and not of Hema and Harsha for whom he knew it was already too late.

He'd done all he could do for them. Perhaps with more time, with the chance to liaise with others, it might have been different but there was no point hoping to change the past. In the box, little more than an oubliette – and perhaps that was how Magnus had decided to dispose of him – he was alone with his memories and his fears. Desperation grew despite the impossibility of escape. If only he could get out, he might have the opportunity to prevent the damage to his girls from being too scarring. With fewer guards around the house and grounds perhaps he'd have one more opportunity to finish Magnus himself.

The thoughts would drive him crazy.

He wasn't prepared to give in to his mind yet. He was still alive, that meant there was still some kind of chance. At the very least perhaps he might see them again. Have the opportunity to say he loved them; to apologise and say goodbye. Such pitiful aspirations. How the town and everything in it had reduced him. How evil his life had been. No matter how he'd tried to absolve himself, no matter how he'd tried to stay pure, he had committed endless crimes and brought the very worst upon his family.

Again, he realised, such thoughts were deadly.

There was one good thing in the town. One good person that had wrought at least a little change – John Collins.

Prophet John. The man who had shown him miracles were possible, that there were other ways to live for those compassionate and loving enough to try. It was crazy, what John Collins had been teaching, but Shanti believed it. In fact, belief didn't fully define it; he knew *in his body* that it was true and possible. He knew it because he'd begun the same journey himself and it had not killed him. He had not eaten anything but light and air for many days and he was stronger and healthier than he'd ever been. He'd noticed in the mirror that, far from emaciating himself since he had stopped taking vegetables and rice, he had filled out. Not much, but enough to notice. His muscles were larger, his chest more expanded and able to hold more air. John Collins said that one day, when enough wisdom and love had been acquired, even the need to breathe would become a thing of the past. People would understand they were immortal, that they had always possessed the potential without realising it.

Of course, if Magnus knew that Shanti no longer needed to eat to stay alive, he might keep him in this stinking hole until he drove himself insane.

No.

He had to survive and to do that, he had to think right. He had to prepare.

First he checked out the painful places on his body. His nose was broken – he was fairly sure it shouldn't be as mobile as it was. A couple of his front teeth were loose. His ribs were sore on both sides and he remembered being kicked a lot when he regained consciousness only to black out again. His legs were fine but his hands and elbows were cut and bleeding where he'd made contact with the teeth of some of Magnus's men. There was a lump on the back of his head and that, more than any other injury, gave him cause for serious concern. It made his whole head hurt inside and out when he touched it. There was a swelling there and he didn't know what it was filled with. His fear was that Magnus's blow had cracked his skull and that his brain was exposed below the skin. If that was the case, he knew he could die at any moment. And if he didn't, and if he made it out of this box, he might not live beyond standing up.

Instinct told him that he should try to heal himself. Was it instinct or was it something else? He felt a small pressure in his gut, right in the very centre of himself. He knew what it meant. He would try to be ready.

Lying on his back in the stinking filth of Magnus's primitive cell, Shanti drew the light stored in his abdomen and sent it up to his skull. He prayed that it would fuse his broken cranium.

***

Bruno led his unfit brigade of guards up the long driveway praying, yes praying, that they were in time.

They rounded the final bend in the approach and he saw what he'd hoped not to. Ranged around the mansion in twos and threes were Collins's raggle-taggle followers. They were dressed in clothes that might have been worn for decades at a stretch. Torn, faded, in some cases patched, in others not. They were no better than vagabonds. Scruffy urchins that had escaped the town's attention for far too long. He would have laughed at them but for three things.

He was so winded he couldn't spare the breath. He had seen what they'd done to the Parsons.

And every man he'd left behind to guard the mansion had fallen.

As he came around that final curve in the driveway, the followers heard the stomping footsteps of nigh on seventy men in hobnailed boots and turned to face them. No matter what happened now, Bruno and his men were committed. There was no need for a command, every black-coat could see the enemy; a force they outnumbered more than two to one. Bruno let the machete drop into his right hand and raised it in the air.

With what breath they had left in their lungs, Magnus's men released their war cry and fell upon the acolytes of the Prophet.

***

When the growling stopped, they tensed and dug their fingers into each other's skin. They bit their lips against the fear. They heard grunts and felt movement. Heavy footsteps dragged past them. The footsteps stopped not very far away. In the background they could hear shouting; a crowd of men swearing and pushing each other. There was a sound like their mother opening a heavy drawer of cutlery in the kitchen and the uproar from far away became much louder.

Then they heard the voice, the terrifying voice that wheedled and cajoled and commanded. The voice of the man who wanted so much to hurt them. In the darkness, still safe, they didn't know what to do. Was it time to run? Would he hear or see them?

'What should we do?' asked Harsha as quietly as she could.

'Don't know.'

'Maybe we should just have a look.'

Harsha went to push the lid of their hiding place open and Hema grabbed her arm.

'It's okay,' said Harsha. 'We're only looking. We don't have to run yet.'

As silently as they could manage, they shifted around until they could both peep over the lip of their secret place.

They saw the hairy man, naked and yelling, with his back to them at the window. They looked at each other. Words weren't necessary now. This was their chance to escape. They crawled up and out as quietly as snakes but Harsha, believing Hema had hold of the coffer's lid, let it go. The lid slammed shut hard. The hairy man jumped and began to turn.

A look passed between them and they both remembered the courage of the brothers in the story their father had told them. Instead of running away, they ran at the hairy man. Ran at him as hard as they could, arms outstretched in front of them, palms spread wide.

***

Magnus woke with a start to the sound of boots stomping gravel and the cries of men in battle.

He grunted and tried to get out of bed. Even simple movements like this were getting harder and harder. Finally he hauled his bulk upright and slid his legs over the side of the bed. The noise from outside was furious. Bodies and blades fell against the spiked railings that surrounded the main building. Right below his own bedroom window he could hear men cursing and roaring as blows landed and pain blossomed.

There were shouts of frustration and failure.

He pushed himself upright and staggered. Reaching out a hand, he steadied himself against one of the bed's four posts until the dizziness receded enough for him to walk. His legs were weak and unsteady as he shuffled to the great window.

Outside, his men were lashing themselves against the enemy like the sea against the rocks. He felt a brief swell of pride over them. These were his best and they were fighting for Magnus and everything he stood for. The pride faded quickly as the reality of the situation became clearer.

His men were tired. Their lunges and attacks were no longer crisp and sharp. They moved heavily, the more effort they put in, the slower they seemed to move. Great, wide, sweeping arcs of machetes missed their targets by inches or feet. Punches didn't land or were ineffectual. Kicks were easily avoided. His guards outnumbered the opposition by more than double but already they were hitting the ground, felled by blows so swift they might have been imaginary but for the damage they inflicted.

And this enemy! They looked so thin and tattered they might have been beggars from the streets. But they didn't behave like pitiful vagrants. He had seen this kind of movement before and he knew what it meant. These were Collins's followers, his fighters. They were fast. They gave no quarter. As he watched, more of his men fell to their birdlike hands. The odds evened.

He had to do something. Struggling with the weight of it, Magnus pushed up the sash window. His men needed encouragement. They needed direction and he could see a way for them to land more telling hits if only he could speak to them. With the window fully open, he wedged it in position with a block of wood and leaned out.

'Bruno! Timing, man! It's all a matter of changing your rhythm.'

He saw that Bruno had heard him, but the man dared not look away from his opponent. He watched as Bruno backed out of range and then darted in with a light left jab. The man he was fighting took the bait and blocked but Bruno was already swinging his machete. Even with a head start and the ragged man off balance, the blade only caught his jaw and not his neck as Bruno had hoped. The machete opened the man's face to the mandible and there was a brief flash of white bone before the blood flowed.

Unheeding of the wound and turning immediately into the attack, Bruno's opponent hit back with strobing hands. Magnus wasn't sure he saw the blows connect until Bruno stumbled backwards, his mouth a crimson grimace.

'Don't stop!' shouted Magnus. 'Take the initiative!'

The man did not close on Bruno, letting him regain his composure instead. Bruno's pride was wounded worse than his face. He seemed not to notice that he'd been given a chance and he advanced as though upon a child he intended to whip. All around the gravelled driveway, men in long black coats were crumpling; their frustrated blades still clean.

'Fucking imbeciles,' Magnus muttered. He began to think ahead a little. What if they got into the house? How many men did he have left inside?

He heard a sound like a heavy wooden door slamming behind him and the patter of feet over carpet. He turned to face the intruders but never quite finished the manoeuvre. Instead he felt small hands pushing him back.

As he lost his balance, he heard giggles. Then he was spinning, falling.

Twenty-five

Collins wasn't used to fighting but it didn't make any difference. A kind of pulse thrummed between all of them and somehow their movements were coordinated. They fought as if they were a single being, each part communicating with every other. The pulse had a rhythm and, in most cases this rhythm moved them *out* of sync with those they faced. The result was the enemy got hurt but they didn't. It was like a dance. Only the bad dancers were struck.

He felt nothing for the enemy. No pity or respect. He knew none of his followers did either. The people that opposed them were a lower order of humanity. They'd have done better to step aside.

When Rory Magnus fell from a second floor window of the mansion, Collins caught the movement like a shimmer across one side of his body, peripheral vision of his very skin. He kept fighting but his black-coated opponents were suddenly distracted and moments later, all the fight went out of them. Their leader hung by impaled legs upon the spiked railings that surrounded the house; a means of protection that had turned against him. As Magnus's men fell back towards the house and the fighting stopped, Collins took in the scene.

Forty men lay dead or unconscious around the gravel driveway. None of them was his. There was only one sound now, signalling the fight was finished: Magnus screaming.

If he'd fallen a little further from the mansion, he'd have landed on his head and might have died instantly. As it was, he'd caught the rusted steel spikes of the fence just above his knees. About a foot below the points, a flat, horizontal brace had prevented him from sliding to the ground. He was a heavy man and the spikes had not simply pierced him. Because of his forward and downward momentum, the spikes had torn the flesh from mid-thigh to kneecap before penetrating through to the backs of his legs. Two spikes through each limb protruded redly upward from the wounds. Both patellae were dislocated onto his shins, the flesh of which was scraped to the bone. His full weight was suspended there, inverted.

Even as Collins watched, the pain and realisation of the damage was sinking into Magnus's diseased mind like volley after volley of falling arrows. He begged to be let down, his voice hardly recognisable as human any more. The blood was rushing to the fat man's head, worse with every forced-out scream, and Collins could see the veins standing out on his neck, his cheeks close to bursting with pressure.

Bruno moved towards his boss and a few other guards made motions to follow. Collins held up a hand and it was enough to stop them. Meanwhile, Magnus tried to free himself. All he could do was push down on the lower ends of the railings, hoping to force himself up and off their points. But the rusted poles were wet with his blood and his hands slipped again and again, dropping his weight more firmly onto the spikes each time. It was clear that he was too fat and weak to succeed but *You never know*, thought Collins, *people become capable of extraordinary feats when their survival is at stake.* They would see what Magnus was made of.

The man's great bulk shook now as he cried tears of frustration and agony, as he moaned and begged for help that wouldn't come.

Collins gestured to Staithe and Vigors.

'Take these men inside.'

His followers herded the exhausted guards in through the front doors.

'Wait,' said Collins to Bruno. 'Not you.'

Bruno turned back and Collins approached him.

'Take me to Shanti.'

***

The light hurt his eyes, forcing him to keep them closed. Magnus or his men had come for him and the ordeal, whatever was planned for him, was about to begin.

The hand that reached into the cell and pulled him up was full of warmth and strength and its touch was enough to assure him he was safe. The hand belonged to John Collins.

'Let's get you cleaned up. Can't have your daughters seeing their father in this condition.'

'You've found the twins. Are they...?'

'You can see for yourself as soon as we get this filth off you. Come on.'

Without power, the pressure washer was no worse than a hosepipe. With Collins holding the jet on him, Shanti stripped and washed himself with brisk, vigorous strokes.

'Put these on,' said Collins. 'They're not exactly you but they'll do for now.'

He handed Shanti the clothes and boots of a fallen guard. Knowing there was no choice, Shanti hardly hesitated before slipping into the clothes. With the black coat over it all and his beard and long hair, he looked exactly like one of Magnus's men.

'Did you find my wife?'

Shanti could see that there was more Collins wanted to say or at least that he wanted to say something other than the truth. In the end his words were plain:

'She died, Richard. I'm sorry.'

Shanti placed his right palm over his mouth, as if making some kind of judgement.

'Her body's still in the house," said Collins, his face saying more about the condition of Maya's remains than his words. "I can show you if you want but we'll have to be quick.'

Shanti looked up.

'No,' he said. 'That won't be necessary.'

Collins led him out of the basement and up to the ground floor. Hema and Harsha were waiting in Magnus's living room. When they saw him, they ran straight to him. He knelt and gathered them in, kissing their heads and stroking their hair. He couldn't find a way to ask them what Magnus had done. When he was able to speak he said, 'Did he hurt you?'

They shook their heads and his tears began afresh. Collins placed a hand on his shoulder.

'I'm sorry, Richard. We have to go. All of us. When the townsfolk realise there's no Meat Baron, they'll panic. They'll go and kill the Chosen themselves. There'll be chaos. The Parsons won't be able to stop them and there are far too many for us to deal with. If we're going to do this, it has to be now.'

Shanti nodded and stood up.

'We're all going on a long walk,' he said to the girls. 'Mr. Collins and I are going to go ahead because we're faster.' He gestured to the followers who had been sitting with the girls.

'You'll be safe with them until you catch us up. Do exactly as they say. Understand?'

'We want to come with you, Papa,' said Hema.

'I know, sweetheart. I'll be waiting for you. I promise.'

He leaned down, kissed them both again, then turned away. He couldn't let them see the heartbreak in his eyes. To regain them like this and then let go again; it was almost more than he could bear.

In the hall he said to Collins, 'Surely there's a truck left with some gas in it.'

Collins shook his head.

'They've used it all up. There may be some stashed somewhere but we'd be wasting time looking for it. If the townsfolk got here before we found it...well...'

He slit his throat with his index finger.

'You're right. Let's go now. Run with me.'

Together they sprinted for the main door. Shanti stopped when he saw Magnus, still trying to free himself from the railings that had impaled his legs. His weight had snapped him at the knees and now he hung not at an angle but straight down. He wept manic, disbelieving tears. Shanti walked over and stood beside him. He had worked in an environment of pain all his life and had a keen sense for it. He could feel the waves of suffering emanating from the hanging giant next to him. He looked down and caught the man's inverted eyes. Streaks of tears and blood ran from his face to his forehead and into his hair. The whites of his eyes were yellow and cracked with broken capillaries. There was insanity there.

'Have pity, Ice Pick. You're a man of compassion. I understand that now. Release me from the spikes, I beg you. Lay me down on the ground here to die quietly. Do the right thing, Mr. Shanti, please. Help me down.' The big man snivelled and shook, more tears coming from a place that he could not resist. 'Down, down, down,' he said. And then. 'Forgive me, Ice Pick. Please forgive me.'

Shanti looked into Magnus's mad eyes for a few seconds longer. Magnus saw the hesitation and hope sparked behind his staring pupils.

Shanti turned away.

He and Collins ran down the gravel driveway. Twenty followers fell into step behind them. The rest left the mansion at a fast walk to escort the twins. Inside, the remainder of Magnus's men and the maids were locked in the basement. Both Collins and Shanti knew they'd find a way to get out eventually but by then it wouldn't matter.

At the entrance to the mansion they turned right onto the main road out of Abyrne. When the sound of boots, some running, others walking on the cracked tarmac faded, the town seemed very still. But something ugly was rising up behind them and each of them knew it.

***

The Grand Bishop sat behind his desk and appraised the three Parsons standing on the other side of it. They seemed no different than three schoolboys in a headmaster's study. There was apprehension. And something else.

Fear.

Not fear of a caning. Not fear of losing their jobs. Not even, and it would have been a most appropriate emotion at that moment, the fear of God. He knew, therefore, that it wasn't merely the breaking of the news to him that had them so stirred up.

Parson Atwell had led their scouting mission and the Grand Bishop addressed his questions to him.

'What did you find?'

'Nothing, Your Grace.'

'Nothing?'

'Not exactly nothing but certainly no enforcement party. What we found were their gowns and their weapons. That's all.'

'But where Atwell? In what condition?'

'Forgive me, your grace, I still don't understand it myself. We found their garments littered as though they'd fallen in battle but there were no bodies. Not one.'

'What do you think happened?'

'They may have been overcome and taken prisoner, their gowns arranged over the ground as...some kind of message. Or they were thoroughly bested and their bodies taken away – again with the clothing left as a sign.'

'A hundred of our best Parsons captured or killed by thirty tunnel-dwelling starvelings? I don't believe it.'

He'd meant the outburst as a challenge, to get Atwell to speak up. It had the opposite effect. Atwell looked down, clamping back an angry response. Nor would the other two Parsons meet the Grand Bishop's eyes. He softened his tone.

'All right, Atwell. I wasn't there and I didn't see it for myself. You can imagine how it must sound to my ears, though.'

Some of the tension went out of Atwell's jaw.

'Of course, Your Grace.'

'I want your assessment. What do you think happened out there?'

Atwell hesitated, glanced at his two companions and then appeared to realise it was no use looking for answers there. He faced the Grand Bishop.

'I think they're dead. All of them. I believe Collins and his followers are far stronger than we've given them credit for. I also think they plan to take over the town.'

'Do you?' said the Grand Bishop. 'Do you really?'

He was angry but not with his scouts. In his heart he believed exactly the same thing. How could he have let all this happen right under his nose?

'Where in God's name did they acquire this strength?'

'I can't answer that, Your Grace.'

'I know, Atwell. I'm sorry. Just thinking out loud. What else have you discovered?'

'We're fairly sure Magnus was tipped off about Collins's whereabouts because we watched seventy of his men returning from the tunnels. They were tired but looked unhurt. I don't think they found him.'

'Unless he sent a hundred and seventy men and only seventy returned.'

'That wasn't how it looked, Your Grace.'

'I know, I know. Dear Father.'

The Grand Bishop sat back and closed his eyes for a moment. It was difficult to think.

'Your Grace?'

He opened his eyes.

'You can go now, Atwell.'

'No, Your Grace. I...haven't finished.'

'What else, then?'

'It's only a rumour – we haven't had the time or the manpower to go and check for ourselves yet – but it seems that Magnus's men did meet Collins in combat and also suffered defeat. Magnus himself was seriously wounded. The townsfolk know something is wrong. Word passes quickly. It's only a matter of time before they begin to demand order. Already people are clearing out the butchers' shops in expectation of a shortage of meat. When the butchers run out, the townsfolk will go up to MMP in numbers too great to control. If we're going to prevent that, we need to act now and put a curfew in place.'

'Yes. See to it immediately.'

'There was just one other matter, Your Grace.'

The Grand Bishop no longer tried to maintain his stature and sighed openly.

'Go on.'

'Doctor Fellows reports that Parson Mary Simonson is no longer in the convalescent room. He thinks she's been gone some time.'

'Not there? But she's far too sick to go anywhere.'

'Apparently not, Your Grace.'

'All right. Thank you, Atwell.'

The Grand Bishop waved a hand at them. They bowed and retreated.

When they were gone he stood and went to a slim closet where he kept his gowns. Hanging beside them was a heavy femur club, jaundice yellow and long untouched. He unhooked it and felt the weight in his right hand. Long-dormant aggression rose in him at the touch of cool bone in his palm. Stepping back, he swung it left and right until some of the strikes he had been so adept at returned to him. He'd never expected to need it again.

Twenty-six

Magnus was thankful for Bruno. There was a man he'd picked for the right reasons. There was a man that was loyal. When they'd broken out of the cells, Bruno was the first there. He directed four of the others as they freed Magnus from the railings.

Magnus didn't like to remember it. After so long hanging there, the spikes were almost part of his legs. It had taken three of them to hold his weight and an extra man to wrench free each leg. The pain was different, worse: his wounding in slow, jerky reverse. He'd vomited and then, mercy of mercies, passed out.

Now he was on his bed, legs washed and bandaged by Doctor Fellows – another good man worth every illegally-supplied bullock. Fellows said that he was a strong man and there was a chance he would make it. A chance. That was all Magnus wanted. That was all he'd ever needed to make things work for him. Magnus could do with slim chances what others could not. Most of the men Magnus knew didn't even know a chance when they saw it.

He might heal.

He might not lose his lower legs. He might walk again.

And if he could do all that, there was no reason he couldn't carry on running the town by controlling every single cut of meat that would ever be fried.

But his stomach was a vice of tension as he tried to ward off the pain that owned everything below it. The level of the pain varied from intolerable to insane-making. He rose and fell with it. The thing that surprised him most was how it had cleared his mind of all peripheral concerns. He was thinking more clearly than he had for months.

His plan was a simple one. Bruno would take every surviving guard in Magnus's employ and go immediately to MMP. There they would join up with all the stockmen and workers from the plant. They'd number at least three hundred men. That made the odds against Collins and Shanti ten to one. Not even Collins was good enough to survive those kinds of numbers. Finally, through the simple violence and force that had always ruled the town, Magnus would regain control. But that wasn't the end of the plan. With the crazies eliminated, Magnus would take all his men and storm the Central Cathedral. They would capture the Grand Bishop first, as an insurance policy and to weaken the will of the Parsons. Then there would be a pogrom in which Magnus planned to end religious influence in the town overnight. They would burn every Book of Giving and every Gut Psalter in Abyrne and atop the conflagration cook the bodies of every Welfare worker. Perhaps they'd eat them too. It would have the desired effect on the minds of the townsfolk. In fact, yes, that was what he'd do: he'd eat the Grand Bishop's roasted heart in front of every person in the town. They'd never forget the image of his flame-illuminated face, feasting on the core of his enemy.

Bruno had already left. The plan was in effect. Only time lay between Magnus and the new future of Abyrne. Only waiting and pain. He'd survived the worst of that already at the hands of Shanti's demonic twin bitches. Those girls and their father would live a lifetime of pain before he let them die. He'd see to it personally. He knew how much their suffering would aid his recovery.

He looked down at his legs. Already the bandages were soaked through with fresh leakage. It was spreading gradually out onto the white sheets. He had lost a lot of blood and though Magnus wasn't short of anger to fuel the ensuing weeks and months of convalescence, Doctor Fellows had expressed concern over the blood loss. 'If anything kills you now,' he'd said, 'it'll be the life blood you lose and how quickly your body replenishes it. Because you were inverted, the wound did not bleed as much as it might have. You're fortunate to be alive.'

Fortunate wasn't a word Magnus would have used to describe his situation. But he could accept the benefits of the second chance Bruno and Fellows had given him.

A symphony of agonies swelled upwards from his legs and he closed his eyes against this new tide. This was how it had been ever since they'd lain him down. Something to do with the blood trying to flow in places where it could not, the doctor had said. Magnus clamped his eyes tight but couldn't prevent tears escaping. His yellow teeth showed through the fur of his beard as he grimaced. The pain was so loud he didn't hear the door open.

When he opened his eyes, he was looking at the Grand Bishop. Behind him stood the full complement of his housemaids, ten of them. Magnus was too shocked to speak. The Grand Bishop approached, the femur club held casually at his right side. From time to time it twitched to the clenching of his fist.

'I'll make a religious man of you yet, Rory.'

The Grand Bishop smoothed his gown from his buttocks and sat down on the edge of the bed. The movement made Magnus cry out through his clenched teeth.

'Your domestic staff have been telling me of your mistreatment of them. It's more than just heavy-handedness, apparently. They say you wilfully and knowingly force them into all manner of degradations. Bestialities, one might even say.' The Grand Bishop raised the femur club and brought the head of it to rest in his left palm. He tapped it there a few times very gently. He leaned very close to Magnus. So close

Magnus could smell the rot on his breath.

'We have laws against that sort of thing in this town you know.'

'When have you ever adhered to a single law?' said Magnus through his teeth.

'You'd be surprised just how pure a man I've been all these years.'

The Grand Bishop moved the head of the femur club a little closer to Magnus's knee. Magnus caught the motion and tensed. Even that caused the oceans of pain to rise up. His breaths shortened against the threat.

'Seeing as you've ruled this house without a thought for law or decency, I'm going to allow it to rule you in exactly the same way. I will accompany you to your basement where your female staff will be free to make use of you in any way they see fit. And I mean *any* way. I will be there purely to offer the succour of our God and to accept your conversion before the end of your life.'

The Grand Bishop tapped Magnus's shin with the tip of his club. Magnus screamed.

'I must say, Rory, I'm rather looking forward to it.'

The maids approached and the Grand Bishop moved out of their way. Magnus saw the looks on their faces. There was still fear there but they were rapidly overcoming it. When it flipped into anger, he would be lost.

'Please go ahead, ladies,' said the Grand Bishop.

Looks passed between the maids and they stepped forward. Hands reached out and caught Magnus by his hair and beard. They yanked and he screamed again. More hands took hold. They pulled him to the edge of the bed. As one, they hauled him off. His torn legs landed heavily and the screaming reached a new pitch. Magnus tried to make himself understood but no words would form through his agony. In this way, they dragged him along the upper hall, through his study and bumped him down the stairs. Each of the women grabbed tools from the walls and drawers.

They jostled to be the first.

She'd have slept badly anywhere in her condition but the wind at the top of the wooden observation tower, had troubled her all night. Cold and insistent it had whined through the gaps in the tower's planks and chilled her back no matter which way she lay. She was grateful for dawn's grey arrival; staying awake would be less of an effort than trying to sleep.

The pain and unsteadiness in every part of her body were constant companions now and she decided it would be safer to stay up in the tower than to try and come down. It had been dangerous enough climbing up there. The towers weren't used or maintained much any more and some of the rungs were missing on the access ladder. She'd risked it because she realised there was no way she could get close to any of the barns where the Chosen slept.

When they sensed her approach, a rigid tension rippled through the herds. It passed from one field to another and through every barn until it was quite clear they all knew she was there. Ten thousand of them setting their minds against her. Perhaps they sensed her sickness and would not tolerate it. She believed that for a while. In time, though, the reality settled over her making her original assumption seem very foolish.

It was simple. They could smell the flesh of their own upon her gowns and probably from her very skin. They knew that she was one who ate them, one for whom they died. Why would they want her near? Why should they let her shelter with them?

There wasn't long to wait now and she knew it. She had begun to look at things differently in these last few days. There had been time to think, time to be most terribly afraid of what lay beyond her physical end. She was separated from a God who did not speak to her. She was therefore cut off from every other Parson, even the Grand Bishop – this was not something that could be discussed with any of them. She was the natural enemy of Magnus and every MMP worker because she had religious power over them. She was the enemy of the townsfolk because she was an enforcer of the Welfare's protection.

Surely now, as she finished her life, she could at least be honest with herself.

When the light was strong enough to see by, she stood and looked over the slatted wooden wall of the tower. Down in the fields a thin mist lay between the hedges. Above it rose the well-defined edge of every field and the walls of the barns. In every field around her, the Chosen began to leave the barns. They walked with a crippled gait, rolling a little to each side. Once outside they stretched and yawned. In every field the Chosen stood next to each other, touching. Some leaned their heads together. Some used the stumps of their fingers to rub at the necks and backs of others. This was the kind of contact she had never known.

But she did not envy them.

Here were creatures that spent their short lives herded and controlled by the stockmen. Naked and downtrodden they lived every day of every season outside or in a barn. They were mutilated from birth to suit the townsfolk's purposes, to suit the laws in the Book of Giving and the Gut Psalter. Finally, they were systematically unmade to feed the hungry mouths of Abyrne. And many mouths there were. For generations it had been so.

Silent in her tower, she watched them as the sun came over the horizon, watched the way they faced it – every single one of them – and seemed to absorb its light. Minutes later, before the stockmen arrived, they broke into random groups or re-entered the barns, behaving once more like animals.

The Parson lay down again when the stockmen came. She didn't want to be seen or challenged. She lay down on the damp, slowly decaying boards and wept.

For she knew her truth was no truth at all. No God would ever answer her calls.

***

The loss of a hundred Parsons was in part to blame but even with the extra muscle they'd have lent, it might not have been enough. The townsfolk were fractious and anxious. They'd been shocked by the blasts at the gas facility. The realisation that there was no more power in the town – not even for the wealthiest areas – had hit hard. Rumour spread from house to house about the struggle for supremacy between their Meat Baron and the Welfare.

Other stories made the rounds. Prophet John had a band of warriors and planned to starve the town into converting to his insane ways. The supplies of the Chosen were dwindling. Prophet John had friends at MMP who had already begun to dump meat by the truckload and bring on a famine. Other tales told of a mass slaughter that had begun; to reduce the Chosen and push the prices of meat up further. Abyrne would then be split between the rich and the hungry. Most of the townsfolk had suffered a little hunger from time to time; a week or two in a year when meat was in short supply. And it was true, a few people did live at the edge of starvation but there'd never been a threat like this hanging over Abyrne. The Chosen existed in huge numbers – God's sacrifice for his people to live upon. If the numbers of the Chosen were reduced too greatly the whole town might face a famine.

The grain bosses heard the rumours too. They had their own spies and the stories they'd heard were closer to the truth. They couldn't let the slaughter take place if they were to continue to supply grain in previous quantities. They didn't care what occurred in Abyrne as long as the town survived. It was the grain bosses' men, more organised than the average dwellers in Abyrne, who led the townsfolk in a column to Magnus's mansion. Their demands were simple: No culling of the Chosen. No discarding of valuable, usable meat. A guarantee that Prophet John would be brought to task and executed.

It said much about the balance of power that they went to Magnus and not to the Grand Bishop.

The delegation started out as a few hundred of the more outspoken and courageous townsfolk. As they marched through the streets of Abyrne, their numbers swelled. People stepped out of their houses to watch them pass and, when they learned where they were going, soon decided to join them. By the time the front of the column reached the road out of the centre of Abyrne there were thousands of people in it.

When they found the mansion empty but for the stringy remains of Rory Magnus, they wrecked it. A couple of youths set fire to the curtains in the drawing room and the big old house began to smoulder. The defilers ran out and watched the flames take hold. When the house began to collapse in on itself, releasing huge upward gusts of sparks and flame, they took that fire into themselves and turned away.

They marched out to the road and, jeering and chanting, turned away from the town. The grain bosses and their workers were lost in a mass of townsfolk they could no longer control. The column flowed out of the mansion's grounds and towards Magnus Meat Processing.

***

Parfitt decided to smoke his cigarette outside. The atmosphere in the dairy was nasty now, worse than the sense of doom in the slaughterhouse. Each cow that came for manual milking struggled and ended up being not only restrained but beaten too. The new dairy boss made no effort to control the violence. It made Parfitt sick.

The greyness of the morning had never really lifted and though it was brighter now, the clouds hung like a low ceiling, pressing down on everything, suffocating it all. He walked away from the dairy block so he wouldn't have to listen to the thrashing of bodies and the curses of his co-workers. He walked to the fence line to look out at the road and across the fields to the wasteland beyond.

If he hadn't picked that moment, he realised, he wouldn't have been one of the first to see Shanti and Prophet John arrive with their tiny entourage. They ran with a very particular kind of intention, focussed and purposeful steps bringing them swiftly towards the gate. His only thought at that moment was that they must have come here knowing they would die, a misguided suicide squad whose deaths would change nothing. He felt nauseous despair. He feared for them.

Across the space between the front gate and the nearest buildings of the plant came Torrance with a crowd of stockmen and dozens of Magnus's black-coats. Dull grey reflected off every blade, chain and meat hook. Fearing he'd be seen, that he'd be expected to lend a hand, Parfitt backed away along the fence line and crossed to the rear corner of the dairy from where he could watch unseen.

There seemed to be some words exchanged between the mismatched factions; Shanti and Collins speaking for their group, Torrance for the superior number. Collins's and Shanti's people did not enter the main gate. None of the stockmen stepped outside it. Torrance's faction became by degrees more frustrated and belligerent. They began to taunt their opponents. Soon every hand with a weapon in it was raised and shaking as the guards and stockmen jeered. Parfitt could even see some of them laughing. If he'd been with them, he'd have been laughing too. The band of skinny, ragged tramps standing outside the gate had no more chance than the Chosen.

As he had the thought, Torrance took the fight to the Prophet. He released a group of thirty or more stockmen and they charged through the gate. Parfitt didn't believe what he saw next, didn't even understand it. Faster than he could follow, the stockmen fell. Blades swung and whirled but made no contact. Instead of the tramps being hacked up, the stockmen were cut down by blows Parfitt wasn't convinced he'd even seen. Machetes and boning knives clattered onto the road, dropped by dead or unconscious men – Parfitt couldn't tell which from this distance.

The jeering inside the perimeter of the plant died away to silence.

At the same time Parfitt saw a smaller group approaching the Prophet's band from further down the road. They were running. Two of them, a little further back than the rest, were giving very similar-looking little girls a piggyback. An extra ten bodies and two children, thought Parfitt. It still wasn't enough. They'd tire and the numbers would be too great for them.

News of the arrival of Prophet John had spread and now Parfitt turned to see stockmen and other workers, armed with whatever tools they could find, running from every part of the plant to join to the defensive force. Torrance had told them to expect it. No one had realised it would come this soon. The pack of men in the forecourt grew and, having not seen the recent defeat of their own colleagues, the new additions brought fresh enthusiasm to the ranks. The shouting began again, louder.

There seemed to be some confusion on the part of Torrance about how best to take on the Prophet. Getting his own men to retreat from the front gate further into the plant's grounds would be difficult enough. They wanted blood. Most especially they wanted Richard Shanti's blood. Parfitt heard the man's name shouted again and again. They hated him for being a traitor. Fingers and blades were pointed at him, threats to gut him, castrate him, promises to saw off his living limbs.

Weakness buffeted Parfitt and he swayed for a moment. A sick sweat broke all over him. This was the end for the

Prophet and Shanti. All of them would die today. Then the town would get back to the way it had always been, ruled by blood-lust and greed. He felt he was on the brink of some final possibility, a gesture in the name of a last stand. He didn't know John Collins, nor did he really know Richard Shanti but he believed in them more than he believed in the mob of MMP stockmen, more than he believed in Magnus and his guards. Why, he didn't know.

It was seeing another party approach from the town that made his mind up. He recognised the feared figure of Magnus's closest man, Bruno, at the head of more black-coats. Shanti and Collins and their tiny group of rebels would be trapped.

Parfitt backed away from it all.

***

The Grand Bishop watched the smoke rise with a swelling sense of dread. He stood in the road halfway to the MMP plant with every remaining Parson. They numbered about two hundred and none as skilled or experienced as those he'd already lost. His grip of Abyrne was slipping. He cursed himself as he stood there with his Parsons spread out behind him. He couldn't afford to appear weak in front of them but he couldn't take his eyes from the uprush of black fumes.

The curfew he'd ordered wasn't working.

Now he found himself trapped between the workers he would come up against at the plant and the angry rabble that would soon be following them along the road. Circumstance was funnelling him into a narrow corridor. He'd run out of choices.

Turning away from the fire, he set off toward the plant. In the distance he could see fields where the herds of the Chosen roamed and the barns where they sheltered. He gave no command to his Parsons.

He knew they'd follow him.

They had no more choice than he did.

***

Shanti and Collins stood amid the bodies of the first group Torrance had sent out, each of them serene.

In front of them was the main gate and just inside it a raucous crowd of combatants that was growing larger all the time. The crowd swore and taunted and waved their various weapons. Shanti saw clubs of wood and bone, cleavers, meat hooks, machetes and chains.

He glanced back down the road and saw the second party arriving at a run with Hema and Harsha being carried. Trouble couldn't be far behind.

'What's the plan?' he asked Collins.

'For me, for my followers, this is it. We make our stand in front of these workers and all those townsfolk that will no doubt soon arrive.'

'Yes, but what's the plan?'

Collins smiled but it soon faded.

'The plan is to never be *forgotten*, Richard. The plan is to martyr ourselves.'

'Maybe there's another way to do this. You might win. You haven't lost a single man yet. Maybe you can come with me.'

'We can't. I can't.'

'But if you triumph, there's no need for you to stay.'

'We're not going to triumph.'

'John, come on. Of course you won't if you talk that way.'

The second group arrived and Shanti's girls ran to him. He bent and kissed each of their heads, then stood and held them beside him.

Collins turned to him.

'I would have liked to get to know you better, Richard. I wish we'd had a little more time. But you have to see that all of us are making sacrifices today. Some will be in blood, others in service. You have your place in this and I have mine. The scales must be balanced and this is only the very beginning of the repayment that is owed.' Collins looked down the road and saw Bruno and the rest of Magnus's men approaching in the distance. 'You have all the knowledge you need now and you know what to do. Take your girls and hide. Don't let anyone see you. Go quickly now.'

Collins put out his hand and Shanti grasped it. There were many words that passed in that silent communication, but not enough. Shanti took a hand of each girl and together they crouched and ran away from the gate and the shouting mob, away from the road where Bruno and his men would soon arrive. They crept into the long grass and down into the ditch below the hedgerow. From there they half ran, half stumbled away from town following the smell of rot.

***

Parson Mary woke to the sounds of angry shouting, of men spoiling for affray.

It wasn't clear how long she'd slept for. This time she'd entered such a deep sleep that it might have been a few hours of blackness or a whole day. Her first act was to vomit but nothing came except the pain of spasms contracting around the growth inside her. Crying, she stood up. Weakness of the legs and a fog of dizziness brought her straight back to her knees.

So. The rest, no matter how deep, had done little for her.

None of this was going to be easy.

With more will than physical power, she used the top of the tower wall to haul herself up. Once there, the top of the wall came to just above her waist. Its only function, she assumed was to stop stockmen from falling. She was grateful for it.

Her vision cleared and she saw it all.

To her right, the MMP plant and the burgeoning gang of workers and black-coats that thronged near the entrance. Beyond the gate, she saw –

finally – Prophet John Collins. There was no mistaking who it must have been. A smooth-headed man dressed in rags and a band of two or three dozen others that looked much the same. They stood calmly whilst the men inside the plant appeared close to frenzy. She felt that Richard Shanti should be there too but there was no sign of him. She wanted him there, somehow. The idea of his presence comforted her but she knew the reality would be that Magnus had done away with him or was about to. It was a terrible pity.

In front of her, a few fields away, was the road connecting the plant and the town. Along this she could see three distinct groups. The first, nearest Collins, was another group of black-coats. Some distance behind them, far enough that the former group might easily not have been aware of them, was a huge band of Parsons led by a man she recognised even from this distance. The way he walked, the tilt of his head and the set of his shoulders; she knew the mannerisms all very well. And yet not well enough.

The final group was the largest and still quite distant. As far as she could make it out it was simply a huge crowd of townsfolk. The head of the column advanced but the tail never ended. It stretched right back into Abyrne. There was no way to calculate how many there were.

Everyone heading to the MMP plant. Everyone ready to spill blood.

She was weary of it. Surely there had been enough blood let in this town. Enough to fill a river that stretched to eternity. Suddenly, everything she recognised and understood was wrong. Not just flawed, but so completely warped it made no sense at all.

She turned her attention back to the tiny group made up by Collins and his followers and felt a fierce, protective instinct for them. They must each have known with utter certainty that they would die, and there they stood ready, steadfast. Only one other creature shared such nobility.

Perhaps they still had a chance, though.

She turned to go to the ladder and tripped over the hems of her gowns. She landed badly, not able to react quickly enough to protect herself, and hit the side of her head against the opposite wall of the tower. It stunned her. There was more pain but that was easy to ignore now. Pain was the essence of her reality from waking until sleeping. Urgency flared in her mind and she remembered Collins.

She had to move fast. Ignoring the blood trickling into her right eye, she lowered her legs to the rungs and began to climb down. Three steps from the bottom she committed to a rung that wasn't there and didn't have the strength to hold herself. She fell the rest of the way landing on her back in the churned mud of the field.

She rolled onto her side, grabbed at one of the tower's supporting legs and pulled herself upright. A few paces away was a high bolted gate. One of many that kept the Chosen secure. She hobbled to it. It took all her mental effort to pull open the bolt. Then, leaning away from the gate and using only her diminishing weight, she hauled it open. Further along the dense hedgerow, there was another gate.

She staggered down to it.

***

The Grand Bishop led the Parsons at a fast walk but it wasn't fast enough to stay ahead of the column of townsfolk drawing up behind.

The crowds that had set out from so many doors across Abyrne were fuelled by fear and anger. Their huge numbers lent them a shared strength and stamina. Not long after leaving the mansion, those at the front had broken into a trot and everyone else that was able had followed suit. Seeing the hurrying group of Parsons up ahead did nothing to slow them down.

The crowd sensed the power of its numbers and began to pursue the Parsons rather than merely follow. They were hungry for meat and ready for confrontation in order to get it.

The Grand Bishop heard the hurried panic in his own footsteps and realised he had to make a decision. If they tried to open the gap now, the crowd would run them down. His only option was to turn and face the townsfolk, talk to them as he had so many times before in the streets, in the squares and in the Central Cathedral. He'd give them God's word they'd receive everything they required. He held his hands up to the Parsons behind him and stopped. He wanted time to regain his breath before the townsfolk caught up to them.

Atwell was right behind him.

'What are you doing, Your Grace?'

'Trying to prevent the end of the world. If we don't turn and face the townsfolk, we're finished. When we're gone, the town will destroy itself.'

'But wouldn't it be safer to outrun them and take refuge at the plant? Then we can address them from safety.'

'No. If they've chased us all that way, they'll have no reason to listen. They'll have lost all respect. We must face them.'

252

The Grand Bishop pushed his way back through the panting Parsons. Then, with his back to the fast approaching crowd he said to them, 'Stand firm. Don't give an inch or show any emotion. The Welfare is the highest authority in the town, God's voice to His people. Let's act like it.'

He turned to face the oncoming throng of townsfolk and grain workers. When they were still two hundred yards distant, he held up his hands with his palms to them. He set his expression in stone and waited.

The front ranks approached quickly. They were thinned out by their pace but they were only the vanguard. Hordes were close behind them. They saw the Grand Bishop but continued to run. Their faces were full of rebellion and disrespect, twisted by a feral mob spirit, knowing anything might happen and that nothing could stop it once it began. The Grand Bishop noticed many of them were armed with iron bars or lumps of rubble and brick. He filled his lungs in a final attempt to control his breathing.

He made eye contact deliberately with as many of the approaching men and women as he could. He kept his face stern and imperious. The crowd's pace slowed. The front ranks thickened as more drew up behind them. They became a wall of faces.

He noticed how thin and hollow-faced so many of them looked while the Parsons were plump, robust and ruddy cheeked. He knew his voice would only reach the first few hundred, possibly a thousand townsfolk. After that, word would have to pass back on its own. He waited until he was sure the column had stopped and that enough folk had caught up to hear him.

'Townsfolk of Abyrne, you are God's children in God's town. As His representative, as the keeper of your welfare, I tell you this: a great blessing has come to pass this day. Rory Magnus, the man who kept the town on the edge of starvation because of his greed, Rory Magnus is dead. He is dead because God wants a righteous town where everyone eats and no one starves. He wants a town where there is order and piety through compassion, not violence. He decrees -'

'What about meat?' shouted a voice. He couldn't see who'd said it.

'You shall have it. The whole town shall have meat. Go back to your homes. Allow my Parsons and me to continue to the plant where we will regain control of all production. Then we can distribute God's divine gift of nourishment fairly and abundantly.'

'But we're hungry now,' someone else shouted. 'What are we going to eat right now?'

He knew he shouldn't have considered the question, allowed it to linger in his mind. He should have just continued and ignored it.

'Yeah,' yelled another voice. 'We want meat today. Now. Not some fucking distribution.'

More voices joined in.

'He's right.'

'No distribution.'

'Give us meat.'

'We'll not starve.'

'We want it now.'

The Grand Bishop raised his hands once more to placate the agitated voices.

'Please, please. That's enough. You shall all have full stomachs, as God is my witness.'

A couple of the Parsons to his right backed away from the crowd. Just a couple of inches, more of a flinch really, but the townsfolk sensed it even if they didn't actually see it.

'Stand firm,' hissed the Grand Bishop from the side of his mouth.

'We want meat.'

'I've already told y-'

'We want meat.'

A chant had begun.

'We want meat.'

'Good townsfolk, I implore you...' He was losing control.

The chant intensified and spread back through the crowd. Anger flared in their eyes again.

'WE WANT MEAT.'

Someone threw a broken brick. It hit Atwell between the eyes making a loud, damp thud. Something had broken inside.

The chant stopped.

Atwell staggered half a step back, unsure what had happened. Blood cascaded from the wound, down his face and onto his robes staining them an even deeper red. He dropped to his knees and fell on his face.

The chant began again, spoken quietly now, not shouted.

'We want meat...We want meat.'

Boots and bars tapped the broken road surface in time with the syllables.

'We want meat...We want meat.'

The chant gained power, townsfolk from far, far back giving their voices to it.

Someone threw another brick. The Grand Bishop saw it coming and ducked. He didn't see which of his Parsons it hit but he heard the cry of pain.

There was a moment; it stretched long between chants. In the moment both sides knew something was about to happen. It rose like an invisible wave. At the end of the moment every Parson turned away and started to run. At the same time, missiles shot from the mob and thundered into their turned backs. Stones hitting heads, rocks hitting backs and legs. The Parsons began to fall and the suddenly rushing mob trampled them into the tarmac with its thousands of stomping feet.

The Grand Bishop lifted the hem of his robes and fled.

***

The ditch was just deep enough that, if they kept their heads down, no one would see them from the road or from the plant. From time to time, Shanti stopped and peeped up over the long grass and weeds that grew unchecked along the verge.

Collins and his followers had split into two lines. One faced Bruno's men, the other the MMP gate. Bruno's arrival had emboldened Torrance and the stockmen anew – their enemies were now trapped in a pincer as well as outnumbered. It couldn't be long before someone made a move on them. Shanti didn't want to see them butchered but going back to help would do no good. He had his part to play, as Collins had said. There were no more choices now.

Further ahead on the other side of the road was the rear perimeter fence that surrounded the meat packing plant.

Shanti knew it was old and poorly maintained. Breaking through would be easy. He knelt down.

'Girls, I want you to stay here. Lie down in the ditch or go further back into the hedge, but whatever happens, do not come out to look for me. No one must see you. Understand?'

Two solemn nods and with them, quiet tears. He hugged them tight.

'If there was any other way of doing this, a way that meant we could stay together, I'd do it. But there isn't.'

In his mind he said to them: *But if we survive this, it must be without either of you seeing the inside of this plant. No one should ever see such a place again.*

'So, hide now, my sweethearts, and I'll come back for you as soon as I can.'

He gave them each another kiss, telling himself it would not be the last.

Then he scrambled farther along the ditch, far enough that none of the fighters at the gate would see him. Finally, he darted up over the lip of the ditch and across the road. The fence was completely broken down in one place and he ran straight over it to the wall of the first building. The wall was made of wood. He pulled nine thimbles out of his pocket and pressed his eight fingers and one thumb into them.

Then he began to tap, loud and hard, on that wooden wall, like a madman playing a tuneless piano.

***

Collins stood beside Staithe and with his back to Vigors.

In the road right behind them stood Bruno and his crew – ready to go at it again but with reservations. Ahead were too many men to count. The followers stood back to back with eyes on each faction. It was fine to die this way and Collins was more than ready. His life had gone on far longer than he'd planned. He might have died that day back in Magnus's study had it not been for the realisation that he could do so much better, so much more.

However, he didn't mean to give the opposition an easy victory. He and his followers would take as many as they could and hold the rest off for as long as possible. But the light in their bellies would not last forever. Sooner or later the energy would be spent, and at that moment they'd succumb to the odds.

He harried himself over how best to use their small numbers. Finally it came to him. He spoke into Staithe's ear and the message passed swiftly. Unseen by their opponents, they all put their hands behind their backs and touched for strength and friendship one final time.

'NOW!' cried Collins.

The thirty lean, rag-attired followers all faced the front gate and rushed in past the barrier. They split, fifteen slipping past the right side of the mob, fifteen passing to the left. Collins saw the look of outraged disbelief on Torrance's face as he flitted past the man. It had been the perfect move. Now the stockmen and black-coats had to fight on two flanks and Bruno's men would have to join them rather than having the advantage of attacking simultaneously from behind.

At no time in their brief fighting past had the followers needed to land the first blow – Parsons and black-coats had needed no invitation. Stockmen were no different. The attacks came furiously; hate propelling the swipe of every weapon. The faces of the followers were serene as they danced between the slashes and thrusts.

Twenty-seven

Parfitt unlocked another gate.

Skidding from one bullpen to the next, he slammed open the bolts, bruising his palms with each new impact. He was sweating, panicking. There wasn't enough time. Halfway around the pens he realised there was no movement. No bulls were coming out of their pens.

Too frightened. What to do?

Come on, Parfitt, think.

No use, he had to get all the gates open first. He sprinted to the next one. Within two minutes he'd opened every bullpen. Still no movement. It was then that he heard the tapping. It sounded like the idle noises the herds sometimes made on the panels and fence posts but this was much louder, more staccato. It didn't mean anything to him, though. He had to get the bulls out; that was all he could think about.

'You're free! Run away! Fight them!'

He pounded on the walls of the nearest bullpen. Then he looked inside. It was empty.

He ran to the next one in the row. The same.

'Shit. Oh, shit no. Already?'

He sprinted along to another row, turned the corner and ran straight into a huge naked form. The gut repelled him like a rubber wall and he fell on his arse in the straw. Looming in front of him was the giant figure of a bull that everyone knew well: BLUE-792; the father of the herds, the strongest bull among the Chosen.

Behind him, others were emerging. Not quite so magnificent, not quite so imposing but all of them dangerous. Each three times the weight of a good-sized stockman and a whole head taller.

Parfitt laughed.

'Fucking brilliant.'

The laughter dried up. He was a lone stockman with zero bull experience lying on the ground in front of a dozen of the brutes. He remembered the way the fighting bulls had stamped on each other's heads to finish their opponents. BLUE-792 advanced and the others fell in behind him. The barn was silent. The tapping had stopped. All he could hear was his own hammering heart and the shuffle of four-toed feet across straw.

He began to babble.

'Wait,' he said. 'I'm the one who let you go. You don't want me. It's them out there you want. Down by the gate. You'll see 'em. Can't miss 'em.' He scrabbled backwards across the floor and tried to stand up at the same time. He came up against a pair of legs.

'Did you let them out?' said the owner of the legs.

Parfitt twisted to look up and saw Rick Shanti, the Ice

Pick. All he could do was nod.

'Then you've bought us a few extra minutes. Come on, let's go do the rest.'

Parfitt gestured to the advancing bulls.

'What about them?'

'Oh, they know where they're going.'

***

When all the bulls were loose Shanti led Parfitt to the corralled dairy herd. One bolt was all it took to set every one of them free. Parfitt never stopped looking over his shoulder to see what the bulls would do. So far they'd followed Shanti as though he were the biggest bull among them. When they saw the cows flooding out of the corral, they tensed at first. Then the bulls were among the dairy herd, touching frantically and sighing in the most urgent tones. He saw BLUE-792 make straight for WHITE-047 and the calf that had been allowed back on her since the power outage. Parfitt had never seen the Chosen hug before. It made his soul shiver. He clasped a hand over his mouth.

'There's no time for that, son,' said Shanti. 'We have to get the gates to the fields open. We've got to let them all out.'

Parfitt nodded, unable to speak.

Shanti went to one of the railings of the corral and began to tap there with his thimbled fingers. The rhythm tinkled brightly and penetrated the air. Shanti breathed his hisses and sighs. The Chosen fell silent and listened. It was something Parfitt had never believed possible. Shanti was talking to them and they were taking it all in. When the tapping stopped, Shanti ran, keeping to the rear of the plant. Parfitt struggled to keep up with him and the herds fell in behind them.

When they reached the last building, the slaughterhouse, Shanti held up a hand. They all stopped behind him. He leaned his head around the corner of the slaughterhouse to check no one was watching. Out in the yards, the fighting was chaotic. Two huge hordes of armed men were attacking the two tiny groups of followers. As Shanti watched, the larger mobs encircled each small knot of followers so that they could attack from all sides. For the moment, the followers appeared to be dropping stockmen and black-coats as efficiently as ever, taking little or no damage. Shanti still hoped there would be time to change the odds before Collins and his people ran out of power.

But there was no way he and the herd behind him could cross the space between the slaughterhouse and the fields without being seen. Nor did he think he could run alone without being spotted.

He drew back and leaned against the wall.

'What now?' asked Parfitt. Shanti shook his head.

'I don't know. We could risk one of us running to the fields to open the gates, maybe. Or we could deliberately take the herd across as a distraction.' Even as he said it, he knew he wouldn't do it. The herd was unarmed, could not even hold weapons in their foreshortened hands. He would never put any of them at risk of the stockmen so needlessly. What they needed was divine intervention and Shanti knew the God that created Abyrne would not be keen to provide it. But perhaps there was a greater God than that, a benevolent, merciful God that wanted peace as much as he and Collins wanted it.

He looked around the corner again to see if there was some other way of crossing the gap. That was when the first of the followers fell. Through a gap in dozens of heads and shoulders, he saw a meat hook rise high and drop fast. It took one of Collins's followers full between the neck and the shoulder. Shanti heard the cry of triumph after what must have been a thousand useless blows against them. The moment the hook caught the ragged figure, the wielder hauled the man into the morass of stockmen. Blades reflected dull in the afternoon gloom, first ashen then bloody.

Shanti closed his eyes and made ready to run.

A figure moved awkwardly towards them from the fields. She was dressed in red, though that was hard to see because there was so much filth and mud clinging to her. She was gaunt and pale of face, not at all how he remembered her. Behind her, streaming slowly and confusedly up from the fields were the herds of the Chosen.

All of them.

Bless you, Parson Mary Simonson, he thought.

He turned and began to tap on the wall of the slaughterhouse. He nodded and hissed at the bulls and cows beside him and one by one they joined him. Thousands of finger stumps padded in unison the message that

Shanti wanted the rest of the herds to hear. Hundreds of throats rasped out coded sighs. There wasn't enough space along the slaughterhouse wall for all of them, so many pattered their rhythms on the metal fences further back, others on the corrugated iron walls of storehouses and lean-tos.

Parfitt watched the response of the arriving herds as they heard the rhythms that suddenly sounded to him like a strange kind of music. He saw the Parson collapse near the perimeter and saw the smile on her face; a sadder expression he hadn't seen. The herds flowed forward and he lost sight of her.

Ten thousand Chosen flooded through the fence and into the yards.

The fighting stopped.

Twenty-eight

The Chosen, responding to the beats and breaths of the bulls and dairy herd, poured into the MMP yards.

Shanti saw astonishment on the face of every black-coat and stockman as the numbers of Chosen swelled. The mass of pale human cattle mushroomed towards the two groups of combatants. Armed men began to back away towards the gate. There was no hint of malice in the expressions of the Chosen but neither was there a dipped head among them or a trace of fear or subservience. Chins up and eyes meeting any and all gazes, the Chosen shuffled forward.

Almost simultaneously two scuffles broke out among the stockmen. At first Shanti thought they were fighting each other. Then, to the front of them came all the surviving followers and Collins himself, every one secured by a man on each side.

Torrance and Bruno stepped in front of them. He pointed his finger at the corner of the slaughterhouse.

At him.

'This is all your doing, Shanti. I've been watching you, my friend. You can talk their language, can't you? You're controlling them.'

It was like having a spotlight turned on him. Everyone would hear his words.

'This has been coming for years. If it hadn't been me it would have been someone else.'

'Bullshit. You and Collins are uniquely fucked up. If it wasn't for the two of you, everything would be fine in this town. When we get rid of you, everything's going to get back to normal.'

Torrance nodded to two of his men. They stepped away from Collins and Torrance whipped him in the back of the legs with a crowbar. He fell to his knees in the dirt. Torrance kicked him with the sole of his boot, knocking him onto his side. 'Hold him down.' He took a thin-bladed boning knife from a sheath at his side and held it up. 'They're all going to die, Shanti. Unless you call off the herds and send them back to the fields where they belong.'

Collins found Shanti's eyes with his own. He closed them and shook his head almost without moving. Shanti was the only one to see it. Collins's eyes were calm when he opened them again but somehow on fire with joy. Shanti could see the light inside him shining.

'Look at the numbers, Torrance,' said Shanti. 'Even with your weapons, the Chosen outnumber you. A few may die but in the end, you'll be overcome.'

'You're not listening, Shanti. Let me explain it another way.'

Torrance knelt behind Collins and pressed one knee down on his head leaving his neck exposed. Shanti noticed for the first time the faint scar that ran vertically between Collins's Adam's apple and the notch between his collarbones; the mark of an incomplete ritual procedure. He didn't have time to think about it. Torrance laid the boning knife against the smooth skin of Collins's neck and began to saw as if Collins were already dead.

Shanti saw his friend's eyes widen in shock and terror. Torrance didn't pause. He was already through the arteries and veins and had severed Collins's trachea. A shocking, unbelievable out-rushing of blood covered Torrance's hands and Collins's face. The ground absorbed it. Collins tried to fight down his survival instinct but he couldn't do it. He began to struggle knowing the rear part of the blade was already approaching his neck bones. Suddenly the tension in his body released, he slackened, eyes still wide, as Torrance's knife slipped between the fourth and fifth cervical vertebrae. The sawing, laboured now, continued until Torrance had the head off. There was no hair to lift it by so he stuck his fingers in Collins's mouth and raised the head upside down.

'Now do you see, Shanti? Now can you understand what I'm trying to tell you? This is over. You send the Chosen back to the fields. Then maybe, just maybe, we'll do the others the humane way. I might even have you do it. You're the expert, after all.'

Shanti was crying, nauseated despite his years in the slaughterhouse. He couldn't allow Torrance to kill the rest of them like that. He could see the faces of the followers, each sallow with this new anticipation. Nor could he let the Chosen come this far and then return to their lives of sacrifice and subjugation.

He would send the herds in. It was time.

He raised his hands to the wall of the slaughterhouse ready to play the order and release the Chosen upon the stockmen and black-coats. He felt sure Torrance would believe he was giving in, sending them back to the fields.

His fingers never made the first tap, his throat swallowed back the first sigh.

His hands dropped.

Bruno pushed his way through the still panting mob.

He dragged Shanti's daughters into view by the hair. He was grinning. 'Look what I found.' Torrance was delighted.

'Perfect,' he said, as he looked the girls over. 'I think they've put on a bit of weight, don't you, Shanti. Must be all the meat they've been getting recently. Healthy little girls, aren't you?' He pinched Hema's rosy cheek. She was flushed with tears. 'Your mama liked a bit of meat too, didn't she?' He looked back at the Chosen. They were shifting their weight from one foot to another. He'd seen this impatience in them before. Usually in the crowd pens where they wanted their deaths to be over as quickly as possible. 'Better hurry up and give that order, Shanti. Or I'll have to decide which girl to do first. Shouldn't be too difficult, they're both the same, aren't they?'

Shanti stopped thinking then. All he could do was save his girls. A man had no choice in such a matter. He raised his thimbled fingers to the wall. The yard was quiet now; the rest of the herd had stopped signalling while the factions negotiated. The eye of every Chosen was on Shanti now. He knew it and he knew what they were waiting for. What they had waited generations for. The simple freedom to live as humans again, as they had before what the Welfare called the creation and what Shanti and many others secretly believed was the opposite: some kind of cataclysm that had ended a much larger world and left only the portion now known as Abyrne.

His first taps were swallowed by the sound of hundreds of running feet approaching and the noise made by a blood-hungry multitude. It approached quickly and grew louder. The stockmen and black-coats turned towards the gates and the road. They saw the last of the Parsons, led by the Grand Bishop, running and stumbling ahead of the townsfolk. Thousands of townsfolk. The fastest were at the front but many more were catching up. The column stretched out of sight towards Abyrne.

The Parsons, including the Grand Bishop, were all cut by the crowd's improvised projectiles. Some of them had little strength left. For a moment they appeared relieved to have reached the gate of the plant. Then they saw that the yard was full of stockmen and black-coats and their faces fell.

But still they ran because death was right behind them. They did as Collins had done and ran past the edges of the armed workers and guards to put some barrier between them and the townsfolk. Only then did they stop and turn.

Bruno and Torrance took it all in as the front lines of the crowd came to halt at the front gate. Rapidly, their numbers expanded.

'What the fuck is this?' said Torrance to no one in particular. The chant began again.

'We want meat, we want meat.' It gained volume.

Fast.

'WE WANT MEAT! WE WANT MEAT!'

While the stockmen's backs were momentarily turned, Parson Mary Simonson staggered through the herds and towards Shanti's twins. The look on her face was one of crazed determination, the look of someone going beyond what was possible for their body.

'No,' said Shanti quietly. 'She'll get them killed.'

He didn't really register that someone had pushed past him until he saw Parfitt racing to stop the Parson. He was younger and quicker but the Parson had too much of a start on him. She reached the girls and tried to pull them out of Bruno's grasp. Of course, in her state, it was impossible, but there was some unrelenting strength inside her that would not quit. She took a hand of each girl and pulled. Bruno, facing the wrong way, turned and spiralled the girls closer. The Parson fell to her knees but wouldn't let go.

Parfitt arrived having swiped a fallen chain from the ground. He raised it and whipped it straight down onto Bruno's head. The grip on the girls released. The Parson fell back, letting go also. Bruno held his head in his hands and swayed. Torrance turned, his knife rising. Other men turned. Parfitt caught the girls' hands and hauled them away, back towards their father and the Chosen. Torrance swiped and missed.

Outside the plant the chant grew angrier. The crowd could see the Chosen, many of them standing within the perimeter of the yard. They could see their meat. They assumed the stockmen were there to prevent them getting to it. They began to advance through the gate.

Parfitt had opened a gap between him and the men behind him. He was smiling as he brought Hema and Harsha towards the protection of their father and the vast herds of Chosen. Shanti willed him the speed to succeed. The smile turned to a look of puzzlement and then disappointment. Parfitt's hands released the girls and they kept running to their papa. Parfitt couldn't run any more. He stopped and wavered and collapsed forwards. Behind Parfitt was a grinning stockman, one who had let fly his cleaver to maximum effect. The heavy blade had somersaulted forwards through the air and sunk cleanly into the back of Parfitt's skull.

The shock of it was erased when Shanti's girls ran right into his arms. He didn't allow the hug to last.

'Get out of sight behind the wall here. No one will come near if you stay with the Chosen.'

The girls didn't speak. They pressed themselves against the wall. There, for the first time, they saw bulls and cows in the flesh, up close. There too, they saw calves pressed close to their mothers. Some of the calves were the same size as the twins. Their eyes met. The twins saw the calves for what they truly were.

Children.

***

Parson Mary Simonson felt something tear inside her as she fell back to the ground.

It made her cold.

She saw Bruno finally succumb to the chain blow and join her in the blood-washed dirt. She saw Parfitt fall too but she watched the girls to safety. Soon the stockmen would take their weapons to her. There was no need. Whatever had given way within her abdomen would kill her, she knew it quite certainly. The details no longer mattered. The pain was no worse than the pain she'd lived with for the past many weeks. The inner breaking felt like a release.

From the ground she saw angry, vicious men above her but she could not hear them. She saw their knives and clubs fall upon her body, but she felt none of it. Now she would return to darkness and unknowing. She would stay there forever. It didn't matter. The question she'd been asking was answered in the martyring of the Prophet.

She lay facing his severed head, looking into his eyes as silent blows crashed down upon her. Collins bore a scar at his throat. Shanti was missing one thumb. Arnold Shanti had committed a crime of interference, a crime so grave it could never be acknowledged. He'd liberated twin male calves. He'd raised one as his own but both had grown up as townsfolk, neither knowing the other existed.

'Brothers...' she whispered to John Collins. '...Chosen.'

She gave herself to the nothingness that came for her.

***

'Ha, Suu. HAH, SSUUUUH.'

Led by BLUE-792, ten thousand pairs of hands tapped out their message. They tapped it on their own thighs, upon each other's backs, they padded it against walls and fenceposts; they beat it on the ground. As one, they breathed.

The noise was greater, more penetrating than the shouts of the townsfolk or the retorts of the stockmen and black-coats holding them back. It was like soft thunder and a rising wind. The crowd lost its voice. The armed factions stopped their threats.

Everyone listened.

But only Richard Shanti understood.

Your time comes. Surely it comes. May you go forward into your time with great dignity. We who gave will give no longer. We have seen the distant tomorrow. We have seen the land where pain is not even a memory. A land where what we gave will never be asked for again. We follow the man of peace to this land. He is one of us. He has given. We who gave salute you. Ha Suuh! Now your time comes.

The herds moved forward as one. Shanti led them.

At first Torrance stood fast. He held up the boning knife in one hand and a crowbar in the other. Beside him and behind him, stockmen and black-coats were stepping back, stepping away. He looked right and left.

'Come on you fucking cowards. You're not going to let your dinner push you around, are you? Hey, you! Stay with me. We'll send them back to the fields in pieces. We'll carve them up and hand out steak to the townsfolk right now.'

No one stood by him.

They backed towards the Parsons and the Grand Bishop who in turn backed further into the yards of the plant. Outside the gates, the crowd of townsfolk realised the size of the approaching herds. Most of them had never seen the Chosen alive and up close. The hairless bodies and stumpy fingers. The pale limbs. They stood like people. But for their damaged feet, they moved like people. A ripple of unease spread through the crowd. They began to retreat. Further back the crush caused others to fall over or be pushed into the ditches and hedges of blackthorn.

Shanti breathed and tapped his fingers on his head. BLUE-792 peeled away from the herds with a couple of hundred other bulls. They passed the Grand Bishop and his bleeding Parsons. He watched them in disgust. He couldn't hold his thoughts in.

'This is an abomination. It's the deepest heresy Abyrne has ever witnessed.'

'This town is the abomination,' said Shanti 'The crimes committed here for generations are unforgivable.'

The Grand Bishop laughed incredulously.

'But they're animals, man. They're God's gift to us. His sacrifice to prove His love for us.'

'The Book of Giving was written by men. It contains no truth about God or anything else. It merely serves those who wield it.'

The Grand Bishop saw it as an opportunity to hold forth once more in front of the townsfolk. To show them his superiority.

'How dare you speak such blasphemies? I will see to it that your status is revoked forthwith. You, Richard Shanti, are no longer among the townsfolk. You have become meat.'

Behind the exhausted Parsons, the bulls began to reappear. They came from the veal yard and on their backs they carried the weak, blind calves.

The Grand Bishop exploded.

'What in God's name do you think you're doing, Shanti?'

'You'll see soon enough.'

When all the bulls had rejoined the herd, Shanti walked out of the front gates of the plant.

He turned right. Away from the town.

No one understood. Not the stockmen, not Magnus's black-coats, not the Parsons, not the townsfolk. Shanti smiled. Without him and Collins, without the followers, without the Chosen, they would never understand. He was glad.

No one dared interfere with the herds as they passed. The surviving followers patrolled the edges of the herd as it left the front gate and followed Shanti. If anyone made a move against the Chosen, Collins's followers would die defending them.

The Chosen passed through the gate in droves for a long time.

The Grand Bishop panicked and ran after Shanti. He caught up to him beyond the dump where so many Chosen lay rotting. Not much farther, the road became broken beyond usefulness and after that it disappeared.

'Shanti,' he panted as he caught up. 'Where are you going?'

'The Chosen are free now. We're leaving.'

'Leaving? To where?'

Shanti pointed into the wasteland.

'But there's nothing out there, man. You'll all starve.' Shanti permitted himself to look at the Grand Bishop one final time. There was dried blood caked to the back of his head. It looked like dirt. His robes were filthy, his face an expanse of worry and questioning. This was the man who would go back to the townsfolk with the job of explaining what had happened. Shanti doubted there was anything in the town's religious books that covered the exodus of the Chosen.

He smiled at the Grand Bishop, turned and kept walking. Some of the gathered townsfolk shouted to the stockmen and black-coats.

'What's happening?'

'Why don't you stop them?'

'Quick, before they're all gone.'

'Just grab a few from the back.'

But no one made a move.

***

By evening, all the Chosen had stepped from the road into the wasteland. Behind them came the last of the followers.

The Chosen walked with the great dignity that they often spoke of to each other. They were no longer afraid to hold up their heads and let their eyes scan the horizon. It was hard on their mutilated feet but they did not falter. The land was like no land they'd ever seen; black glass sculpted into razor-backed dunes. Across these solid obsidian waves a black dust blew at the will of a constant wind. Where the dust came from or where it blew to, none of them knew.

They only knew that they were free now and that with Shanti's knowledge and the knowledge of the followers, they would survive until they reached a land where pain was no longer a memory, a land where what they had given would never be asked for again. They knew it existed.

The town of Abyrne lay distantly in the west now while the Chosen walked eastward.

Not one of them looked back.

Afterword

For the record, I'm not a vegetarian.

Yet.

Nor am I on some kind of animal welfare crusade. I'm just one of those people who can't help thinking about things.

Because I do all the shopping and cooking, I see to it that most of our meals don't include meat. When they do, the meat is expensive; in other words it's organic and from animals raised and slaughtered respectfully and humanely.

If you don't have the stomach to kill, gut, skin and dress an animal, you ought not have the stomach to eat it either. Much of the impetus for this book arose from that double standard. Consumers are very happy to pick and choose their cuts of meat after they've reached the butcher shop or supermarket. If they ever think about the process that got the meat there, they must put the truth out of their heads in order to enjoy their rib-eye, neck fillet, belly or breast.

Having researched the subject and watched hours of gut-churning footage, my conclusion is simple. All over the world, animals are farmed and brutalised for slaughter in the most appalling conditions and in numbers no one wants to consider. I won't go into it here. There are plenty of websites where you can find out for yourself. You might try typing 'slaughter footage' into a search engine and see where it takes you.

Or you might decide not to. I could understand why.

In MEAT, I put humans through abattoirs for the freak-factor, for the sheer horror of it. But all the time it was the animals I saw in my mind's eye, animals waiting in lines in narrow steel corridors, waiting for death at the hands of men with targets to meet.

Believe me, they don't go quietly or willingly. Who would?

Joseph D'Lacey

Also Available

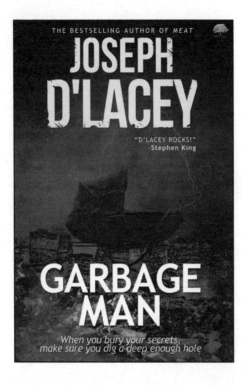

Shreve, a dead-end town next to the UK's largest landfill. There's nothing the bored residents won't stoop to in an attempt to spice up their pedestrian lives. All wannabe model Aggie Smithfield wants is to escape before Shreve swallows her ambition along with a million tons of rubbish and dirty little secrets. Desperate, Aggie asks renowned but reclusive ex-photographer, Mason Brand, for help. The deal they make might be the only thing that can save her when the town's fate catches up with it. Beneath everyone's feet, something born of the things we throw away is awakening. And when the past is reborn, there will be no escape.